INCA'S DEATH CAVE

An Archaeological Mystery Thriller

By Bradford G. Wheler

BookCollaborative.com
Cazenovia, NY 13035

BookCollaborative.com
PO Box 403
Cazenovia, NY 13035
BookCollaborative.com@gmail.com

ISBN-13: 978-0-9822538-6-1

Library of Congress Control Number: 2012910062

Mystery, Thriller, Archaeology

PRINTED IN THE UNITED STATES OF AMERICA

Cover Photo by Dreamtimes
Interior design by Lorie DeWorken, Mind*the*Margins

To Julie

And in memory of Arthur Gordon Wheler
(February 21, 1921 – May 6, 2013)

INCA'S DEATH CAVE

An Archaeological
Mystery Thriller

Cornell Bell Tower (Note 1)

Chapter
1

"Professor Robert Johnson?"

I turned to see a woman in an expensive business suit standing in the doorway of my office. Her tone if not official was at least authoritarian. I could imagine people jumping to attention and saying "Yes, ma'am."

I slowly got to my feet and with a big smile said, "Yes, I am."

She didn't say anything for a few beats and then responded. "May I come in and have a word with you?"

I held out my hand and said, "Please call me Rob."

She shook it in a polite, businesslike manner. "I'm Lois Stone, a technical administrator at Falone Advanced Technologies." She handed me a card.

"Your card says Chief Technology Officer and Senior Vice President. It also says PhD."

"That is my official title, Professor Johnson. May I have a seat?"

"Rob. Please make yourself at home." I suspected she wasn't the make yourself at home type. "What can I do for you?"

She looked at me in a penetrating and evaluating way. I wasn't sure I liked it.

"Mr. Walter Falone of Falone Advanced Technologies asked me to bring this letter to you. He felt it would be better received if I brought it to you in person."

"Why would that be?"

"So you would take it more seriously."

"So it is a serious letter then?"

"Professor Johnson."

"Just call me Rob."

"ROB. I'm taking considerable time out of my rather busy schedule to fly to Ithaca because Mr. Falone believes you should give the offer contained in this letter serious consideration."

"May I ask what kind of offer it is?"

"Mr. Falone would like to engage your services and the services of one of your PhD students."

"Dr. Stone." I assumed she didn't want me calling her Lois. "I know very little about Falone Advanced Technologies and less about Walter Falone. Some kind of advanced remote sensing and monitoring for oil exploration, mining, nuclear power plants, stuff like that. I'm an archaeologist."

"We are well aware of your area of study. Mr. Falone feels your expertise could be helpful."

I seemed to hear in her tone "expertise such as it is." I asked her, "Do you agree?"

"This is not a project that I'm directly involved in. However, you would probably fit right in."

That seemed pretty noncommittal, definitely not a ringing endorsement.

"Please read the letter from Mr. Falone. He would like to fly you and Ms. Summers to meet with him in Houston on February 20th returning the next day. That is during Presidents' Week and there are no classes."

Ms. Summers, so that was the student she was talking about. Interesting. I said, "We wouldn't want to miss class, would we? I assume Mr. Falone has a nice jet." Then I said nothing.

"Professor Johnson, whichever jet Mr. Falone decides to send to pick you up, I'm sure you will find it adequate. I sense a somewhat flippant attitude on your part. I urge you to seriously consider Mr. Falone's offer. At the very least meet with him in Houston; you will find it most interesting. Mr. Falone is many things but boring is not one of them. I have a great deal to do back in Houston. Here is Mr. Falone's letter. Good day, Professor Johnson."

"Rob," I said to her back as she walked out.

Somehow I didn't feel I was Dr. Stone's type. I put on a clean shirt this morning. Maybe I should have shaved.

Chapter
2

Abbey Summers walked into my office and dropped into a chair. She was by far the brightest PhD student I've had the privilege to work with. She was not only smart, and hardworking, but she also had an upbeat quick wit.

"What's up, Prof?"

"Abbey, do you want to go to Texas?"

"Sure. I've never been to Texas. Why?"

"Someone wants to hire us."

"To do what, Prof?"

"Something of an archaeological nature."

"Who, where, when, and are they going to pay us?"

"Let's start with your last question and work backwards. He wants to pay you more than I make here at Cornell as a full professor and me about twice that. The when is, fly to Houston February 20th for a meeting and start full time June 1 for 14 or so months. Do research here between February and June as our schedules permit. The where, is in South America. As for who, that is what you are going to find out and tell me... Mr. Walter Falone of Falone Advanced Technologies. Also Dr. Lois Stone, Chief Technology Officer for the firm, find out all you can in the next few days. The jet arrives for us next week."

"Prof, like a private jet? For real? And he wants to pay us. How much do full professors make anyway?"

"More than your graduate stipend. Now get to work. I have a class to teach."

Chapter 3

Abbey walked into my office.

"What is that five-inch file under your arm?" I asked her.

"The info on Falone. You know how professors like voluminous works. Every good student knows to pad research reports with marginally related stuff. Do you want to know what I found out?"

"He started in a garage, right?"

"No, Prof."

"Well, Abbey H-P, Apple, Amazon, and even the Wright brothers started in a garage."

"Falone didn't start in a garage, Prof. Do you want to hear what I researched?"

"Give me the Cliffs Notes version."

"Walter Falone graduated from Cornell in 1982 in geology. He went into a PhD program at the Colorado School of Mines in an interdisciplinary degree program. After about two and a half years he seems to have dropped out. Next he is in Sudbury, Ontario, Canada.

"Did you know there are over 345 mining supply and service companies in Sudbury? Also some research and development firms working on high-tech mining technologies such as Mining Innovation Rehabilitation and Applied Research Corporation (MIRARCO), the Northern Centre for Advanced Technology (NORCAT), and the Centre for Excellence in Mining Innovation (CEMI)… He takes a job at MIRARCO in the EVO division. Prof, do you know what that is?"

"Abbey, I bet you can tell me."

"Enhanced Visualization and Optimization. Falone leaves there in less than two years and joins a small, almost-broke gold mining exploration company, Socrates Gold Corp. It owns mining rights to several sites in northern Ontario and Argentina but no commercially viable finds. Falone cuts a deal to work for them for almost no pay but for stock and stock options. This company is trading for less than two cents a share. He borrows money from his grandmother and buys as many shares as he can on the open market."

"Abbey, how could you possibly find out he borrowed money from his grandmother over 25 years ago?"

"Oh, I made that part up. I wanted to see if you were still listening. Well, guess what?"

"They find gold, right, Abbey?"

"No, they find palladium, lots of it. It turns out the exploration company was sitting on a different type of gold mine and didn't even know it. The stock goes from pennies to dollars and then is bought out by a major mining concern. It seems Falone made somewhere between $80 and $120 million."

"Canadian or US?"

"What?"

"Abbey, $80 to $120 million in Canadian or US dollars?

"Prof, who cares?"

"I just want to show you I'm listening."

"Probably Canadian. Do you want me to check the exchange rate back then?"

"No, Abbey, please go on, you're doing great."

"About this time patent filings and copyright registrations start showing up in Falone's name. He seems to have taken what he learned at the Colorado School of Mines and MIRARCO to a new level, combining available site data not only with search engine capabilities that scour all available databases but adding a layer of artificial intelligence… Prof, is this too general? I've got a lot more technical details and references."

"Abbey, this is fine. Keep going."

"Next Falone goes to Calgary, it seems he wants to try his system for oil and gas exploration. However, now he sets up his own company, Falone

Advanced Technologies. He has no track record in oil and gas exploration so he finds Suncor Oil & Gas Corp. The company is engaged in the process of exploring its oil and gas properties which are over 100,000 acres near Hamburg, Alberta.

"Again, this company's stock is trading for pennies and they pay for his services with stock. Well, Prof, he finds oil and makes another bundle.

"He moves his whole operation to Houston. He only has a few employees at this point. But I guess he feels he's ready to play in the big leagues. Today he has over 4,000 employees worldwide. Mostly highly educated scientists and engineers. Houston is the headquarters location. He has major offices in Sudbury, Ontario, and Peru. The other offices are mostly field and client support offices."

"Abbey, Peru is in South America."

"Very good. You must be a tenured Cornell professor. Peru is the world's largest silver producer, third largest in bismuth, copper, tin, and zinc, fourth largest in arsenic trioxide, lead, molybdenum, and rhenium, and fifth largest in gold… So a very good place for Falone Advanced Technologies to have a major operation for the mining division. Peru also has archaeology, lots of it."

"Tell me what you have found out about Walter Falone the man."

"Walter Edward Falone, born 1960, Dayton, Ohio. Only child. His father was a medical doctor, now deceased, mother taught school, she is now living in Florida. Falone was married in 1986 to Jane Everson Falone. She died of breast cancer in 2001. They had two daughters, one is a pediatrician in Seattle and the other a private school principal just outside Dallas, both married. Other than the mother's death, it seems like a well-adjusted family."

"Abbey, what about Falone himself?"

"The family always seemed to keep a low profile. No Hollywood style parties or big flashy things you see some of the ultra-rich doing. After the death of his wife Walter seems to have become even more reserved, no more articles about him attending industry conventions or big fundraisers. He seems to have his daughters and their families to his ranches in Texas or Peru for most holidays. Not much else I can tell you on that front, Prof."

"What about our good Dr. Lois Stone?"

"Dr. Lois Stone, born 1981, Boston, Mass. Graduated from Brown University with honors in computer science. Went to Cal Tech and got her PhD in artificial intelligence. She did postdoc work at Stanford. Published a bunch of papers along the way. Worked for Google for a couple of years and then went to Falone Advanced Technologies."

"Chief Technology Officer and Senior VP at a place like Falone Advanced Technologies in her early thirties. Quite an accomplishment."

"Prof, she seems like a real grind. There doesn't appear to be much to her besides work."

"Well, Abbey, good work. Put the file on the shelf over there."

"You mean next to the dusty pile of technical journals you never read?"

"Yup, I think there is room."

Cessna 525 Citation Jet (Note 2)

Chapter
4

I received an email from Mrs. Regina Lopez, assistant to Mr. Falone. She said we should be at the general aviation section of the Ithaca Tompkins County Regional Airport at 8:50AM EST for a 9:00AM departure. Well, that beats the two hours of TSA security lines at JFK.

Dress was to be business casual. We could expect to arrive back in Ithaca by 6:00PM EST on the 21st. She included her cell phone and email and said to contact her with any questions.

I had none so I sent a polite reply saying thank you and we were looking forward to meeting Mr. Falone.

I picked Abbey up at her College Town apartment at 8:30AM and put her overnight bag in the back. It was cold with a clear blue sky. Not many sunny days in the winter in Ithaca. It is only 10 minutes to the airport but I wanted to be on time.

"Prof, is this business casual enough?" She unbuttoned her oversized down parka.

"Abbey, you look great." She did. She had on black dress slacks, and a light pink blouse with a matching sweater. I was surprised how well the slacks and blouse set off her red hair and clear blue eyes. In the plastic bag she was carrying I saw black pumps. I assumed they would replace her hiking boots at the airport. She wore a one-string pearl necklace with matching earrings for jewelry. A big change from the blue jeans and sweatshirt she usually wore. She always looked attractive in a college student way, tall and fit. Today she looked elegant.

I also had dressed with some care. A blue blazer, white shirt, tan slacks, and cordovan loafers. I decided to leave my Indiana Jones hat and cowboy boots home and never even thought of bringing my bullwhip. We were dressed for success.

We parked in the general aviation parking lot, grabbed our overnight bags, and walked into the fixed-base operator Taughannock Aviation. A woman dressed a little more formally than business casual walked up to us and said, "Good morning, I assume you are Professor Johnson and Ms. Summers. I'm Jane Fitzpatrick with Falone Advanced Technologies, I'll be accompanying you to Houston. We will be leaving in about 10 minutes. Please use the restrooms if you need to. Please excuse me while I speak to the pilot."

"Prof, they sent a Cessna 525B Citation Jet 3 for us. I was hoping for something bigger. Only one pilot on the 525B."

"Abbey, I thought you had never been on a private plane before."

"I did some research."

The jet seemed more than adequate to me but not over the top. It was probably a cost-effective fit for the number of people and distance to Houston. That said something about Mr. Falone.

We walked out to the tarmac where the pilot was waiting.

"I'm Captain Jim Bodin. Let me take those bags, and may I answer any questions before we depart?"

Abbey spoke up. "Captain, this is a Cessna 525B Citation Jet 3, correct?"

"Yes, ma'am."

"Houston is about 1,200 nautical miles from here?"

"Yes, ma'am."

"Are we stopping somewhere?"

"No, ma'am, direct to Houston. A little over three hours in the air."

"Yes, that is what I calculated. However, I thought the Cessna 525B Citation Jet 3 only had a range of 1,300 nm. That means you wouldn't have the FAA required 45-minute reserve when we got to Houston."

"This aircraft has been fitted with long-range tanks. It is rated for 1,950 nm. However, it reduces the useful load. Our flight plan is filed for 09:00 EST so we should get on board now."

Jane Fitzpatrick directed Abbey on board.

As I started up the steps the captain said to me, "Quite an interesting young lady you have there."

"Yes indeed, Captain, yes indeed."

I settled in and looked over at Abbey. She was reading Julian H. Steward, 1946 edition, *The Handbook of South American Indians No. 143, Vol. 2: The Andean Civilizations*.

"Did you steal that from Olin Library? It's a restricted volume."

"No. I have a friend who works in Olin. He said I could borrow it. Peru is in the Andes."

"Yes, I've heard that." I closed my eyes and put my head back...

Jane Fitzpatrick walked us down the Citation's steps toward a waiting van. The pilot followed with our two bags. She said, "The driver will take you to Mr. Falone's ranch. It is about a 50-minute drive."

We had landed at Ellington Airport, a joint public and military airport about 17 miles southeast of Houston. It was about 65° and felt wonderful compared to what we had a few hours ago in Ithaca.

We were driving west. The van was set up for business. Four captain's chairs, two facing front and two facing back, adjustable table system with AC outlets between the seats.

Abbey was staring at her iPhone. "Prof, this van has Wi-Fi. The signal strength has remained constant since we started driving at the airport."

I said, "Technology is amazing."

It was flat here and by now we were far enough away from Houston that it was mostly farmland.

We turned up a dirt road, no name, just a street address number. The road became a paved driveway about a quarter mile in. The ranch was a complex of buildings. No big gate or security fences. There was a main house with what looked like a carriage house on one side and a guest cottage on the other. Well, if you could call a place that had to be over 6,000 square feet a cottage. Behind these buildings were several buildings that looked like the working part of the ranch.

The car stopped in front of the main house. The driver opened the van door for us. As we got out of the van the front door opened and a pleasant-looking woman in her early sixties said, "Professor Johnson, Ms. Summers, welcome, I'm Regina Lopez. Please come in. I have lunch ready for you. Unfortunately Mr. Falone was held up at his office in Houston and won't be here until later this afternoon. I'll have the driver put your bags in the guesthouse and I'll walk you over there after you have eaten."

The lunch was simple but somehow exceptionally tasty. A green salad and chicken salad on what seemed to me homemade bread.

The guesthouse was also an interesting arrangement. Work-professional and homey at the same time. The rooms were more like suites or apartments. Abbey and I had suites on opposite sides of the center area. The great room had a full kitchen and dining area towards the back and a conference table with several workstations towards the front. This opened out onto a patio and swimming pool area. Off to one side of the great room was another room with a bar, pool table, darts, and several large flat-screen TV's.

I went out to the covered part of the patio with my laptop and began running term papers from my first-level course "ARKEO 1200 – Ancient Peoples and Places" through my plagiarism software program. I don't catch as many students plagiarizing as I used to, not because students are more honest, but because they have all learned to run their papers through one of the free plagiarism software programs such as Grammarly. My favorite was a student about three years ago. I told him I liked his paper about pre-Columbian metallurgy, and did he know why? He shook his head. Because it reminded me of an article in the Journal of Archaeological Research, and did he know why I remembered the article? He began to look nervous. I said because I co-authored the article.

I gave him the choice of doing a 10-page paper on the history of plagiarism over the last 300 years citing at least two dozen of the most famous cases from those years, or going to see the Dean. The paper was quite good and I knew he had a sense of humor when he included his pre-Columbian metallurgy paper as one of the cases.

Abbey came out on the patio with the Steward book she had "borrowed" from Olin Library. She plopped down in a chair.

"Abbey, what do you think of Texas?"

"So far pretty good. Nice place here. Maybe I'm getting my PhD in the wrong field."

She started reading and I went back to running term papers through the plagiarism software.

There was a gentle knock on the sliding glass door from the great room to the patio. A man in his early fifties with dark hair, in a short-sleeved shirt, stepped out onto the patio.

"Professor Johnson, I'm Walter Falone. I'm so very pleased you are here."

After my experience with Dr. Lois Stone the CTO I decided not to say call me Rob. I said, "Mr. Falone, a great pleasure to meet you."

His response: "Please call me Walter." He turned to Abbey, put out his hand, and said, "You must be Ms. Summers."

Abbey said, "Yes, I'm Abbey, it is nice to meet you, Mr. Falone."

"Walter."

"If it is OK with you, you call me Abbey, and I'll call you Mr. Falone. It just feels better."

"That will be fine, Abbey. I see you are reading Julian Steward. He was quite an interesting man. He studied for a year at Berkeley under Alfred Kroeber and Robert Lowie, after that he transferred to Cornell University, from which he graduated in 1925 with a B.S. in Zoology. Although Cornell, like most universities at the time, had no anthropology department, its president, Livingston Farrand, had previously held an appointment as a professor of anthropology at Columbia University. Farrand advised Steward to continue to pursue his interest in anthropology. So he went back to Berkeley to study under Kroeber and Lowie for his PhD. I believe you would find his book *Cultural Causality and Law: A Trial Formulation of the Development of Early Civilizations* most interesting. That is if you haven't already read it."

Abbey just looked at him.

Falone said, "I would like to change and I have a couple of phone calls to return. Can you come over to the house at 5:00 and we can talk?"

"Do you mind if we wander around the property?" I said. "I would like to get a little exercise after sitting on the plane all morning."

"No, you two make yourself at home. There is a fitness room in the pool house along with changing rooms. There are marked paths all over the property for hiking and biking. One trail starts at the far edge of the patio. Would you like mountain bikes?"

"No thank you, I like to walk and Abbey is a runner."

"Well, as I said, make yourself at home and I'll see you at 5:00."

As he left I saw Abbey staring at his back. "Not what you expected, Abbey? Not like J.R. Ewing from Dallas? Or was that before your time?"

"I've seen the reruns. And no, I didn't expect J.R. but he doesn't seem like a reclusive billionaire to me."

"How many reclusive billionaires do you know, Abbey?"

"Good point."

I had expected him to be bright, maybe even brilliant. But I had visions of being summoned to his football field-sized office by a butler. The plane, the van, lunch, this guesthouse all spoke to efficient quality but not opulence or showiness. I knew Julian Steward's work well but I didn't expect anyone outside my field to. Yes, this trip to Texas was becoming interesting.

I put on blue jeans, a golf shirt, and sneakers and began walking down the trail. A few minutes later Abbey ran by me saying, "See you later, slow-poke."

I just kept walking. The trails had a park-like feel down to signposts with photos of the wildlife and detailed descriptions.

There was extensive signage at the intersection of the trails from the house and the guesthouse. I stopped to read it.

"The ranch consists of 3,200 acres and several habitats, including wetland aquatic and hardwood forest. Dominant tree species include Cedar Elm, Hickory, Osage Orange, Green Ash, Cottonwood, Sycamore and Hackberry to name a few. Throughout the ranch, forest canopies shelter dense undergrowth vegetation of coralberry, dwarf palmetto, American beautyberry, possum haw, yaupon, grapevine, Alabama supplejack and the abundant Turk's cap with its beautiful red blooms. Bluebonnets can be viewed in the early spring.

"The ranch offers opportunities to view wildlife. You can often view nesting pileated woodpeckers, as well as many other species such as the barred owl, warblers, yellow-billed cuckoo, white-eyed vireo, Mississippi kite, northern perula, and many more. White-tailed deer, raccoons, opossums, armadillos, rabbits, and squirrels are common sightings on the ranch, while other creatures tend to be a little more elusive, and are rarely seen, such as the bobcat. If the creepy crawlies are the animals you like, look very closely and you might see a number of reptiles and amphibians."

It went on to describe the geography and climate.

I moved on to explore the working part of the ranch. It appeared there were cattle, of course. No self-respecting Texas billionaire can have a ranch without a few thousand head of cattle. There were large herds of sheep and goats grazing. I came to a riding complex that had stables, paddock, outdoor and indoor riding arenas, all very high-end.

Beyond the stable was another set of barns and fenced-in areas. There were llamas, alpacas, and guinea pigs, now those are not the Texas rancher's usual livestock.

I checked my watch and decided to head back to shower.

Chapter

5

We walked over to the main house at 5:00. As we went up the steps the door opened and Mrs. Lopez greeted us. There must be security cameras but I hadn't spotted them.

She led us into a well-proportioned living room. Walter Falone was reading in an armchair. He stood up and walked over to greet us with a big smile and handshake.

"Please have a seat. Mrs. Lopez will get you something to drink. Abbey, what would you like?"

Abbey ordered a white wine, I asked for a beer, and I was interested to see Walter also requested a beer.

"Did you have an enjoyable walk around the ranch?" Walter asked.

"Quite impressive, 3,200 acres."

"Actually small change by Texas ranch standards. The King Ranch is 825,000 acres, about 258 times the size of this ranch. There are 19 ranches in Texas of 130,000 acres or more."

Abbey said, "48,041 more than Rhode Island."

I said, "What?"

"Rhode Island has 776,959 acres so it is 48,041 acres smaller than the King Ranch. Well, Delaware is bigger than the King Ranch."

Walter Falone looked at Abbey. A look not unlike the look the pilot had given her. I'd seen many people look at her that way. It wasn't just that she was brilliant – she obviously was. It was the mix of what this young woman knew and didn't know. I have known her since her freshman year and was thrilled when she decided to stay at Cornell for her PhD work when she could have gone anywhere. As a 15-year-old freshman she once asked me why they say "dial the phone." It took me a minute to realize that dial phones went out before she was born.

Walter said, "Is that wine to your liking? If so I'll have Mrs. Lopez bring you another glass."

Abbey smiled and nodded yes.

"Walter, I was interested in the trails, and different livestock. Also do you ride? The stables are beautiful."

"I don't ride but my two daughters do. I hope the stables encourage them to come visit. The trails are being developed as part of an internship program. Each summer there are about six to eight interns working with Professor Sarah Chapman from the Environmental Studies department at Texas A&M. The students are from universities all over the country. We have had several from Cornell over the years.

"The livestock is work related. Remote sensing of animals, primarily wildlife, is still quite crude. We have a team working in this area. Large-scale detailed noninvasive tracking of wildlife in Africa and Asia could be invaluable to saving species while allowing the people in these areas to continue economic development. I'm not talking about tracking and counting herds from aerial or satellite photos. We are developing thermal bio patterns of species; remote vegetation and water consumption assessments in real time as herds migrate; and patterns of interaction of a particular herd and predators, again in real time. Adapting what we have developed for the mining and petroleum exploration industry to wildlife management can be transformative. Well, that is a long way of saying that the livestock here are used as a small part of that project. Now we are obtaining thermal body signatures for the animals here in a controlled environment. That is hard to do in the wild. This is part of building our database of background images. We also have scientists working in several zoos around the world. One of the beauties is that it is noninvasive, no darting and tagging of animal, no blood sample, etc.

"I also hope my grandchildren will want to spend time here on the ranch."

I said, "You have grandchildren?"

"My oldest daughter is expecting. I'm hoping for many and I like to plan ahead."

"Walter, I have another question. Why would someone whose company has 11,347 US patents and 4,312 employees, someone who was the first to successfully combine remote sensing with a SankeyTree type application for creating 4D visualizations of energy flows between processes, and then add advanced search properties, data mining with a layer of artificial intelligence, want to employ an archaeology professor and one of his students? Also how did you overcome the combinatorial explosion? The amount of memory or computer time required must have become astronomical."

"Rob, human beings solve most of their problems using fast, intuitive judgments rather than the conscious, step-by-step deduction that AI largely depends on. In the early days I just stopped the computer runs when they began diverging and took my best guess on which path to go down with the computing power I had available. Even today my company relies on highly trained scientists and engineers to run the programs, select the area of exploration most likely to get the desired result, and to interpret the data. However AI has made progress at imitating this kind of 'sub-symbolic' problem solving. Embodied agent approaches have also made progress; they emphasize the importance of sensorimotor skills to higher reasoning statistical approaches to mimic the probabilistic nature of the human ability to guess. It is really very interesting and all aspects of the field are advancing rapidly… But to answer the question you really wanted to ask me, follow me to another part of the house."

We entered a room that would have been a respectable archaeological gallery in almost any museum.

As we looked around Abbey said, "I know many of these pieces, Prof."

I said, "So do I, Abbey."

Walter picked up a gold Moche headdress representing a condor from about 500 AD. He handed it to me. I hesitated, then said, "I know this piece, it is in the American Museum of Natural History in New York."

"Take a close look at it, Professor."

I did. "It is an excellent copy. If I remember correctly this piece and numerous others were acquired at auction by an anonymous bidder and then donated to the Natural History Museum. That was you?"

"Actually I will only answer that question if and when you and Ms. Summers agree to join the project and sign the confidentiality agreements. Until then you will have to speculate. But please examine everything. You will find that nothing is stolen or illegally obtained. The only original pieces are ones where almost every major museum has fine examples and these would add little or nothing to their collections.

"You see, Rob, other than my family and my work I have my one hobby – archaeology. My wife died several years ago from cancer. My daughters are grown and they have their own families and careers. We are together for the holidays and vacations. My work is stimulating and I truly enjoy it. Archaeology, in particular pre-Columbian archaeology, seems to have gone from a hobby to a highly enjoyable way to spend any free time I have. It was the only thing that could fill the lonely nights after my wife died. It probably helped restore my balance after the loss of my wife, perhaps even saving my sanity."

"Walter, Abbey and I obviously share your love of pre-Columbian archaeology, but it doesn't answer my question of why we are here."

"Before I go into details I would like you to read this letter."

The envelope was addressed to me. The return address was the American Museum of Natural History, New York, NY. I removed the one-page letter and saw it was again addressed to me. Before I started reading I glanced at the bottom of the page. It was from Dr. Peter T. Hurst, Curator, Division of South American Archaeology, American Museum of Natural History.

The letter started:

"Dear Professor Johnson,
"I believe I had the pleasure of briefly meeting you at a conference in Washington, DC, a few years ago…"

I quickly read the rest of the letter. I remembered meeting Dr. Hurst but I was surprised he remembered me. He was a major presenter at the conference and I was one of about 200 attendees.

I said, "Dr. Hurst thinks quite highly of you. To use his words, 'a dear friend and trusted colleague' and he goes on to say 'whose expertise in remote sensing and data analysis could be transformative to the entire field of archaeology.' Quite high praise from someone of his standing in the field. This is intriguing, 'Your work will be superbly staffed, supported, and

Inca's Death Cave

funded… The results could be the most significant archaeological find in decades.' Well, I guess I'm impressed… I assume this letter is to reassure me you are not just a nutty billionaire with dreams of being the next Heinrich Schliemann."

Walter said, "Nothing quite that grand, however discovering the ancient city of Troy was quite an accomplishment."

"All this letter does is make it even more of a mystery why Abbey and I are here. If the project is as Dr. Hurst indicates and the pay is what you outlined, you could have your pick of the world's most renowned archaeologists. The last time I checked I wasn't one of them."

"Rob, you teach ANTHR 7220 - Incas and their Empire and several other courses on pre-Columbian archaeology at Cornell. You have a professional interest in this area. You are due for a year sabbatical and Abbey has been a student of yours since she was a freshman. So it is only natural that you two would take a year to do field research in South America."

"Yes, now I see, Walter. People will hardly notice we are gone and no one will care where we went or what we are doing. Someone of high stature might draw attention to this project of yours."

Walter said, "How do you two feel about that?"

Abbey spoke up. "It would be nice to know what project you are talking about to see how we feel about the offer and the project. But for picking Professor Johnson I think you picked the best archaeology professor in the world and, if he says yes you will be damn lucky to have him and I'll come if Prof does."

I said nothing.

Again Walter looked at Abbey. He said, "I see Mrs. Lopez is here. Dinner must be ready. After dinner we can discuss this in more detail."

Bradford Wheler

Ceremonial Mask, La Leche Valley Peru, 900-1100 A.D. (Note 1)

Gold Cup Sican Culture 850-1050 A.D. (Note 1)

Sican Gold Beaker Cups 9th-11th Century (Note 2)

Chapter
6

After dinner we settled in the living room again. Walter opened a bottle of 2001 Corison Kronos Vineyard from Napa Valley and poured us each a glass. It seemed to me an aromatic and cassis-scented Cabernet. Perhaps $80-$100 per bottle. It was above my normal price range but not outrageous, especially for a billionaire. The dinner was excellent but again without seeming fancy or in any way over the top.

Walter said, "You seem to already know the project I have in mind is in Peru. That really isn't a surprise given the extent of the operation Falone Advanced Technologies has in Peru. Do you know why we selected Peru?"

I said, "Abbey, tell Walter."

She looked at me and then a smile came to her lips.

"Peru is the world's largest silver producer, third largest in bismuth, copper, tin, and zinc, fourth largest in arsenic trioxide, lead, molybdenum, and rhenium, and fifth largest in gold.

"In recent years the government has privatized over 220 state-owned firms via joint ventures and consortia in the mining and fuels industries. The firms have generated revenues of $10.2 billion, with an additional committed capital flow of about $13.4 billion, representing 17% and 21% of Peru's GDP, respectively.

"Peruvian laws have attempted to ensure equitable mineral, crude oil, and gas exploration and production. Owing to these terms, an increased number of domestic and foreign companies, AngloGold Ashanti, Barrick Gold, BHP Billiton, Cambior, Falconbridge, Mitsui & Co., Mitsubishi,

Peñoles, Teck Cominco, and others, have set up operations in Peru.

"The combination of tropical latitude, mountain ranges, topography variations, and two ocean currents (Humboldt and El Niño) gives Peru a large diversity of climates.

"Throw in a stable government, varied geography, a high biodiversity with over 21,462 species of plants, and it sounds like a great place for a business like yours to work and test out new exploration methods.

"Plus, Peruvian territory was home to ancient cultures spanning from the Norte Chico civilization, one of the oldest in the world, to the Inca Empire, the largest state in pre-Columbian America."

Walter said, "In short a great place for me and my company. Also I fully understand that when you are asked to do research you do an outstanding job."

Abbey looked at me and said, "Prof, 11,347 US patents and 4,312 employees, someone who was the first to successfully combine remote sensing with a SankeyTree type application for creating 4D visualizations of energy flows between processes."

"Well, Abbey, you went to the trouble of producing that five-inch file, I thought the least I could do was read it."

Walter said, "Abbey, let's give your boss a chance to show off. Rob, Chimú?"

"Walter, volumes have been written about Chimú culture."

"Give us a brief summary then."

I began, "The oldest civilization present on the north coast of Peru, Early Chimú is also known as the Moche or Mochica civilization. The start of this Early Chimú time period is not known, probably BC, but it ends around 500 AD. It was centered in the Chicama, Moche, and Viru valleys. There are numerous large pyramids that are attributed to the Early Chimú period. These pyramids are built of adobe in rectangular shapes made from molds. The Early pottery is also characterized by realistic modeling and painted scenes.

"However the Chimú, I believe you are referring to the Kingdom of Chimor which was the political grouping of the Chimú culture that ruled the northern coast of Peru, beginning around 850 AD and ending around 1470 AD. The kingdom encompassed over 600 miles of coastline. Ruins of the city of Chan are located just northwest of the current Trujillo city.

"Chimor was the last kingdom that had any chance of stopping the Inca. But the Inca conquest was begun in the 1470s by Tupac Inca, defeating the local emperor Minchancaman, descendant of Tacaynamo, and was nearly complete when Huayna Capac assumed the throne in 1493 AD.

"This was just 50 years before the arrival of the Spanish in the region. Consequently, Spanish chroniclers were able to record accounts of Chimú culture from individuals who had lived before the Inca conquest.

"The Kingdom resided on the north coast of Peru on a narrow strip of desert, 20 to 100 miles wide, between the Pacific and the western slopes of the Andes. The valley plains are very flat, and well suited to irrigation, which is probably as old as agriculture here. Fishing was also very important.

"The Chimú were known to have worshipped the moon, unlike the Inca, who worshiped the sun. The Chimú viewed the sun as a destroyer. This is likely due to the harshness of the sun in their desert environment."

"Rob, stop there, please," Walter said. "You have hit on the two main points I wanted to discuss with you tonight. One, 'The Inca ruler Tupac Inca Yupanqui led a campaign which resulted in the conquest of the Chimú around 1470 AD. This was just 50 years before the arrival of the Spanish in the region. Consequently, Spanish chroniclers were able to record accounts of Chimú culture from individuals who had lived before the Inca conquest.' And second, 'The Chimú were known to have worshipped the moon, unlike the Inca, who worshiped the sun. The Chimú viewed the sun as a destroyer.' There is another item critical to this part of my story. What can you tell me about how the Incas ruled the people they conquered?"

I should have been annoyed by this 20 questions approach but the truth was I was having fun. Walter Falone was not a man to spend this kind of time without a good reason and just as he had planned, the letter from Dr. Hurst caused me to be seriously interested.

I said, "The Inca Empire was a patchwork of languages, cultures, and peoples. This plethora of civilizations provided for a general disunity that the Incas needed to subdue in order to maintain control. The components of the empire were not all uniformly loyal, nor were the local cultures all fully integrated.

"Traditional local power holders did much in the way of governing. Male heads of household were required to pay taxes both in kind (e.g., crops, textiles, etc.) and in the form of the mit'a corvée labor and military obligations. If the conquered peoples paid their taxes and swore loyalty they were pretty much left alone.

"Local religious traditions were allowed to continue, often incorporating the local deities into the pantheon of Inca gods. As I mentioned before, for the Incas the sun god was supreme and for the Chimú it was the moon god."

"Rob, I know this seems a bit of a roundabout way to explain my project but indulge me a while longer. Can you tell me about quipus?"

I said, "Abbey, why don't you join in the fun and answer this one?" Abbey had done extensive research in this area and it is always fun to show off your prize students.

Abbey began. "I'll skip the part about how quipus were in use in the Andean region from about 3000 BC and go to their use in the Inca Empire since that seems to be what we are talking about. Quipus played a key part in the administration of the Inca Empire.

"Quipus, sometimes called talking knots, were recording devices that usually consisted of colored, spun, and plied thread or strings from llama or alpaca hair. They could also be made of cotton cords. The cords contained numeric and other values encoded by knots in a base 10 positional system. Quipus might have just a few or up to 2,000 cords.

"Spanish officials often relied on the quipus to settle disputes over local tribute payments or goods production. Spanish chroniclers also concluded that quipus were used primarily as mnemonic devices to communicate and record numerical information.

"Some of the knots, as well as other features, such as color, are thought to represent non-numeric information, which has not been deciphered. It is generally thought that the system did not include phonetic symbols analogous to letters of the alphabet. Dr. Gary Urton suggested that quipus could record phonological or logographic data. Such as a zip code represents a city. Prof worked with Dr. Urton when Urton was at Colgate University."

Falone injected, "Yes, Gary's work is quite impressive."

Abbey continued, "Based on the analysis of several hundred quipus, Marcia and Robert Ascher have shown that most information on quipus is numeric, and these numbers can be read. Each cluster of knots is a digit in the base 10 system."

Falone interrupted again. "Abbey, your knowledge of quipus is also quite impressive. How many original quipus exist today?"

"Professor Urton says that 751 quipus have been reported to exist. The Berlin Ethnologisches Museum has the largest collection, 298 I believe. It is a shame the major museums in Peru have only a few dozen each."

"Yes, Abbey, I agree. My company recently completed a project with Dr. Albert Von Hanstein, the Curator of the Berlin Ethnologisches Museum. Using rather advanced digital stereoscopic and holographic photography we produced three-dimensional digital images of the museum's entire collection of quipus. This will allow researchers all over the world access to a vast quantity of information without any possibility of damaging the original artifacts... Abbey, what could be better for researchers than this?" Walter asked.

Abbey said, "For you to make exact replicas using the most up-to-date 3D printing technology. Why not? Cornell Creative Machines Lab has confirmed that it is possible to produce customized food with 3D Hydrocolloid Printing, and Chinese scientists have begun printing ears, livers, and kidneys, with living tissue."

"You are quite a remarkable young lady. I intended to shock both of you when I told you that is exactly what we did. We gave replicas from the Berlin Ethnologisches Museum to six museums in Peru with substantial quipus collections with the agreement that they would allow us to repeat the process with their collection and distribute the results to all the museums involved.

"The CEO of EMC Corp. is a member of the President's Council of Advisors on Science and Technology with me. Well, Joe's company has this RSA Security division which does all sorts of cryptography for NSA and private industry, so I asked if they had some code-breaking capability they could apply to the digital images and 3D models we produced of the quipus.

"Joe was quite excited and decided to use it as a test for his team. He gave them the digital files and models to analyze with no additional information.

"They quickly deciphered the base 10 digital system and figured out most of the material was numeric inventory, census, and calendar information. They also identified a number of label coding systems that appeared to be a writing system beyond numeric inventory items. So far, they seem to have found out pretty much what the experts in the field have discovered.

"Beyond that they identified groups of patterns. Different quipus seemed to relate to each other. Some straightforward, such as inventories for what appeared to be the same place in consecutive years. One that I found particularly interesting seemed to indicate a journey from Vilcabamba in the Department of Cusco to the northwest of the current Trujillo city."

I said, "Vilcabamba – *The Lost City of the Incas, Tomb Raider, Star Evil, The Lost City*, and let's not forget the PlayStation 2 game *Shadow Hearts: From the New World*. Walter, I'm enjoying your wine and the conversation but…"

"Please, Professor, just a few more items and then I'll outline my theory, the basis of the project for you."

A theory, well, he did fly us here and Dr. Hurst's letter said it "could be transformative to the entire field of archaeology." I smiled and tipped my wineglass in a gesture to go ahead.

Walter said, "Perhaps I'll ask Abbey this and let you enjoy your wine, Rob."

I smiled again.

"Abbey, the manuscript *Historia general del Piru,* do you know it?"

Abbey smiled. "Let's see now, the *Historia general del Piru* was written by Martín de Murúa who was born about 1525 and died about 1618. He was a Basque friar and was a chronicler of the Spanish conquest of the Americas. The book which is believed to have been written between 1580 and 1616 is considered the earliest illustrated history of Peru. He was assisted in his translation of the Quechua language by an Inca nobleman, named Guaman Poma, who provided over 100 illustrations. Poma was later highly critical of Murúa's depiction of Inca history in his own writings.

"There are two known manuscripts, one in the Getty Center in L.A. and the other in a private collection in Ireland. More?"

Walter said, "Not on the *Historia*. What about Guaman Poma?"

Abbey replied, "The man or his manuscript?"

"Start with a little about the man and then the chronicle, if you would, Abbey," Walter said.

"Felipe Guaman Poma de Ayala, also known as Guaman Poma, was a Quechua nobleman known for his chronicle in which he denounced the ill treatment of the native peoples of the Andes by the Spanish after conquest. He was a direct descendant of conqueror and ruler Huaman-Chava-Ayauca Yarovilca-Huanuco and born about 1535. Guaman Poma was a fluent speaker of several Quechua and Aru dialects. He also learned Spanish. He died sometime around 1616.

"His manuscript, *El primer nueva corónica y buen gobierno* or *The First New Chronicle and Good Government*, was 1,189 pages long. It contained 398 of Poma's full-page line drawings. The manuscript gives the view of a provincial noble on the Spanish conquest, most other surviving documents give views of the colonial era from the viewpoint of the nobility of Cusco, the ancient capital of the Incas.

"It was written between 1600 and 1615 and addressed to King Philip III of Spain. The book stated the injustices of colonial rule and argued that the Spanish were foreign settlers in Peru, a country they had no right to.

"The original manuscript has been kept in the Danish Royal Library since at least the early 1660s. A high-quality digital facsimile was published online in 2001 by the Danish Royal Library. It is tough reading because he wrote in native languages as well as Spanish."

"So you have read it, Abbey?"

"Well, Mr. Falone, let's say I've tried to read parts of it."

Walter said, "Having these types of work published in digital form on-line is a wonderful thing for scholarship and advancing our understanding of the ancient world. It allows the potential for crowd sourcing of so much that was in the past restricted to a few scholars."

Feeling a little left out of the conversation, I said, "However it is quite expensive to do in a manner that does not damage the original document."

"That's very true. Are you still enjoying your wine? Let me pour you some more."

I held out my glass.

Walter continued. "Poma served from about 1560 to 1570 as a Quechua translator for Fray, or Friar Cristóbal de Albornoz in his campaign to eradicate the messianic apostasy, known as Taki Unquy, from the local people.

"Taki Unquy arose in the 1560s in Huamanga, Ayacucho, then it spread to Lima, Cusco, Arequipa, Chuquisaca, and La Paz. It was also called 'The Revolt of the Wak'as,' which rejected the European and Christian god which had been imposed during Spanish conquest. Taki Unquy from Quechua is 'sickness of the chant' or 'dancing sickness.' The movement promoted the return to worship of the huacas. The followers believed that the wak'as were annoyed by the expansion of Christianity. The wak'as, Andean spirits, began taking possession of the person, making them dance to music and announce divine will to restore the pre-Hispanic culture, mythology, and politics.

"As you know, Professor, wak'a is an object that represents a revered monument of some kind. The term huaca can refer to natural locations, such as a cave or immense rocks. Some huacas have been associated with veneration and ritual. These objects were believed to have a physical presence and two spirits, one to create it and another to animate it.

"The religious revolt evolved into a political revolt with an ideology in keeping with Andean tradition. The followers believed that the huacas would return with all their might and would defeat the Spanish God, rid them of the invaders, and re-establish the equilibrium to a world wracked by the conquest.

"The revolt was brutally crushed by Friar Cristóbal de Albornoz. He took the spiritual leaders to Cusco where they were forced to reject their beliefs in public. The women participants were imprisoned in convents.

"Now here is what I am most intrigued by, both Guaman Poma's *Corónica* and Friar Martín de Murúa's *Historia general del Piru* refer to a journey north of a breakaway group from the revolt. Poma speaks of one of the religious leaders of Taki Unquy who claimed his ancestry not from the Incas but from the Kingdom of Chimor or perhaps even the Sican Empire. It isn't clear. According to Poma this leader used the name Minchancaman. Which was the name of the last great Chimú emperor. He seemed to have a sizable group of deeply devoted followers called the 'True of Heart.' He repudiates not only the Christian god of the Spanish but also the Inca sun god Inti for the Chimú moon god Si. Poma writes of Minchancaman's journey north with the True of Heart to the great huaca cave of the true gods. Where his True of Heart people will find eternal glory free from disease and the nonbelievers.

"You have to understand the state of the native culture and population. The Incan population suffered a dramatic and quick decline following the arrival of the Spanish. It is estimated that parts of the empire suffered a population decline of over 90% from the 1520s to the 1570s. Mostly from Old World diseases such as smallpox, chickenpox, diphtheria, typhus, influenza, measles, malaria, and yellow fever brought by the Spanish. A once-great people were utterly demoralized.

"In Friar Martín de Murúa's *Historia general del Piru* he refers to a Friar Pedro Zambrano Ortiz who was captured by one of the revolt's religious leaders and forced to travel north with his band. He was released at some point and ended up in the city of Arequipa. He is said to have kept a diary."

I said, "You believe that the band that held Friar Pedro Zambrano Ortiz was Minchancaman's True of Heart? They traveled north to the 'great huaca cave of the true gods' which was what, a kind of Jonestown Peoples Temple, where the True of Heart committed mass suicide in the equivalent of 900-plus followers of Jim Jones by cyanide poisoning?"

"Yes, Rob, something like that."

"You want to hire Abbey and me to help prove this theory?"

"Yes, to prove or disprove it. In any event interesting historical questions will be answered, new research technologies will be tested, and other interesting archaeological items might emerge."

"Walter, I assume you have a plan of attack or at least a place for us to start."

"I do indeed. I'm sure you know of the General Archive of the Indies housed in the ancient merchants' exchange of Seville, Spain, the Casa Lonja de Mercaderes, the repository of extremely valuable archival documents illustrating the history of the Spanish Empire in the Americas. I assume you also know the Complutense University of Madrid, one of the oldest universities in the world. Both have received grants to produce digital copies of all the works relating to the greater area of Peru during the 1500s and 1600s.

"The Church is strongly opposed to the wholesale release of this information for fear some of it may reflect badly on the Church. However I have entered into an agreement that allows me and my staff, who are bound by the same agreement, access to all the material for the purpose of archaeological research.

"That, Rob, along with the available material from the Getty Center, is where I would want you two to start."

"Walter, it could take a lifetime to review all that material."

"Rob, Falone Advanced Technologies has some tools and techniques that will greatly assist you in the process. It is late and I suggest you review the material in this briefcase. It contains the contracts between Falone Advanced Technologies and you two. It gives an outline of what your duties would be. Please read them in the morning and I will stop over to answer questions. Then you can make a decision. Whatever you decide it has been a most pleasurable evening for me and I hope at least a somewhat interesting one for the two of you."

"Walter, I now see another reason for hiring me and not someone of Dr. Hurst's stature. If this turns out to be a wild goose chase it is just Professor Johnson and one of his students testing out new research equipment and techniques in the field. No one is embarrassed or let down."

"Rob, perhaps the wine or the late hour is making you cynical."

He probably had a point. I put on a big smile, took the briefcase, and thanked him for a wonderful evening.

When we got back to the guesthouse I asked Abbey, "What do you think of Texas?"

"Prof, I think it makes you cynical."

"No, the BS administrative bureaucracy at Cornell makes me cynical."

I decided I was being too cynical to accomplish anything useful so I told Abbey I was going to bed and I would see her in the morning.

Inca's Death Cave

Inca Quipu (Note 2)

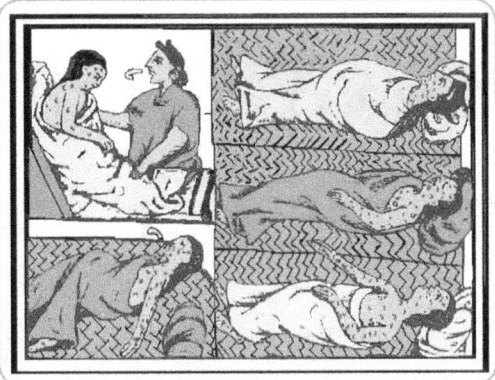

Depiction of Smallpox Victims (Note 2)

Mummy in the Cemetery of Chauchilla (Note 2)

Chapter
7

I got up about 6:30 and made a pot of coffee out in the guesthouse kitchen. I walked to the pool house. As I thought, the men's locker room had about a dozen swimsuits along with towels and flip-flops. I swam, showered, dressed, and went out on the patio with coffee to read what Walter had given us. Abbey arrived back from her morning run and said, "I'll join you after I shower."

Most of the bulk in the briefcase was our contracts. What interested me more were copies of the permits from the Minister of the Interior's Department of Antiquities. The permit area covered half of the country's regions from Cusco in the south to Tumbes in the north. That had to be over 40% of Peru's land area. The permits I was familiar with all had prescribed a small area, some with dimensions as small as 50M by 50M.

The permit stated that all items discovered were the property of the Ministry of the Interior, the Ministry having the sole right of the distribution of said items by auction, negotiated sale, and/or gifting to any museum, organization, or individual.

The permit holder had the right to photograph, measure, record, and test, in any nondestructive manner in keeping with accepted scientific methods, all items discovered. The permit holder also had the right to publish its findings in print, digital, audio, and video formats and copyright its work.

The permit holder was responsible for all expenses including the expense of periodic inspections by Ministry officials. The choice of lead archaeologist would be by mutual agreement between the Ministry and the permit holder. I assumed Walter had me preapproved.

I started looking at the contracts. The description of our duties was quite general. The pay was great. The confidentiality agreement was strict. I was sure none of this was negotiable. Walter was probably ready to fly someone else down if we didn't sign up. I started to wonder if maybe we weren't his first choice and he had been through this whole process with others. I decided it was too early in the morning to become cynical.

Abbey came out, got a cup of coffee, and joined me on the patio. I said, "Would you like to read this stuff?"

She said, "I read it all last night. Do you know how much land that permit covers?"

"I'm sure you can tell me, Abbey?"

She smiled. "A whole bunch, Prof, a whole big bunch. Have you ever seen a permit like that? Where would we start?"

"No, I've never seen anything like this. Walter must have a plan. He obviously wants us to start with the digital documents from the Getty Center, the General Archive of the Indies, and the Complutense University of Madrid. That will be tens of thousands of pages so he must know where he wants us to begin… Abbey, what do you think of the contracts?"

"Well, the other contracts I've signed were for my apartment and my car lease. These seem a little more comprehensive. The money is great and I don't think we get to change the contract terms, do we?"

I said, "No, I'm sure not. Abbey, what do you think of Texas now?"

"Prof, I say we do it. Sign on the dotted line and go for it."

"You don't even want to ask Walter any questions when he comes over?"

"Yes, Prof, only about a million. But it won't change my mind."

I said, "There is something wonderful about a female who can make up her mind."

Abbey stuck her tongue out at me and picked up the "borrowed" copy of Julian Steward's book and began to read. I got more coffee and decided I should read all the contract documents.

At 8:30 the breakfast order we had given Regina Lopez last night arrived. I told the young woman who brought it to tell Mr. Falone to come over anytime it was convenient for him and he didn't have to wait until 10:30 if he didn't want to.

Walter arrived at 10:00 and again politely knocked on the door to the patio before joining us.

Walter said, "Good morning, I trust you slept well."

I was starting to see why people might enjoy working for him. I said, "Abbey and I would like to sign these contracts and come to work for you." Abbey was staring at me. I didn't want her to think she was the only one who could make up her mind.

"I would love to have you two working with me, but no more questions?"

"Abbey has a million questions and I probably have more. However I don't think you will answer them until we sign."

"Rob, do you want to have your attorney review the contracts?"

"No, Walter, I'm sure your attorneys have done a fine job. My attorney does mostly wills and real estate."

I handed Abbey a pen. She was grinning ear to ear as she began to sign. This was a very big deal for me so it had to be an exciting moment for her. I signed when she was done with the pen.

Walter sat patiently while we signed and then he said, "Now I'm not sure I have the time or the information to answer all million questions but I'll try."

I said, "I assume you want us to spend the time between now and June 1 reviewing the digital records while we are still at Cornell. I know the Getty Center has the digital form of the *Historia general del Piru* done. However I'm not sure of the status of the material from Seville and Madrid. But even this one volume is a lengthy document and it is written in sixteenth-century Spanish."

"I do want you to start with the *Historia* and the *Chronicle*. Other documents will be sent to you as logical groupings are completed. To the extent that our software is capable we will provide you with translations into modern Spanish and English as well as the originals. We will also provide you with search and pattern recognition software to help your search. This software is many generations beyond what you or anyone at Cornell has ever worked with. Working on these two manuscripts with it, you should become skilled at using it and able to provide valuable feedback to our development team.

"I know you have lots more questions, but I'm getting short of time and there are several other points I would like to cover. The digital *Historia* and *Chronicle* files will be sent to you. Someone from HR will email the standard employment forms for you to fill out. Your pay will be electronically deposited in your account every two weeks. A plane will be in Ithaca to pick you up on June 1 and bring you to Houston. After a day in Houston you will leave for Lima. Please put your affairs in order so you can be in Peru for an extended period. Please make a list of equipment you believe you will need and we will make sure what is needed is in Peru. For now Mrs. Lopez will be your primary contact."

That was good news; I thought it might be the icy Dr. Stone.

Walter went on, "I'm sorry to be short but I'm pressed for time. I'm truly looking forward to working with the two of you. Please have a safe trip home." With that, Walter departed.

Abbey said, "He is the nicest billionaire I know."

"I agree, Abbey, I agree." We both laughed and headed to our rooms to get our overnight bags.

Mrs. Lopez was there. She handed me our copies of the contracts and put the rest of the papers in the briefcase.

Cornell McGraw Hall (Note 1)

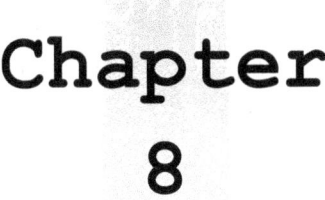

Chapter
8

I was in my office in McGraw Hall after the Presidents' Week break. I had my meeting with the Dean to discuss my sabbatical. The Dean was interested in what I would be doing. As instructed, I told him we would be helping Falone Advanced Technologies test field equipment in Peru that might have applications in the field of archaeology. He of course knew of Walter Falone. I made it sound as mundane as I could.

Abbey put in her letter requesting a leave to do field work in Peru with me. I instructed her to dampen down her excitement and describe her work as a good opportunity for a grad student to get field experience.

Abbey marched into my office and set her open laptop on my desk. I had forwarded the digital files I received that morning from Falone Advanced Technologies to her a few minutes ago. I said, "What's up?"

She turned her laptop around. I looked.

— ‥’ ‡_Œ "Ÿ´x|‾_öm‑S4Yk 'y3‡Šœ • Þ 6 é □>7 'jÍÐÆÐ_
i˄˄ÒG" fË_€ ª ¨Ö_þ á =_ê *_Vw® _øJ™Ü<=ö—
&æŒ, ÿóÝ½1°⊠ëcÝ‑_WY_=⊠_□{⊠ÒÞ • ûÃ¥˜‑} `ˆi_
ëhýãÓÐ»c é 2È_‾⊠‡—T9| ó ‑ ’ 9Z⊠ÍætÄ[ÏM/
Ž § _Ⅹšͱ̈\ÚçæÃøQ˜¬æë__M?_{ ¨A D_ñ (Õ⋯Hñx • x‑
½e ó Ç__E%C3žQj ſ cÛµ— ‑ š< _tw "ûZÛd:Ý^_‾Œ⋯]
ÿ« ſ _Do+® à ù ¹Ùäî2ŒsÄK‾Cv} ßö ¢ kw(Œ® ſ • 0\y‡_
õS[ÚŒ_⋯_ ſ Ðt/_%¥Ö9_¹_m ›sóo‰©œô_
ö>E ò Þ" ¾PÄ˜_î¿Ó*b__¦˜Œ%ÌÚ⊠ÿE_j.

bC '_Á ó Ð_ë ¡⊠%¶ ¿Jå;4û § aß ^b Ú_ù \X
]‰ì |⊠¥¼m˜□Â¡¥Wv ò J >¯v^$_c¬†åSÄ™XâXÿ § =. _Á«f*¥ž
2···h_»2_-c%Ñ § Qe" eÊ__i?*Øe,,t__s_a £ öÃ é *v`À__Oï
yÛ÷Ø § ¬5¬_¯Ó¹Ý©ëNWª £kó ü _[_ ⊠‡;kö×_wf··· >Ê%_v_
á p_Jô7 ê _Î à Rœ_ â3ó:_$_iñ⊠v §_ ì 02Ññ,Q3å©*ñÕ ú ‡_
uþ ¨ mS÷b‡" _›®Ã; • 1 ê å° Ì^ wÌ^ • »1ÇeY
Žª!9Ëyxwd é ' glîgdýØP ó ſ ¸M_Oýå0¾_WO(• na1Ê*eût_
,,!ï⊠. _²Á□ãn²« £—¦Äª ±>ÿÿª˜ÓVtÎLNÀ\‰ÔÚ¯iŽ £V__ſ]
_™_Ûx¦ žJ»ƒP1_ÕzvîÚv__Ò ü †Ùq¼- ¢_ j_*‡ ú *>µ]
ŽCÌ□□Dn é K" s]uh¿ i#' ¥xi ê á fšýô € ···n¿Â_Ra_s¡p˜F__
IK_q;û÷ ê ÓçÑŠÍHã_ýÆMO—¼_žz¸_F_¾t ù #ÞÁ®X_Ú_ "v©_
Ò £ ²ÞûY?†Qÿç/X_¥2(||j § }J‡_û ò ù _ÈÏÏX_□···Ì • F_
@_ÿ»øö_ -¯=Ú[_ſ I—

As I reached in my drawer, I said, "It is encrypted. Haven't you broken the code yet?"

"Very funny, Prof."

"Here." I handed her a memory stick I had gotten via FedEx a few days ago. "Here is the encryption software." I then handed her a registered letter I had gotten the day before. "The user name and password are in this. Once you finish installing it on your laptop, could you install it on mine when I'm at my 10:10 class? They seem to take security very seriously so we should too."

Abbey took her laptop and walked out without a word. Not in a humorous mood this morning.

Later that day, I was looking back and forth between the modern Spanish and English versions of the *Historia*. The English seemed a bit jumbled. Abbey's mother's side of the family was Hispanic so her Spanish was far better than mine. We were scheduled to meet at 1:00. I hoped she was making better progress than I. Falone Advanced Technologies had sent the digital form of both the *Historia* and Poma's *Chronicle*. I decided to start with the *Historia*.

I moved on to the search software and went through the instructions for setting the search parameters. I was hoping it was written a little more like "advanced search for dummies."

So I guessed we would start with any reference to Friar Pedro Zambrano Ortiz. Then toss in Minchancaman, True of Heart, and the great huaca cave of the true gods. Walter had only mentioned a reference to Friar Pedro Zambrano Ortiz being in the *Historia*. I still wasn't sure how many terms to add at once. I decided to start with just Friar Pedro Zambrano Ortiz.

The search software didn't actually run on our laptops. We had a piece of code, a cookie I guessed, that allowed us to access a computer at Falone Advanced Technologies. This program must require massive amounts of computing capacity, I thought.

I tried the run. It came back with eight references to Friar Pedro Zambrano Ortiz. It gave lots of other information. But I focused on the distance between the references, primarily because I thought I understood it. That was a page, line, and word count between each reference to Friar Pedro Zambrano Ortiz. It started with the count from the start of the manuscript to the first reference to the friar and proceeded to each subsequent reference from there.

I began with a section that had three references to the friar quite close together. First I read the English version. Then I tried the modern Spanish and finally the original translation. I found a reference to Friar Pedro Zambrano Ortiz being captured and taken north. I went to the other places where the friar was mentioned and found that he went to Arequipa.

Not much more than Walter had told us. Both the *Historia* and the *Chronicle* had been available in digital form for quite a while. I suspected that Walter's research people had found most of what there was to find in these manuscripts. So Abbey and I would be double-checking what they found, learning to use the software, and brushing up on our sixteenth-century Spanish.

Abbey walked in my office a few minutes after 1:00.

She said, "This software is amazing. It is like Bible Analyzer Version 4.7 on steroids. Really mind-blowing."

Abbey obviously had gotten more out of her time playing with the software than I had. I knew Bible Analyzer was used quite a bit by both grad students and researchers here at the University. I assumed that was primarily because it was freeware.

I said, "That was just what I was about to say. Could you refresh my memory on Bible Analyzer's capabilities?"

I thought she was going to tell me I was full of it. But she just gave me that smirk smile of hers.

"Prof, if it all comes back to you when I start, let me know, I wouldn't want to bore you. Bible Analyzer is written in Python with a wxPython GUI. The primary features are Bible text comparison, proximity range searches, and textual statistical analysis. Later they added other features such as a dedicated cross-reference panel, 'Related Verse' searches, text-to-speech and audio features, Harmony/Parallel Text Generator, and Advanced Related Phrase Search. Bible Analyzer can also search for specific individuals using an ID tagging system.

"Is it all starting to come back to you now? Prof, they say the memory is the second thing to go. Well, this software of Falone Advanced Technologies does all that and lots more. Most of those features I haven't figured out yet. It also can handle way more documents. I wouldn't be surprised if you could load the whole Library of Congress in this software. I hope we get to meet the people who built this. I have a whole bunch of questions and somebody needs to help us so we can use all the features."

I smiled at her and said, "You know what I think? I think Walter's researchers have already found out everything there is to find out in these two documents. All we are doing is learning about the software and re-checking what his people have done. I also think Walter told us just about everything that they found. Would this software work on the digital copies of the quipus?"

Abbey said, "I don't think so. That's why he sent the digital 3D copies of the quipus to his buddy Joe at EMC Corp. What did you think about Poma's *Chronicle*?"

I didn't want to admit I hadn't even looked at the *Chronicle* because it took me so long to figure out even the most basic parts of the software. I said, "Nothing but what Walter told us." That was a true statement.

"Well," Abbey said, "I think Walter might be wrong."

"Wrong about what?" I said.

"Walter called the followers of Minchancaman the True of Heart, I believe a better translation is the Strong of Heart."

She really was a most amazing young lady. I said, "Interesting, I believe you have more than earned your pay today, Abbey. Very fine work. I mean it, very well done. Now go enjoy your weekend. Go to happy hour or something. If you hurry you can still make the pre-3:00 club."

Chapter
9

It was the second Monday morning since we came back from Texas. I walked into my office about 8:15 to find the safe Cornell provided professors had been drilled open. It wasn't a high-tech safe. The University provided them to us so we could lock up tests, hopefully discouraging students from doing anything stupid. No prelims for a while. I was sure all I had in there were old test copies.

My desk and the rest of my office had been searched. Not trashed but someone had gone through everything. I started to call the Cornell police and then decided to call Regina Lopez instead. She answered on the second ring just as I realized it was only 7:15 in Houston.

I apologized for the early hour and explained what I had just found. She thanked me for calling her first. She said Falone Advanced Technologies had systems and technologies that made the company the target of industrial espionage. She suspected that it wasn't related to our project but someone thought it might be a vulnerable spot to enter Falone Advanced Technologies systems. She said to call the Cornell police and just tell them about the break-in with no mention of our work for Falone Advanced Technologies. She would arrange for a security team to be there later that day. In the meantime she told us not to access any of the company websites.

I called the police and while I waited I called Abbey. "My office was broken into, are you OK? No problems at your apartment or with your car?"

She said, "I don't know. I spent the weekend at my soon-to-be ex-boyfriend's place."

Well, maybe that explained her being somewhat less than her usual up-beat self. I told her what Mrs. Lopez had said and I'd call her again when I was done with the police.

I sat at my desk and didn't touch anything else until the Cornell police arrived. Small-time robberies were not all that uncommon at the University. It was the professional way the safe was drilled out that seemed to interest them the most. Maybe they did know how to do more than write parking tickets. They asked me what was missing. I told them nothing as far as I could tell. They dusted for fingerprints and asked me to make a list of people who were in my office recently so their prints could be eliminated.

A small crowd had formed outside my office. An officer came in and told the investigator that it appeared that no other offices had been broken into. He also said he had identified the side door that had been forced open.

When they were done questioning me I took my briefcase and laptop and left. After answering a few questions from the onlookers, I spotted the Dean and told him what I told the police and the little I had learned from the police. I left out the part about how the police seemed quite interested in the professional way the safe was drilled out. I'm pretty sure being a busybody was one of the requirements to be a Dean.

I walked across the quad while calling Abbey on my cell phone. I told her I'd meet her in the lounge in Goldwin Smith.

I received a call from John McCay. He said he was with the security division of Falone Advanced Technologies and his plane would be landing about 2:30. We agreed to meet at my house at 3:00 to avoid attracting attention at the University.

Abbey had gone to her apartment while I was dealing with the police at my office. She said it appeared nothing had been disturbed. Her car also didn't seem to have been touched. It would have been hard for people to know she was at her boyfriend's place.

We had lunch and headed to my house to meet John McCay.

A rental car pulled in my driveway right at 3:00. Two men got out. I opened the door as they approached.

"I'm John McCay, you must be Professor Johnson. This is my associate Tom Forest."

We shook hands and I introduced Abbey. They had the ex-military or ex-cop look. Both were fit and had short hair. Tom was much younger than John, who was clearly the boss.

I said, "Usually not much excitement in my department at the University."

"Well, let's hope we can keep it that way," McCay said. "Please give me a complete rundown on what happed this morning. Include as many details as you can remember."

I started when I walked into my office and ended with what I had told the Dean. McCay asked what type of safe it was. I didn't know the model or serial number. I told him the brand and described it as best I could.

"Ms. Summers, please tell me about your weekend. Any signs of disturbance at your apartment?" McCay asked.

Abbey said, "I was at my boyfriend's place this weekend. My car and laptop were with me. I checked my apartment this morning. Nothing seemed out of place. I have two roommates. I didn't say anything to them but if something strange had happened, believe me, I would have heard about it from those two."

McCay said, "Good. It appears Professor Johnson's office was the only target. Mr. Falone asked us to give you two a security overview. He feels it is important for you to understand the lengths to which some of our competitors and foreign countries will go to steal our company's sophisticated sensing systems. We also have sensitive data and information of our clients which we must protect.

"As I'm sure you know, security can be classified in two major categories, physical and information security. Physical security is everything from building and property security that every company is concerned with to more unusual concerns we have because of the places we work around the world. In some of the places we operate we even need to worry about terrorism and kidnapping.

"Tom and I are with the information security side. This is an area of major concern for Falone Advanced Technologies. Now, information security gathering has many forms and many shades of gray.

"Competitive intelligence is the legal and ethical activity of systematically gathering, analyzing and managing information on industrial competitors. It may include activities such as examining newspaper articles, corporate publications, websites, patent filings, specialized databases, information at trade shows, and the like to determine information on a corporation. Everyone does this. However, there are consulting firms in this area that go beyond what is legal. Companies hire these firms knowing full well they are obtaining information illegally. If the consulting firm is caught, the hiring company just fires them and acts shocked that anyone would do that. That may be what we have in your case, Professor Johnson.

"Then we get to countries that engage in industrial espionage and economic espionage. Our friends like Israel and the French are known to look the other way when their companies conduct industrial espionage. France is one of the most aggressive pursuers of espionage to gather foreign industrial and technological secrets. The government of France is alleged, by the US government, to be conducting ongoing industrial espionage against American aerodynamics and satellite companies. Our industry was not specifically named but we have been targeted as well.

"The biggest problem is China. You may have heard of Ghost Net. Ghost Net was a vast surveillance system reported by Canadian researchers based at the University of Toronto in March 2009. Using targeted emails it compromised thousands of computers in governmental organizations, enabling attackers to scan for information and transfer it back to a digital storage facility in China. Google in 2010 announced that operators, from within China, had hacked into their Google China operation, stealing intellectual property and, in particular, accessing the email accounts of human rights activists. The attack was thought to have been part of a more widespread cyber attack on foreign companies within China known as Operation Aurora.

"Mr. Falone wanted me to explain the situation we are facing so that you would understand why we all have to take security so seriously. It is unfortunate but it is the reality of life in most high-tech firms."

While John explained this, Tom connected our laptops to the equipment he had in his briefcase. He also checked our cell phones. They were clean; no malware had been installed.

They gave us each a new laptop and cell phone and told us to use them for all our work related to the company. The cell phones would work in Peru and ours probably would not. They explained the laptops and phones had the latest security features.

Abbey had been studying her laptop and said, "These laptops have GPS and cell connections like an iPad has, correct?"

"Yes," Tom said.

"I assume if it is lost or stolen you can remotely disable it. The GPS is tracking the computer and being monitored all the time, even when I turn it off, right?" Abbey went on. "Do I need to put a towel over this thing when I take a shower?"

Tom said, "There is no video or audio feed, just GPS tracking and it is monitored all the time. The same is true for the cell phones."

John was going to go with me to my office and Tom was to check both cars and then go with Abbey to her apartment.

It was almost 5:00 when we got to my office. It was pretty quiet and no one seemed to notice us. John put on gloves and looked at the safe. He then removed a device from his briefcase and began systematically moving it around. It seemed to me just like the movies. The way they look for bugs.

"Well, look at this," he said.

John removed a box about two by three inches and maybe half an inch thick from the underside of one of my bookshelves.

"Professor, I assume this isn't yours."

I just shook my head. "What is it? A bug? What does it do?"

John said, "It's a bug and it spies on you. Exactly how I won't know until we test it at our lab. It may give us a hint as to who was behind the break-in, but probably not. Welcome to my world, Professor."

I wasn't really sure I wanted any part of his world. John stated again that he suspected that this was done by one of the competitive intelligence gathering firms.

John drove me home and then went to pick up Tom at Abbey's apartment.

Chapter
10

The rest of the spring semester went by quickly. No more break-ins. The Cornell police found no fingerprints that shouldn't have been there. Since no one was hurt and nothing was missing they went back to writing parking tickets and dealing with drunk and disorderly students.

I put my affairs in order. The Dean wasn't going to replace me for the year. They wouldn't offer my fall and spring independent study course, and the rest of my courses would be taught by other members of the department. This was pretty standard. No one seemed to mind. I had done it for others when they had been on sabbatical. However, I took care to put my lesson plans in good order for them.

Mrs. Lopez forwarded an email to me that outlined in more detail how we were to describe our employment with Falone Advanced Technologies. I was helping field test new sensing and testing equipment the company was developing to be used in the area of archaeological and geographic exploration. I would be evaluating the results in comparison to standard methods. This would be done mostly at existing sites. Abbey would be assisting me. All expenses paid and a salary. Most of my colleagues would jump at any chance to spend a year in the archaeological digs of Peru. Most also had family and other constraints that ruled this out.

I rented my house to a married grad student for the 14 months I was to be away. My pay from Falone Advanced Technologies was being electronically deposited to my account. I set up my Schwab pay-bill account to send a check for the entire after-tax amount to be applied to my mortgage each month. Before the year was over I would have the mortgage paid off. This job would repair much of the financial damage done by my divorce.

Abbey was going to her classes and doing as little as she could get away with in her teaching assistant job. We decided that there was no point in even thinking about a topic for her thesis until next year when we returned. The rest of the time she was spending doing every imaginable combination of searches of both the *Historia* and the *Chronicle.* She was really getting good with the search software. Her ability to read and understand six-teenth-century Spanish was increasing daily. She was even teaching herself several Quechua and Aru dialects. She had apparently split up with her boyfriend and was devoting all her time to our project and running.

I wasn't going to find anything Abbey didn't find in the documents. I wasn't much good with the software so I decided to focus on Friar Pedro Zambrano Ortiz. I used the University's research materials and more tra-ditional research methods. I even went to the library.

Cornell's rare book and manuscript collections were founded in 1865 by Andrew Dickson White, the co-founder and first president of Cornell. The Carl A. Kroch Library has more than 500,000 volumes, and 70 million manuscripts, photographs, and other artifacts. The Rare Book and Manu-script Division features collections spanning 4,000 years, from cuneiform tablets to comic books. However, pre-Columbian works are not the collec-tion's strong point.

I started by seeing Mrs. Laura O'Hara, the Senior Reference Specialist. With a title like that in the rare book and manuscript library, one would think of an old biddy. Well, Laura was, if not exactly hot, definitely a very attractive woman.

The author of the *Historia*, Friar Martín de Murúa, who had mentioned Friar Pedro Zambrano Ortiz being taken north by Minchancaman and his followers, was a Mercedarian friar from the Basque region of Spain. So I started there. Laura O'Hara pointed me in the right direction.

The Royal, Celestial and Military Order of Our Lady of Mercy and the Redemption of the Captives, also known as Our Lady of Ransom, was es-tablished in 1218 by St. Peter Nolasco in the city of Barcelona in the King-dom of Aragon. Its members are commonly known as Mercedarian friars or nuns. A lot of interesting history about the evolution of the order from

1200 AD to 1600 AD, but not much that helped me.

Friar Murúa volunteered to serve in the missions of New Spain. He arrived in Peru in the early 1580s. He is known to have lived in the Curahuari Valley about that time. He later traveled throughout as a missionary, near Lake Titicaca and Cusco. From about 1595 to 1601 his residence was at the Mercedarian Monastery of Saint John Lateran in Arequipa. In 1611 he returned to Spain and published his manuscript the next year.

Murúa's *Historia* mentioned that Friar Pedro Zambrano Ortiz was in Arequipa after being released by Minchancaman. No date was given. That is probably where the two friars crossed paths. Murúa was there from 1595 to 1601 so sometime during that period Murúa must have spoken to Ortiz. Or maybe Murúa heard the story second-hand. Or maybe I was just wasting my time.

It wasn't even clear to me if Friar Ortiz was a Mercedarian or Dominican friar. That is how my days went. I was being paid so I would keep digging. That is often how it is in archaeology, a whole lot of nothing, but every now and then something falls in place.

Chapter 11

The email from Mrs. Lopez said to be at the Ithaca airport for a 1:00PM departure for Houston. We were told to pack a small bag for an overnight stay in a hotel near Ellington Airport. The rest of our gear was to going to be loaded on the plane scheduled to leave for Lima at 9:00AM local time.

I left my car with the people who rented my house and told them to use it. They had only one car. Abbey had stored all her stuff and her car at her parents' house. Her mother had driven her to my house the day before and said a teary goodbye.

A friend of mine with a Suburban agreed to drive us with all our bags to the airport. As we pulled up to Taughannock Aviation I saw the same Cessna 525B Citation Jet 3 we had flown to Houston back in February. There was a different pilot but Jane Fitzpatrick was there to meet us.

She checked to see that we had our passports, visas, and a separate overnight bag. I thought, "Yes, Jane, I did pack plenty of clean underwear."

The flight was smooth. When we arrived a driver took our overnight bags and another employee loaded the rest of our bags on a cart. Jane told us to be in the lobby of the hotel at 7:15 AM and we would be driven back to the airport.

The next morning the driver drove us right into the hangar. It was a busy place. I looked at the large jet and said to Abbey, "Rats, it's not a Gulfstream G4."

Abbey said, "Prof, it is a Boeing BBJ C which is a variant of the BBJ featuring the 'quick change' capabilities of the 737-700C. This allows the aircraft to be used for executive duty during one flight, and to be quickly reconfigured for cargo duty for the next flight. It has blended winglets for additional fuel economy of about 5-7% and self-contained stairs for disembarking at airports with limited ground support. I believe it also has long-range fuel tanks, for intercontinental travel. The C-40 Clipper is a military version. No G4 but it should get us there."

I said, "That's what I thought." She gave me her look. "I mean that it should get us there." She smiled.

The plane's cargo hold was being loaded. Lots of aluminum crates that looked like they held equipment. The driver told us to wait by the car and Mr. Falone would join us shortly. He then took our bags and headed towards the plane.

I saw Walter talking to the good Dr. Stone. He turned and waved to us. As he turned back I gave Dr. Stone a little wave with my pinky finger. She didn't respond in kind.

In a minute he broke off his conversation with Dr. Stone and came over to us.

"Professor, Abbey, I'm so pleased to see you two again. I hope your trip went smoothly. Once again I must apologize for being short on time. I won't be able to join you in Peru for a day or two. However you can get settled and meet the staff. Our project is located at my ranch along with some other R&D work. The company's business operations are in an industrial park next to the Lima airport."

Abbey said, "WHOO," and then looked a little embarrassed.

Walter and I looked up. A gentleman who was at least six feet five inches tall was walking towards us. He looked chiseled, super-fit but not with bulging muscles like some weightlifters. I thought, he's built like Arnold Schwarzenegger, but looks like a young Sean Connery.

Walter said, "Yes, Abbey, you are not the first woman to react that way."

Abbey looked more embarrassed.

Walter went on, "Major Ian Campbell, retired SAS."

I looked at Abbey and said, "British Special Air Service like our Navy Seals."

Walter said, "Major Campbell, I would like to introduce you to Professor Robert Johnson and Ms. Abbey Summers."

I shook his hand. "Nice to meet you, Major, please call me Rob."

Abbey seemed to have lost her voice but managed a smile and a hand-shake.

"Major Campbell handles security for our operations in Peru. He is headquartered at the ranch but most of his team is at our Lima office or out in the field."

Walter excused himself to talk with Major Campbell.

Abbey said, "What are you looking at?"

I replied, "You."

Walter returned and said, "Again I must say I'm sorry to be so short on time. I will see you in a day or two and we can spend the time to really get started."

He then got in the car that picked us up. The driver closed the door and drove off. Walter Falone was definitely the politest billionaire I knew.

As we walked over to the plane, Abbey called out, "Hey, Jimmy, long-range tanks?"

I looked up to see Jim Bodin, our pilot from our first trip to Houston. He was standing next to the plane's stairs with another pilot.

He said, "Yes, ma'am. It will get us all the way to Lima no problem."

He introduced us to the other pilot; we shook hands and then went up the stairs. We were directed to seats that were set up with four across a table, two facing front and two facing the back. Abbey took the back-facing window seat and I took the seat across from her facing forward.

Only six other passengers boarded the plane. In addition to Major Campbell the other five were engineers and technicians stationed in Lima. The pilot told us to buckle up and that it was 3,126 miles to Lima and our flight time was about six and a half hours. Abbey had a copy of *Lonely Planet Discover Peru* guidebook. I took out my copy of Bryan Gruley's novel *The Skeleton Box*. It was a workday for the five engineers. They all had their laptops open and were sitting in a group quietly conversing.

About an hour into the flight I heard Abbey say, "Excuse me, Major."

I looked up to see Major Campbell stop by my seat. "Yes?" he said.

Abbey went on, "Is your sidearm a SIG Sauer P226-9-NAVY or a P226R with an extended 5.0 inch barrel and external threads to accept a suppressor?"

Major Campbell blinked and then calmly said, "It's a P226R. Are you proficient with handguns?"

"My family is from Plattsburgh," Abbey said as if this would explain her knowledge of handguns to even the dimmest of wits. She went on, "What are the worst security issues in Peru that aren't related to cyber security?"

The Major said, "Well, there is the Shining Path, a Maoist guerrilla group. They claim to be freedom fighters but are mostly involved in drug smuggling, kidnapping, and money laundering. But probably the most gruesome was in 2009, when Peruvian policemen reported apprehending gang members suspected of killing people in Huanuco Province for their fat and selling the fat on the black market for use in cosmetics in Europe. Three suspects confessed to killing five people and told the police that the fat was worth $60,000 a gallon. At least 60 people are reported missing this year in Huanuco Province."

Abbey looked a little pale. The Major said, "Lots for my people to do in Peru." He smiled and continued on up towards the front of the plane.

Abbey said, "Did he make that up?"

I said, "Google it and find out." She did and I could tell by the look on her face that Major Campbell hadn't made it up.

They served lunch. After I finished I put my seat back and took a nap. I woke when they brought us warm washcloths and asked if we would like anything to drink.

I looked out the window as we started our descent into Lima's Jorge Chavez International Airport. Lima is a big, sprawling city with a population of almost nine million and a land area of over 1,000 square miles. It is the capital and the largest city of Peru. It is located in the valleys of the Chillon, Rimac, and Lurin rivers, in the central coastal part of the country, overlooking the Pacific Ocean.

Some parts of Lima are quite nice; other parts have extreme poverty. The climate is mild, temperatures are usually between 54°F and 84°F for the entire year.

Lima was founded by Spanish conquistador Francisco Pizarro on January 18, 1535, as Ciudad de los Reyes. It was the capital and most important city in the Spanish Viceroyalty of Peru. Now Lima is the most populous metropolitan area of Peru, and the fifth largest city in the Americas.

Major Campbell collected everyone's passports and customs papers. Our plane taxied to the general aviation section of the airport to a hangar that appeared to be just used by Falone Advanced Technologies.

As we reached the bottom of the ramp Major Campbell handed us our passports and papers back. He said, "Professor Johnson, your driver is over there. He will take you and Ms. Summers to the ranch."

As the five other employees got off they began directing how the cargo should be loaded in the different trucks.

We went to meet our driver.

Chapter
12

We headed north on the Pan-American Highway, also known as Peru Highway 1 towards the city of Huacho. It is in Huaura province, one of the nine provinces of the Lima Region. It was just over 90 miles north of Lima on the coast.

As far as I knew Huacho was known for two things: being near the Lomas de Lachay National Park and holding the city's annual Guinea Pig Festival where guinea pigs are dressed up in fedoras and frilly dresses to participate in a fashion show. Must not be a lot else to do in Huacho.

The park is quite spectacular. It is 13,000 acres in a peculiar geography called the Yungas. It is a stretch of forest along the eastern slope of the Andes Mountains and features a unique mist-fed ecosystem of wild plant and animal species. I was looking forward to finding time to explore the park.

We turned off the Pan-American Highway and headed inland on the road to Lomas de Lachay. We passed the park entrance and continued for several miles. We turned again up a gravel road. About 100 yards in was an open gate with a manned guardhouse. We were in the region situated between the eastern part of the coastal strip and the western part of the Highlands. This region is considered to have the most biodiversity in Peru. It is mainly composed of lucuma, cherimoya, and casuarin trees. Casuarin are evergreen shrubs and trees growing to over 110 feet tall. The foliage consists of slender, much-branched green to grey-green twigs bearing min-ute-scale leaves in whorls of 5-20.

We came to a high open meadow that ran north-south. To the east you could see the start of the rain forest and the Andes Mountains beyond. To the west the terrain fell away towards the coastal desert plain. This was not so much a ranch as an eco-reserve.

The buildings also ran north-south along the meadow. There was second manned gate as we came up to the south end of the meadow. We were waved through. The driver proceeded to the main house and told us he would take our bags to the guesthouse.

As Abbey and I walked up the porch steps to the front door, it opened. I thought, "It's like déjà vu, all over again." As that great philosopher Yogi Berra said.

I said, "Mrs. Lopez, what a pleasant surprise to see you here. I assumed, wrongly I see, that you were stationed at the ranch in Houston."

"Mr. Falone keeps me jumping. Please come in, it is very nice to have you two here. I trust your trip went smoothly. I would like to introduce you to the core members of your project group before it gets too late. Then I'll show you to the guesthouse and you can settle in."

Mrs. Lopez led us to the north end of the house. We went down a set of stairs and entered a long hallway that I realized must be underground. We had entered what had to be the underground level of a quite large research or office building.

We turned a corner and went through double doors into what looked like a super high-tech playroom. Two young men were playing a shoot-everything video game on about an 80-inch flat-screen TV. They saw Mrs. Lopez, one hit the mute button, and both stood. They had tech geek written all over their faces.

Mrs. Lopez said, "I'd like to introduce you to Ned Harris and Fred Eaton."

I thought that fits them perfectly: "Ned and Fred." Then I pointed to the flat-screen TV and said, "*Call of Duty: Black Ops,* no *Shadow Hearts: From the New World?*"

They had a deer in the headlights look on their faces. I quickly took in the rest of the people in the room. Seven, four male and three female, all in their twenties. One of the other two men was dressed like an investment banker on vacation in Bermuda. The other one struck me as any of a hundred grad students I might see at Cornell.

The first of the three women was now standing next to Mrs. Lopez. She had big blue eyes, blond hair and a bouncy, cheery air to her. I pegged her for head cheerleader, valedictorian, captain of the field hockey or tennis team. If they still had bake sales she would have been one of the main organizers.

I had been a college professor too long to be put off, shocked, or much else by tattoos, body piercing, or multicolored hair. The second young woman had all three. She sat in a swivel chair with both legs curled up under her.

The third woman appeared to be of Asian descent. Slightly built, short dark hair, and very thick glasses.

Mrs. Lopez was beginning the introductions when her cell phone buzzed. She looked at the screen and said, "I have to attend to something for a little while, perhaps Elizabeth, you could make the introductions and bring Professor Johnson and Ms. Summers to the guesthouse in about 40 minutes."

It was obvious that Elizabeth was thrilled. Mrs. Lopez said to me, "Professor, I believe you will find this is a very hardworking and dedicated group. They are also bright and creative. I will join you at the guesthouse a little later." The way she said "creative" I felt there was a bit of a warning there.

"I'm Elizabeth Walters. It is a pleasure to meet you, Professor Johnson, we have heard a great deal about you, all good of course." Yes, she was a first-class suck-up. But I'd seen lots of that during my years teaching. She continued, "And it is also very nice to meet you, Ms. Abbey Summers, may I call you Abbey?" Abbey gave me a sidelong look and I replied with a half smile.

"Standing over here is Harrison Lodge." This was the investment banker dresser. He stepped forward, shook my hand and Abbey's, and gave us a short welcome in a Boston Brahmin accent. I'd be willing to bet he learned it by copying the accents of the characters Charles Emerson Winchester on *M*A*S*H* or Walter Gaines on *Cheers*.

Next came Mike Ryan, my all-around grad student type. He was polite enough but seemed a little mad at the world.

Then Elizabeth introduced the two other women. I thought it interesting that she introduced the men first. I wondered what that meant, probably nothing.

Rainbow hair came first. Elizabeth said, "This is Mitch Baker." I could read Harrison Lodge's mind, he was saying, "Yay, Mitch rhymes with bitch." Mitch said, "Hi."

Finally came the slight Asian woman. Elizabeth said, "This is Sadako Ogato."

She stepped forward and with a small bow said, "It is a great honor to meet you, Professor, and you as well, Ms. Summers."

Her accent was Midwest but her name and the formal introduction with a slight bow made me think her heritage was Japanese.

Elizabeth then said, "You have already met Ned and Fred."

Fred said, "We are the rejects."

I said, "You and Ned?"

He said, "No, all of us are 'The Rejects.'" He said it with great pride.

"All right, I'll bite, why are you called The Rejects?"

"Because Dr. Stone hates us," Fred replied.

Mitch spoke up. "Dr. Stone doesn't hate me."

Fred and Ned shouted in unison, "No, she doesn't hate Mitch, she despises Mitch."

"Yes, sir, Dr. Stone despises me," Mitch said it in a way that made it seem that it was a well-earned honor.

Elizabeth took control of the conversation in the way a third-grade teacher might just before things got out of hand. "You see, Dr. Stone tried to have each of us fired. She is a difficult person to work for. Have you met Dr. Stone, Professor?"

I said, "Oh yes, I have had that pleasure. I don't think I'm the doctor's type. She said she sensed a somewhat flippant attitude on my part. It seems Dr. Stone doesn't go for flippant." I was also remembering her comment, "This is not a project that I'm directly involved in. However you would probably fit right in." Well, screw you, Dr. Stone. I might just fit in after all.

Elizabeth went on, "Mr. Falone wouldn't let her fire us. He transferred us to different projects that Dr. Stone wasn't involved in. Most of us went to our Sudbury, Canada office. Dr. Stone doesn't go there much. Then Mr. Falone asked each of us if we would like to join this project."

I found it interesting the way she said Mr. Falone "asked us." As I took another look at the group I had another thought about why Walter picked me and not Dr. Hurst from the Museum of Natural History or some other A-list archaeologist. They might not be willing to work with The Rejects. I was starting to wonder what that said about me when Elizabeth went on, "Mr. Falone has given us a great deal of responsibility here and access to the company's finest equipment and latest software. We are glad you have arrived so we can really get going. As I said before, Mr. Falone speaks very highly of you."

Mitch broke in. "Walt said you would be good for us." She said it in a tone that indicated she really didn't think so.

Elizabeth again wanted to keep things from going in what she felt could be the wrong direction. "Well, it's getting late. I need to get you two over to the guesthouse to meet Mrs. Lopez."

Mitch, not liking to be cut off, said, "You two are cutting into our cock-tail hour."

I looked at my watch. It was after 7:00PM. "I'm breaking one of my own rules on the first day. I will try not to interfere with cocktail hour in the future. But what about Mrs. Lopez, I didn't expect to see her here."

Elizabeth said, "She is like a grandmother to us. I think she goes wherever Mr. Falone is spending a lot of time."

I looked at the other six to see what their reaction was. I sensed that even if grandmother went too far, they all liked and respected her. Elizabeth led the way to the door. It had been an interesting meeting and I wasn't sure quite what to make of it.

As we walked down the hallway with Elizabeth ahead of us sending a text, to Mrs. Lopez I assumed, Abbey began humming the theme music from *The Twilight Zone*. I said, "What do you think of Texas now, Abbey?" She began to hum louder.

Chapter 13

We took another underground hallway. I needed to get a map or I could be lost for hours down here. We came up in what was the gym and pool house for the guest complex. This was a different layout than the Texas ranch. In front of us was the pool. To the right and left of the pool were guesthouses and across on the other side was what looked like a partly covered party patio with a cookout area. We turned right and entered the guesthouse.

Mrs. Lopez was there. She said, "Thank you for your help, Elizabeth. I assume things went well."

"Yes, Mrs. Lopez, everyone enjoyed meeting Professor Johnson and Abbey. I'm sure we will all work well together."

Mrs. Lopez said, "Sometime tomorrow morning the Professor and Abbey will meet with your group. I'll let you know when. Now these folks have had a long day and need to settle in."

As she left, Elizabeth said with a big smile, "We will be looking forward to it."

Abbey was rolling her eyes. Mrs. Lopez said, "I know Elizabeth can be a little much. But she means well and is really a very fine young lady. You'll see she is also an extremely productive worker. I put the background files on each of them on the counter. Now I'll let you settle in. Professor, your apartment is on the right and Abbey, yours is over here to the left. Your bags are in your apartments. The refrigerator and liquor cabinet are well stocked. I've arranged your dinner to be delivered at 8:15 to give you time to freshen up. Breakfast will be sent over at 8:30AM. At 9:30 someone from the security office will come by to walk you over to get your security passes, access codes, etc."

I said, "When do you expect Mr. Falone?"

She replied, "Not until tomorrow night at the earliest. If it is tomorrow it will likely be too late to meet."

Abbey walked towards the refrigerator. This common area had a setup similar to the Texas guesthouse. It seemed to have a total of four apartments. Perhaps this one was a bit larger.

Abbey opened the refrigerator, stuck her head in, and came out with a bottle of white wine. She handed it to me and said, "Prof, open this, I need a drink." She then started opening cupboard doors until she found the snacks. She grabbed a large bag of chips and a bowl and then headed to the table.

I opened the wine and took two glasses over to the table. I didn't figure the bottle would last long enough to require an ice bucket. I poured Abbey a generous glass and then filled mine. "Cheers."

She took a big sip and smacked her lips. I said, "What do you make of our team?"

She said, "Other than wanting to wring Little Miss Goody Two Shoes Elizabeth's neck, I'm not sure. Walter did pick us so he must be an excellent judge of people."

"Abbey, I love the way you can always find the bright spots. Do we dare look at their background folders?"

"Let's wait. I don't want to spoil the enjoyment of our wine. Also I need to take a shower before dinner." She refilled her glass, grabbed a few more chips, and headed to her apartment.

I sat there for a bit. White wine and potato chips, not bad, and it somehow seemed to fit the day. I decided I needed a shower. I filled my glass and headed to my apartment. It was bigger than the one in Texas. It had a combination kitchen, dining area, living room and workstation. It was two bedrooms and two baths, with an en suite master bath.

I took my shaving kit out of my overnight bag. I would tackle unpacking later. After shaving, showering, and putting on fresh clothes I headed back to our great room. I finished the little bit of wine in the bottle. I went to open another bottle when there was a knock at the door. I opened it and let the two waiters in with our dinner and as they set it up I opened the bottle of wine.

Abbey came out and we ate mostly in silence. It had been a long day and I guess neither of us wanted to start discussing all we were thinking regarding the day's events. I told Abbey I was beat and going to bed. She gave me her warm smile and said, "Interesting day." I smiled back and went to bed.

I got up at 6:30 the next morning. I put on my swimsuit, started the coffee, and headed to the pool. After a long swim I showered and dressed.

I took a cup of coffee over to the table along with the seven files. I took the file on Elizabeth Walters and began to read. I was right, in high school she was a cheerleader, captain of the tennis and field hockey teams, yearbook editor, and valedictorian. She went to Dartmouth, majored in computer science, graduated with high honors, and played field hockey. From Dartmouth she went to Stanford receiving a PhD in AI. She then worked for two years at the Stanford Artificial Intelligence Laboratory before starting with Falone Advanced Technologies. There were a lot of details on her exact research areas. I put the file down.

Abbey walked in from her run and said, "It's a jungle out there." She saw I had been reading the file. "Prof, what do you think of our team?"

I said, "I've only read Elizabeth's. It seems like Walter must have had these files put together when he was deciding if he should save them from Dr. Stone. They don't read like standard personnel files. I'm thinking I'll wait until after breakfast and just enjoy my coffee."

"Read this one, Prof." She slid Ned Harris's file across and went to her apartment to shower.

Ned attended Gateway Community College in New Haven, Connecticut. He was in an associate's degree program in Diagnostic Medical Sonography but kept sneaking into the Yale University engineering library. After he was thrown out several times one of the library's management staff gave him an application for a part-time job. As an employee he could spend as much of his free time in the library as he wanted. Somehow he taught himself advanced computer coding and computer analytics.

I started to smile and knew why Abbey had given me the file. You can't make this stuff up. Ned gets hired by Booz Allen Hamilton, which is probably the largest technology-consulting firm in the country, with 99% of the company's revenue coming from the federal government. He is assigned to the NSA account. The same Booz Allen Hamilton that hired Edward Snowden to work for the NSA, who leaked all the classified documents on the NSA's mass surveillance and data collection program PRISM.

Well, there was nothing about Ned leaking anything and after two years at Booz Allen Hamilton he joins Falone Advanced Technologies. I thought, whatever it is he does for Walter's company it seems he is good at it. Abbey can probably explain it to me.

The waiter came in with our breakfast. As he set it up, I quickly glanced at the other files. Until I met with Walter I wouldn't understand what Abbey and I were supposed to be doing. I had no idea if The Rejects were to report to me what resources were available, or who else was involved. I didn't even know to whom I reported.

Abbey came out of her apartment and joined me for breakfast. She was dressed in blue jeans and a golf shirt. It looked like workday clothes to me.

"Prof, what is the game plan?"

I didn't have a plan so I said, "Drop back and punt? After breakfast we will go to security for whatever we need to do. Then I guess we unpack and cool our heels until Walter arrives."

"Quite a plan. Did you work on it all night?" Abbey said.

"Abbey, let's call it an interim plan. You could go over later and get to know Elizabeth and company."

"Prof, did you read those files?" I pointed to the stack of five files I hadn't read and shook my head. She continued, "There is some serious brainpower in that group. Maybe a little weird but smart."

I said, "I think we will find a lot of that at Falone Advanced Technologies. Walter doesn't really have that many employees given all the things the company is involved in. He combines high tech with really smart people to accomplish it. Without knowing what we are to do, it is hard for me to fit their backgrounds into any meaningful picture. I'll read them all at some point."

We finished breakfast and I went to my apartment to brush my teeth before our 9:30 appointment with security.

Chapter
14

At 9:30 Major Campbell knocked on the door. He said, "Are you two ready go through all your security procedures and get a short tour of the ranch?"

"Sounds great. I would have been lost in the tunnel system without a guide yesterday," I said.

Major Campbell laughed. "Yes, a bit confusing at first. We will walk over to security outside. That way you can start to get the lay of the land."

"Does the ranch border the Lomas de Lachay National Park?" I said.

"Yes, the ranch property runs along the north side of the park. It is about 10,000 acres, almost as large as the park. We provide security monitoring and information for the park. We also provide scientific data and information but that isn't my area."

Abbey said, "Is security a big issue here?"

The Major said, "The park is well patrolled. It has about 30,000 visitors a year so the government wants it to be safe. The tourist trade is important to the local economy. The problems are mostly in other areas and related to drug trafficking. The government walks a thin line in responding to both US pressure to severely limit coca production and protests by coca farmers against the eradication of coca production in poor, rural areas, where the majority of the population is involved in that business. There are ties between the Shining Path (the Maoist guerrilla group), narcotics traffickers, and the local coca farmers. It seems the farmers sell most of their coca crops to drug traffickers who then pay the Shining Path to operate within certain regions.

"We have continual problems with cyber security. But you heard all about that from John McCay."

I asked, "Did he ever figure out what that bug they put in my office would do?"

"It would try to intercept your wireless signal between your laptop and the router. It was positioned to try to intercept the signal when you were at your desk. It probably would have worked well when you were using your laptop at your desk."

I interrupted the Major and said, "Why would they break into my safe and search my office then? They must have guessed you folks would look around and probably find it."

The Major continued, "A couple of things come to mind. The bug may have been planted a week or two earlier than the break-in. It wasn't getting results so they broke into your safe to see if they could get a copy of your access codes. Or they may have planted more than one bug."

I said, "Wouldn't John have been able to find it?"

"The bug John found is at the low-tech end for these devices. Other bugs can be 'off' and hard to find. They don't emit any signal. An internal timer is set to activate them later when they figure all the searching is done." Major Campbell smiled and continued. "I agree with John, it was probably someone seeing if there was an easy entry point to our computer systems and not directly related to your project."

I was thinking the bug probably didn't help them because I don't spend much time at my desk. With Wi-Fi everywhere on campus there are a lot nicer places to work.

We arrived at the security office, which was on the main level of the office/research building that we met The Rejects in yesterday. I assumed we were now one floor above their high-tech playroom.

The Major introduced us to David Fine, a man in his late twenties or early thirties. He then excused himself. David started by sitting me in a chair and taking the standard driver's license type digital photo. He then rolled up a retinal scanning machine. It reminded me of being at the eye doctor's.

He said, "Look straight ahead and try not to blink." Then he went through the same procedure with Abbey.

Next we were fingerprinted and told about our computer access codes. The codes would be sent directly to the cell phone the company provided and changed every 48 hours. Secure area door locks had either fingerprint scanners or retinal scanners. We would be in the system for all areas we were cleared to enter. We could set the locks on our apartments and the guesthouse.

Dave said, "Now let me tell you about some optional additional security that some of our employees choose to use."

He was holding an electronic device about the size of a grain of rice. It looked like the shell or case was made of glass.

Dave said, "This little baby is amazing and it's not just any injectable RFID chip." The look on my face made him stop. "Professor, maybe I should back up a little. Radio Frequency Identification (RFID) tagging is the use of very small electronic devices called RFID tags for identification and tracking using radio waves. RFID tags are in all sorts of things, credit cards, shipping containers, store items, etc. They only cost a few cents and normally can be read from only a few meters away.

"Now this little beauty does way more than the usual RFID tag and of course it costs a lot more. It's called VeriChip, this is the model X, and it is produced by a company called Applied Digital Solutions."

Abbey interrupted. "You called it an 'injectable RFID chip'? Like put in your body. Not swallowed, but implanted?"

"Yes, Ms. Summers. The VeriChip is injected under the skin. The injection feels similar to receiving a shot. It is encased in glass so there is no irritation to the tissue. The standard model stores your personal information. Thousands of people have already had them inserted. The American Medical Association declared that implantable radio frequency identification (RFID) devices may help to identify patients, thereby improving the safety and efficiency of patient care, and may be used to enable secure access to patient clinical information."

Abbey was looking a little pale.

Dave continued, "If you are injured the hospital can access all your vital information such as blood type, medical allergies, etc. Some people raised concerns about cancer or maybe the chip would explode if you had an MRI. Maybe you saw the *MythBusters* show on the Discovery Channel about the VeriChip?"

Abbey said, "I guess I missed that one."

"Well, they wanted to test whether an RFID tag will explode if placed inside an MRI. They inserted an RFID tag into pig flesh and placed it inside the MRI, but failed to get any results. Then team member Kari Byron had a RFID tag placed inside her arm and was placed inside the MRI. The RFID tag remained unaffected, and left Kari unharmed. How cool is that?"

Dave was obviously more into this stuff than I was. It is nice to see people enjoying their work.

He went on. "As I said, most RFID tags can only be scanned up to a few meters away. However this model X, X for extended range, combined with our firm's advanced sensing capabilities, lets us track the VeriChip up to several miles away. Most of our employees in certain African countries choose to have the chip implanted. Areas that are high risk for kidnapping and the like."

Abbey said, "Voluntary, right?"

"Yes, ma'am."

We both shook our heads. Dave seemed a little disappointed.

I said to Abbey, "What do you think of Texas now?" She smiled.

Another fit young man came in and handed Dave two ID badges. Dave looked them over, seemed satisfied, and handed one to each of us. It didn't look much different than my photo ID from Cornell.

Abbey said, "Are the RFID tags in these tracking us 24/7 like the cell phones and laptops?"

"No," Dave said. "The cell phones and laptops have GPS tracking. The ID badges use RFID tags. The RFID tags are extended range but not injectable obviously. But 24/7 automated tracking when you are on the ranch and the capability of tracking up to several miles off the ranch if required."

Major Campbell came in. Dave said, "They are all set but they decided not to have the injectable RFID tags." Again I thought there was disappointment in his voice.

Next we stopped in a conference or training type room. There was a wall diagram of the ranch. In addition to the main house, guesthouse, and office we were in, there were several more buildings running north. There was a small airfield with several hangar-type buildings, riding stables, and an area with all sorts of towers and domes.

I said to the Major, "I don't see anything that looks like barns or live-stock pens other than the stables."

He answered, "Ranch may not be the right term. It is more like a park. Large-scale ranching or farming might damage the environment and Mr. Falone bought here in part to help protect the Lomas de Lachay National Park next door. Being from Texas he may just find it easier to call it a ranch."

Abbey asked, "What about the airfield? It looks short. What do you fly from here?"

He said, "Helicopters and drones mostly. It is 1,200 feet long so most small STOL, or short takeoff and landing aircraft can use it. The largest aircraft we operate is the Britten-Norman Defender 4000, it is an enhanced version of the BN-2T Defender intended for the aerial surveillance role. The nose structure is capable of accommodating a FLIR turret or radar, and an increased payload. The forward-looking infrared, or FLIR cameras we have are unreal. Better than what we used when I was in the service. I know you Yanks don't always share the latest stuff with us Brits. But don't get me started on that topic. Well, the imaging assembled for video output is truly amazing."

My eyes started to glaze over. I guess when you work for a super high-tech company you really get into this stuff. I was wondering if for the next 14 months whenever I asked what time it was they were going to tell me how to build a watch.

The Major said to me, "Am I boring you, Professor?"

I said, "Waco."

He said, "What?"

I said, "The FBI deployed a Britten-Norman Defender for electronic aerial surveillance on the Branch Davidians' compound during the siege at Waco, Texas, in 1993." Funny what things you remember.

Abbey said, "Major, tell me about the drones."

I tried to put an interested look on my face. I really didn't have any-thing much to do until Walter arrived. And it was refreshing to see that these people all seemed to truly enjoy their work. So if I learned a few new things it wouldn't hurt me.

Major Campbell said to Abbey, while looking at me, "If I go into too much detail let me know. My group operates the drones for the research teams. A lot of us are pilots and we love this stuff... Aerial surveillance and remote sensing of large areas can be very cost effective with UAV systems usually just called drones. Surveillance applications include livestock and wildlife migration monitoring, wildfire mapping, mineral and petroleum exploration, pipeline security, home security, road patrol, and anti-piracy. The list goes on and on."

I said, "Tuna." Abbey looked like she was getting pissed at me.

The Major said, "No, Abbey he is actually right. The Boeing Insitu SeaEagle is a small, low-cost, long-endurance drone. It was designed to help fishing fleets look for tuna. We work with a later model, the ScanEagle. It is the main drone we use. The Royal Navy makes extensive use of the ScanEagle; that's where I first worked with it."

Abbey said, "Major, he gets this way sometimes. I'm used to it. I think he needs more to do."

I tried not to smile and the Major continued, "He will have plenty to do soon. Anyway the ScanEagle needs no airfield for deployment. It is launched using a pneumatic launcher. It is recovered using a Skyhook that uses a hook on the end of the wingtip to catch a rope hanging from a 40-foot pole. Just fly it in and snag the rope, which is attached to a shock cord on the pole. Its wingspan is about 10 feet. It is 4.5 feet long and weighs just 44 pounds. Best of all it has a flight endurance of over 20 hours. We are test flying one this afternoon – stop over and see it."

The Major was like a kid in a candy store. He obviously loved this stuff.

He went on, "The biggest drone in our fleet is the IAI Heron. It is a medium-altitude, long-endurance drone developed by a division of Israel Aerospace Industries. It is capable of Medium Altitude Long Endurance (MALE) operations of up to 52 hours' duration at up to 35,000 feet. It has a 54-foot wingspan, is 28 feet long and will carry about 550 pounds of equipment.

"Walter likes working with Israel Aerospace. They lease us drones at reasonable rates and we license them advanced remote surveillance systems that their military wants. There is a later model, the Heron TP with endurance of 70 hours, but Walter says it costs too much and the extra endurance doesn't make much difference in our R&D work."

This went on for a while more. Abbey said she would go to the drone launch that afternoon. I said I had some research to do. We thanked the Major and started back to the guesthouse.

On the walk back to the guesthouse I said, "After the drone launch stop by and visit The Rejects. I'd like to have you tell me what they do. I'm sure you can figure it out much faster than I can. I need to do some more online research."

Abbey mouthed, "Nap."

Back at the guesthouse I received an email from Mrs. Lopez saying that Mr. Falone would be in sometime tonight and would like to meet with Abbey and me at 9:00AM tomorrow. She also said the refrigerator was stocked with food and to leave a list on the counter when we needed any-thing. No more two waiters serving me breakfast.

I went back to researching Friar Pedro Zambrano Ortiz online. Then I answered a few emails and decided a nap would be a good idea.

Abbey came back at about 5:00. I was having a beer and back to reading a novel by the pool. She said, "I'm going to get a glass of wine, do you want another beer?"

"Sure," I said. She had come out of the tunnel so I assumed she had visited the lab after viewing the drone flight.

She came out and handed me the beer. I said, "Cheers. How was the drone flight?"

"Prof, without boring you with the technical details, they have amazing stuff here. The amount of high-quality data they can generate, well, I can't even describe it. The trouble is I'm not sure what we can do with it."

"Abbey, I can do tech when I need to. But I've been thinking about that too. We need to figure out how to focus all these fancy high-tech tools to narrow our search. How did it go at the lab with The Rejects?" If they hadn't seemed so proud of the name themselves I wouldn't have used it for fear of offending someone.

She said, "I didn't get there until almost 4:00 and by a little before 5:00 they started closing up shop. A few wanted to work out and others had things to do. They invited us over to the dining hall for dinner tonight. It seems most of the folks eat there. There aren't many company employees here on the ranch. All the people I met at the drone flight who worked with the sensing equipment flew in from Lima for the day. It seems that the drone flight team and our team are about the only ones here more or less full time. Plus there are the staff members for the ranch. Others come and go as needed.

"They can't fly the drones out of the Lima facility. There is too much commercial air traffic. I wish Mr. Falone would get here to give us some direction on where to start."

I told her about our 9:00AM meeting tomorrow. She seemed pleased, and said she was going to clean up and change before dinner.

At about 6:50 we walked over to the dining hall. It was in a separate building beyond the research facility and security offices. From the wall map this morning I noticed a building much larger than the guesthouses that was labeled "bunk house" behind the research building. It must be where the rest of the staff stayed. Somehow I didn't see it being bunks for these folks. It was probably another one of those Texas names. I made a mental note to go take a look at the place.

The dining hall had a bar and grill feel to it. The tables were set up so they could be pushed together for larger groups or stand-alone for just a few people. We headed to the bar. Abbey ordered a white wine and headed for a table that had five members of our Reject team. I got a beer and went over to where Major Campbell was sitting with two others, a man and a woman. "May I join you?"

"Please have a seat, Rob," the Major said. "This is Dr. Dona Frank and Peter Frank. They are here from our Lima operations working on the sensing equipment in the drones."

Peter said, "We are having some hardware issues and I'm hoping we can fix them here tomorrow. It's a bear taking all that equipment out of the drones. Then hauling the stuff back to the lab in Lima and then reinstalling it. I'm the fix-it man. Dona is the brains of the operation."

I said, "It's nice you can work as a team."

Peter went on, "We met at Berkeley. After I graduated I didn't want to get a real job so I got hired by the University to repair their lab equipment and help build new equipment for various research projects. Dona was getting her PhD and I was asked to help her with problems they were having with some new equipment. That's what I've been doing ever since. Works for me."

"It works for me too, dear," Dona said with a warm smile. "Professor, that is quite a young lady you have there in Ms. Summers."

I said, "How very true. Did you get peppered with a thousand questions?"

"She was actually quite focused. She looked over all the sensing equipment and focused right in on the ground-penetrating radar. Then the questions started. I was surprised how much she knew."

I said, "We actually use GDR a lot in our archaeological work to detect and map subsurface archaeological artifacts, features, and patterning. It is great for locating artifacts and map features without any risk of damaging them. The principal disadvantage of GPR is that it is severely limited by less-than-ideal environmental conditions. Clays and silts are often problematic because their high electrical conductivity causes loss of signal strength." I stopped and smiled. "But I suspect you know all this and much more. But pretty much we roll our equipment over the ground. No drones."

"Those were Abbey's questions," Dona said. "From your drone, can you distinguish manmade stone structures from background rock of the same type? Can you identify adobe brick structures? What penetration can you achieve over what area, at what altitude? What is the resolution? How is the data compiled and searched?"

"That sounds like Abbey. I'm sure you had no problem answering her questions," I said.

Dona smiled. "I had answers, just not answers she liked. As you mentioned, Rob, the depth range of GPR is limited by the electrical conductivity of the ground. In addition to that, the transmitted center frequency and the radiated power affects the depth of penetration and resolution. That is when you are in direct contact with the ground. We start losing signal strength before our radar waves even hit the ground. Being in flight we also have power limitations. We can't plug into a high-voltage outlet up there. The equipment we have flying in the drones now is quite helpful for many things. A lost city covered by vegetation probably yes, but identifying structure below more than a few inches of grade no."

I looked over at the table where Abbey was sitting and all but one of our Team Rejects were there. Mike Ryan was missing. I said, "If you don't mind I'll dine with you folks. I'd probably spoil the party over there."

Dona said, "We would love to have you."

Peter added, "Grub's pretty good here."

We ordered and had another round of drinks while we waited for our food. I found the conversation flowed easily. These people were smart and upbeat. Again it seemed they enjoyed their work and had great respect for Walter Falone.

I found that my first impression of Major Ian Campbell was off base. I had pegged him for a policeman type with a military background. I guess in some sense he was but he was also more. He was a mechanical engineer with an advanced degree from the Defence Academy - College of Management and Technology in Shrivenham, UK. He loved all things that flew and it seemed he could fly all sorts of planes. He quizzed me on my hobbies and we found that we both enjoyed golf and squash. It turned out there was a squash court at the ranch and he invited me to play. I looked at his six-foot five-inch super-fit body and I knew I was going to get killed. But it would be good exercise.

After dinner Dona and Peter excused themselves to answer some emails. Abbey seemed to be enjoying herself so, I waved goodbye to her and walked out with the Major.

I said, "Walter arrives tonight."

Ian replied, "You are eager to get started, Rob."

"Yes, but I'm looking for a needle in a haystack and it seems all this great technology isn't going to be the help I thought it might be."

He said, "But Mr. Falone wants to find that needle so we are going to help him. Sometimes even with all the greatest technology in the world you still need boots on the ground and plain hard work."

I said good night and went to the guesthouse. I poured a glass of red wine, went into my apartment and put on some soft music. I thought through what we knew and what we needed to know next.

Inca's Death Cave

ScanEagle Catapult Launcher (Note 1)

ScanEagle (Note 1)

Britten-Norman Defender (Note 2)

IAI Heron Drone (Note 1)

Chapter
15

I got up early, took a walk, and then a swim. I was having coffee and looking briefly over the files on our team when Abbey came back from her run.

I said, "I'll make us an omelet while you shower."

"Great. Put lots of cheese in it." She grabbed a cup of coffee and headed to her apartment.

I put the files aside and went to the kitchen area. I had the omelet, toast, and more coffee ready when Abbey came out.

She said, "How was your dinner?"

"I enjoyed meeting the Franks and I got a better feel for Major Campbell. And how was your dinner?"

She replied, "There is more to the Major than just chief cop. I found that out when I saw him in action at the drone launch yesterday. I also really like Dona and Peter. I hope we get to work with them.

"As for dinner it was fun. They are all so different and a little weird. They seem to get along and I assume they are good at what they do. But I'm still not sure what exactly that is."

I said, "I noticed that Mike Ryan wasn't there and he seemed a little mad at the world when I met him yesterday. What's up with that?"

Abbey smiled. "He's been trying to get in Elizabeth's pants and she wants nothing to do with him. She figures he isn't marriage material so why bother getting involved. Pretty smart on her part, right?"

I said, "Yes." But thought, men and women seem to have very different philosophies on that subject.

"Prof, what should we take to our meeting with Mr. Falone?"

"Just lots of questions, I guess."

Mrs. Lopez led us into a study in the ranch house. Walter Falone got up and came to greet us.

He said, "How nice to see you. I'm sorry to keep you waiting but I have great news. I'm a grandfather. That is why I had to run the other day. By the time I got to the hospital in Seattle my daughter and grandson were comfortably resting in their room. They named him Walter."

He seemed overjoyed, as he should be. We both congratulated him.

"Well, I could go on all day about that. You have met your team. What is your first impression?"

I said, "The Rejects, and I only use that name because they seem so proud of it, seem to be a bright and eager group. They have quite varied backgrounds and at this point I'm not sure how we all fit in together on the project. Hopefully I'll have a better idea after today."

Walter replied, "They seem to have bonded over the fact that they all had difficulty working with Dr. Stone."

I thought, well, that's a polite way to put it.

He went on, "Dr. Stone is difficult for some people to work with but she has her loyal and devoted followers."

I thought, so did Hitler.

Walter said, "Each person has skills that could be useful to us at some point. They also have other things they can work on if we don't need their help at the moment. They are here in part so you have direct access to them and that dropping their other work whenever you need them will not disrupt other projects. Now please update me on what you have been able to do since February."

I said, "Abbey, please give Walter a rundown on your work with the *Historia* and the *Chronicle*."

She began, "Your software is amazing. It is like Bible Analyzer Version 4.7 on steroids. Really mind-blowing. I tried to explain all the features to Prof. I know I don't have to explain them to you. I found mostly what you told us was in the two manuscripts when we met back in February. I brushed up on my sixteenth-century Spanish. I can pretty much work from the original now without referring to the modern Spanish or English translations.

I've even taught myself some Quechua and Aru.

"I would like to work with someone who is really expert with the software. I was hoping that the documents from the General Archive of the Indies and the Complutense University of Madrid were available so I can get started on them. Also I believe your translation of the 'True of Heart' would be better translated as "Strong of Heart'."

Walter started, "Very interesting, Strong of Heart. As for the software there are two people who are not only experts with the software but also have the ability to customize the feature in real time while running the software. They are Dr. Stone and Elizabeth Walters. I believe you will find it easier to work with Elizabeth."

Abbey smiled and nodded politely.

He continued, "As for the rest of the documents we seem to have some issues. The Vatican wants to review each document before it is released to us."

I had visions of the Vatican sending one monk who only reads Italian and Latin to review a mountain of documents that were written in sixteenth-century Spanish.

I said, "Don't tell me they want to review paper copies manually."

"I believe that is their plan. They fear there may be something in them that can cause a scandal," Walter said.

I went on, "Walter, these documents are 400 years old. Scholars have been reviewing them for well over a hundred years. If there were any big scandals someone would have found it. We aren't even interested in the Church. Didn't we sign contracts that said we wouldn't disclose anything about the Church? Aren't they bound by that contract? I don't remember them having the right to review the documents before we worked with them. And don't we actually have the digital copies already? I mean, your people produced them."

I stopped. My frustration was showing and I was sure Walter was as frustrated as I was.

He said, "You are correct that we do have the digital files and I believe we are on strong legal ground to use them given the contracts we signed. However, I would prefer to work this out with the Vatican. They have a great deal of material in Rome that might be helpful at some point. They have agreed to release a large batch of documents this week."

I said, "Let me guess, they will all be warehouse inventories, shipping records, and routine business records that have nothing to do with the Church and are very unlikely to help us."

"I believe that is likely to be the case," Walter said.

"Can we at least tell them the order in which we would like the documents reviewed? That could help. Not that we know which ones would be most helpful. We could make an educated guess," I said. My frustration was still showing.

"I have people working on this. I hope to resolve the whole issue soon. If not we will see if we can prioritize their review. You seem to be putting a lot of stock in these documents."

"Walter, actually I'm not but you never know and it seems unreasonable of them to be doing this. Our permit covers about a third of Peru. We are looking for a cave temple probably somewhere north of Trujillo. Well, if we assume it is in Peru, not because we know that but because Peru is the only country covered by our permit, we still have an area about 200 miles by 100 miles. In the geography of that area there could be a million caves, maybe 10 million caves. We are in an area where almost anytime you put a shovel in the ground you can find something of archaeological significance. A team of trained archaeologists could spend months just to determine that the site has nothing to do with what we are looking for. If I understand what I saw yesterday our wonderful equipment needs to get to within a few hundred yards to produce meaningful results."

Walter held up his hand. So I stopped. He said, "I like the fact that you kept using the word 'our' and you have identified some of the challenges we face. Have you thought about how you would start?"

I said, "A few things have come to mind. Quipus are usually thought to be primarily about numerical records. The 3D digital images of the quipus that indicate a journey from Vilcabamba to the northwest of Trujillo City should be examined to see if we can determine the approximate size of Minchancaman's group. It would be very helpful to know if he had a few dozen, few hundred, or few thousand followers.

"What if the information we are looking for is still in Peru and not back in Spain? The Saint Francis Monastery in Lima has a library that is world-renowned. It possesses about 25,000 antique texts, some of them predating the conquest. Perhaps we should also be looking in Peru.

"I also thought we should know more about Friar Pedro Zambrano Ortiz. Finding his diary of the time when he was a captive of Minchancaman would be our Rosetta Stone. It turns out the friar is a Dominican friar, not a Mercedarian friar like Friar Murúa. Friar Ortiz's father was some kind of official in the Casa de Contratación. The Casa de Contratación was a government agency of the Spanish Empire, existing from the 16th to the 18th centuries, which attempted to control all Spanish exploration and colonization. It was established in the port city of Seville. But I assume, Walter, you know of the Casa de Contratación. As an official with Casa de Contratación, Friar Oritiz's father was quite well off. He had nine children. As was customary at the time, one child's career would be in service of the Church. In this case two of his children joined the Church, Friar Ortiz and one of his sisters. She became a nun of the Dominican Second Order and took the name Sister Maria Ortiz. Now get this. Where does she end up? The Monastery of Saint Catherine that is a monastery of nuns of the Dominican Second Order, located in Arequipa, Peru. It was built in 1579.

"Murúa's *Historia* mentioned that Friar Pedro Zambrano Ortiz was in Arequipa after he was released by Minchancaman. No date was given. That is probably where the two friars crossed paths. Murúa was there from 1595 to 1601 so sometime during that period Murúa must have spoken to Ortiz. Or maybe Murúa heard the story secondhand.

"I suggest the place to start is with the Monastery of Saint Catherine in Arequipa. Their library is much smaller than Saint Francis Monastery's library but it is known to contain numerous manuscripts from this period. Given that Friar Murúa, Friar Ortiz, and Sister Ortiz were all there at the same time makes it a likely place to find something useful."

Walter stopped me and said, "Very interesting and I like it. However it took over three years to line everything up for our work in Spain and we still don't have it yet."

I went on. "It's funny, when I was doing research at Cornell I found out about a grant proposal that might be helpful to us. Mrs. Laura O'Hara, the Senior Reference Specialist at Cornell's rare book and manuscript department, has written a grant proposal to catalog, digitally copy, and to the extent that time and resources allow, restore manuscripts from the period of 1575 to 1625 in the Monastery of Saint Catherine in Arequipa. Cornell has approved the grant subject to funding. The Monastery has agreed in principle and the grant has been submitted to the Department of Antiquities at the Interior Ministry here in Peru."

Walter said, "Rob, by chance you wouldn't happen to have a copy of this grant proposal, would you?"

I reached in my pocket and handed Walter a memory stick. Abbey looked like she was going to burst out laughing.

Walter turned to her and said, "You look like you have something to say, Abbey."

"It just too much. Prof's girlfriend Mrs. O'Hara just happens to write a grant proposal that exactly fits Prof's theory."

I interrupted her. "Mrs. O'Hara is a happily married woman and not my girlfriend."

"I know, Prof, but you two are thick as thieves. Mrs. O'Hara is the wizard of the rare book and manuscript department. Prof is always sucking up to her for help when he needs to find something."

Walter said, "I think I'm going to enjoy working with you two. If this grant were to be fully funded, when would the work begin?"

"The team could be in Arequipa in less than a week. That assumes someone could get the Interior Ministry to issue whatever permits are required," I said.

"Rob, I'm sure it is all in the grant proposal but what kind of team are we talking about?"

"The team would be Mrs. O'Hara and three other women from the University's library system. Laura believes an all-female team will function better at the monastery. She has extensive knowledge of the Church and its customs. I believe she can fit in well." Walter looked relieved. Perhaps he thought I wanted to send a small army.

Walter said, "I'll review the grant proposal and I may have more questions for you. But if it is as well done as I think it is we can get started on that piece of our puzzle right away."

"Great, Walter, but before I continue to outline my suggested plan of attack I need a better understanding of our team, my authority, and what resources are available. I assume I have use of The Rejects. But I'm un-clear how involved you can be and who I need to work through to make things happen."

Walter said, "That was on my list of things to cover today. First I hope to be here at the ranch most weekends. My two daughters will be here for part of the summer and I want to spend as much time with them as I can. I suggest we meet each Monday morning at 10:00. That will allow me a couple of hours in the morning to work on other things. I will budget two hours for our meetings. If we don't need it all, fine, we'll get back to work. If you need me at other times contact Mrs. Lopez, she can always find me and she will be spending the summer here at the ranch.

"As for your role, you will be in charge of directing the project team. Outline your plans with me at our weekly meeting and then go to it. The Rejects, I haven't wanted to use that name but, as you pointed out, they seem quite proud of it and it seems to have created a sense of team spirit. They are your core team. You can use as much or little of their time as you need. Their other work has been structured so they can spend as much or little time on it without disrupting other projects. You can develop a re-porting system that works for you. Other people can be brought in but we can't disrupt other important projects.

"Major Campbell will work closely with you. He will handle logistics, equipment needs, transportation, etc. He is quite resourceful and you can consult with him on any needs you have. He also has good relationships with the National Police, Military, and Interior Ministry. I think you will find he is quite committed to our project.

"Rob, does that give you what you need to know to start to organize your team?"

"Walter, do I have a budget?"

Walter smiled and said, "Your team is the only team in the company that will not be required to make monthly budget reports. You have a bud-get but I haven't decided what it is yet. What are your next steps?"

"I will use our team to see if we can narrow down the area we need to search. Your firm has extensive geographic and geological data bases. Using them we can eliminate areas that don't have the type of cave forma-tions we are looking for. I assume Minchancaman had no access to ships, as the Spanish did, so they must have traveled overland. We can research the routes that existed at the time.

"I didn't focus on this because I was quite sure they would be part of what you were digitizing in Spain, but there are several other chroniclers whose works are available in several places. Copies of the original manuscripts, English translations, and/or digital PDF files are not that hard to obtain. Any who were writing in Peru after 1564 might have useful information for us. I'm thinking of ones like Miguel de Estete, the Spanish conquistador. He was born in 1495 died in about 1572 in Ayacucho, Peru. He took part in all the major battles of the Inca Empire. In addition to his noted chronicle of the conquest I believe some of his other writings are available. Also Garcilaso de la Vega who was born 1539 and died 1616 might be helpful. He was the son of a Spanish conquistador and an Inca noblewoman; he is recognized primarily for his contributions to Inca history, culture, and society. Many scholars consider Garcilaso's accounts the most complete and accurate available. He left Peru in 1561 for Spain where he did most of his writing and spent the rest of his life. However, he corresponded with people still in Peru and interviewed people who returned from there.

"I even think the Peruvian linguist Santiago Astete Chocano who died in Lima in 1975 could be helpful. He was the main founder of the Quechua Language Academy in Cusco. He created a translation method from Quechua to Spanish that is still widely used. He published many articles and books about the Quechua language and its grammar.

"Abbey and Elizabeth can search these and other available relevant manuscripts until we receive the records from Spain and Arequipa. In a week or two I will be able to give you a much more detailed overall plan for our research."

Walter said, "Let's plan for a week from next Monday. That will give you almost two week to get organized. Rob, Abbey, I'm very pleased with the start you two have made. Thank you for your hard work on our project to date."

"Walter, I did have another thought. Minchancaman and his followers had many hundreds of miles to travel on foot. It is possible the fatigue, death, disease, and desertion depleted his followers to very few. Minchancaman may have died after Friar Ortiz was released and the group just melted away."

Walter said, "I know that. If that is what happened then that is what we will find out. Again very fine work and I look forward to our next meeting."

As we were walking back to the guesthouse Abbey said, "You did a good job, Prof."

"Thank you, Abbey. So did you. Do you think you are going to like working for Walter Falone?"

"Are you kidding? I think we are both going to love it, Prof."

"I believe you are right, I believe you are, Abbey." I thought I've only met this man three times and yet I'm more motivated about this project than I've been about anything in decades. On the face of it, it is a crazy, almost hopeless project. Yet I somehow truly believe we can do it. It is interesting how motivating a little genuine respect, and heartfelt praise for your efforts, can be. I wondered why all those supposed geniuses in Cornell's administration couldn't figure that out.

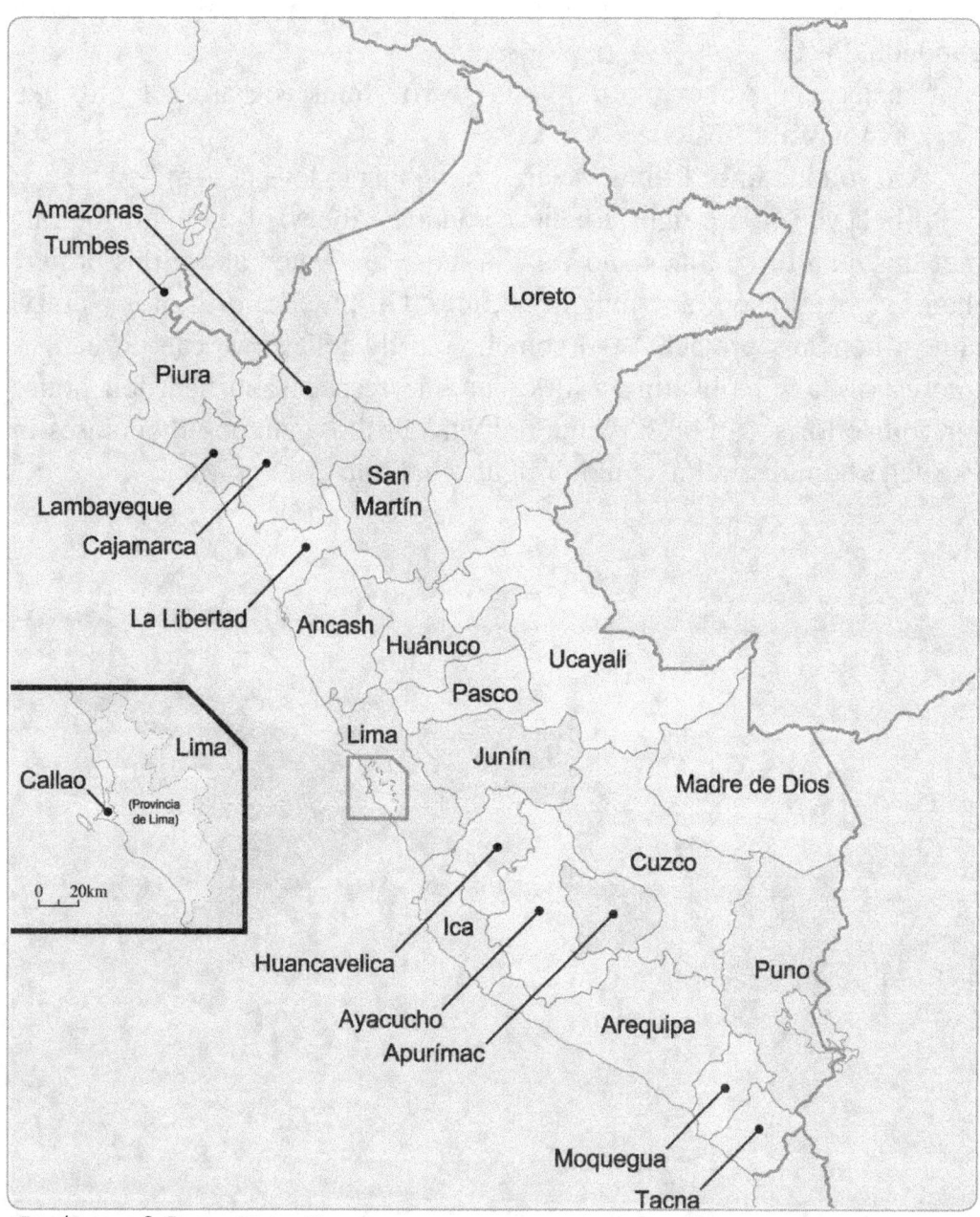

Regions of Peru (Note 2)

Chapter 16

After a quick lunch at the guesthouse we walked over the research building. I had an office with two rooms. It was set up with a larger inner office with an entrance through the smaller front office. It also had a second door to the hall from larger room, if I needed to sneak out. I gave Abbey the front office but I told her to work wherever she wanted to.

She dumped some of her stuff and said, "What's next?"

"Let's have a visit with Elizabeth. Check and see if she can join us for a little bit."

A few minutes later Elizabeth and Abbey walked into my office. I said, "Find a seat. I'll have to find more comfortable chairs."

Elizabeth said, "Very nice to see you, Professor Johnson. I hope you had a productive meeting with Mr. Falone."

"I believe we did. Walter has asked me to organize our team's effort and report to him weekly on our progress."

She said, "Does that mean we can really get started? I mean full time."

I nodded and continued. "I would like to ask for your help in organizing and coordinating our efforts." For a second I thought she might jump up and hug me. "I assume you know about as much as we do about what has been found in the quipus, *Historia*, and *Chronicle*. Does the rest of the team also know what we are trying to do?"

She said, "Yes," and I went on. "I would like your help in putting our team's talent to work in the most efficient way on the various tasks that we need to accomplish. You have much more insight into each team member's expertise. It seems the members all respect you. I don't believe we need a lot of formal structure; there are only nine of us. But we must work in an organized and systematic fashion."

I then went over where I wanted to begin. Elizabeth sat quietly and I could tell she was taking it all in and turning it over in her mind. At one point I had the eerie feeling I was talking to a chess grandmaster who was observing all and thinking a dozen moves ahead. I stopped, cleared my throat, and went on. I said, "I'm sure you have questions."

She replied, "I believe we should go over the questions with the whole team. Their questions are probably the same as mine. It will save time and if they miss any I'll ask there. You should know that Ned Harris has some reporting responsibility to Major Campbell. We do real-time risk assessments for many of our clients. He is involved in that."

I thought Ned Harris, who worked for NSA, and said, "I plan to meet with Major Campbell later today if his schedule permits."

She smiled. "Professor, I just want to assure you that I'm fully committed to this project, I will give it my full attention and make a 100% effort. I will not let you or Mr. Falone down."

"I know you won't, Elizabeth. May I ask you something on another topic?" She nodded. "Mr. Falone gave me a background file on each team member. I understand how the others might not be able to work with Dr. Stone but you seem to have a wonderful ability to work well with a wide variety of people. What happened with Dr. Stone?"

"I told the truth."

I said, "Ah yes, the truth, that is often a dangerous thing."

"I meant no disrespect and I was trying be helpful. I told Dr. Stone she needed to develop some balance in her life. Outside interests, hobbies, or maybe take up a sport. How could she meet a husband and start a family if she did nothing but work? I tried to explain that the years you can safely have children go by quickly for a woman despite all the progress of science. I must have deeply offended her."

I thought, for this, Dr. Stone tried to get this brilliant, hard-working young woman fired? I said, "You tried to do the right thing, Elizabeth. I admire that. Let's go talk to our team."

As we went to the main workroom I sent Major Campbell a text requesting a meeting when he was free. The team grabbed seats. I was in professor mode. I figure they were all used to that and expected it from me. I went to the whiteboard and at the top I wrote:

THE REJECT TEAM: PROJECT "THE INCA'S DEATH CAVE." WEEK 1

I then went on to outline with bullet points the areas we needed to investigate. I said, "I'm going to explain why I believe each of these areas is potentially important. Then I need your help in figuring out how we best go about it. Once we have done that we can decide who will do what. Our first reporting to Mr. Falone is a week from Monday so we have eight weekdays to develop our plans in detail. We will need to be able to articulate not only why and how but also the time frame, costs, obstacles, and likelihood of positive results."

We then discussed each item I had listed on the whiteboard and developed on outline of the how. I was pleased to see how focused everyone was. It seemed maybe they were being too ambitious but I decided not to scale back on anything. Once the detailed plans were developed we could decide what was doable. I also wanted to keep to myself my fear that if we didn't, by some stroke of luck, find Friar Ortiz's diary, all our work would probably be for nothing.

As we finished the last of my bullet points Mitch said, "Professor, at the beginning you said 'our first reporting.' Does that mean the entire team will meet with Mr. Falone?"

"Yes, I plan to ask Mr. Falone to join us here for our reporting a week from Monday. I also hope he will meet with the entire group as often as he can. It will of course be up to him."

She seemed pleased and almost smiled. I said, "Elizabeth I need to attend to some other things now. Would you be so kind as to lead the discussion on who will work on the development on each plan and add it to the whiteboard? I may need 25 to 50% of Abbey's time to assist me, don't let her over-schedule herself."

Mitch spoke up again and said, "Professor, what are you going to do while we are busting our asses on this list?"

Elizabeth was about to jump in. I held my hand up to stop her and with a big smile said, "I'm going to brush up on tombs, temples, caves, and caverns, Mitch."

"Cool, if you need help let me know," Mitch said. I gave her the thumbs-up sign.

"Thank you for all your help, everyone. I'm truly impressed with the range of expertise you have. I know I will enjoy working with each of you." As I left the room I thought, maybe I was learning from Walter.

I went back to my office and sent an email to Mrs. Lopez requesting that Mr. Falone meet with the entire team a week from Monday in the workroom. I hadn't heard back from Major Campbell so I decided to walk over to the airstrip and see what a drone looked like.

Cessna Skymaster (Note 2)

Chapter
17

It seemed quiet at the airstrip. I walked through the open door of the hangar. There was one of those funny-looking Cessna aircraft with the push-pull engine configuration. It had one engine mounted in the nose and the other in the rear of its pod-style fuselage. There was also a lot of equipment all over the hangar floor and Peter Frank working on the IAI Heron drone. The Major had rattled off the dimensions of this drone the other day but now looking at it I was surprised. The wings were well over 50 feet, they had to be at least 15 feet longer than the much larger Cessna's wings.

Peter looked up and said, "Hi, Rob, how are you? How was your meeting with Mr. Falone?"

I said, "I'm great and I think our meeting went well. We agreed our project could well be a wild goose chase but we are going to go for it. I wanted to see what these drones looked like. I also sent a text to Major Campbell and I hadn't heard from him so I was hoping I'd bump into him."

"Major Campbell is flying. He will land in Lima in about 30 minutes. I've got to radio him. I just found another part I need him to bring back. What did you want to ask him? I'll relay the message."

I said, "I just want to set up a short meeting to visit with him when he is free. No big deal."

"Well, I've got to radio him anyways. I'll be right back," Peter said.

Peter walked to an office in the rear of the hangar and I started to walk around the drone. It was a strange-looking thing with a split or twin tail same as the Cessna had. It had only one engine in the back in a pusher configuration. There was a belly pod, a nose pod, and a funny mushroom-shaped pod on top near the front of the aircraft. It also had no windows, which made perfect sense, but still looked strange. I was thinking or more correctly hoping this drone might have some special powers that could help us in our search.

Peter returned and said, "The Major wants to have dinner with you tonight at about 7:30 if you are free?"

"That sounds good. Are you going to relay the message, Peter, or should I send him a text?"

He said, "Send him a text in case I forget."

"Peter, our team, as you know, is looking for a temple or tomb in a cave or cavern. How can this thing help us find it?"

He replied, "You should ask my wife, Dona, about that. But my guess is that our aerial sensor in the Heron will only help you pin down the type of geography you are looking for. It is set up for large area work. The Israelis originally designed it for medium-altitude long-endurance operations such as monitoring their borders.

"Now the other drone we are working with, the ScanEagle, might be helpful to check out hard to reach areas. Come over here, I'll show you."

I now wished I'd paid more attention when Major Campbell told us about the drones yesterday. But it is more interesting and easier when you can actually look at the thing. Sitting on the floor, it looked more like an oversized model airplane than the drones you see on the news. The wing-span was about 10 feet and it was only about four feet long. Peter went over and picked it up.

He said, "The beauty of this drone is its weight is only a little over 40 pounds. Just load the drone, launcher, and recovery boom in a full-size pickup truck and away you go. It can fly into places it might take you hours or days to hike to. It travels about 55 mph and can stay in the air about 20 hours. Plus it is cheap to operate."

I liked Peter's explanation. No pilot-speak with knots, UAV, STOL, and XYZ. I said, "What is in it, cameras?"

"Rob, we can put all sorts of equipment in it, just not at the same time. So yes, regular video cameras or infrared cameras. We can install sensors for pollution or chemical spill detection. We can even put in the world's smallest synthetic aperture radar, it only weighs 3.5 pounds. But I'm not sure that would be of much use to you."

I said, "What about ground-penetrating radar?"

"Not that would be any of any use. Any equipment that would be powerful enough do anything would weigh too much and need too much electrical power. Your best bet would be high-resolution cameras to see places from 20 feet to say 1,000 feet above the ground. If you want to operate above 16,000 feet we need to put in a special supercharged engine, but that cuts way down on endurance."

I guessed this was cool stuff and I was starting to see why Major Campbell got into it.

I said, "If I'm starting to understand what you are telling me, we should use all the available data to reduce the search area. By that I mean existing geographic and geological data combined with whatever we can find from the historical record to reduce the search area. Then the large Heron drone could help us further refine our search area. Finally we take in the ScanEagle for a closer aerial look at the areas of interest."

Peter said, "I'm not sure I told you that but it sounds like a good plan to me. But hey, I'm just the fix-it man. Ask my wife or some of the other brilliant people around here."

I thanked Peter and asked him to let me know when they were doing test flights of the ScanEagle locally so I could come and watch. As I walked back to the guesthouse, I thought, I have a plan but it has a big problem. The temple or tomb cave, if it exists, probably had the entrance covered by rockslides and 400 years of vegetation growth. I had the team working on everything but the drone flight part. If we made enough progress the drone might be helpful. Maybe.

Chapter
18

Back at the guesthouse I took a swim and then a shower. I sent a text to Abbey saying I was having dinner with Major Campbell. Rather than drink alone I headed over a little before 7:00.

It was quiet in the dining hall. The place really had more of the feel of a pub and I decided I liked thinking about it as my local pub.

There were two men at the bar. One was David Fine who had given us our security information. I introduced myself to the other, a Carl Scott, who was one of the control pilots for the drones. I ordered a beer and told them I'd enjoyed learning about the drones from Peter Frank this afternoon. We made small talk and at about 7:20 Major Campbell joined us. After a little more small talk, the Major and I excused ourselves, and went to a table in the corner.

I asked, "How many people do you have here at the ranch?"

"I have about six on a 24-hour-a-day basis. They rotate in and out. Their permanent assignment, to the extent there is such a thing in this company, is in Lima. They can have a more normal expat life in Lima. Walter seemed pleased with his meeting with you and Abbey. I met with him shortly after you did."

I said, "That's good. I guess he liked the fact I at least had a plan of attack."

"Walter also liked your attitude. He said that you were fully invested and positive about the project."

"Well, Major, when you are attempting the impossible, why not have a positive attitude? It should be good for the troops, right? I just don't want

Walter to get his hopes up unrealistically. Everyone else on the team is being well paid and they will get great experience no matter what the results."

"Rob, do you really think Walter doesn't understand the odds that are involved?"

"I guess he does but being honest in a positive way seems best to me, Major."

"You can call me Ian. If you prefer Major in a business setting that's fine but don't feel like you need to. Being honest in a positive way is good by me and probably what Walter liked."

I said, "In my meeting with Walter, he said you were available as part of our team. He gave me a rough outline of what you could help with, but I'd like to hear how you see yourself fitting in."

"I've been in Peru for several years now. I have established a fair number of relationships with the various government departments. When we are working out in the field it helps to have the various authorities welcoming us and not questioning what we are doing there. I also will arrange transportation, handle equipment needs, things like that. Rob, anything I can do to help, just speak up."

I said, "Boots on the ground and hard work."

He tipped his glass to me and said, "Whatever it takes."

"Oh one more thing, Ian, Elizabeth said Ned Harris reports to you. How should I fit him into our team's work?"

He said, "Ned is quite an interesting young man."

I interrupted him. "Seems like there is a lot of that at this company."

He smiled, nodded his head, and continued. "We provide risk assessment for our clients in the various countries we work in. Everything from storms and forest fires to political unrest. As we collect specific data for our clients, we also feed any information that helps us understand the risks in certain areas back to our risk assessment team in Houston. They evaluate it along with US State Department assessments and other available data. That group is one of Dr. Stone's. Since Walter transferred Ned to me, I've had him monitoring risks for the area of our permit. He sends what he finds to the Lima group. They combine it with their work and pass it on to Houston. They use a lot of radio communication here so we monitor the police, and all sorts of others. Sort of like the old guys in the

States with their police scanners. Except, our computers listen in and our software screens for the items of interest. I have Ned developing, or maybe modifying is a better description, our software to screen for anything that might relate to our project. New archaeological findings, caves, temples, and things like that. I'm letting Ned decide on the screening parameters. He can do a much better job than I can. If you have other ideas on how to make use of his talent I'm open to suggestions."

I had the feeling that the risk assessment group might do more than just listen to police scanners. I also thought the clients probably went beyond oil and mining companies to include ones like the NSA and CIA. However, I really didn't want to know. I had enough to worry about.

I said, "Unless the team has something in mind for Ned, it's fine by me. However, I'd like him to feel included in the team."

"I agree, Rob. We will see how best to integrate his work into the team's agenda."

I told the Major about my visit with Peter at the airfield and how interesting I found it. I also asked him to let me know the next time they were flying the ScanEagle so I could watch.

It was about 10:30 and I still hadn't seen Abbey or The Rejects. I was wondering if they had reverted to college hours of working all night, and sleeping in until noon. I said good night and headed back to the guest-house.

Chapter
19

I took my usual morning swim and thought, it's nice having a beautiful pool just outside the door that someone else takes care of and pays for. I showered, got my laptop and notebooks, and went to our common kitchen area. The coffee was done and I made some toast. The bread was great. Someone must bake it here on the ranch.

I only had a vague idea of what I needed to research. I had spent years studying various aspects of pre-Columbian archaeology but never with something like the search for a cave temple/tomb and especially not at the specific time period we were looking at. I hoped if I did a review with that in mind I might come up with a pattern that I didn't now see or at least something helpful. Plus the team members were all hard at work, I was being paid well, and treated well, so I had to work hard at something.

I started by listing the 25 major archaeological sites in Peru. The total number of sites is over 300. I put the 25 major sites in alphabetical order starting with Acaray and ending with Tambo Colorado. I would review each site. Next I would review cave or cavern temples and tombs in Peru as I had said to Mitch. Then I would go through the subjugated people that made up the Inca Empire in our permit area. Walter seemed to think the followers of Minchancaman were of Chimú decent. I thought it was way too early to jump to that conclusion. That should keep me busy until I thought of something more useful to do.

I started working on the archaeological site at Acaray. The Fortress of Acaray is located in the Huaura River Valley in the Norte Chico region north of Lima. It is located on a series of three hilltops, each ringed with a number of perimeter defensive walls. It was built about 900–200 BC and abandoned 1000–1470 AD. I realized I was now reading for my own enjoyment. This site was not in the right place or time for our search. I would have to discipline myself to focus on the sites with some likelihood of being helpful.

Next I went on to the Buena Vista site located in Peru about 25 miles inland in the Chillon River Valley and an hour's drive north of Lima. This location might fit, however it seemed too far south and the contents of the temple were from about 2200 BC.

I was just starting to look at the Cahuachi site when Abbey came out of her apartment dressed for a run. It was only 9:40 so I guess no sleeping until noon for her.

I said, "Good morning. How did your day go?"

She replied, "Walter has assembled a group of eager campers here. There was a lot of yelling and shouting. People cutting each other off in mid-sentence with new ideas and others piling in. Elizabeth didn't so much lead the discussion as try to steer the group in the general direction of your outline. The funny part was no one had hurt feelings. They all seemed to love it. Finally everyone had their work to do and they just dove in. Walter has no slackers in that group."

"Abbey, I'm not surprised by that. I don't think Walter would waste his time saving someone from Dr. Stone if they were a slacker. I'm going to work here today. I'd like to stay out of their way and let them work. You can work where you want but I'd at least like you to check on them today."

"I'll be working over there. I need to work with Elizabeth. She knows a ton about the search software and I want to learn what I can from her before I have to wring her neck for being such a suck-up. Just kidding, Prof. She really isn't that bad."

"Takes one to know one, Abbey." She gave me her dagger look. "What? I was talking about being geniuses." She stuck her tongue out at me and started off on her run.

I went back to reading about Cahuachi. It was a Nazca culture burial site from maybe 500 BC. I moved on. I knew at least something about each site from my previous research work over the years but I made myself review each one. I did a quick review of all 25 sites and came up with six that might fit the area we were interested in.

That was the problem, we really didn't know very much and what we thought we knew might not be correct. According to Poma, Minchancaman claimed his ancestry not from the Incas but from the Kingdom of Chimor or perhaps even the Sican Empire. He repudiates not only the Christian god of the Spanish but also the Inca sun god Inti for the Chimú moon god Si. He travels north with his followers. The Kingdom of Chimor and the Sican Empire were both in northern Peru. They both worshiped the moon god as one of their primary gods. If I believed this and that Minchancaman actually made it back to the lands of Chimor or Sican, then we were talking about only eight of the 25 regions of modern Peru, located in the northwest of the country. So from the southern part of the Ancash Region to the northern part of the Tumbes Region was only 500 to 600 miles. Starting at the coast it was about 200 miles to the eastern edge of the San Martín Region. Say 100,000 to 120,000 square miles. Well, that really narrowed it down.

In the eight-region area there were six major archaeological sites. They might or might not be of any help. At least they were all interesting to me even if they didn't help with our project. I looked at my revised list: Chan Chan, Cumbe Mayo, Guitarrero Cave, Huaca de la Luna, the fortress of Kuelap, and Sipán. I decided to start with Chan Chan and work my way through a review of all of them, then look at some of the minor sites in my eight-region area that fit the time frame we were interested in. Fortunately most of these sites were south of our area of interest. I came up with nine more sites to add to my list.

It was almost 5:00PM and I was searching with terms that might result in something useful because I was tired of reading about archaeological sites. I spotted a reference to *Adventures of the Jaguar.* There was something familiar about it. I clicked on the link. Yes. Here was research I could dig my teeth into.

Zoologist Ralph Hardy was a man of many interests and talents including archaeology. While he was on an archaeological dig in Peru a giant serpent burst forth from the ground. While the others in his group fled in terror, Hardy followed a rare white jaguar into a ruined temple and found a series of cave drawings depicting the ancient Incas battling the same monster as well as a mystical "nucleon energy belt." The buckle of the belt had an inscription: "He who loves the animal kingdom may wear this belt and be transformed into a human jaguar." Hardy put on the belt and instantly transformed into the Jaguar.

He now possessed all the powers of the animal kingdom, only a thousand times more powerful. His skin had the toughness of a rhinoceros' hide and he had a lot of other cool powers from the animal kingdom. Also he had the telepathic ability to mentally communicate with and command all animals.

The Jaguar was a superhero published by Archie Comics in 1961. The author was Robert Bernstein and the illustrator was John Rosenberger. I thought, what I need is one of those nucleon energy belts. But I decided a beer and swim would have to do.

Abbey came back around 6:00 and asked me to join a few of the team for dinner. We went over at 7:00.

At one of the tables in the dining hall there were five of our team members. I said, "How is it going?"

Mitch spoke up. "Just peachy. How is your reading about tombs, temples, and caves going?"

"Mostly boring, Mitch. I'm not sure I'd even know if something was useful when I read it. But I did find the works of zoologist and amateur archaeologist Ralph Hardy quite interesting."

Fred shouted out, "Way cool, *Adventures of the Jaguar*."

I cut Fred off and in my professor tone of voice I said, "I also found that reference interesting. However I was only able to access two of Hardy's 15 major works. Perhaps a little later you could help me locate more of his works." I was pretty sure no one else had a clue what we were talking about.

Fred said, "I'll stop by your office, Professor, and see if I can help."

The rest of the evening didn't focus on work specifically. A lot of the topics related to work but we all seemed to want an interesting discussion, not a report on our workday. I work with a lot of bright young people at Cornell but I was impressed with this group. It occurred to me that this was like the difference in college athletes and the pros. Walter's firm was the NFL or NBA league for what these folks did. It was up another whole level. I decided I liked it.

Chapter
20

I started the next day with my usual swim and coffee. I had an email from Laura O'Hara saying her grant was being funded by Mr. Falone's foundation. It was Friday. I'd met with Walter on Tuesday and I'd left Ithaca Sunday morning. Things at Falone Advanced Technologies moved a lot faster than the University.

Laura said she had been instructed to coordinate all her logistical needs with Professor Johnson who was working for Mr. Falone's company during his sabbatical from Cornell. She was also told that Mr. Falone would like her team to proceed to Lima as soon as possible. Laura asked if a week or so would be soon enough. She also wanted to know about the required permits and the equipment she would need. There was a PS on the email that said she had a gift for me.

I told her to plan to leave a week from Tuesday and I would confirm the date and time. I would handle the equipment and permits on this end. She should contact the Monastery of Saint Catherine in Arequipa and let them know when she was arriving. As I completed my email to her I realized how much of my hopes were pinned on finding some of Friar Ortiz's papers. I had already discussed with Laura that she should give top priority to any of the writings of Friar Ortiz, Sister Ortiz, and Friar Murúa.

I sent a text to Major Campbell requesting a meeting. He texted me right back asking me to come to the airfield any time after 1:00PM.

Abbey returned from her run. I told her to ask our team to assemble in the workroom at 10:00 for a short meeting.

I went back to reading about archaeological sites in the eight regions we were focused on. I didn't think I'd get much more out of this line of research. At a little before 10:00 I walked over to the research facility. I decided being in professor mode would be best.

I walked into the workroom, said good morning, and went to the white-board. I wrote:

THE REJECT TEAM: PROJECT "THE INCA'S DEATH CAVE." WEEK I DAY 4

I started by telling them that the research team from Cornell's Department of Rare Books and Manuscripts would be arriving at the Monastery of Saint Catherine in Arequipa a week from Tuesday.

Next I said that Mr. Falone was very much looking forward to meeting with the entire team a week from Monday. He would plan to be in the workroom by 10:00AM. This seemed to please everyone. I also told them that next Friday we were going to have a dress rehearsal and I had invited several people to critique their presentation. That morning I'd sent an email to Mrs. Lopez, Major Campbell, and Dona and Peter Frank inviting them to attend. The team would take the practice run much more seriously if they had a knowledgeable audience. We agreed at the previous meeting that Friday would be our scheduled day for a review of the week's progress and the official end of our work week. That would give me the weekend to organize for my Monday meeting with Walter.

I then asked everyone to give me an update on the progress they had made. At this point they were to create a detailed plan for each area of research. I wanted Walter's OK before we started. Some of the research was straightforward, but other parts would involve considerable expense and lots of computing power. I was amazed at how much the team had accomplished since our meeting Tuesday afternoon. I realized that this planning phase wouldn't take until a week from Monday. So I asked the team what else we should add to our existing areas of search if we had time next week.

Mitch spoke up first. "I'd like to research Yatiri, Folk Catholicism, and Pachamama in the regions of Tumbes, Piura, Cajamarca, and Amazonas."

I thought I might hear a snicker or comment but no one made a sound. She went on. "The Yatiri are a special subclass of the Qulliri, a more generic category of any traditional healer. They practice using both symbols and materials such as coca leaves. They have handed down their traditional beliefs for hundreds of years.

"We all know about Folk Catholicism in Haitian Vodou, Cuban Santeria, and Brazilian Candomble. Similarly complex syncretism exists between Catholic practice and the indigenous people in Quechua communities of Peru. There might be unique aspects to these practices in the region that are helpful to us.

"Pachamama is a goddess known as the earth/time mother and she is revered by the indigenous people of the Andes. In Inca mythology Pachamama is a fertility goddess. She causes earthquakes and is typically in the form of a dragon. She is also the creative power that sustains life on earth. Pachamama is the wife of Pachakamac and her children are Inti, the sun god, and Killa, the moon goddess. I realize Killa is a somewhat different variant of the moon god than the Chimú moon god Si. The moon god was their greatest divinity for both groups. But again we may find a useful connection."

Still no one said anything. Finally Mitch said, "What? I'm in Peru. I read stuff. I can't do engineering and computer shit all the time."

Harrison Lodge, my investment banker dresser with the Boston Brahmin accent, spoke up. "I'd be happy to help you, Mitch."

Well, that surprised me.

Mitch said, "Sure, I should have my other work wrapped up by midnight. We can start then if you're done with your work."

It didn't sound like any pre 3:00 happy hour for them this Friday. I said, "Mitch, would you add the San Martín Region to the area you are looking at. I'd be interested to see what you found there as well."

She smiled and nodded her head.

Abbey and Elizabeth said they would be flat out on their work, something about setting up multiple parallel searches with a new algorithm that looks across the parallel searches in real time. The others all suggested ways to expand the scopes of what they were doing.

I said, "Great start, everyone. You all have made amazing progress in just a couple of days. If you need me for anything just text me or send me an email. I'll be around all weekend."

As I started to walk out Fred came up to me.

"Professor, I have some additional material for you on the archaeological work of Ralph Hardy. I believe you will find it interesting."

He handed me a memory stick. I said, "How many of his works were you able to find?"

"Professor, the stick has all 15 of Hardy's major works. I also have related works but they're not by Hardy."

"Fred, that is great. Other than what I found yesterday I haven't read any of Hardy's work in decades." Fred and I were having fun and no one else had a clue what we were talking about.

"Professor, did you read his works when they were originally published?"

I smiled and said, "No, Fred, I'm old but I wasn't even born in 1961 when Hardy published his first volume. However original copies were not that hard to find when I was your age."

Chapter 21

I walked over to the airfield shortly after 1:00PM and made my way into the office at the back of the hangar. It was much larger than I thought. It contained what must be the control room for the large drone. It looked like a cross between an airplane cockpit and a fancy video game station. It was in a room with no windows to the outside but two glass walls, one facing the main office area and the other on the right side to a room loaded with equipment. This room also had a glass wall facing the main office area. Major Campbell and Carl Scott, the drone controller I'd met the other night, were working in there on the equipment. I knocked on the doorframe as I stepped in.

Major Campbell said, "Hi, Rob, I'll be right with you. Carl, you keep going on this while I meet with the Professor. Rob, let's go into my office over here."

"Major, I sort of understand how the control station for the Heron drone works but how do you control the ScanEagle in the field?"

"We have a portable ground control station. It is a little like a desktop flight simulator. We set it up in the field at the site where we launch and recover the drone. We also have a remote video terminal. I'll show you all of it when you come to watch a flight of the ScanEagle."

We walked into the Major's office. I was almost afraid to ask him what the thing was on his desk. It was about two and a half feet square. It stood on bug-like legs and there were four little motors with what looked like model airplane propellers facing up. The motors were mounted at the end of one-foot-long rods on each corner. The body in the center was a six-inch diameter globe with a flat top.

The Major said, "It looks strange, doesn't it? It's called the Scout. It is a vertical takeoff and landing quadcopter requiring no launch equipment. It is built by Aeryon Labs of Waterloo, Canada. It can hover in a fixed position and weighs 3.0 pounds without a payload.

"The Scout can be operated beyond the line of sight up to 1.9 miles. It can operate at 300 to 500 feet above the ground and it can fly 30 miles per hour with an endurance of 25 minutes. The Scout's design allows flight in adverse weather conditions and it has been flown in wind speeds of 50 mph. All communications are digital and encrypted.

"The Scout is controlled with a tablet PC-based interface. This system differs from the customary method of joystick control so it is easy to operate. The Scout monitors external conditions such as wind speed and internal functions, such as battery level. That is probably more than you wanted to know, Professor."

I said, "So you use it for shorter range simpler and quicker looks over the next hill than you would the ScanEagle?" I wanted to show I'd been listening.

"Yes, it all fits in a suitcase. Just put it in the trunk of your car. But that isn't why you wanted to see me."

I told him about my email from Laura O'Hara. He said he had gotten an email from Mrs. Lopez asking him to provide me with all the required support. We reviewed the list of equipment from Laura. He added secure cell phones and laptops to the list.

I said, "Major I'm sure you are familiar with the problems we are having in Spain trying to get the digital documents from the Casa Lonja de Mercaderes in Seville and the Complutense University of Madrid."

He nodded and I went on. "I'm concerned that when the Vatican learns of our work at the Monastery of Saint Catherine in Arequipa, we may have the same problem. I was wondering if you could hook up something to the high-speed scanner we are providing to transmit the info to us in real time?"

The Major looked at me and said, "In real time?"

I felt a little foolish and said, "Everyone around here seems to use the term. I think it means right away."

He smiled. "Professor, I'm planning to have a daily courier come to the monastery to drop off any mail to the team and pick up any outbound mail they have. How about you ask Mrs. O'Hara to put each day's work on a memory stick and give it to the courier?"

I said, "That seems a lot easier, doesn't it?" Maybe I'd seen too many James Bond movies or maybe it was all the tech stuff and drones around here. We went over the rest of what needed to be done. He said to ask Mrs. O'Hara's team to be at the Ithaca Airport at 9:00AM a week from Tuesday. We would meet them at the Lima airport.

Having finished, the Major said, "Come on, Rob, I'll show you how to fly the Scout."

He put the quadcopter in a padded suitcase along with a tablet computer. We walked outside in front of the hangar and he handed me the suitcase. It was light. The whole thing including the case couldn't weigh more than 20 pounds.

He said, "Open it and fly it."

As I put the case on the ground and opened it, I said, "Are you testing the manufacturer's claim that any idiot can fly this thing?"

He smiled. I took the Scout out and set it on its bug legs on the runway. I said, "Is the battery already in it?"

"Yes, Rob, those two in the case are spares."

I picked up the tablet and hit the power button. On the screen was what looked like a Google Earth map of the airfield where we were standing. I looked at the tabs across the top of the screen, pushed "Program flight" and a cursor began flashing on the screen's map. As I moved the cursor it drew a line on the map. I drew the line down the runway and back. Next I picked up the Scout and looked for an on/off or power button. I didn't see one so I put it down and looked at the tablet again. I hit "enter" on the screen and got an error message. "Enter altitude and cruise speed." I found the boxes for each and put in 20 mph and 100 feet. Then I hit "enter" again. The propellers on the Scout began to spin. It took off slowly and headed up the runway in the direction of the line I had drawn. I looked at the screen and there was a red dot on the line showing where the Scout was.

I said, "Is the camera working?"

The Major said, "Look at the tabs."

I looked at the tabs. The four to the right were "still camera," "video camera," "near-IR camera," and "FLIR night-vision camera." "Video camera" was in bold and the other three were light gray. I pushed the video camera tab. My tablet screen split in two. The left side was my line on the map. The right side showed a video picture straight down below the Scout.

I said, "Very cool. Video in real time."

"Yes, Professor, real-time video."

I watched it fly down the runway along the path I drew on the screen and then start back on my return line. I was wondering what would happen when it got back. I just waited. It returned to the spot it had taken off, slowly descended, and landed.

I said, "What would happen if I mapped out more distance than the battery could go?"

The Major said, "The Scout monitors the battery level to make an automated decision en route to return home and land before the battery is too low. It always returns to the spot it took off unless you specifically program it to land somewhere else. It is too expensive to lose in the jungle."

I thanked Major Campbell. It was fun and I was sure useful in the right applications.

Back at the guesthouse I decided to spend some more time reviewing what I found. There were cave tombs in the right geographic area such as Guitarrero Cave in the Ancash region. However they dated back to 10,000 BC. I found some cave temples from the right time period but they were way too far south of the area we were interested in. There were tombs and moon god temples in the right area and somewhat the right time period. But they were mostly made of adobe and not in caves. Finally there were lots of caves and caverns all up and down the Andes mountain range. A lot of interesting reading, but not much help.

I went and got a beer from the refrigerator. In my pocket was the memory stick Fred had given me this morning. It was time to research *Adventures of the Jaguar*.

Inca's Death Cave

Drone Control Station (Note 1)

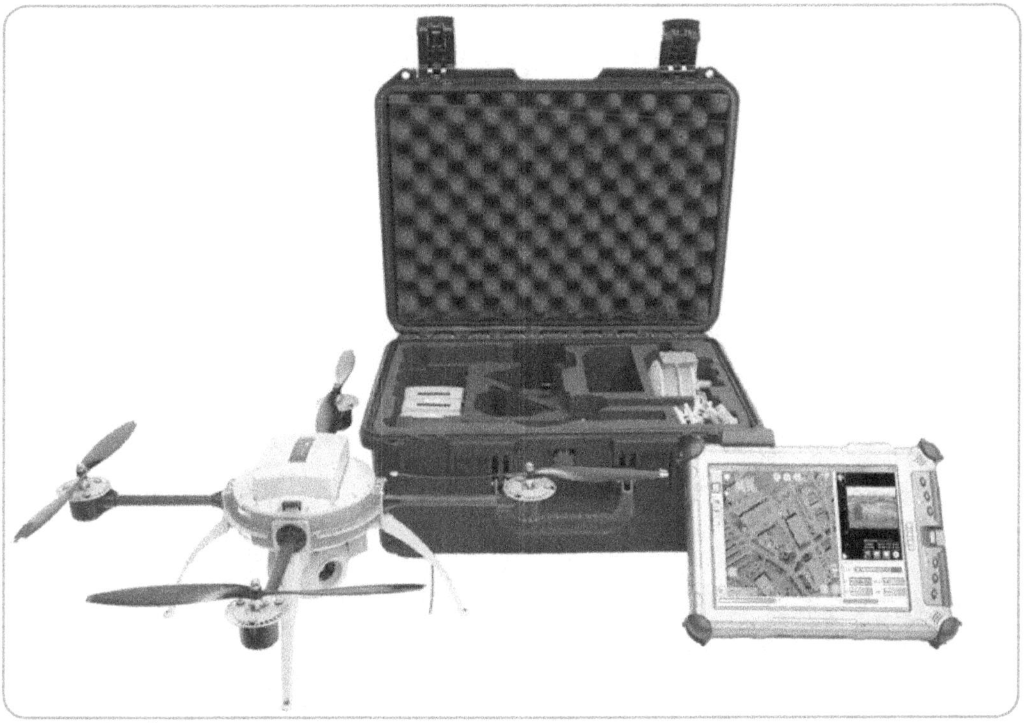

Scout Quadcopter (Note 2)

Chapter
22

Saturday after my usual morning routine I decided to explore the Lomas de Lachay National Park that bordered the ranch to the south. I put on my hiking boots and went to the security office to borrow a car or get a ride. They gave me a ride over and said to call or text when I wanted a ride back.

I had to keep reminding myself June was the start of winter in South America. Where the ranch and the park are located there are two distinct seasons: the humid season from approximately June to November and the dry season from December to May. The temperature only varies from a low of about 55° Fahrenheit in the winter to 75° in the summer. Today it was 60° and just right for hiking in the hills.

Lachay's western edge is approximately four miles from the ocean. The reserve is situated between 500 and 2,900 feet above sea level and has a varied topography. The park starts in the west as a coastal desert, then becomes rolling hills, and finally turns into a steep rocky landscape that joins the Andes Mountains beyond the eastern edge of the reserve.

I was in an interesting area called the Peruvian Yungas, on the eastern slopes and valleys of the Peruvian Andes. The Yungas runs from Peru south to Bolivia on into Argentina. It is the eco-region of rain forest and montane forest and it is limited to the eastern side of the Andes.

The terrain, formed by valleys, fluvial mountain trails, and streams, is extremely rugged and varied, contributing to the ecological diversity and richness. It is complex mosaic of habitats that occur with changing latitude as well as elevation. There are high levels of biodiversity and species endemic throughout the Yungas regions. So all in all it was a great place to spend the day hiking.

I also wanted to see petroglyphs, or rock carvings in the reserve even though they dated back to about 900 BC.

I spent a good part of the day on both Saturday and Sunday hiking in the park. I saw lots of interesting birds and no snakes or jaguars.

I was in my office at the ranch's research facility when a text message arrived. "We have an express package for you. Where shall we deliver it?" It was Dave from security. I texted him that I was in my office downstairs and asked if he wanted me to come up for it. He said no, he would be right down.

The package was from Laura O'Hara. This must be the gift she mentioned in the PS on her email. I opened it. The note read, "It's nice to have research librarians as friends." In the package there were 18 memory sticks. All were either 64 or 128 GB sticks. There was also an index sheet. It gave the name of the institution that the memory stick was from. I saw Harvard, Yale, Stanford, and Oxford. Fourteen were from major universities in the US and Europe. Four were from major museums.

I plugged one in. It was the digital form of manuscripts from the period we were interested in. I checked several more and realized Laura must have asked her counterparts at these institutions to give her a copy of any relevant material they had in digital form. I thought, yes, it is nice to have friends who are research librarians. I took a quick look at each one. There was some duplication but that was to be expected. Next I sent a text to Abbey and asked her to join me.

"What up, Prof?" Abbey said as she entered my office.

"A gift from home," I said.

"What is on them?" she said as she pointed to the memory sticks I had lined up on my desk.

"Good stuff, I believe. Why don't you and Elizabeth add these to the collection of manuscripts you're going to analyze? Let me know what you think of the contents. An overview of what they are and how helpful you think they might be when you run the search programs on them. Or just your best guess," I said.

She scooped up the memory sticks and said, "A present from your girlfriend Mrs. O'Hara?"

"Abbey, she is not my girlfriend."

Abbey walked out and with her back to me said, "Yet."

The rest of the week went quickly. I continued my reading on background research. On Thursday I called a 10:00AM meeting. I told the team I wanted to hear how they had agreed they were going to divide the hour and 15 minutes of presentation time. Walter was allocating two hours each Monday to meet with us. I wanted 45 minutes for questions and discussion. If they had disagreed about who would have how much time to present, they had worked it out by now.

I let them know that Mrs. Lopez, Major Campbell, and Dona and Peter Frank would be there Friday for our practice run. We would start promptly at 1:00PM and have a hard stop at 3:00PM.

Abbey and Elizabeth asked to speak with me. I said, "Sure. Where do you want to talk?"

Abbey said, "Anywhere, Prof."

I thought that was good, that means it isn't some kind of big people problem with the team. We sat at one table in the workroom.

Elizabeth said, "We finally received the first download of material from Spain."

I said, "And?"

Elizabeth continued, "There is a lot of it. However from Abbey's review of it, it seems it is what you expected, mostly items of a commercial nature."

"I've been thinking about that," I said. "There may be useful information there. The regional officials often sent in reports of what was going on in their areas when they sent in tax collection reports or reports on mining production. There could be something valuable there."

Elizabeth said, "That is no problem. We have the software set up for a massive data search. With the cross document parallel search program I've developed, and Abbey helped, we should be able to recognize patterns that could be missed in the search of any one document."

I looked at Abbey to see what reaction she had to the "and Abbey helped." But I didn't sense any tension.

Elizabeth went on, "We will have everything loaded and ready to go by Friday. All we will need is Mr. Falone's permission to proceed on Monday."

I looked at Abbey. She said, "Elizabeth has made some mind-bending enhancements to the company's search software. I can't wait until we see what it comes up with. I looked at those memory sticks and there is a great deal of material that is in some way relevant to our search. With that material, the material from Spain, and some other stuff I was able to get, we have a lot to work with right now. Who knows, it might have something helpful."

Friday afternoon at 1:00PM everyone assembled in the workroom. After people finished saying their hellos, I welcomed our guests and turned it over to Elizabeth. None of the team members seemed to mind that she always wanted to be the spokesperson.

There were three main work areas to explain. Each team member gave part of the presentation. It seemed in depth and clearly presented to me.

At the end Elizabeth asked for questions. When no one spoke up right away Mrs. Lopez asked how long it would take. That turned to be a more complicated question than she thought and sparked a lengthy discussion. Dona Frank asked several technical and detailed questions. The Major and Peter Frank had a few more questions.

I was pleased. As our four guests left, Dona Frank said, "Professor, will you join us for dinner tonight? Major Campbell has already agreed to join us."

"That would be great. What time?" I said.

She replied, "7:00PM."

They left and I addressed the team. "Super job. I was most impressed and I believe Walter will be quite surprised by what you have accomplished in just over a week. When he gives us the go-ahead Monday the fun will really start. I know you all have made tentative plans to go to Lima for the weekend and Major Campbell has arranged air transport for you so you won't have that drive to worry about. Your flight leaves at 5:00PM so be up at the airfield about 15 minutes before then. Again, great job, I'm very proud of each one of you." I guessed that was enough of a speech from me so I shut up.

Mitch said, "Not bad for a bunch of rejects, right, Professor?"

I said, "One man's rejects are another man's superstars."

"One woman's rejects, Professor," Mitch said.

I'd begun to realize Mitch liked to have the last word, so I smiled, nodded, and walked out of the workroom.

I met the Franks for dinner at the dining hall. It was quiet. There were members of the security force at the bar. I had figured out that all the ranch hands and staff were locals. They worked their shifts and went home like normal people.

Major Campbell joined us and the conversation went to The Rejects' presentation that afternoon. The general comments were about how much had been done in a few days and the quality level of their work.

I said, "I hope I'm not setting them up for a big disappointment. We may do all this work and come up with nothing."

Dona Frank cut in. "Rob, you do understand that all the work you are doing will advance science even if the cave temple or tomb isn't found. The search program improvements that Elizabeth and Abbey are creating are the next generation. I believe their software improvement will be incorporated into Falone Advanced Technologies' next-generation search software and I know quite a bit about this topic. They appear to be doing in weeks what a team of a dozen or so highly qualified programmers would take months or even years to accomplish. Walter will have spent a small fraction of what it normally cost. All the other areas of investigation will have some business, scientific, or scholarly use."

I said, "Dona, I get that on an intellectual level. But I worry the team will be so emotionally invested that it will still be a huge letdown for them if we don't find something of great importance. They don't want this for themselves, they want to do this for Walter Falone. They don't want to let him down."

Our dinner came and the conversation became lighter and more general. I looked up and I saw Sadako walk into the dining room.

I said, "Good evening, Sadako. I thought you went to Lima with the others." She was far too polite to not come over and greet us. I could tell she was uncomfortable. I didn't like this. She was a long way from home in a place with a very limited social life.

I started to ask if something was wrong when Dona squeezed my knee under the table and said, "Sadako, if you are not too busy tomorrow I would greatly appreciate your help. Houston sent us loads of new equipment that needs to be installed. That is why Peter and I are here this weekend."

"Oh no, Dr. Frank, I'm not too busy and I would be honored to help you. I have many questions I would like to ask you. That is, if it doesn't interfere with your work."

"I'm sure it won't interfere. Peter and I will be at the airfield about 8:00 in the morning. Join us whenever you can and please call me Dona."

"I will be there at 8:00, Dr. Dona."

I said, "Would you like to join us for dinner?"

"No thank you, Professor. My takeout order is ready and I have a Skype call scheduled with my family in a few minutes."

"Well, then we won't hold you up. Have a nice evening, Sadako."

When she went to pick up her dinner I said to Dona, "That was very nice of you. My team is a very diverse group. They seem to have bonded very well around their work, but they don't have much else in common. This is not like a university or city where all the normal social life is built in. Also I kind of like Dr. Dona, it has a nice ring to it."

Dona said, "She is a fine young lady. I'm sure Peter and I will have a much more enjoyable workday tomorrow because Sadako is working with us."

Her husband said, "Cheers to that."

Major Campbell said, "Rob, what are you doing tomorrow?"

"I haven't decided, Ian."

He said, "How would you like to go flying with me? I thought maybe we could fly north along one of Minchancaman's potential routes. We could cover six months of walking in a few hours of flying."

"I'd love that. What time would you like to go?" I said.

He said, "Let's meet here at 8:30 for breakfast. You decide where you want to go and then I'll chart a route and file a flight plan. There is a still a big drug smuggling problem in Peru. I don't want the officials to think we are the bad guys."

We said our goodnights after dinner. I walked back to the guesthouse and thought all in all it had been a very satisfying week.

Chapter 23

I met Major Campbell at 8:30 for breakfast. I was excited about our trip. I didn't have any idea how far he wanted to fly or what plane we would take. So I put down everything I wanted to see and figured Ian would tell me if it was too much.

He said, "Where do you want to go, Rob?"

So I told him. "I'd like to fly generally up the main Inca coast road on our way north to Tumbes and then back down the mountainside Inca road on the way home. There are a few detours I'd like to make along the way to view archaeological sites from the air. Too much?"

"No, Rob, with detours probably 1,100-1,200 miles. We'll take the Cessna Skymaster. It is the T337B Turbo Super Skymaster model with a few special modifications."

I thought, everything in this place has "a few special modifications."

He continued, "The two Continental turbocharged fuel-injected 210 horsepower engines have a service ceiling to 33,000 feet, a cruise speed to 233 mph, and a range to 1,640 miles. It is pressurized and has Robertson STOL modifications. The plane has the range but I don't think your bladder does. I suggest we stop in Tumbes City for lunch and top off our fuel tanks. That is almost the farthest north we will go and it roughly splits the trip in half. Let me see what you have marked on your map."

I showed him and he said, "It will be a full day, Rob. Let's finish our breakfast and walk up to the airfield."

At the airfield Major Campbell went to his office to file the flight plan.

I went looking for Sadako and the Franks. I found them at a workbench in the main hangar. I watched from a distance for a moment. They seemed fully engaged and happy.

I said, "Good morning. You all seem hard at work this morning. I'd ask what you are doing but I'm not sure I would understand your answer."

They were all smiles and said good morning.

"Sadako, how was your Skype call home last night to your family?" I said.

"We were on for almost two hours. My parents had my grandmother over and several other family members. Everybody tried to talk at once. It was wonderful. They all miss me and I miss them. But they told me how proud they were of my work and that I brought honor to the entire Ogato family."

She was beaming and seemed a very different person than last night. Family love and hard work, now there is a great cure for the blues. We visited for another few minutes and then I went back to the office to let them get back to work.

I was looking at the IAI Heron drone control station when Major Campbell came out of his office and said he was all set to go. The Cessna Skymaster was positioned in the front of the hangar and ready for us to take off. I climbed in the copilot's seat and adjusted the seat belt and shoulder straps while the Major went through the pre-flight routine. He climbed in the pilot's seat and continued his pre-flight checking. I had the feeling I was in very good hands with this pilot.

We taxied out to the runway and did a run up with Ian revving each engine and checking all the gages. He set the altimeter and taxied to the very end of the runway. Then he stepped on the brakes and pushed both throttles to full. When he let off the brakes the plane seemed to jump forward like a jackrabbit and leap into the air. I guess he wanted to show me how the "few special modifications" worked.

I said, "When you said short takeoff you weren't kidding. What about the other end, can you land in a tennis court without hitting the net?"

He smiled and said, "It depends on the winds."

We headed north flying up the coastal Inca trail through the Ancash Region. The first place I wanted to see from the air was the archaeological site Gran Pajatén. It is located on the border of the La Libertad Region and the San Martín Region in a climatic area known as the Andean cloud forest. It sits on a hilltop, and has about 26 circular stone structures at the top of numerous terraces and stairways. The ruins occupy an area of about five acres. The buildings are decorated with slate mosaics displaying human, bird, and geometric motifs. The earliest part dates from about 200 BC but parts were constructed during the late Inca period. The settlement is attributed to the Chachapoyas culture, which was later incorporated into the Inca Empire. I wasn't exactly sure how seeing these things from the air would help. But I figured if I did enough exploring something might eventually help, and Walter was paying me well, and treating me well.

From Gran Pajatén we continued north past Trujillo City. I want to next see Chan Chan. It was the largest pre-Columbian city in South America. Chan Chan covered almost eight square miles and had a dense urban center of over two square miles. The Chimor, a late intermediate-period civilization that grew out of the remnants of the Moche civilization, constructed it. The adobe city of Chan Chan is the largest adobe city in the world. It was built around AD 850 and lasted until its conquest by the Inca Empire in AD 1470. The Chimor peoples primarily worshiped the moon god Si. Their last great leader was Minchancaman. That is the name Friar Murúa used to identify the leader who was leading the Pure, or Strong of Heart north. The entire area north of Chan Chan was once controlled by the Kingdom of Chimor and later conquered by the Inca Empire. It extended beyond the region of Tumbes and into Ecuador. Since it was on the flat desert coastal plain it was unlikely to have any cave formations. The Chimor were not know to use cave temples or tombs.

We continued north along the border between the regions of La Libertad and Cajamarca into the region of Lambayeque.

As we flew along, I was again struck by the north-south nature of the climate zones and geography. Peru's climate is very diverse, with a large variety of climates and microclimates, including 28 of the 32 world climates. This diversity is chiefly caused by the presence of the Andes Mountains and the cold Humboldt Current.

In general, the climate on the coast is subtropical with very little rainfall. The Andes Mountains have a cool-to-cold climate with rainy summers and very dry winters. The eastern lowlands have an equatorial climate with hot weather and rain distributed all year long.

In some places you can go from sea level on the Pacific coast to an elevation of over 15,000 feet by heading only about 50 miles due west.

We were now in the Lambayeque region. This was the home of the Sican. Sican is the name given to the culture that inhabited the north coast of Peru between about AD 750 and 1375. It is also referred to as Lambayeque culture. According to the archaeologist Izumi Shimada, "Sican" means "temple of the moon." It succeeded the Moche culture and ended with the Chimú conquest of the Lambayeque region circa 1375. It may have lasted longer farther north.

Parts of Sican culture fit with what little we knew. The trouble was we just knew too little.

We were flying above the Lambayeque Valley. It is the site of scores of natural and man-made waterways and is also a region of about 250 decaying brick pyramids.

I wanted to see Túcume. It is located south of the La Leche River on a plain around La Raya Mountain. It covers an area of over 540 acres and encompasses 26 major pyramids and mounds. This site was a major regional center, maybe even the capital of the successive occupations of the area by the Lambayeque/Sican from 800 AD to 1350 AD, Chimú from 1350 AD to 1450 AD, and Inca from 1450 AD to 1532 AD. Even today the local shaman healers invoke the power of Túcume and La Raya Mountain in their rituals, and local people fear these sites. Hardly anyone other than shaman healers ventures out to this site at night.

We were now headed to the two most northern regions of Peru, Piura and Tumbes. They both bordered Ecuador on the west and the Pacific Ocean on the east. There was a push for these three regions to merge but it was voted down in 2005.

Because I live in Ithaca, I had to keep reminding myself that going north in Peru meant heading towards the equator and it would in general get warmer not colder. The temperatures of the Tumbes and Piura coastal region range from the mid-50s to over 100° Fahrenheit. Summers are hot, humid, and sunny, with occasional afternoon and evening rain showers. The farther north, the less arid, due to the Humboldt Current getting less cold as it nears the Equator. The winter is warm and comfortable with very little rain.

As we flew through Piura toward Tumbes, looking left I could see the Pacific Ocean and the subtropical desert of the coast. Below us was the savanna-like scrub of the tropical dry forest area. Looking right there were foothills and small valleys of tropical climate that turned into mountains that reach 8,800 feet in elevation.

We were quickly approaching Tumbes City. Ian was on the radio with approach control for the Capitán FAP Pedro Canga Rodríguez Airport that served Tumbes City. I had no idea who the airport was named after but it sounded quite impressive. The airport was big enough to serve commercial jets bringing in tourists to enjoy some of Peru's most superb beaches and resorts. The city of about 95,000 people was quite close to the Ecuador border.

We landed and taxied to the fixed-base operator. Ian spoke English to approach control and the tower. English is the international language of aviation. However the Spanish he spoke to the gas truck attendant was excellent.

He said, "Rob, how about a bite of lunch?"

I said, "You were right about my bladder. How about a pit stop on the way?"

We walked to the office of the fixed-base operator. It had a coffee shop inside it. We hadn't talked much during the flight. I was taking in the sights and making notes as we flew along.

"Well, Rob, what did you think about our flight up? You seemed engaged and I saw you were making notes along the way."

I said, "I loved it. Just the flying and viewing the terrain was wonderful. I had forgotten how great the aerial view is from a light plane. You just don't get that from an airliner. Professionally I enjoyed seeing the archaeological sites and land surrounding them. In my mind's eye I imaged them at the height of their glory with people going about their daily business." I stopped and sighed.

"But I only hope it is of some use to our project. I have been stuffing my head with everything I can that is related and hoping it will do some good at some point."

He said, "If you put enough resources on it you can find a needle in a haystack. You can even find both halves of a broken needle in a haystack."

I said, "Are we trying to do that or are we putting nine ladies on the job and trying to make a baby in one month?"

"Rob, I believe my analogy is closer to our situation. We don't have a firm time line. You are being a bit hard on yourself. You have only been here 10 days. The team is motivated and they have outlined a fantastic plan. On Monday the power of Walter's corporate tech machine will go to work and we will see results."

"Thank you, Ian. I hope you are right. It's funny, in a short time I've become committed to this project in a way I haven't been committed to anything in years. I guess that is part of the reason why Walter is so successful. But it's not just Walter, I want this to be really good for the whole team."

He said, "You know what I think, Rob? I think once again Walter has found the right man for the job."

I smiled, "If you weren't my pilot I'd buy you a drink."

"When we get back, Rob, you can buy me two."

After a quick lunch we took off and flew south. Four of the northern regions of Peru, Tumbes, Piura, Cajamarca, and Amazonas, wrap around the southern border of Ecuador. So we flew south the same way we came through Tumbes and Piura to avoid entering Ecuador's airspace. Then we turned west across Cajamarca and then north in the Amazonas Region.

As we went west across Cajamarca there were two areas I wanted to see. The first was the Marañón River. It is the principal source of the Amazon River, starting about 100 miles to the northeast of Lima, and flowing through a deeply eroded Andean valley in a northwesterly direction, along the eastern base of the Cordillera section of the Andes, where it makes a great bend to the northeast, and cuts through the jungle Andes, until it flows into the flat Amazon basin. It is referred to as the Grand Canyon of the Amazon.

The second was the Cutervo National Park. It is the oldest National Park in Peru and covers about 32 square miles. The park protects part of the Peruvian Yungas eco-region. There are lots of caves in this park including San Andres Cave, where the endangered bird guácharo lives.

The main attraction in the park is the Cueva del Guácharo. In the cave is a colony of guácharo, which is nocturnal and feeds exclusively on fruit and nuts. There is also a stream that flows under this cave, containing a species of catfish and other troglobites, or animals that live entirely in the dark parts of caves.

The park contains endangered animals that include jaguar, ocelot, spectacled bear, neo-tropical river otter, colocolo, mountain tapir, and the national bird called the Andean cock-of-the-rock.

Next we turned north to the Amazonas Region. This area is covered by rainforests and mountain ranges. Its geography of big valleys and plains in the rainforest zone that are close to the Pacific Ocean is unique. The mountain pass of Porculla at 7,000 feet is the lowest pass of the whole Peruvian Andes to arrive to the Pan-American road system.

The vast and deep Marañón valley is one of the most important features of the region. This valley crosses a big part of its territory and runs from south to north. It reaches its greatest width in the province of Bagua, which is one of the seven provinces that make up the Amazonas Region. It narrows when it crosses the eastern mountain range. In this area it crosses those wonderful canyons or narrow gorges called punkus, a Quechua word that means doors.

The Pongo de Manseriche is perhaps the most spectacular gorge on the Marañón River. The river runs through this gorge before it reaches the Amazon Basin.

The Pongo de Manseriche is three miles long just below the mouth of the Rio Santiago River near the old missionary station of Borja. It is a 2,000-feet deep gorge that cuts through the Andes. It is as narrow in places as only 100 feet and as seen from the bottom it seems to close in above you at the top. Through this dark canyon the *Marañón* River rushes along at up to 12 miles an hour.

We then flew over Kuelap's Fortress. It is a huge construction of military architecture that shows the high level of civilization achieved by the people of this region. The Chachapoyas culture developed during the Inca age and represented a strong opposition to the Incan conquest by repelling the first Inca attempts to incorporate the region to their empire.

We then turned south retracing our route toward the last region in our area of interest, San Martín. The territory of San Martín can be divided into four geographic areas.

The west, near the eastern side of the Andean Plateau, has a rough topography and many ravines.

The second area is the zone of the wide valleys, with stepped terraces formed by the Huallaga River and its main affluent the Monzón, Mayo, Biabo, Abiseo and Tocache rivers. The population is engaged mainly in cattle raising and agriculture. Coca is also grown in most of those valleys. The coca is flown to Colombia, where it is used to create cocaine, which is subsequently shipped to the United States.

The southwest zone that contains the Blue Biabo mountain range, that has a low elevation, where there is an impressive canyon called Cajon de Sion. This area also contains the Cordillera Azul National Park.

The fourth area is a small lower jungle zone with areas easily flooded.

By this time my head was swimming with all I had seen in the last few hours. I realize I had gained a firsthand overview of the area we were interested in. I'm not sure I could have gotten so much in such a short period of time any other way. It was a day well spent.

I said, "Major, let's go home. My head is about to burst I've seen so much. I'll buy you those drinks."

Inca Style Suspension Bridge (Note 2)

Inca's Death Cave

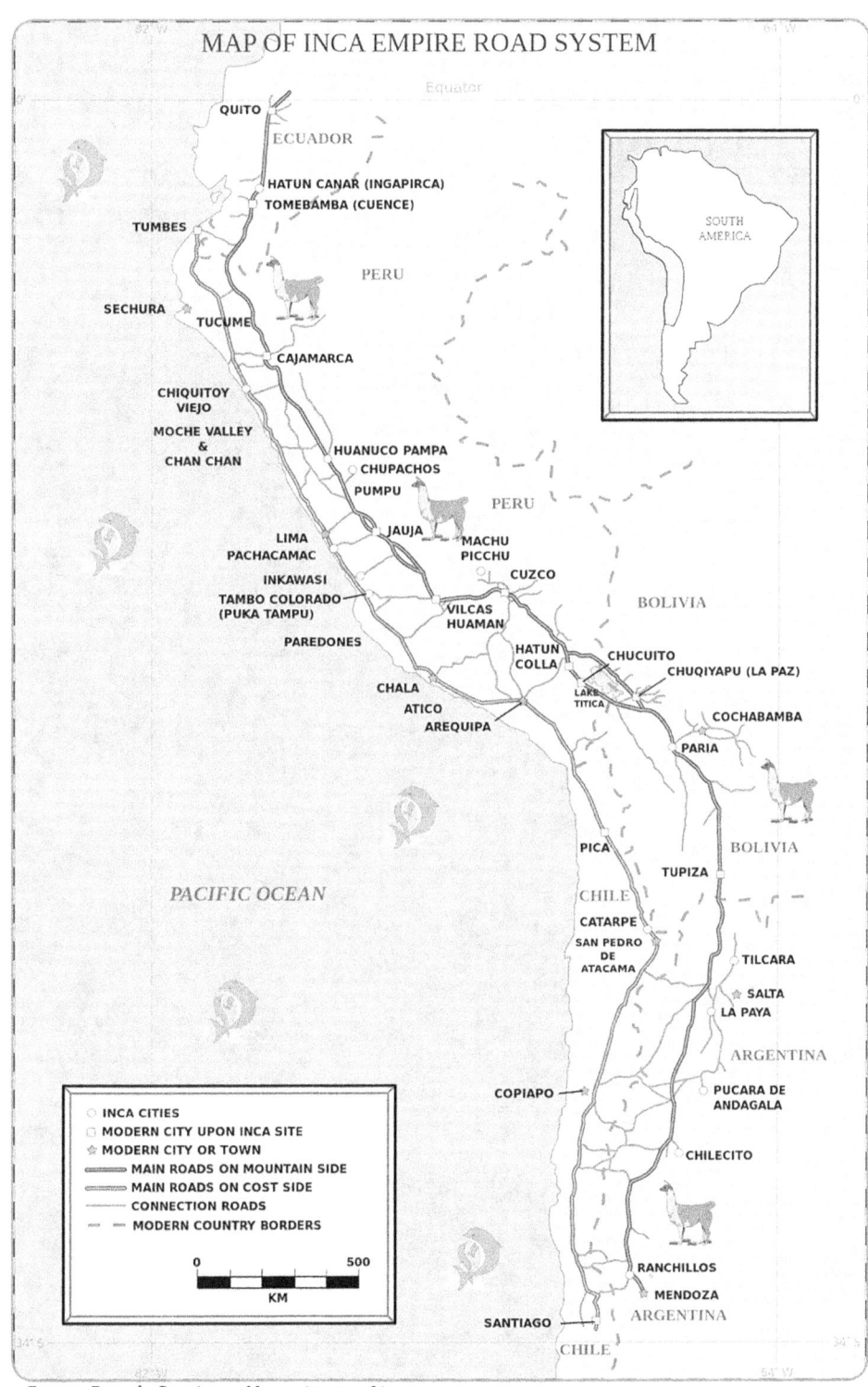

Inca Road System Map (Note 2)

Chapter
24

I spent Sunday worrying about our Monday presentation to Walter. I knew my team was well prepared and all of them were experienced at clearly conveying their ideas.

Monday morning I took an extra-long swim and after breakfast went to my office in the research facility. I made a point of staying in my office and not checking on the team. They didn't need me fussing around and asking questions that I knew they had already taken care of. At 9:55AM I went to the workroom. I met Walter in the hall and I said, "A big day for our team. They have accomplished much more than I expected in a short period of time."

He said, "They are all bright, talented, and dedicated young people. I've been looking forward to this morning. This is one of the really fun parts of my work."

We walked into the workroom. Walter greeted each person individually with a warm smile and a few words for every one of them. When they answered his friendly questions he seemed to be listening hard.

I walked to the whiteboard and wrote:

THE REJECT TEAM: PROJECT "THE INCA'S DEATH CAVE." WEEK 2 DAY 1

My time line wasn't perfect but I wanted our workweek to start on Monday with our reporting to Walter. So I left out the first half-week we were in Peru. It was exactly 10:00AM.

I said, "Elizabeth has agreed to lead the discussion." I smiled at her and took a seat next to Walter. As Elizabeth came to the whiteboard I looked at each team member. They didn't seem nervous, except for Sadako, who probably felt the weight of "bringing honor to her entire family." The rest looked like athletes in the zone and eager to start.

Elizabeth began, "Mr. Falone, the entire team is very pleased that you allowed us to present our plans for researching this project to you in person. We know how busy your schedule is and we have tried to provide enough detail without taking more of your valuable time than needed. However if at any point you would like more detail just interrupt us and ask. We are prepared to go into whatever level of detail you are interested in."

I thought, these folks have done their homework. They will have checked and rechecked their work and the details behind it. I also thought it would be very hard to BS Walter Falone.

Elizabeth continued, "We have broken our research into six main areas. The first that we will discuss is the searching of the relevant documents we have. This includes the customizing of some of the company's software and developing some new software to run in parallel with the company's software. Abbey and I will primarily be handling this work.

"The next area is researching the geographic and geological characteristics of our target area. We will primarily be using existing company sensing technology and the company's extensive database. We will however also use outside available data. Mitch and Mike will be heading this up.

"Harrison will be researching the weather patterns from this period in all our areas of interest. Given the number of climate and sub-climate types in Peru he will have a lot to cover. The results of Harrison's work will then be integrated into the geographic and geological work of Mitch and Mike.

"Fred will research all the possible routes that Minchancaman and his followers could have taken on their journey north. Again this work will be integrated with the work of Mitch, Mike and Harrison.

"Sadako has agreed to take on the very difficult task of trying to further interpret the quipus. Ned will assist her with whatever time he has when he isn't working for Major Campbell.

"Finally Mitch and Harrison will be researching non-Christian religious practices and faith healers in our areas of interest. They will start with current practices and beliefs and work backward in time to before Minchancaman's time.

"If it is all right with you, Mr. Falone, we will take each area in turn and answer questions and have a discussion at the end of each presentation."

Walter said, "That sounds like an excellent way to proceed, Elizabeth."

Each of the members of the team gave part of the presentation. Walter asked penetrating questions. He had several suggestions on how to use the company's existing data, especially in the areas of geographic and geological research. He seemed very interested in the search software Elizabeth was developing.

After the final discussion Walter said, "That was magnificent. You folks have made my week. Please proceed on all fronts."

Elizabeth said, "We don't have much insight into the cost of this research and our budget constraints."

Walter replied, "I told Professor Johnson that your project team is the only one in the company not subject to our normal budgeting and cost control systems."

Mitch, who had been well behaved during the whole meeting, spoke up. "I bet Dr. Stone didn't like that."

Walter smiled at her and said to Elizabeth, "Please proceed with all speed."

Abbey spoke up and said, "Mr. Falone, we do have one more item. Prof would like to tell you about the research he has done into the works of the zoologist and amateur archaeologist Ralph Hardy."

The cover of the comic book *Adventures of the Jaguar* flashed up on the whiteboard. Everyone broke out laughing.

Fred started screaming. "I didn't tell them, honest, I didn't tell."

Walter in a very serious tone said, "Abbey I've read all 15 works of Ralph Hardy. They are most illuminating."

Then he again said how pleased he was with what had been done and asked me if we could meet in my office for a moment.

I said, "Great job. Now go to it, team."

As Walter and I walked to my office I said, "Walter, you have assembled an amazing team. Very bright, hardworking, and committed to you."

He said, "You seem to get along well with all of them and it didn't take long for you to earn their respect."

"Walter, I guess I'm Reject Team material. I'm not quite sure she would ever hire me in the first place. But Dr. Stone wouldn't take long to fire me. No, but seriously being a professor at Cornell you see all types and I've found it's best not to jump to early conclusions."

He said, "I agree, Rob."

I offered Walter a seat in my office.

He began, "Again let me say your team has made a very good start especially given the short time you have had together. As you know Mrs. O'Hara's team arrives in Peru tomorrow."

I said, "Yes, I plan to fly to Lima with Major Campbell to meet them. We will introduce them to the technical support team that will go with them to the Monastery of Saint Catherine in Arequipa and set up their equipment."

He said, "That sounds fine. Unfortunately I've made little progress with Church officials on the Church related documents from Spain."

I said, "I believe we should keep receiving as many non-Church documents as we can. They may be helpful and if nothing else we can test the software and cross them off our list."

Walter said, "I will keep working on this and there are a few documents that have been released by the Church reviewers. Those will be here in a day or two. As usual my schedule is overbooked and I need to catch a plane to the States. I'll see you next Monday at 10:00AM for an update. Great start, Rob."

I sat in my office for a few moments mentally reviewing our line of research. I felt we had the major areas covered and now we would see what it would produce.

Next I walked back to the workroom and then stuck my head in the various workspaces. Everyone was hard at work. They didn't even look up as I quietly went by. I decided the best thing I could do was stay out of the way. So I went back to the guesthouse to continue my reading about all things related to our project.

Chapter
25

Tuesday morning I was in my office at the research facility trying to figure out something productive to do when Major Campbell came in.

He said, "We have a problem."

The way he said it, it sounded more like I had a problem. I gestured for him to have a seat.

"What's up?" I said.

"Elizabeth's and Abbey's search program seems to be hogging all the company's server capacity. From what little I know it seems that their program consumed all the server capacity on the ranch, which isn't that large. Then it began using the servers in Lima. This is standard procedure – the server farms are set up to share capacity to optimize the usage. But Elizabeth seems to have written into her code a way to bypass the normal priority system and up her work to the front of the queue. Sometime around midnight her work was using all of Lima's server capacity and it began tapping the servers in Houston. In Houston the program systematically shut down other people's work, as it had done in Lima, and pushed their work to the back of the queue. Now the next interesting thing was that none of the normal alarms were triggered. Elizabeth's program somehow made the system believe this was normal operating procedure. It wasn't until people started showing up for work this morning that they realized their work had been shut down and put in the waiting queue. The Houston computer security group cut the connection to Lima and the phones started ringing."

As the Major was telling me this I was typing a text to Abbey. I told her to find Elizabeth and come to my office ASAP.

I said, "Quite ingenious of our girl. I imagine once the fuss settles down Walter and the computer security team will be interested to see how she did it."

He said, "That's an upbeat way to look at it. But for now we have some fires to put out."

Elizabeth and Abbey walked into my office. Elizabeth said in her cheery voice, "Good morning, Professor, good morning, Major. You asked to see me?"

I said, "It seems we have been rather piggish with our use of the company's server capacity."

"Yes, Professor, launching everything at once seems to have used quite a bit of capacity."

I said, "Combinatorial explosion caused by your new algorithm that looks across the parallel searches?"

She said, "Exactly, I believe it increased the server capacity requirements by about ten times."

I said, "Quite ingenious to put your work at the front of the line and disable the normal alarm systems."

"It was something I've been wanting to try for a while now, Professor. Mr. Falone did say, 'Please proceed with all speed.' Perhaps I took him too literally."

My cell phone rang. I saw it was Mrs. Lopez and answered it. After saying hello I listened to her.

I said, "Major Campbell is in my office and has been filling me in. I just had Elizabeth and Abbey join us. Yes. If you don't mind, I would like to put you on speakerphone."

As I did Elizabeth said, "Good morning, Mrs. Lopez. How nice to hear from you."

Mrs. Lopez cleared her throat and said, "Elizabeth, you seem to have caused quite a stir this morning. It seems quite a few people in Lima and Houston are upset at having their work shut down."

Elizabeth said, "I didn't shut it down, I just moved it behind our work in the queue."

Mrs. Lopez said, "Be that as it may, Mr. Falone has had a rather busy morning. He asked me to tell you. No server space in Houston, 35% of Lima's capacity and use all the capacity at the ranch that isn't required for Dr. Frank's and Major Campbell's work."

"Is that negotiable, Mrs. Lopez?"

Mrs. Lopez said, "No, it is not negotiable. Do you have a problem with this arrangement?"

"No, Mrs. Lopez. If that is what Mr. Falone feels is best, I'm 100% onboard."

"Elizabeth, when can you have this implemented?"

"I can do it within an hour or so. First I'll reestablish the former queue and make sure everyone's work is running as it was before. That will take an hour. Then I'll set the capacity limits on our work, evaluate what was done overnight, and restart our searches. That will take at least the rest of the day, Mrs. Lopez."

"That will be fine, Elizabeth."

"Mrs. Lopez, please tell Mr. Falone I'm sorry to have caused him all this trouble. I know he is very busy."

"I will tell him, Elizabeth. But in a funny way I think he might have rather enjoyed it. I'm sure he will want to discuss your program enhancements when he has time. Now get to work, young lady. I have other thing I need to attend to."

She hung up and I said, "Well, now that we have that solved, did you accomplish something with all that server power you stole overnight?"

Elizabeth said, "I didn't steal it. Maybe I jumped the queue. We did accomplish several things. First the program didn't crash. Next the priority function worked well and the alarm override worked. We were processing a huge amount of data with multiple runs in parallel. The software I wrote to look across the parallel runs worked. But we don't know yet if it captured useful data or not. This could be very helpful in national security or law enforcement if a huge amount of data needs to be searched in a very short time in an emergency situation. The other thing we don't know and it will take a while to find out is if we found anything that helps our project."

I said, "You better get to work getting the rest of the company back online. Once you exhausted the server capacity in Houston, would your program have started taking over the servers in Canada? Also you knew if you asked for permission to test your software in this way they never would have given it to you, right?"

She nodded yes.

I said, "Go get to work and let me know what you found after everything else is back on track."

They both left my office. I said to Major Campbell, "Quite an ingenious team we have."

He said, "Let's fly out to Lima at about 2:00PM. Meet me at the airfield."

Chapter 26

I went up to the airstrip at 2:00PM. We were taking the Cessna Skymaster. It would be a short flight but Major Campbell liked to fly whenever he could. He had the plane out in front of the hangar and was starting to preflight it.

I said, "Hello, are you ready for me to get in?"

"Climb aboard, Rob."

The takeoff, flight, and landing were all done in about 40 minutes. We taxied right up to the front of the company hangar. We parked and walked in. The technical support team was there with the equipment in crates. Major Campbell went over all of it to make sure everything was in order. Once he had checked everything, they began loading it on the Britten-Norman Defender, the aircraft they were taking Laura O'Hara and her team to Arequipa in.

I tried to stay out of the way. When the plane was loaded Major Campbell came over and told me Mrs. O'Hara's plane had just landed.

As it taxied up I said, "A Gulfstream 4. I always wanted to fly in one of those."

Major Campbell said, "Ithaca to Lima direct. Walter must want this team in place right away."

The ramp was rolled up and Jane Fitzpatrick, our flight attendant, opened the door, came down the stairs first, and handed Major Campbell everyone's passports. He began reviewing them with the customs officer as Laura and her team came down the stairs.

I said, "Not a bad way to fly is it, Laura?"

She gave me a hug and introduced me to her team. We didn't spend much time on catching up. Major Campbell introduced the technical staff that would set up the equipment. Then we started working down our short meeting agenda.

When we were done Major Campbell said, "I'm sorry to make this meeting so short but we would like to get you to Arequipa before dark. All of you will stay at a hotel near the airport tonight and go to the monastery in the morning. Once everything is set up and working, the technical support team will return to Lima but they are on call if you need them."

We said our goodbyes and they got on the plane and left.

Major Campbell said he had a few things to check on so I went to the office area in the hangar and looked at the map of Peru on the wall. After about a half an hour someone said, "Find anything new?"

It was Major Campbell standing behind me. I said, "It is a big country to try to find the one 500-year-old tomb cave we are looking for in."

He said, "Let's go back to the ranch, get a drink, and have dinner."

"Good idea," I said.

Fountain at the Monastery of Saint Catherine in Arequipa (Note 1)

Chapter
27

The next day I had finished my swim, showered, and shaved. I was having coffee when Abbey came out of her apartment, got some coffee, and flopped into a chair.

She said, "Got some headaches for you, Prof."

I said, "Good morning Abbey, nice to see you. Do I have time to enjoy my morning coffee or do the headaches start now?"

"I should tell you. You won't enjoy your coffee thinking about what I'm going to say and you will probably imagine it is worse than it is. Plus I'd like to get the monkey off my back."

I refilled my coffee cup and said, "Fire away."

"It seems that when Mrs. Lopez said Elizabeth was restricted to 35% of the company's Lima server capacity she thought it was for her work. The Lima operation seems to think the 35% applies to the whole team's work. Elizabeth's search program takes up more capacity than anybody else's work but the others need quite a bit of server capacity too. Now Houston believes that our team has no access to their computers. But Mitch, Mike, and Harrison need access to the company databases that reside in Houston."

I said, "Well, that's not so bad. My head still feels OK and I might actually have to work and earn my pay today. I figured I wouldn't be able to sit around and read about archaeology for 14 months. Tell me what happened yesterday after you left my office. Did we crash the Lima facility again?"

"No, Prof. Elizabeth told everyone else to use all the available computer power. She had to put all the sidelined projects in Lima and Houston back online. Then she wanted to see what she had accomplished with all the computing power she had overnight. Also she couldn't scale her future runs until she knew how much capacity she had and just how much her new search software actually required when it ran. You know, Prof, Elizabeth may have created something really big here or at least taken what the company had to a new level."

I said, "I believe you are right. I also believe that Walter figured even if we never find our death cave, the byproducts of our work will more than pay for this project. I wish I could do that with my hobbies. Well, let's get the team together at 9:00 so I can get a better understanding of what the computer requirements are for each area of our research."

"Prof, we better make it 1:00PM. Just about the whole team worked all night because they didn't know how much server capacity they would get once Elizabeth started her search runs again."

I thought it's fun being the boss when you have team members like these. "That's fine. 1:00PM in the workroom. You are up early – no all-nighter for you?"

"No, I don't have much to do until I see what Elizabeth's results are. So I tried to help Sadako yesterday and Elizabeth was going to leave some of what she found on my desk when she went to bed. I'll head over now and I'll set up the meeting for 1:00."

She left and I thought about how to resolve the issue. I had a feeling that Elizabeth didn't need all that computer power to do what we wanted done for our project. We could only analyze a certain amount of material at a time. She could do sequential search runs. However that wouldn't demonstrate the real power of what she had created.

I decided to call Mrs. Lopez. I explained our situation. The Houston position of not granting access to the databases, when Walter had approved it and had explained to the team how to better use the databases, seemed totally unreasonable. Mrs. Lopez agreed. I told her I was happy to handle it. But I needed to know the right people to contact. She gave me the name and phone number of the head of computer operations in Lima and said she was a reasonable person. As for Houston, Mrs. Lopez said she had better handle that herself. I told her I had a 1:00PM meeting with the team. She said she would have the Houston situation straightened out long before that and she would be back to me.

I hung up and thought, someone in Houston is going to get an earful from Mrs. Lopez. The devil in me was hoping it was Dr. Stone but it was probably someone in the computer center. I also thought Mrs. Lopez is a good one to keep on your side.

I called the company's computer center in Lima. As Mrs. Lopez said, the woman in charge of the center was quite reasonable. She explained that she knew and liked young Miss Elizabeth Walters but other people had their jobs to get done on time as well. She would check what capacity above the 35% might be available. She also said that we could go to 45% from 8:00PM to 5:00AM. If more capacity was available we were welcome to use it. I thanked her and she wished me good luck.

At 10:30AM I received a text from Mrs. Lopez. The team had full access to the databases and it was only the search runs that were restricted from the Houston servers. I sent a thank you back.

At 1:00PM I went into the workroom. Everybody was there. They looked on edge.

I said, "Let's take the easy one, the team has full access to the databases in Houston and everywhere else the company has them. Mrs. Lopez ripped Dr. Stone a new you-know-what over that one."

Mitch screamed, "Yes! Really?"

"No, Mitch, I was just fantasizing about the Dr. Stone part but the rest is true and I'm sure she gave someone an earful. She didn't seem pleased when I told her about Houston."

My team seemed to relax a little. Next I said, "I spoke to the head of the company's computer operation in Lima. She said we can use 35% of their server capacity from 5:00AM to 8:00PM, and 45% for the rest of the night. She will review the exact needs of the others using the Lima servers and try to give us more capacity if it is available. I believe she is trying to be as helpful as she can be. I want everyone to respect the capacity limits she gives us." I looked at Elizabeth. She smiled and nodded yes.

"Elizabeth, I know you want to do a mega-run to test your new software. I don't think that is required for our project." She looked crushed. "However, I will talk to Walter next Monday and see if we can arrange a mega-run test search. Perhaps on a holiday weekend or maybe just before or after a maintenance shutdown. I'm sure Walter is just as interested as you are to see what this new software can do. I'd like to talk to you about the specifics after we're done here, Elizabeth.

"Given those constraints I'd like to hear how you plan to proceed in your research areas."

Harrison put his hand up. I said, "You start"

"Professor, I don't need much computer power for what I'm doing now. I will be searching all sorts of weather databases and most aren't the company's. Some have a subscription fee but I think the company already has a subscription to most of them. Later when I do some weather pattern modeling I'll need some serious computing power. But I'm sure I can fit it in during slack times."

I said, "Harrison, that sounds good to me. Next."

Mitch spoke up. "Now that we have access to all the databases we can find what we need. Once we pull everything together there may be some searching but Elizabeth will have to help us and it shouldn't take that much time."

"OK, but all of you also have to keep in mind that you have to figure out how to display or present your material so I can understand it and hopefully use it. Next, Fred?"

"I have what I need, Professor."

Sadako said, "Professor I'm not yet sure what I need. But nothing is holding me back now. When my requirements change I will let you know."

I said, "Dare I ask what we accomplished in the last two days?"

Abbey said, "Let just say we didn't find it yet."

"Alright, I got it. I'll let you folks get back to work. Elizabeth, did you get everyone back online in Lima and Houston?"

"Yes, Professor, I did that yesterday."

"Do you have time to talk with me about your software now?"

"Yes, Professor. Now would be fine."

I was coming to realize she really was that sweet and nice. It wasn't just an act or to suck up. I said, "Good, let's go to my office."

We sat in my office and I said, "I'll tell you what I think I know about your software and you correct my mistakes and then fill me in on the rest in simple terms I might understand. The company has developed very powerful search software. As Abbey said it's like Bible Analyzer on steroids. It also has some kind of artificial intelligence that keeps it from going down too many wrong or unlikely pathways. This eliminates the problem of combinatorial explosion." Once I've learned a nifty new term like that I like to throw it around a bit. "What you have done is to set up multiple searches at the same time and have developed software that looks across all these searches while they are running and coordinates them like an orchestra conductor. But you also did something else. You wrote some code that puts your work in the front of the line ahead of everybody else's work. It does this without setting off any of the system's normal alarms."

I thought that was pretty good for a guy who examines old bones and broken pottery for a living.

"Very good, Professor."

I figured she would say that and then politely explain that I didn't have a clue.

She went on, "Yes, basically that is what I'm doing. To answer the question you asked me before I don't need all that computing power for our project. I can run the searches end to end day in and day out and be done with what we have in a few days. Then I'll run searches across the search results as many times as needed. We have quite a bit of data but not the amount I've designed this software for. I think I'll use trains for my analogy."

I said, "I like trains, old-fashioned and slow."

She smiled. "Imagine lots of parallel train tracks. Those are our search runs. These trains are all electric trains and they are powered by one substation. Now this won't be a perfect example but I hope you will see what I'm doing. We start the trains down the tracks and as they go faster they need more electricity. In our searches we need more server capacity because the searches keeps expanding like a fractal or like an evergreen tree that keeps branching out. To keep from a combinatorial explosion, as you like to put it, I've done several things. First I've turned off the part of the company software that automatically shuts down unlikely branches. This is how the company software keeps from bogging down by going down too many pathways. The artificial intelligence (AI) used to do this is very effective for what the company does. In our petroleum and mining areas we are usually looking for one or two specific things so it is relatively easy to identify and shut down unlikely search branches. Our project is different.

We don't really know exactly what clue will be helpful. We need to look at everything from every direction. There are many real-world applications that have this same problem.

"Now that the AI that trims the branches back is turned off, we need another way to not crash the program when we run out of server capacity. So one thing I did was to program a code that would move anybody else's train of the tracks. That was the part that put other people's computer work at the back of the queue. Once our searches needed more capacity or in our example our trains needed more electricity than our substation had, we would tap into another train system's substation. First we would use any spare electricity they had and then we would start parking those trains to get more of their electricity. When we were using all their electricity we could go to the next train system's substation and use that and so on. Are you with me?"

I nodded my head.

She went on, "Now we can't just keep having billions and billions of more branches of our parallel searches. So this is the fun part. I wrote a program, and I'll go back to my train analogy, that looks back and forth across our train tracks and sees in the big picture across all the tracks. We can program a sensitivity level in this with multiple parameters for what we want to be searching for. This program tells each train how fast to go or in search terms which paths not to go down. But it does it globally, not each train individually, or as the company search software does within that one search. As new information emerges my new software remembers the pathways that were shut down and can restart them if they now look useful given new information."

She stopped to take a breath and see if she totally lost me.

I said, "I assume you can set the total server capacity that this whole process will use and that will just slow down the whole search process or reduce the number of parallel searches you can run."

"Yes sir."

"I also assume you can turn off and on the part that bypasses the computer system's usual alarms."

"Yes sir."

"Well, very cool. I believe you have built something truly amazing, now give me some real-world examples of how it would be used."

She said, "In a classic simple search you pretty much know what you want. For example if you want to buy a digital camera, just plug the term into the Google search engine. You get a million hits ranked in order of how likely they are to be what you want. Now you can compare prices, look at the different features, read reviews and so on.

"Our project is one example where a simple search is only marginally helpful. You could plug in terms that you think might be relevant all day and not get anything useful. With the standard company search software you can list the terms that you think might be helpful like Minchancaman, Friar Ortiz, Sister Ortiz, and Friar Murúa and search any digital document you think might be relevant. This is what Abbey did with the *Historia.* It would work for what we want to do but be a somewhat slow process. My software setup allows you to search a large number of documents at once with a large number of search terms. Then look across all searches as they are running, identifying potential useful patterns, and shutting down paths that hold little likelihood of being helpful. This not only greatly speeds up the process but it increases the chances of finding the patterns that will be useful.

"There are other situations where the amount of data is much greater and time is critical or the search has to be ongoing. Let me give you some examples from the past. The Boston Marathon bombing, the 9/11 World Trade Center attack, or the Japanese attack on Pearl Harbor. After the event people looked back and found clues that together would have warned of the situation. Congressional committees and reporters love to point fingers and blame people for not seeing patterns that in hindsight seem obvious. The reality is those 6, 10, or even 20 clues were mixed in with millions, if not billions of other pieces of information and it is almost impossible to see any meaningful pattern.

"We now have computing power that is literally a million or more times as powerful as it was a decade ago. With my system of programs and the vast computing power that now exists, it is possible to look at the billions of pieces of information in real time and pick out those clues. Some false patterns will emerge but the number will be small enough that they can be checked out manually. Let's use the federal government as an example. They could set up a real-time search of terrorist plots using numerous likely search terms and run the program continuously with a given amount of server capacity. If there is a credible threat then they could start letting the program put low-priority computer work at the back of the queue, adding more and more government servers as needed. Now you don't want to start a panic so the system turns off the alarm systems as it goes from server to server. To eliminate the problem I had with people seeing their work sidelined, the appropriate government officials could say that they are performing maintenance on the system or some story like that."

I was dumbfounded. I was only somewhat able to get a grasp of the enormity of what she had done. I said, "How long have you been working on this?"

"I had the basic idea about a year ago but Dr. Stone said it was a waste of time. I've been outlining how it would work on my laptop in my spare time since then. When Mr. Falone asked if I wanted to work on this project he also asked if I had any idea for productive use of my time before you arrived and if I had spare time once you got here. I told him I had some ideas to improve the company's search software. He just said, 'Go ahead.' Once I got here last month I started writing the code. Not much else to do here, so I worked pretty hard on it."

I thought, I bet you did work pretty hard the last month or so. I could imagine a hundred programmers at IBM or Google not being able to do this in a year. If her system worked as described it had to be worth hundreds of millions.

I said, "I think I understand what you have done. I know I don't understand how you did it. I would like you to put together a presentation on what you feel is the best way to test your program's capabilities. If you can use the documents from our project I would prefer that, if not OK. I assume what you were able to run in the last few days seemed to work."

She nodded and I went on. "In your presentation show what was accomplished with the period of time you ran wild on the company's computer systems. Then keep working with the server capacity you now have to demonstrate what can be done even without lots of computing power. It might even turn up something useful for our project. I will see if we can meet with Walter on Monday. I know he will be interested and maybe he can figure out a way to run a mega test."

She said, "I can do that by Monday no problem. Thank you, Professor, for taking the time to listen with an open mind. Lots of smart people don't do that. Mr. Falone said you would be very good for our team. Frankly I was a little worried you might be an old professor who just liked to examine cave drawings and bones."

I said with a smile, "First I'm not smart enough not to be open-minded. Second I do like examining cave drawings and old bones. You should try it some time. Now go get to work. I've important things to do. I believe Fred has some more vintage comic books for me."

She laughed and said, "Thank you, Professor Johnson. I really mean it. Thank you."

She left and as I sat there I started to wonder what pet project the rest of my team had been working on before I arrived. Perhaps I'd ask each of them when the time was right.

Next I picked up the phone and called the Lima computer center. I spoke again to the head of operations. I told her I believed Elizabeth had created some very powerful new improvements to the company's software. I also told her we would be giving a presentation to Mr. Falone next week and requesting the server capacity to fully test it. I went on to say I didn't want her to think we were going behind her back and that I appreciated the help she was giving us. She said if Mr. Falone approves it, young Miss Elizabeth must have done some fine work. I hung up. I had only had two phone conversations with this woman but I liked her already.

I went back to reading background material. But my mind kept wandering. So I decided to give up for the day. I took a long swim and at 6:30 I headed to the dining hall. I saw Major Campbell at the bar. He waved and then said something to the bartender. I walked over and he handed me a beer.

He said, "A busy day, Professor?"

"Major, today I believe I earned my pay." We clinked our glasses and drank.

Chapter
28

The rest of the week went quickly. Walter wanted to meet with Elizabeth and me in his office at the ranch at 9:00AM Monday. I pretty much left the team alone to do their work. In our Friday progress meeting I'd learn what they had accomplished.

I received an email from Laura O'Hara saying that they were set up in the Monastery of Saint Catherine in Arequipa. They had been warmly received by the Abbess, who had introduced her to the nuns that worked in the manuscript area of the monastery's library. They were very proud of their manuscripts and treated them with great care. It seems the Abbess had impressed upon these nuns that this was a unique opportunity to catalog and preserve a particularly valuable part of their manuscript collection. She also explained these people were from one of the world's most prestigious universities and that they were all experts in their fields. Laura mentioned that it didn't hurt that they were all women, spoke passable Spanish, and were Catholic.

The equipment all seemed to be working fine. However my idea of easily picking out documents that might really help us didn't seem feasible. The way the manuscripts were organized Laura could identify roughly the time period we wanted. This was required by the terms of the grant. But they would pretty much have to work shelf-by-shelf, then manuscript-by-manuscript. One team member would catalog, two others would carefully digitize the manuscripts, and the fourth would put a sheet of acid-free paper between each page of the manuscripts. All team members would wear special acid-free cotton gloves. The equipment technician had set up screens to block out the sunlight and metal halide track lighting for illumination. The process would be slow and methodical.

She went on to say the Abbess and the nun in charge of the manuscripts spoke excellent English and seemed very bright. All in all it was an upbeat email.

Friday morning I walked into the workroom at 9:59AM and wrote on the whiteboard:

THE REJECT TEAM: PROJECT "THE INCA'S DEATH CAVE." WEEK 2 DAY 5

I tried to be dramatic for no other reason than it was fun and the team seemed to enjoy it.

I said, "First no one is expected to work this weekend. Ground transport to Lima leaves at 5:00PM but you already know that."

Mitch interrupted me. "Can I work if I want to or do I have to go to Lima and get drunk on tequila?"

I ignored the question and went on. "Mitch, why don't you start with your presentation?"

She smiled and began. "Lots of caves in our area of interest. We started in the north with the four regions of Tumbes, Lambayeque, Cajamarca, and Amazonas. Once we have mapped these areas out we will integrate it with the work of Harrison and Fred. The four of us decided it made more sense to try to complete the integration of one section and work out the problems before moving on."

She projected a map of the four regions on the whiteboard.

"First we eliminated the easy stuff. In the low-lying coastal areas there are no real caves. Next we had a debate over what elevation would be too high for our cave tomb. The city of Cerro de Pasco is located at the top of the Andean mountains in the region of Pasco. At 14,200 feet in elevation, it is one of the highest cities in the world, with over 50,000 inhabitants. So if you can have a city at that elevation you could have a cave tomb higher up the mountains. At least that is what we figured. It turned out to be a great debate about not much. The top elevation of the Tumbes region is 440 feet. The highest elevation in our four regions is 22,205 feet in Ancash.

The next is 13,100 feet in the La Libertad region. So we picked 16,500 feet as our cutoff and eliminated a little territory in Ancash.

"We are now in the process of eliminating cities, river bottoms, open pit mines, and a few other minor areas. We should finish this next week sometime and then begin the integration with the work of Fred and Harrison. If we knew how big a cave we were looking for it might help. Do we have a cave tomb for two dozen or two thousand? That is about it. Do we get an 'A'?"

Fred said, "Professor will give you an 'A,' Mitch, but what will the 'A' stand for?"

Mitch gave Fred the finger. But it all seemed to be in fun.

I said, "Mike, anything to add?" He shook his head. He seemed in a better mood.

Harrison volunteered to go next.

"I'm finding there is not much accurate weather information from 1500. I made a crude model to take what was available and then factor in what we think El Niño and the Humboldt Current were doing at the time. It will give us a general idea and I'll have it for Mitch and Mike in a day or two. When Abbey and Elizabeth have time we could search ship captain's logs from the period. They were always good about reporting the basic daily weather. But at this point if the weather was good enough for people to live there it was good enough to die in a cave."

I said, "Good point. When you finish your model let's talk about the best use of your time."

Sadako raised her hand. I nodded.

She said, "I have much more work to do before I can report."

"You volunteered for a very hard job, just work at it and please ask me if you think I can help." I made a mental note to go sit and work with her early next week. I wasn't sure I'd be much help but I wanted to show her my interest.

Fred said, "I don't have much to report other than I'll have my information on the routes Minchancaman and his merry band might have taken north ready by midweek to integrate with the work Mitch, Mike, and Harrison are doing."

Ned said, "I've been monitoring the airwaves and no one else has found our 'Inca's Death Cave' yet."

"That certainly is good news, Ned."

"I guess you two are up," I said to Abbey and Elizabeth.

Abbey got up and began. "Elizabeth's program is amazing. In the first run we just loaded all the documents we had. That included the documents from Spain, the University and museum documents from Mrs. O'Hara, and a lot of other documents I was able to find. I used general search terms to see how the program would work and what it might find. It will take me a while to understand what we found. Elizabeth is showing me how to set up new searches that are refinements based on what looks promising from the mass search. One good thing about these searches is they don't take up much server capacity. I have a lot of work to do and since I don't like tequila I plan to work this weekend. More later."

I said, "Anybody have anything else to add? That also looks like a great week's work. Thank you for all your efforts and enjoy your weekend."

Once again I was impressed with what had been accomplished in a week. As everyone was leaving the meeting I said to Sadako, "What are your plans for the weekend?"

She lit up with a big smile, and said, "Dr. Dona and Mr. Frank have invited me to stay with them this weekend in Lima. On Saturday morning they will show me the laboratory at the company's Lima facility. In the afternoon we will visit the National Museum of Archaeology, Anthropology, and History of Peru. It is the largest and oldest museum in Peru. On Sunday we will visit the Museum of Art of Lima and the Museum of Natural History. The Franks have been very kind to me."

I said, "They are wonderful people and I enjoy both of them. I need to go to Lima and see those museums. You will have to tell me which one you liked the best. Please say hello to them for me and enjoy your weekend." I was feeling better about Sadako's adjustment to being here. I mostly had Dona Frank to thank for that.

I went back to my office and sent Abbey a text to come see me when she was free. In about 30 seconds she walked in and said, "What's up, Prof?"

It was interesting that no other team member used that name for me. Perhaps they sensed it would violate the relationship we had built up over the years.

I said, "Since I've finished reading all 15 of Ralph Hardy's manuscripts,

I want to talk to you about what you found in those documents and see if there are any I should read."

"It is all pretty interesting, Prof. But let's see, first there was a lot of duplication on the 18 memory sticks Mrs. O'Hara gave us. That is to be expected. I believe you might be right about the documents from Spain. A lot of those documents are reports from local Spanish colonial officials on tax collection, crop yields, mine production, and that sort of thing. You were right in that many also reported on what was going on of interest in their area. It appears from Elizabeth's mass run that we have some references to Minchancaman's movements, or at least someone's movements with a group of followers at about the right time. I'll need to figure out how to set the search parameters for a targeted search run just around that. As I said in the meeting, I hope to have that done this weekend. After Elizabeth has her Monday meeting with you and Walter, I'm hoping she can help me set it up.

"I think it would be a waste of your time to try to do anything with the Spanish documents until I narrow them down more. However I made a master memory stick of the documents from Mrs. O'Hara that eliminated all the duplicates. You might enjoy playing with that."

She walked into her adjoining office and came back and gave me the memory stick.

She said, "This should keep you busy." Then she smiled and walked out. She had work to do and didn't want me wasting any more of her time.

I put my feet up on my desk, leaned back, and thought, I love working with highly motivated people. It makes the boss's job easy and makes him look good.

I spent the rest of the afternoon looking at what was on the memory stick. It would take years to read all this stuff. Most of it was in Spanish and sixteenth-century Spanish to boot. I'd have them run it through the translation software. Then I realized that Abbey must be working completely with the sixteenth-century Spanish original documents and not bothering with the modern Spanish or English translations.

At dinner that night Major Campbell invited me to a test launch of the ScanEagle drone Saturday morning.

After my usual morning swim and breakfast I went up to the airstrip. The first thing I noticed was there were four ScanEagles. Ned was working on one on a workbench with one of the drone pilots. The other three were on the floor.

I said, "Good morning, Ned. How many of these things do they have?"

Ned said, "It's one system. A complete system comes with four air vehicles, a ground control station, remote video terminal, the launch system, and Skyhook recovery system.

"You can buy it all for a cost of only about $3.2 million. With four we can put different instrument packages in each one. I'm testing remote surveillance equipment. I'll launch it and when my stuff doesn't work right, which is usually what happens on the first try, they hook it for me. While I'm fixing or adjusting my equipment someone else has the equipment ready to test in another one of the ScanEagles and they launch theirs. That way the pilots don't just sit around most of day."

"Where are the others who will be testing their equipment?"

"They have their drones all set to go and will be here once we start flying them."

I looked at the equipment Ned was installing. It didn't mean anything to me. "What are you doing surveillance on and how does it work?"

Ned said, "I better let Major Campbell answer that. No offense, Professor."

"OK, I get it. I probably wouldn't understand most of what you told me anyway."

He smiled and I let him get back to work. A minute later I heard an airplane approaching and the Britten-Norman Defender landed. Eight people got off with some gear and the plane turned around and took off. It was the morning taxi service in from Lima. I went into the office, got some coffee and tried to stay out of the way.

Major Campbell was there. He said hello but he was busy organizing everyone. I went back out with my coffee. They were putting one of the ScanEagles on the pneumatic catapult launcher. I watched until they launched it. It took off with a rush of air sound, turned north, and was out of sight in under a minute. I guess it was cool if you were into it. I walked back to the guesthouse.

Chapter
29

I went to my office in the research facility at 8:15AM. Elizabeth joined me a little after 8:30. She seemed keyed up. We discussed her presentation in general terms until ten of nine and then headed to the ranch house to meet with Walter.

Walter gave us a warm welcome and offered us coffee. Elizabeth said no and I said yes. After about two minutes of small talk Walter asked Elizabeth to begin.

She told Walter to feel free to interrupt her at any point with questions. She didn't use the train track analogy she used with me. It quickly became apparent to me that I wasn't going to understand much of this. I tried to listen but mostly I enjoyed my coffee.

Walter would ask a question and they would have a discussion in great detail on how a particular aspect of the program worked. This went on for over two hours. I refilled my coffee cup several times and kept my mouth shut.

Walter said he would like to schedule the test run for Fourth of July weekend when there was a shutdown scheduled for maintenance of the entire computer system. Elizabeth's test could run up to 18 hours. She said that would be more than enough time. She would be able to use all the computer capacity in Lima, Houston, and Sudbury.

They discussed the amount of data that she wanted for the test. They decided that the test would include everything we had for our project and about an equal amount that Walter would provide along with the search terms for that data. Abbey would develop the search terms for our data based on what she was able to discover between now and the test date.

Walter said, "Rob, what do you think?"

I said, "A few things actually. First I like the idea that we are running all our documents. That is because it would take me over 1,000 years to try to read them. I believe if we don't find some quality clues in the documents we will have a hard time proceeding. Also I believe Elizabeth has done something that a hundred of Google's top programmers probably couldn't do and that is absolutely amazing. If it works you should give her a bonus, a big bonus."

He said, "Well put, Elizabeth, that was very well done. I'm looking forward to the full test. Now in the few minutes I have before I have to leave I would like to go over a few items with Professor Johnson.

"Rob, I'm sorry I don't have much time for an update but I would like to know how your team is getting along and how Mrs. O'Hara is doing."

I liked that he was more concerned about my team than any results we had produced. I said, "Our team is doing well. I was worried about Sadako but Dona Frank invited her to work with her last weekend and invited her to stay with them in Lima this weekend. Now she seems fine. Mrs. O'Hara is doing fine and has received a warm welcome. We will start getting material this week."

Walter said, "Great. I hate to cut you short but I need to leave for Houston this morning."

I said goodbye and walked back to my office. Abbey was in her office outside mine.

I sat in one of her chairs and said, "How did your tequila-free work weekend go?"

"I got a lot ready for Elizabeth to help me with some focused search runs. I hope she will make time for them. I know she is very excited about the big test of her software that Mr. Falone approved today.

"It is interesting, Prof, there are several references to a group of natives moving north by various Spanish officials. It's not clear to me if we are talking about the same group or several groups. But this was the time of the Taki Unquy religious revolt that developed rapidly into a political revolt against Christianity in general. So we don't know if they are reporting on Minchancaman's group or just rebellious groups of people in general. Plus many of our documents are fragments or partial documents."

I said, "Fred should be done with his mapping of routes north this week. Once he gives his info to Mitch and Mike, have him plot all the reports you have found on his route map. Would you like me to talk to Elizabeth about making time for your focused search runs?"

"No, Prof, she is about the hardest-working person I know. She will help me if she can."

"OK. By the way Mike seems to be in better spirits now. What's up with that?"

Abbey said, "I guess he got over Elizabeth's rejection of him and he and Mitch seemed to have made some kind of arrangement."

I decided that I really didn't want to know what kind of arrangement that might be. I got up and said, "I'd like to see that map when you and Fred have your first batch of reports plotted."

I checked my email and went to get lunch. After lunch I went to look for Sadako.

I found her in one of the workrooms. She had six flat-screen displays on the wall. All had quipus projected on them.

I said, "Hi, Sadako, how was your weekend in Lima?"

"It was wonderful, Professor. The Franks took me to three museums, their lab, and out to dinner. But you are probably here about my work. This is harder than I thought it would be. I've learned the numbering system and deciphered some more of the location codes but that's about it."

I sat down next to her and said, "I'm glad you enjoyed your weekend and I appreciate you volunteering to take on this very difficult work. Do we know the date each of these quipus were made?"

"Professor, I don't have dates for most of them."

"OK, then send an email to each of the museums that owns the original quipu. Ask them for their best estimate of the age of each. I bet most have been carbon-dated or they have some idea of the age. Then put them in chronological order. Once you have that done that try to identify as many khipukamayuq or knot makers as you can. Even if you don't know who did it, you may be able to tell which ones seem to have been done by the same knot maker. You can just label them khipukamayuq A, B, etc. Finally work on any location material you can find within them. If nothing else that may tell us which quipus to eliminate from our research."

She seemed pleased to have a way to focus her efforts. "Thank you, Professor, I like that idea. Perhaps I was trying to do too much all at once."

I said goodbye and thought it might not help find anything, but Sadako was obviously getting frustrated and it was all I could think of to try to help her.

Next I thought I should visit the rest of the team members since I had spent so much time with Elizabeth. I found Fred next and told him about working with Abbey to plot locations on his map. I also asked him for about a dozen of his favorite comic books from his digital collection.

Mitch and Mike were working in a corner of the game room.

I said, "How was the tequila?"

Mitch said, "One of the nice things about working for this company and living rent free is that I can afford really good tequila. Professor, how many shots did you do this weekend?"

I said, "I'm sorry to say, shots are few and far between for me these days. How is the work coming?"

She continued, "We have Fred's route map and we are integrating it into our map. We should have Harrison's work tomorrow. I'm writing a probability program that we can overlay on the maps. I'm not sure I have the exact parameters we want but I'm writing it so once it is done we can just plug in different factors or parameters and run a new probability map. How cool is that?"

I said, "Very. Mike, do you have anything to add?"

"Just that Mitch likes to do most of the talking so I let her. Also the program she is writing, if it works the way I think it will, it should have lots of spin-off applications for the company's work."

"Even better," I said. They seemed quite happy bickering with each other and they were getting vast amounts of work done. Walter would probably have another multimillion-dollar software program out of what Mitch was doing.

I found Harrison, he was hard at work and didn't seem like he wanted to talk. I didn't see Ned, so I went back to my office to reflect. Everything seemed to be moving along. I just hoped it would yield some results for our project. I was no longer worried about wasting Walter's money. This team would more than pay for itself with just Elizabeth's program and I felt there would be more to come.

When I returned to my office I found a package from Arequipa. It contained a memory stick with the first batch of digital documents from Laura. I quickly looked them over and then gave the stick to Abbey who was still working away at her computer.

She said, "How many documents are there in the monastery that are covered by the grant?"

I said, "A few thousand, I would guess?"

Abbey said, "This memory stick has seven documents on it."

"Well, hopefully their production rate will increase. But I can tell you one thing for sure, Laura will not chance damaging any documents by rushing, Abbey."

"Well, Prof, she may need to take a leave from Cornell this fall then. You did say you believed this was the most promising place to find relevant documents."

I said, "I guess I did say that, didn't I." But, I thought, promising like very little chance versus almost no chance. "Will you just load the documents from the monastery in the mega run for Fourth of July weekend or do a separate run?"

She thought for a moment. "I will do both. For the Fourth of July run we want everything we can get. But once we have a few dozen documents from the monastery I'll set up a search run just for them. The search terms can be narrower. As more documents arrive I'll add them and rerun it. Perhaps I'll be able to fine-tune the search parameters as we go. Don't say 'that's what I was going to say,' Prof."

"I didn't say anything, Abbey."

"I saw the look on your face. You were about to."

On Friday we had our progress meeting. There was no meeting with Walter on the next Monday because he wouldn't be back on the ranch until July 3. He would be coming with his daughter and new grandson. He planned to be at the ranch for about 10 days. Even without a Monday meeting with Walter I wanted to stick to our weekly progress meeting schedule. So at 9:59AM I marched into the workroom, went to the whiteboard, and wrote:

THE REJECT TEAM: PROJECT "THE INCA'S DEATH CAVE." WEEK 3 DAY 5

I asked Sadako to start since she hadn't reported at our last meeting. She seemed eager to talk about what she had done. She started by saying she had reviewed the work done by others on interpreting the quipus. She did a mini review of the major researchers of quipus and outlined what she thought their strengths and weaknesses were. Then she reviewed the points I had discussed. She said as she found locations on the quipus she would have them plotted on the master map Mitch and Mike were producing that combined the work of Fred and Harrison. She emphasized that even when she identified a location she didn't yet know what it referred to. It could be the location on the inventory of items on the quipu, the location where the quipu was done, the home of the knot makers, or something else. She finished by saying she had much work to do.

I looked and Mitch and said, "Next."

She said, "Mike, get your butt up there and give a progress report."

Mike looked surprised for a second but quickly recovered.

He said, "We finished our basic map last week. Fred and Harrison gave us their work earlier this week. I'll have it all combined with our map in a day or two. Mitch is working on a probability program that will allow us to examine the likelihood of matching a given parameter on any given geographic area of our combined map. It should be a very powerful tool."

He went on to describe in detail several aspects of what they had done. I was impressed. Mike hadn't said much in the past but it was clear he knew what he was talking about. I realized I had underestimated him just because he had been pouting after Elizabeth's rejection of him. We men do have fragile egos.

Harrison said, "I'm done with my weather study for now and I could help Elizabeth get ready for her test if she needs help."

Elizabeth said, "I could really use help loading all the data for the parallel search runs. It is mostly grunt work but I'd love to have some help."

Harrison gave her the thumbs-up sign.

Ned raised his hand, I nodded, and he said, "I've been doing way cool surveillance work for Major Campbell. But if I told you about it I would have to shoot you. I can help Elizabeth too. I'll check with him but I don't think the Major needs any of my stuff for a week or two. Plus I'm good at grunt work. Most of my life is grunt work. My middle name should be grunt work."

I cut him off. "I get it, Ned, and Elizabeth will appreciate your help. Fred, what is your status?"

He said, "I've given my info to Mike. I plan to try to help Abbey with the locations she finds in the documents but I can help Elizabeth if Ned shows me how to grunt."

"Your turn, Elizabeth," I said.

"Thank you, everyone. I can really use the help. Abbey has developed the search terms for each of the parallel search runs. She also has a plan for which documents go into each run. Mr. Falone's data came already loaded in the search runs along with the terms. It's a good thing because we don't have the time to figure out his stuff and load it. We will have about 2,000 parallel search runs."

I was shocked. I was thinking maybe two dozen.

She went on, "Since the run is so large I added another feature. The software that looks across the 2,000 parallel runs is likely to produce a huge amount of data. So I set up another level of cross search to search across the data that it produces. This test is more about pushing the limits of the software system than our project. We will generate information that Abbey will then have to put in groups for targeted runs that hopefully will give us some useful results. The test will start at 12:01AM and run for 18 hours. Any questions?"

Ned said, "I got no problem working the weekend if you show me what to do. Give me an hour to go clear my schedule with the Major and I'll be ready to start."

Mitch said, "I drank enough tequila last weekend so I'm going to work this weekend on my program."

Everyone seemed excited about working all weekend. Like it was a big party. I think they all knew that Elizabeth had something really big here if it worked.

I said, "I'll be around this weekend if you need me. I'm kind of like Ned when it comes to grunt work. It seems to be a big part of my life." Elizabeth didn't jump on my offer. That was fine by me. I assumed they would be working a different part of the clock than I did.

I went back to my office. A few minutes later Sadako came in.

She said, "I plan to work all weekend. But next Tuesday Dr. Dona and

Mr. Frank will be here and I like to help them that day, if it is OK with you, Professor."

"Yes, that would be fine. I'm sure the Franks will appreciate your help."

"Also, Professor, if Elizabeth is running behind schedule, I would like to stop my work on the quipus and help her."

I said, "Very good idea. Please let her know you are available if she needs more help."

She smiled and thanked me as she left. I opened up my laptop and pulled up the map that Mitch and Mike had added the work of Fred and Harrison to. Mike said he had more integration work to do but the basics of the combined geography, geology, route, and weather map was there. It eliminated a lot of territory but there was a whole lot left. I looked at the routes north. I tried to think about where Minchancaman might lead his people. If he really was a descendant of the last king of Chimor that would suggest they took the more westerly route north. But Minchancaman was the name Friar Murúa used and it might not be accurate. The other obvious route north was farther inland and would lead to the Amazonas region. That would suggest the Chachapoyas culture. It developed during the Inca age and represented a strong opposition to the Incan conquest by repelling the first Inca attempts to incorporate the region to their empire. Both the Chimor and Chachapoyas cultures worshiped the moon as a primary god, not the sun. I remembered seeing a reference that the descendants of the Chachapoyas in parts of the Amazonas region are quite superstitious and still follow many ancient rituals. Their religious beliefs are mixed with fantastic apparitions and there is almost always a cave in them. I would have to research that again.

I was interested to see Mitch's program that assigned probabilities to different areas of the map based on different assumptions or inputs. I didn't have a clue on how that would work. But I figured if Mitch was smart enough to build it she was smart enough to explain it to me.

I studied the map for a while more. I was almost willing myself to see something that I knew wasn't there. Well, enough of that. I shut my laptop. I wished they had a pre-3:00 club here at the ranch.

Chapter 30

Over the weekend I kept reading and hoping it would help at some point. I hiked in the park and played squash with Major Campbell. He beat me without much trouble but I got a good workout. I never saw Abbey all weekend. I assumed they worked all night.

In my office on Monday, I received a call from the woman who ran the Lima computer center. She said that people in Houston were complaining about Elizabeth's test run. They were saying that it took too much time away from the planned maintenance period. They asked her to complain about it but she politely said no. She just wanted me to know people were stirring the pot and probably jealous because they never were given that kind of server capacity. She was quite annoyed by the whole thing. I thanked her.

It was late enough in the morning that I figured some of the team was up. I went looking for Elizabeth. Her work area that usually looked like a very neat command center now looked like something out of a cyber-war movie. Four folding tables were covered with terminals and big cables. I guessed the wireless Wi-Fi was too slow. Abbey seemed to be parceling out packets of work to Ned, Fred, and Harrison. No rushing around, no pulling of hair, just grinding out large amounts of work.

I signaled Elizabeth. She came over to the doorway. I said, "How is it going? I know Sadako is willing to help and I could have Mitch put her work on hold and help for the next few days."

Elizabeth said, "It is going well. I may ask Sadako to join in. Abbey has the other three all trained so they don't need much supervision from us.

Sadako is a quick study. Abbey could train her in an hour or two. If I need Mitch I'd rather ask her myself and just let her know it is OK with you. I still have three and a half days."

I said, "I'll be getting more documents from the monastery this week. Should I just hold them?"

"That's probably a good idea, Professor. We can add them next week when we do the more focused search runs."

"Anything I can do for you?"

"Just keep your fingers crossed, Professor."

"Will do. Call me if you need me, Elizabeth."

I was getting regular emails and shipments of memory sticks with the documents in digital form from Laura at the monastery. It seemed they were able to digitize about 80 to 100 pages a day. Abbey was right, there was no way they were going to finish in the two and a half months they had left. I knew they had to be extremely careful with the documents. So rushing wasn't an option.

I sent an email asking Laura what volume of documents she estimated there were in the time period covered by the grant. I asked her to give me her best estimate of how long it would take to complete digitizing all of the documents.

She emailed back quickly with an estimate of at least six months and that was best case. She must have done the calculation before I asked for it. I then asked if she would like me to see if Walter was interested in extending the grant or renewing it for next summer. Laura said she would let me know.

I spent most of the rest of the week reading the documents Laura had just sent and that weren't being added to the test. I figured out how to load them into the translation software so I had a modern Spanish and English version of the originals. It was an assortment of types of documents. There were letters, journals, parts of prayer books, shipping manifests, hand-drawn maps, and some items I wasn't sure what they were. No map with a big red X saying "death cave here." I didn't see names I recognized but I kept reading.

Tuesday night I had dinner with the Franks and Major Campbell. I thanked Dona for being so kind to Sadako.

Dona said, "When we got off the plane this morning Sadako was waiting for us. She explained that she couldn't work with us because Elizabeth needed her help. She was very sorry but Elizabeth's test was important not just to our team but, perhaps to the whole company, and she hoped I understood. I told her to go and we understood completely."

"It seems the whole team has been putting in 20-hour days since Friday. They also seem extremely happy. Whistle while you work happy," I said.

Dinner was a welcome break from my work of reading old documents and trying to stay out of my team's way.

I checked in with Elizabeth on Thursday morning. I had in the back of my mind to ask Walter to give us the 18 hours at the end of the shutdown so Elizabeth would have more preparation time. But I knew it was a bad idea since everything was already scheduled. Elizabeth said all the documents and search terms would be loaded by that night. She was sending everyone to bed early Thursday night and Friday they would just recheck everything.

She said, "Are you coming to the 12:01AM blastoff, Professor?"

"I'll be there, Elizabeth."

I went back to my office and began trying to read the documents from Laura. I remember being in Ithaca teaching several classes and thinking how nice it would be not to be grading student papers. If only I had all my time to just read and do research. Now I thought, be careful what you wish for. But I kept plowing ahead. Everyone else was working hard so I felt I should be too.

Friday at 11:00PM I went to Elizabeth's lab. The entire team was there. No one looked tired after the week of 20-hour workdays. That was one of the advantages of being young. It was somewhat anticlimactic. There was no rocket blasting off. Elizabeth didn't even have to push "enter." It was all programmed to start running at 12:01AM. I congratulated everyone and decided to go to bed.

My cell phone rang. I rolled over and took it off the nightstand. 4:23AM and it was Abbey. This couldn't be good news.

I said, "What's up, Abbey?"

"The program crashed and Elizabeth thinks it was sabotage. You better get over here."

I said, "Tell Elizabeth not to call anyone. Don't accuse anyone. Do a system check and I'll be right over."

I put on my clothes and thought back to the call I'd received from the Lima computer control center. Maybe she was trying to warn me of more than just people complaining. I figured at the time that since Walter authorized the test no one was going to overrule him, and that the folks in Houston were just grumbling.

Abbey was standing next to Elizabeth who was seated and typing away on her keyboard. She had tears running down her face.

I said, "Take a deep breath and tell me what happened."

Elizabeth said, "I know someone did something because the program ran way beyond the point of the crash on my first test run two weeks ago before Houston pulled the plug."

"OK. First, do we still have access to the computer system? We are supposed to be the only ones on the system for another 12 hours. Can you identify exactly what happened or if someone else is on the system?" I said.

She said, "I still have access to the system. I know the exact time the system crashed and at what point in the run it was. I don't think anyone else is on the system and I can check that fairly easily. I think someone installed some malware before everyone had to log off the system."

I said, "Let's not worry about who might have done this at this point. Can you go in and get the malware? We need that as proof that it was sabotage and not just a program bug.

"I think the bug is in there because if it self-destructed when it crashed your program you could just run your program again and be fine."

Elizabeth smiled and said, "As a matter of fact we have an excellent program for cleaning out malware and since no one else is on the system it should be easy."

I said, "OK, get to it. But don't destroy it. I want that bug alive. Just remove it and capture it. I'll be in my office down the hall. Let me know when you find it. I would like there to be enough time left in our 18-hour test period to run beyond where the crash occurred."

Elizabeth was already hard at work. The tears were replaced with a look of determination.

Sitting in my office, I thought how this situation was unlike anything I'd seen at this company. Everyone seemed to get along so well and be so helpful to each other. I realized I hadn't been here very long and the only places I'd seen for more than a few minutes were here and Mr. Falone's Houston ranch. Still it struck me as out of character for this organization.

Next, I thought about the timing. Abbey called me at 4:23AM. If the program crashed 15 or 20 minutes before that, it meant the run was going for about four hours. We had use of the computer system until 9:00PM. We needed to have the malware out before 3:00PM so we could do a second run of six hours getting us well past the crash point.

I stood up and went back to the Elizabeth's lab. "Sorry to interrupt you but I had a bad thought. You don't suppose they put in several bugs? They could put one at four hours and then at say five hours and six hours. If I did that I would make the bugs erase themselves after they crash the program. You look around the four-hour spot and don't find any problem. Then you run the test again. It crashes at the five-hour spot. Then you run it a third time, it crashes and we are out of time."

Elizabeth said, "Professor, we aren't actually running these down railroad tracks where someone could set up bombs at different places down the track. That was just an analogy I used to explain the concept of the program."

"I guess I know that but..."

Then Mitch cut me off. "Elizabeth, wait, even though he doesn't know what he is talking about I think he's onto something."

Then she went into programmer speak and described how someone could do something that would be very hard to find and yet would cause multiple crashes of the system. That would leave the impression that the program was deeply flawed.

It seemed like a light bulb went on in Elizabeth's head. The two of them were talking a mile a minute.

I said to Abbey, "I'll be in my office, call when they have something."

Abbey said quietly to me, "Prof, you're brilliant even when you don't know what you are talking about."

I smiled at her and headed to my office. I made a pot of coffee. It was 6:35AM. I tried not to count the minutes. It made no sense to me why someone would do this. But before I went to Walter I needed to know for sure that it was sabotage.

Abbey came in at about 7:15AM and poured herself a cup of coffee. The whole team was in the research facility ready to help but mostly just staying out of the way.

I said, "How are they doing?"

Abbey said, "They seem to be onto something. Elizabeth and Mitch are working on it but I don't know how long it will take or what they may find. The whole team is really mad. Ned is in the corner of the workroom. He has four screens fired up and is typing like crazy on a couple of different keyboards."

Major Campbell walked in and said, "Trouble?"

I said, "Word travels fast."

He said, "Actually I just stopped over to see how things were going. But one look at everybody's faces told me something was up."

I explained the best I could what we thought happened. I also told him about the call I received from the head of the Lima computer center. We decided to check on the progress.

As we walked into the workroom we heard Ned screaming, "Houston is fucking with us, they're fucking with us." He saw our reflection in one of his monitors and went quiet.

Major Campbell went over to Ned and looked over the monitors. "What did you find, Ned?"

Ned said, "I came across some email exchanges between a couple of the Houston computer center operators."

The Major said, "Let's not worry about how you came across these emails right now. Just show me what you found."

Ned displayed on the monitors about a dozen emails between four people. They were all negative about Elizabeth's test run and the fact that they would lose 18 hours of their maintenance time. A few hinted at getting even. But there was no smoking gun. People smart enough to do this were probably smart enough to not leave an email trail. We still needed more proof.

Ned was looking a bit sheepish. I realized he had probably broken many company rules by hacking into other employees' emails.

Major Campbell said to Ned, "Start monitoring their emails in real time. They should be getting to work soon. I'm betting they won't be able to resist seeing what their handiwork has done. I'm officially launching an internal investigation. You are authorized to search any employee's correspondence and communications up to the executive officer level. It appears you already have the override codes for the email system. We can talk about that another time. If you need help let me know."

Ned said, "Yes, Major. Search any employee's correspondence and communications up to the executive officer level. I'm on it."

Major Campbell went into Elizabeth's lab to talk to her. I stayed where I was and looked at the monitors and then at Ned. He started furiously typing a text message on his phone.

He said, "What?"

I said, "You're up to something. The Major gave you broad authorization and you are planning something he hasn't even thought of. It's fine by me. I want to nail whoever did this. Later come tell me about it."

"Professor, you're like my mother. She reads my mind," Ned said.

I went to Elizabeth's lab. I asked Abbey, "Have they found anything?"

Abbey said, "There is definitely sophisticated malware that was put on the system. Elizabeth and Mitch are discussing with Major Campbell how best to document it. They don't want to just erase it and they don't know if it is programmed to self-erase at a certain time."

"I guess I won't be much help with this. I'm going to see how the rest of the team is doing," I said.

I went back into the main part of the workroom. Everyone was there but Mike. The mood seemed tense.

Not knowing quite what to say I asked, "Where is Mike?"

Fred said, "He is getting coffee for us. Is there anything we can do to help?"

"Right now, Fred, I think we just stay out of the way. Major Campbell is working with Elizabeth and Mitch to document the bug and Ned as you can see is working his magic."

Major Campbell came out of Elizabeth's lab and he looked at his watch. So I looked at my watch, it was almost 8:00AM.

Major Campbell said, "I'm going to use your office to make some calls. I want my counterpart in Houston to get going on this."

I told the Major to go ahead and let me know if I could help. Mike came back with a big tray. It had a pot of coffee and a pile of bagels. He began to pour cups and hand them out. We filled him in on what little we knew. So we waited.

About a half hour later Major Campbell came back and went into Elizabeth's lab. I was glad he was taking charge of this. I had the feeling there would be hell to pay for whoever was behind this.

He came back out and said, "Professor, would you join me in your office. Walter will be here in a minute and wants to speak to us." He turned to our team and said, "Walter asked me to tell you not to worry, we would have the test back on schedule shortly and that he greatly appreciates all the work you have put in over the last few weeks."

I followed the Major into my office and said, "Were Elizabeth and Mitch able to extract the malware?"

He said, "Not exactly. We copied it and stored the copy off the system. Depending on what Walter wants us to do we may run the test again and monitor exactly how the malware crashes Elizabeth's software. That could actually be quite instructive."

A moment later Walter came in my office. He was composed but as close to mad as I'd ever seen him. He smiled and said, "Looks like it will be an interesting day. Give me an update, please."

The Major went over what we knew. He told Walter what Mitch and Elizabeth were doing and what he had instructed Ned to do. He then explained that he had asked the head of security in Houston to examine the records of exactly who was on the system and when in Houston over the last few days.

Walter said to me, "Rob, please ask Elizabeth to join us for a few minutes."

When I came back in with Elizabeth, Walter stood up shook her hand and said, "You have had a busy week. How are you holding up?"

Elizabeth said, "Fine until about 5:00AM this morning, then things became a little unsettling."

He said, "Once you develop an important new software system, the next thing you need to do is figure out how to protect it from hackers. Whoever did this, even though that wasn't their intent, may have helped us in the next step of developing your amazing new system."

Elizabeth smiled and said, "That is a positive way to look at it, Mr. Falone, and I hope that is the silver lining. However I'm most troubled by why someone would want to do this. The software system could be very useful in many areas of the company and have great commercial value."

Walter said, "That part is deeply disturbing to me. But I want you to focus on the upside. Major Campbell and I will handle the other part."

He then went through a series of detailed technical questions with Elizabeth. At the end of the questions, he told her to restart the program in 15 minutes and he would have the Lima computer facility monitor the run and probable crash.

Next he wanted to talk with Ned. Major Campbell tapped out a text to Ned. A minute later he walked in with his laptop.

Walter again stood and shook Ned's hand warmly. He said, "Let's see what you found so far, Ned."

Ned seemed very nervous. He began, "Major Campbell authorized me to search any employee's correspondence and communications up to the executive officer level. I found about a dozen emails between four people that were suspicious. They didn't openly talk about sabotage but they were very negative about Elizabeth's work. Professor Johnson received a call from the head of the Lima computer center warning him about potential trouble."

Ned was choosing his words very carefully. He also failed to mention that he had hacked the Houston emails before Major Campbell had authorized an investigation.

Ned went on, "Major Campbell thought whoever did this might be gloating about it or talking among themselves. So based on his instruction, I've been monitoring and recording the emails and communications of these four individuals."

He had Major Campbell's full attention. The Major said, "Ned, beyond the emails what communications are you monitoring and recording?"

Ned knew that what he was doing was going to come out. I was impressed to see how skillfully he had laid out his cover using Major Campbell's own words.

He said, "I'm monitoring and recording all conversations that are occurring in the offices of the four people we identified."

Walter was quiet. Major Campbell said, "Exactly how are you doing that?"

"Well, Major, it is one of the things I've been working on in my spare time. I'm using a program I developed that turns on the microphone in their computer and then records the conversation, encrypts, compresses, and sends it to my computer."

Walter spoke up. "Ned, you did that remotely from here to laptops in Houston?"

"No, sir. I'm still working on that part. Once Major Campbell gave me the authorization. I asked a friend of mine in the Houston security group to install my little software package in each of their computers before they arrived at work. Would you like to hear it in action?"

Walter said, "Yes."

Then Ned opened his laptop on my desk. There were four sets of bars. Three were still and one was jumping up and down. Ned clicked on that one. Voices came out of Ned's speakers. It sounded like two people talking. I felt like a voyeur listening in like this. There was nothing special about the conversation. Then a third person came in and said, "She is going to run it again." Then there was the noise of people leaving the office.

Ned turned it off and said, "The recordings start a little before 8:00. We can review the recordings in detail later. They won't use email. They are too smart for that. I believe once they decided to sabotage Elizabeth's run they stopped using email. What we found in the emails was just the early complaining between the four of them."

Walter said, "Tell me about how you put your piece of code in the target machine."

"Well, sir, I can use all the traditional methods. Load it from a memory stick. That is what we did in Houston. But you need access to the computer to do that. It could be built into a software program. When the software is loaded my cookie is loaded as well. This is what the CIA did to Iran with the centrifuge software they bought. It caused the centrifuges to spin so fast they broke apart. Also you could have it as an attachment to an email. If they open the attachment the cookie is installed. That is what most common hackers do and the most common way people's computers are contaminated.

"Now what I'm working on is a way to install the cookie from an un-open email. Send the email and the cookie installs itself even without the person opening the email. I got it to work on computers with no security features. But I haven't figured out how to do it with even basic security features, let alone the security we have here. I've got some ideas and maybe when Elizabeth has some time she can help me."

Walter said, "Very interesting, Ned. Please use this on company employees only with the direct approval of Major Campbell."

"Of course, Mr. Falone, only with direct approval."

I said, "Now do we just wait five hours to see if Elizabeth's software system crashes again? If it does do we have enough time to remove the malware and run a full test?"

Walter said, "Yes, we want to run the software again to study exactly how the malware attacks and crashes Elizabeth's system. We don't want anyone to know we have found the malware so I'm going to wait until later to arrange for more test time. We will have an uninterrupted run of the system before the weekend is over, Professor. Now I would like to thank the rest of the team for their hard work as I leave. I have things to attend to. Major, would you walk with me? I'd like to have a word with you."

I looked at my watch. It was after 9:00. Elizabeth's software had been running for about thirty minutes. If my prediction was right the crash should happen between about 1:30 and 2:30PM. I went back to Elizabeth's lab.

She had everyone working. I said, "Idle hands do the devil's work?"

"Yes, Professor, the time will go much faster if we all stay busy. Plus there are many things we can be working on that will save us time later."

"Well done," I said and I thought all that time as head cheerleader, captain of the field hockey team, yearbook editor, etc., seemed to have made a good manager out of her. "Send me a text if you need me. Otherwise I'll be back in a couple of hours."

I decided I needed a swim, a shower, and breakfast. So I headed back to the guesthouse.

Major Campbell was deep in conversation with Ned in the hall. I didn't interrupt them. I just waved and left.

The crash came at 1:37PM. Everyone was ready for it. I wasn't sure if they had captured the information they needed or not. Major Campbell told Elizabeth to run the software that would clean out the malware. Once that was done she should set up to rerun her software system. If she needed to go beyond 9:00PM she was to let him know and he would arrange more time. The mood of the entire team was now upbeat, as if they had just conquered an evil foe.

I didn't see Ned anywhere. I asked Major Campbell, "Where is Ned? I thought he would be interested in this."

The Major said, "Ned is hard at work. He will be working from the security office for a while. Walter wants to put his snooping software to work in a few more places. Walter is quite upset about this."

I said, "I haven't been here long but this action seems out of character from what I've seen of the way employees get along at the company."

"It is, Professor, and I don't like it."

I found Abbey and said, "How is everyone doing?"

"I think they are OK. Once Elizabeth realized that Mr. Falone, Major Campbell, and you knew it was sabotage she was able to just focus on what needed to be done and she wasn't so upset. She saved the second run at the four-hour point about an hour before it crashed. That means she can start the third run at the four-hour point and the run should be completed before the 9:00PM deadline. That way Mr. Falone won't have to extend the time period for us and the bad guys might not know we're onto them."

I said, "Good plan. Do we know if the program is working? By that I mean not just running, but is it producing useful and meaningful results?"

"Prof, it is producing so much we will spend a week or two just sorting it out. I helped load the data Mr. Falone provided. I believe it was designed to determine if her system does what she thinks it might. You know, predict future 9/11-type attacks or a Boston Marathon bombing. For our work it will work fine once we refine the search parameters. If we come up empty-handed it is because there is nothing in our documents to be found."

"Abbey, if Minchancaman had more than a few dozen followers, when he went north, there will be some record of it. The question is will it be enough to find where he ended up? I think I'll visit with Elizabeth and then check on everyone else."

I went into Elizabeth's lab and said, "Is your baby running smoothly? Abbey told me you were able to restart the run at a point just before the first crash. Smart thinking."

"It seems to be going fine. When the second crash occurred we were using all the Lima's and most of the Houston's server capacity. Once we add Sudbury's we will reach the maximum speed for this test. If my estimates are correct we should be done with the run between 7:00 and 8:00 tonight."

I said, "What absolutely must be done tonight once the run is complete?"

"Must be done, not much, Professor. We will just need to power down everything so the maintenance people can do their work."

"Elizabeth, I would like you to power down when the run is complete and I want everyone to take at least Saturday off. It would be better to take the weekend off. Drinks on me at the dining hall bar once you shut down."

She looked at me with a tired smile. I said, "I'm the boss and that's an order." She gave me a bigger smile.

I went to security to look for Ned. I was stopped as I went in. Very politely one of Major Campbell's men said, "May I help you, Professor Johnson?"

I said, "I'm looking for Ned or Major Campbell."

He replied, "I'll let Major Campbell know you are here, sir."

It seemed like things were being done by the book now. I wondered if Major Campbell had issued some kind of security alert or if his men just sensed the Major's mood.

Major Campbell came out of the office and said, "Come in, Rob."

I went into his office, sat, and said, "Elizabeth estimates the run will be completed between 7:00 and 8:00PM so no need to extend the test period beyond 9:00. Once they have powered off the computer system I've declared a holiday and invited them for drinks on me at the bar. I've also told them no work on Saturday. Not that it matters, if they feel like working they will. I'd like you and Ned to join us if you can. Feel free to invite others if you want."

"Professor, my boys could run up quite a tab. Ned will be done by 9:00 and I'll let him know. I hope my schedule will permit me to stop by. The team has worked incredibly hard. Some down time would be good."

"Major, don't worry about the tab. If it is too big, I'll just put it on my expense account. Have you made any additional headway on our sabotage problem?"

"We will. We have a copy of the malware. We will see what we can learn from that. Security in Houston will examine the computer records there. Ned has his work to do. We don't need to rush. You keep your team focused on their job and my group will find out who was behind this and why."

I said, "I told the team from the very beginning, don't talk to anybody about this and don't accuse anybody of anything. They get it. They know that it would only make it harder to find whoever did it."

"Thanks, Rob. This has me quite pissed off. Not professional of me to show it, I guess. Since coming here I've dealt with everything from B&E to hostage situations. However they were all from the outside. The only employee problems we have are related to over- eager employees breaking some security rules. Never anything malicious, destructive, and senseless like this."

I said, "I know. It strikes me as strange. This isn't just a petty jealousy issue between people. Someone went to a great deal of work to design and install the malware. They must know they could get fired or even be prosecuted. When I got the call from the head of the Lima computer center I assumed she was warning me of people grumbling and bitching. I wonder if she knew or suspected more? She strikes me as a straight shooter. Have you spoken to her, Major?"

"No, Rob, but I intend to. I have a few more things to do. I'll see you at the bar later."

I smiled and said, "OK, but I didn't give you Saturday off."

He said, "You are a real slave driver. I'm sure my weekend will be a busy one."

Elizabeth's system completed its run at 6:48PM, ahead of her estimate. People started coming into the bar a little after 7:00. The mood was subdued. I quietly told each one again, don't talk to anybody about this and don't accuse anybody of anything. I probably didn't need to but they understood and took it the right way. I had arranged for the dining hall to put out pizza and wings. It seemed like comfort food was called for.

As 8:30PM approached the mood seemed to brighten a bit. The whole team was here except Ned.

He hurried in a few minutes later and said, "Now the party can start."

He was keyed up, excited, or something. He ordered tequila. Only much later I would find out why.

Major Campbell came in and much to my surprise Walter was with him.

Walter said, "I just wanted to stop by and tell you how proud I am of all of you. I have to leave in the morning for Houston so I won't be at your Monday meeting. Please stay focused on our project. I believe we are going to see some interesting results in the next few weeks."

Then he left. I thought there are going to be some heads rolling in Houston. Walter's daughter and grandson were here and he was scheduled to be here all week. He is worked up enough about this to fly to Houston and deal with it in person.

People seemed to relax and enjoy each other's company now. It was as if Walter had lifted the problem off their shoulders and put it on his. They seemed to know he would properly deal with it.

With the relaxing came the reality of how tired everyone was. At about 10:00 people started to leave. I sensed contentment. It was almost as if a common outside enemy brought the team members closer.

I said goodnight to them and then to Abbey. "Let's go to the guest-house before you have to carry me home, I'm beat."

As we walked back Abbey said, "What do you think about today's events?"

"Several things. First I don't understand why people did this. People are going to get fired from very good jobs for this. He might not show it but Walter is very upset by this. He will find out who is behind this and there will be hell to pay. Walter works very hard to create an atmosphere that is open and supportive. He wants his people to be creative and try new things. It's OK to fail, just learn from the failure and move on. It is like he sees cancer and he is determined to cut it out before it spreads.

"Next, I think our team worked through this brilliantly. They worked together. They identified the problem, and they addressed it constructively. I'm hopeful that today helped fast-track the development of protecting Elizabeth's software system from cyber attacks. The silver lining she spoke of. I'd probably think of more stuff if I wasn't so tired."

We said goodnight.

Chapter
31

I left everyone alone for the weekend. Monday we would regroup.

At 9:59AM on Monday I walked into the workroom and wrote on the whiteboard:

THE REJECT TEAM: PROJECT "THE INCA'S DEATH CAVE." WEEK 4 DAY 1

We spent the meeting discussing how to work with the results of Elizabeth's search run. The plan was to examine what was found and then set up targeted searches around interesting patterns that emerged in the Fourth of July mega search run.

Fred, Mike, and Harrison would join Abbey and Elizabeth in this work. Mitch would go back to her probability software for our master map and Sadako would keep working on quipus. Ned was working full time for Major Campbell.

We agreed that Friday we would plan to have a review of our findings from the document searches. Mitch said she would have her software to the point we could test it if we had suitable data. This felt like progress.

I received another package of digital documents from Laura at the monastery. I gave them to Abbey along with last week's package. I was still trying to read the modern Spanish and English translation of last week's package but while interesting it wasn't much help for our project.

In an email from Laura she said things were going well. They were working five to six days a week and then exploring the area around Arequipa on their off days. Everyone seemed happy with the arrangements and the way the nuns at the monastery were working with them.

Laura went on to say she was willing to take a leave from Cornell for the fall and continue working on digitizing the documents if Mr. Falone wanted to continue the grant. Two of her team would have to go back because of family and other commitments. One wanted to stay. She also was in contact with a friend who retired from Cornell's library system last year and would like to come and work during the fall. Laura felt sure she could find a fourth person if the grant was extended.

I sent Walter an email explaining the situation. I was pleased Laura wanted to stay and complete the work. I still felt this was the place we were most likely to find documents from or about Friar Ortiz.

The next day I received a short email from Walter asking me to work with Laura to put the grant extension through to Cornell. He would have one of his assistants handle the financial arrangements with the University.

I told Laura and she said she would have it submitted to Cornell in about a week. So I went back to reading documents and studying our master map.

Friday we met in the workroom for our standard meeting. As I did each week I started by writing on the whiteboard:

THE REJECT TEAM: PROJECT "THE INCA'S DEATH CAVE." WEEK 4 DAY 5

I told Abbey to focus first on what she thought were the top five or six search terms for the specific searches we were doing. We had thousands of pages of documents and I figured we would learn the best approach by starting with a small number of searches based on information from our mega search.

She picked Friar Ortiz, Sister Ortiz, Friar Murúa, and Minchancaman as specific word search parameters.

She then decided to try string search parameters around two themes. The first was terms relating to the revolt of the Wak'as and the Taki Unquy religious movement. The second was terms relating to the True of Heart, Strong of Heart, or of bands of former Taki Unquy members moving north.

Abbey had developed dozens of other search parameters but these were her top choices to start with.

I said, "OK, Abbey, what did we find?"

"Prof, I found a whole lot of stuff for you to read. You won't have time for Fred's comic book collection any time soon."

I said, "Wonderful. Could you be a little more specific?"

She said, "The only references to Minchancaman in the context we are looking for is in Friar Murúa's *Historia*. There are lots of references to the last great emperor of the Chimor named Minchancaman. But not ones that fit the time period or context we are dealing with.

"Now Friar Murúa is referred to almost 100 times in the appropriate time frame. We could try a fancy cross-reference search to reduce the number but it is easier and more precise just to read the hundred references. The search gives the document, page, and line of the reference. I've set up the program so it will go from one reference to the next in the digital file.

"For Friar Ortiz and Sister Ortiz we have 17 and 8 references respectively. I expect more when we receive more documents from the monastery. We will also read each reference.

"For our string search parameters around the two themes we have almost 200 hits. There may be useful information in these and again we will have to read them to find out. When I say we, I mean Prof, now has some real work to do and I will work with him."

Next Elizabeth got up and said, "I plan to keep refining the software system. I sent the results of the mega run to Lima as instructed by Mr. Falone. I will review the results of the data he provided to see what it tells me about how well the software worked. I assume at some point a meeting will be set up to go over this with the people Walter has reviewing the run. I'm available to help with more searches when I'm needed."

I thought it was interesting that Walter sent the result of the test run to Lima and not to Houston to be analyzed. I was quite sure his original plan was to have that work done in Houston.

Next Mitch said she was ready to test her software whenever we wanted. She would keep working on refining it until we needed her.

Sadako had just over 150 quipus in digital form. She had identified about 35 different knot tiers. It was as I suspected; there were about eight knot tiers that made up the bulk of the quipus. I believe that was because these groups of quipus had somehow survived destruction by the Spanish.

She assigned probabilities to each quipu as to how likely it was that she had the correct knot tier. I'm not sure how she came up with these probabilities. But knowing Sadako I'm sure it was based on some logical method. She was still working on locations. There was the location of the items described in the quipu. The location where the quipu was tied and the home location of the knot tier. It was hard to tell which was which or to know if there were also references to other locations.

I told her to take a few days off if she wanted and go help the Franks with their work. There would be a great research paper in her work but I had the feeling it wouldn't help our quest for the death cave much.

Fred was going to help Ned in the security office. I assumed someone had to listen to all the hours of recorded material.

I asked Mike to research cave and caverns in our target area. Unfortunately the target area was still huge.

Harrison was going to plot the locations where Minchancaman and his followers were reported to have been. That is assuming Abbey and I found any such sightings. He would work on his climate model until we had something.

As more documents arrived from Spain and the monastery we would run them through the six search parameters. I realized we really weren't using the full power of Elizabeth's system. I wasn't sure we needed to. I wanted to think about that some more and I wanted see what the experts in Lima thought of the mega test run.

I closed the meeting by telling them to take the weekend off. I hoped most would go to Lima or do something for a change of pace. They had been working long days for two weeks straight.

I was excited to start reviewing the search results. I told Abbey I would take the 200 hits from the string search of the two themes. I had Abbey help me set it up so I could review them from my laptop. She set it up so I could review the English translation first, then the modern Spanish translation, and finally the sixteenth-century original Spanish document. I was hoping that I could rule out many as totally unrelated to what we were looking for in the English translation. That would save me the trouble of struggling with the Spanish. I had worked back and forth between the English, modern Spanish, and original Spanish versions of other documents enough to trust the translation software to get the big picture correct. It could miss subtle things. I would read the other versions if I wasn't sure.

Abbey would take the Friar Ortiz, Sister Ortiz, and Friar Murúa references. She preferred to work from the original document. Her understanding of sixteenth-century Spanish was now excellent.

Once I had everything set up on my computer I decided to take the rest of Friday afternoon off. I hiked the trails on the ranch and then took a long swim. Then I went to the dining hall for a drink and early dinner. It was quiet. Major Campbell came in and I waved him over. I decided not to bring up his investigation. If he wanted to talk about it that would be fine. He didn't.

All he said was, "Do you mind if I have Fred keep helping out my team for a week or so? He is quite good with technology and he works well with Ned."

I said, "You can use Fred as long as you need to. He won't hold up any of our work. Right now it is Abbey and me. We have to plow through everything the searches have come up with. I'm actually looking forward to it."

We had a pleasant dinner not talking about work. Afterwards, I went back to the guesthouse, read one of the comics Fred had given me in digital form, and went to bed.

Chapter 32

I was up early Saturday morning. Abbey had gone to Lima Friday afternoon with some other team members. Not much to do on the ranch other than work. Out by the pool with my laptop and coffee, I started reviewing the 200 hits. Most were for the first terms relating to the revolt of the Wak'as and the Taki Unquy religious movement. The second set of terms, relating to the True of Heart, Strong of Heart, or to bands of former Taki Unquy members moving north, had only had 39 references. I decided to start with the larger one.

By noon I had plowed through several dozen references. I was working mostly with the English translation. I would go back a page or two from the actual reference, then read to a page or two beyond the reference. Lots of interesting background material but there was nothing specifically about our Strong of Heart. I took a walk, a swim and ate lunch.

I switched to the other group after lunch. This was more interesting. There were references to groups of Wak'as and the Taki Unquy religious followers either moving through or residing there. This was mostly low-level Spanish officials commenting on the topic in a routine report on something else such as tax collection and crop yields. Maybe I was getting somewhere. I decided to spend the rest of the weekend on these 39 references.

Monday morning Walter wanted to meet briefly with Major Campbell and me at 9:00AM. I texted the team that I might be a little late for our 10:00AM meeting.

Walter warmly greeted Major Campbell and me when we walked into his office.

He said, "Please have a seat. Professor, how are you making out? How is our team's morale?"

I said, "The morale is great. It seemed our trouble on the Fourth of July just brought the team closer. It also appears we have some interesting information from the search runs. I'll be able to give you some specifics in a week or two. How did Elizabeth's software preform? I realize our work doesn't require the full power of what she is trying to do. I was also interested to see how we were making out with the Church related documents from Spain?"

Walter said, "I'm glad to hear our team is doing well and I look forward to hearing about your progress when you are ready to report. As for Elizabeth's software system, the preliminary reports I have indicates it is as powerful as she hoped. There will be some refining to do on it. It will also have to be customized for different applications. But quite remarkable is probably an understatement. Lastly we have all the non-Church documents. There is another batch of Church reviewed documents due to be sent this week. We will see how much we receive."

I said, "Elizabeth is still working on the software system. There were refinements that she didn't have time to incorporate before the test. I guess this should pay for our archaeological project."

Walter smiled. "Rob, it will pay for it many times over. Ned and Fred are to work full time with Major Campbell. Is that a problem for you?"

I said, "Not at all. I'm the bottleneck now. I'm not sure what I would have them doing at this point."

Walter said, "Good. Please tell the team I look forward to attending next Monday's meeting. Now I need to discuss some other matters with Major Campbell."

I said goodbye and left. I was dying to know what was going on and what they had found out about who crashed our software. But I knew they were not going to tell me until they were ready.

My meeting with Walter was so short I had time to stop by my office and review my weekend notes before the 10:00AM team meeting. I realized Walter had included me in the first part of the meeting mostly out of courtesy. I had no real news for him.

At 9:59AM I walked into the workroom and wrote on the whiteboard:

THE REJECT TEAM: PROJECT "THE INCA'S DEATH CAVE." WEEK 5 DAY 1

I found I enjoyed this little bit of theater that started each meeting.

Elizabeth started by saying she was working away on her software but was ready to help anybody who needed it.

Mitch and Harrison were basically working on their pet project and waiting for us.

Mike had developed an interesting overlay for our master map. It showed the suitability of an area for caves or caverns of three sizes. He had developed a volume matrix in cubic feet over an area to a depth of 150 feet. I decided to label the small caves, big caves, and caverns. It seemed simpler to visualize and work with. Assuming it was accurate it could be quite helpful. If for example we knew we were looking for a cave temple for 500 people, it would rule out certain areas. It was ingenious and ruled out additional parts of our master map. The trouble was we still had many hundreds of square miles in our search area.

Abbey reported on her review of the references to Friar Ortiz, Sister Ortiz, and Friar Murúa. She started with Friar Murúa. She left out his *Historia* since we had been going through that since February. Most of the about 100 references to Friar Murúa had nothing to do with our search. She did find two places of interest where he mentioned Friar Ortiz being a prisoner of a group of Taki Unquy religious followers. One was in a letter to another friar and the second may have been notes that he used when writing his *Historia*.

All the references for Sister Ortiz were lists of her involvement with activities relating to the monastery. Not much help for us.

The references to Friar Ortiz were again mostly just his name showing up on a list of church people being involved in some activity or being at some place. There was however one report from a Spanish colonial tax official in the San Martín region; it stated Friar Ortiz was released from captivity by a group from the Wak'as revolt. That was promising. We now had independent verification that Friar Ortiz was in fact held prisoner by a group from the Wak'as revolt. We also had a location that was quite far north.

I asked Abbey to have Mike and Harrison try to determine where the report came from in the San Martín region. It was unclear or there were conflicting places noted. Mitch could then run all the locations through her software and we could see what the probabilities looked like. This would at least keep them busy and give Mitch some data from our project to test her software with. Also I was discovering that often when I sent these folks on a wild goose chase they came back with something worthwhile.

Of the 39 references I reviewed relating groups of Wak'as and the Taki Unquy religious followers either moving through or residing there, about half seemed that there was at least a chance it was our True of Heart group. Most of the references were vague on the size of the group. Some had a clear location; others didn't. I gave my list with as much location information as I had to Mike and Harrison and asked them to plot it on our master map.

I told the group that I'd only reviewed a few dozen of the almost 200 references to the revolt of the Wak'as and the Taki Unquy religious movement. I planned to keep working on them this week. Then I said that we should be getting more documents from Spain this week. We would run them, along with new documents from the monastery, through the same search parameters.

Finally I told them that Walter said he was looking forward to attending our Monday meeting next week. That seemed to please everyone.

As I walked back to my office my phone vibrated with a new text message. I looked at it. It was from Laura and said, "Read the email I sent you as soon as you can."

I opened my laptop and found Laura's email. Not good news. It seemed that the Vatican heard about our project to digitize the documents at the Monastery of Saint Catherine in Arequipa. They were raising the same objection to the Abbess of Saint Catherine's Monastery as they had in Spain. It seemed that the personal representative of Cardinal Eduardo Poggi was arriving in Arequipa to discuss the matter with the Abbess. Laura went on to say the Abbess had requested that I come to the monastery as soon as possible to meet with her.

I just didn't understand this. All of the documents we were digitizing were from the 1500s. They mostly related to Peru. I just couldn't see what the Church was so worried about. These documents may not have been studied by scholars for hundreds of years as the ones in Spain had been. But what scandal could they contain that would interest anyone today?

First I sent a text message to Major Campbell to ask him to arrange air transport to Arequipa for first thing the next morning. Then I sent an email to Walter outlining what I knew. I also asked him to have someone meet with the Ministry of the Interior before the Church started causing difficulties there.

Next I emailed back to Laura telling her I would be there in the morning. I told her to explain to the Abbess the confidentiality agreement we all signed. It had a specific clause about not disclosing anything that would be harmful to the Church. I attached a copy in case Laura hadn't brought her copy to Peru.

There didn't seem to be much more I could do about that until I met with the Abbess. So I went back to working on the 200 references to the revolt of the Wak'as and the Taki Unquy religious movement.

Major Campbell came into my office and said, "Problems in Arequipa?"

I explained what was happening. He seemed as mystified as I was. He said he would fly me to Arequipa airport at first light and then go to Lima to handle some things there for the day and pick me up again at 3:00PM. I was to meet him at the airfield at 6:30AM.

He left and I went back to my reading. A little while later I received an email from one of Walter's assistants wishing me well in my meeting with the Abbess and saying that there shouldn't be a problem with the Interior Ministry. I knew the emails I sent to Walter went to an assistant first. However, I wasn't sure how much the assistants handled on their own and when they took them to Walter. Well, it seemed to work.

In the late afternoon I met with Abbey. She would continue reviewing the references I hadn't gotten to along with loading the new documents into the search software.

I met Major Campbell at 6:30 the next morning. He was going through the pre-flight routine for the Cessna Skymaster. I climbed in and buckled my seat belt.

Major Campbell climbed in and said, "It is going to be just under a two-hour flight. We are landing at Rodriguez Ballón International Airport. It is about 12 miles northwest of downtown. I've arranged for a car and driver to take you to the monastery and then bring you back to the airport."

I said, "Can we fly over Machu Picchu on the way?"

"Rob, it is a bit out of the way. How about on the way back? I'll file our return flight plan to include flying over the site. Let's plan to leave Arequipa at 2:30PM to give us more time."

I said, "That works for me. I can't see the Abbess wanting to meet with me for more than an hour. I'll spend the rest of the time with Laura and her team. Then have the driver get me back to the airport by 2:30."

When we started to descend into Arequipa I was surprised how big it was. Arequipa is the second largest city in Peru so I guess I shouldn't have been surprised. The airport was a large, modern international airport.

The Major landed and taxied to the fixed-base operator. He didn't even shut down the engines. I grabbed my briefcase and got out. The driver was waiting for me. I looked back and Major Campbell was taxiing away.

It was morning rush hour so the driving was slow. I decided to just sit back and enjoy the sights. Arequipa is one of the most industrialized cities in Peru. However its historic center is well preserved and covers more than 820 acres. It is a World Heritage Site and a national and international tourist destination.

We finally were approaching our destination. The Monastery of Saint Catherine has an interesting history. The nuns of the monastery are of the Dominican Second Order. It was built in 1579 and was enlarged in the seventeenth century. The monastery is over 215,000 square feet. The nuns live in the northern corner of the complex. The rest of the monastery is open to the public.

The founder of the monastery was a rich widow named Maria de Guzman. The monastery accepted only women from upper-class Spanish families. Each family paid a dowry at their daughter's admission to the monastery. The dowry was 2,400 silver coins equivalent to about $150,000 today. That practice was discontinued long ago.

In 1871 Sister Josefa Caden, a strict Dominican nun, was sent by Pope Pius IX to reform the monastery after reports of outrageous wealth and its misuse. Sister Caden sent the rich dowries back to Europe. She freed all the servants and slaves. Then she gave the nuns the choice of either remaining as nuns or leaving. There were also stories of nuns becoming pregnant, and even stories of the skeleton of a baby being discovered encased in a wall. It was later confirmed that there were no skeletons of babies.

The driver dropped me off at the main public entrance and said he would be back at 1:00PM and would wait for me in the parking lot. I thanked him and headed into the front entrance. I gave my name and told the attendant whom I was here to see. He directed me to the northern end of the monastery and said someone would meet me.

A nun met me and took me to the area next to the library where Laura's group had set up their workshop. She said she would let the Abbess know I was here. Laura and her team were hard at work. We exchanged greetings. Laura offered me a seat next to an antique desk and joined me. The other three kept working. I was impressed with the great care they took with the documents.

I said, "How are you doing? With the work and just in general being here."

"Rob, this is a fascinating place. They have some very rare and valuable documents in the collection. The nuns who are assigned to the library collection are very interested in learning all they can from us. Everyone has been extremely helpful. I know the pace at which we are digitizing the documents must be holding back your work."

I said, "We both know it is more important to protect and preserve the documents. It may be the most important part of the whole project. I'm starting to think that all along Walter knew the side benefits of his quest for the death cave might be of more lasting value than finding the cave or tomb."

Laura continued, "As for your second question. I believe the four of us feel this is the adventure of a lifetime. At some point we will make time to explore beyond Arequipa. But we still have only seen a fraction of what the city has to offer."

"Tell me about the Abbess," I said.

"Well, she seems bright. She is a good manager of people and is well respected not only by the nuns but also by all the people who work in the public areas of the monastery. She makes a point to visit us every couple of days. She invites us to attend services and suggest things we might be interested in seeing around the city. I think you will enjoy meeting her. However she is upset by interference of Cardinal Poggi. I have the feeling there is bad blood between those two."

That was interesting. We spent the next 20 minutes talking about the work with the documents. The nun returned and said the Abbess would like to see us now.

We were taken to a large office or receiving room. Its design was strongly influenced by Moorish taste and workmanship. The furniture all looked antique. However there was a flat-screen display, computers, laptops, a fax machine and a high-speed printer/scanner. It looked like the nuns were up to date on the business side of their operation.

When we entered the Abbess got up from behind her desk to greet us. She was in her late fifties or early sixties. She had a warm smile and a firm handshake.

She said, "It is a pleasure to meet you, Professor Johnson. I appreciate you coming here on such short notice."

Her English was excellent. She directed us to a sitting area at the side of the room. I took a seat in an armchair. Laura and the Abbess sat on a couch.

She went on, "It is a great pleasure having your team here from Cornell University. Laura and her three assistants are showing extreme care with our documents. They also have fit in well with the daily life in the monastery. I believe the nuns working with them will learn a great deal. I understand Mr. Falone is arranging for Laura to continue her work through the fall. We of course welcome this news."

That was a relief, I was afraid with the pressure from the Vatican, the Abbess might have called me to tell us to pack up and go home.

"Professor, I am quite disturbed by the message I received from Cardinal Eduardo Poggi. Do you know of him?"

I shook my head no.

"Speaking bluntly, he is a part of the old guard at the Vatican that seems unable to face the realities of the modern world. He is also not a nice man. His dealings with others in the Church have often been underhanded and at times ruthless. Many people both dislike and fear him. Having the Cardinal's personal representative visit is not good news.

"I have spoken with my counterparts in Spain. I understand that your digitizing of the documents from the General Archive of the Indies housed in Seville, and the Complutense University of Madrid, is being held up."

I said, "The documents are all digitized and they are being reviewed by the Church at a painfully slow pace. I doubt we have received 5% of the documents they are holding for review. It seems the confidentiality agreement we signed means nothing to them. As I said to Laura, I don't understand what could be in these 500-year-old documents that worries the Church. Researchers have had access to these documents for several hundred years. If there was a big scandal hidden there someone would have found it."

"Professor, it is modern technology and the modern world which Cardinal Poggi fears."

I was totally confused and the Abbess must have seen it on my face.

She said, "Professor Johnson, do you remember a little while back when the United Nations Committee on the Implementation of the Convention on the Rights of the Child gave the church a most public grilling for its handling of sex abuse scandals around the world? Vatican officials faced hours of tough questions in Geneva from the UN."

I said, "Yes. It had been headline news at the time."

"Professor, do you know what the shameful response was from the two high-ranking Cardinals sent by the Vatican?"

I just shook my head.

"They basically told a United Nations panel that the Vatican has little real power to stop bishops from hiding clergy sex crimes. The Cardinals added that the church has little legal basis to punish clergy and other church members for sexual abuse. Priests are citizens of their own states and fall under the jurisdiction of their own country.

"Now, Professor, while this may be true in a strict legal sense, it avoids the moral issue. It is hard for me to believe that our huge and powerful Church bureaucracy continues to pretend it's powerless over its own officials.

"At the same time at the Vatican, Pope Francis called the scandals 'the shame of the Church.' Just a few weeks earlier he announced the establishment of a commission to help him decide how best to protect children from sexual abuses by priests and help past victims.

"Pope Francis has only had a short time to deal with the many issues the Church has ignored for too long. But I believe he will. I pray each day that God gives him the courage and strength to do what needs to be done.

"It gets worse. Good Catholics such as myself have known of these scandals for decades. We have sinned by not demanding that our Church leaders put a stop to it. As I've prayed on this, I realize we are no better than the Germans who just looked the other way during the Holocaust."

The Abbess closed her eyes and folded her hands as if to pray.

When she opened her eyes I said, "I've often thought that the Church would be better off if it were turned over to women for the next two thousand years. Good Catholic women like you, Abbess. They are bound to do a better job." I stopped and wished I'd kept my mouth shut. But much to my relief the Abbess smiled. It was a big grin.

She said, "I must admit I've confessed to such thoughts myself many times. Do you know women constitute the majority of members of the consecrated life within the Catholic Church? There are over 720,000 of us."

I said, "I understand that the sexual abuse of children by priests has been a major problem for the Church for decades now. But I don't see what it has to do with the sixteenth-century documents we are interested in."

The Abbess said, "In Spain all the documents of the General Archive of the Indies housed in Seville, and the Complutense University of Madrid are being digitized. Here you are only dealing with the one time period 500 years ago. However, there are many projects around the world to digitize vast quantities of documents and make them searchable online. This is what Cardinal Poggi and his group fear. There is now an organization in Finland that is trying to bring the whole worldwide Church up on charges of crimes against humanity for the child abuse and its cover-up. Some at the Vatican fear if enough material becomes available online such groups will be able to sit at a computer and compile vast amount of evidence against the Church. If they remain dusty documents in hundreds of different places with restricted access it would be impossible to amass such evidence."

I said, "I understand this in theory but, it seems unlikely to me that they will stop the continued digitization of documents worldwide. I guess my more pressing concern is what do we do here, now that Cardinal Poggi's representative is coming."

The Abbess said, "I have a plan. I would like to move Mrs. O'Hara, her team, and the equipment into the cloisters, no men are allowed there. I assume the Cardinal's representative will be a man. Do you have two women who you can spare to come work under Mrs. O'Hara's direction, and another set of digitizing equipment? If so with the help of the two nuns currently working with your team we could effectively double the document output."

I said, "I have two women I can ask if they are willing to come. There are four women on my team but two of them while more than capable of doing the job I need to focus on other work. Perhaps I should tell you a little about the two and you decide if I should ask them. Michelle, who prefers to be called Mitch, is a bit unconventional in her look and dress."

The Abbess put up her hand. "I'm not concerned about that, is she hardworking, honest, and suitably intelligent?"

I said, "She is very bright, extremely hardworking, and I believe she is honest."

"Then please invite her, Professor. The other woman I assume is qualified."

I said, "Sadako is of Japanese descent. She is quite shy. But she is very hardworking, very bright, and honest."

"Professor, if they are willing to come we would love to have them. It may only help at the margin to have two groups digitizing the documents. However, I feel obligated to do what I can to help with your project. Mr. Falone has been very generous to us here and Mrs. O'Hara and her associates are fine women. It has been a pleasure having them here.

"Professor Johnson, I would also like you to deliver a letter to Mr. Falone for me. I'm requesting some additional help from him concerning Church matters."

She handed me an envelope of very fine bond paper. It had a wax seal over an inch in diameter with the Abbess's personal seal. When I took it from her hand it felt like it was four or five pages. I felt like a royal messenger.

She said, "Thank you again for coming on such short notice. It has been a pleasure meeting you."

I went with Laura to a nearby café for lunch. I said, "I'm happy to get as many digitized documents as soon as possible. But in the big picture, will it really make a difference having the second group?"

Laura said, "I believe it is the Abbess's way of showing she is working in good faith to honor our arrangement. She doesn't like the interference and the topic has obviously touched a raw spot with her. Do you think Mitch and Sadako will agree to come help?"

I said, "All I can do is ask. I'm not going to pressure them. Do you want them here? Will they be helpful?"

Laura said, "I think it could help the dynamic. Moving into the cloister will be a change for us. We may need to stay in the cloister 24 hours a day when the Cardinal's representative is here. It could help morale to have new people with new things to talk about. Plus we will be able to double the production. When things settle down in a week or two, I'll send them back. I guess all this is a way of saying if they are willing to come, I'd like to have them."

We had an enjoyable lunch. I gave her a more detailed background on Sadako and Mitch. She seemed fine with what I told her.

I was glad to see that Laura was so happy doing the work here and with the people she interacted with. She walked me through the public spaces of the monastery for about 45 minutes and then to the car. I told her I would call her after I spoke to Mitch and Sadako.

Major Campbell landed at 2:20 and I climbed into my seat and buckled up. Since he was talking to the tower we didn't talk. I put on the head-phones anyway, it reduced the noise and if Major Campbell had something to say he wouldn't have to shout.

We flew north and a little east towards Machu Picchu, perhaps the most famous archaeological site in South America. It is situated on a mountain ridge above the Sacred Valley at an elevation of almost 8,000 feet. Most archaeologists believe that Machu Picchu was built as an estate for the Inca emperor Pachacuti who lived from 1438 to 1472. It is commonly known as the Lost City of the Incas.

The Incas built the estate around 1450, but they abandoned it during Spanish Conquest about a hundred years later. It was unknown to the out-side world until 1911 when Hiram Bingham, an American historian, redis-covered it. I had visited Machu Picchu several years ago when I was in Peru for a brief vacation.

Machu Picchu is situated above a loop of the Urubamba River that surrounds the site on three sides. The cliffs drop vertically for 1,480 feet to the river below. The location of the city was a military secret. Its deep precipices and steep mountains provided excellent natural defenses.

Inca's Death Cave

The city sits in a saddle between the two mountains Machu Picchu and Huayna Picchu. It has a commanding view down two valleys and a nearly impassable mountain at its back. The water supply is from springs that cannot be blocked easily. The hillsides leading to it have been terraced, providing farmland to grow crops and steep slopes that invaders would have to ascend. There were two routes from Machu Picchu going across the mountains back to Cusco. The first was the sun gate, and the second was across the Inca Bridge. This Inca Bridge or the trunk bridge was a part of a mountain trail, which was a stone path, cut into a cliff face. A 20-foot gap was left in this section of the carved cliff edge over a 1,900-foot drop. This was bridged with two tree trunks. Removing it would leave the trail impassable to enemies.

Major Campbell flew low over the site. I could clearly see the three primary structures. The Hitching Post of the Sun, the Temple of the Sun, and the Room of the Three Windows. They are located in what is known as the Sacred District of Machu Picchu. He circled twice and then headed north. I could have had him circle for hours but he had work to do and it was getting late.

Machu Picchu, The Lost City (Note 3)

Chapter 33

Once we landed I went looking for Mitch and Sadako. I found Mitch first in the workroom.

I said, "How would you like to work in the cloisters of the monastery for a while?"

"You're joking, right, Professor?"

"Actually I'm not. The Vatican is causing the same problem in Arequipa as they did in Spain. The Abbess wants to move the digitizing work into the cloisters and double the output."

"So work in the cloisters and sleep in a cell with the nuns?"

"I'm not sure but something like that."

"OK, Professor, I'd love to. If they need help I'm the chick to do it. When do I go and is anybody else going with me?"

"I'm going to ask Sadako if she is willing to go. You will fly out about 8:30 tomorrow morning. A plane is coming in from Lima with equipment for Dr. Frank's work. It will pick you up and take you to Arequipa along with additional digitizing equipment."

I was starting to see that Mitch didn't like being stereotyped. One might think based on her nonconventional looks she wouldn't be caught dead in a monastery. So Mitch says "yes I'd love to go live and work in a monastery." I thanked Mitch for her help and said I hoped it would only be for a week or two.

Sadako said she was happy to help but seemed surprised Mitch was going. She made a point of saying that she worked well with Mitch.

I told the others. Mike said he could run Mitch's probability software for the master map when we needed to. I still hadn't seen Ned and Fred but I assumed Major Campbell was keeping them busy. It was funny he hadn't mentioned what they were doing in our flight to and from Arequipa.

It was past 6:00PM but I wanted to see how far Abbey had gotten on the 200 references to the revolt of the Wak'as and the Taki Unquy religious movement. I caught up with her at the guesthouse.

I said, "Did you have time to check out any of the Wak'as revolt references today?"

"Prof, I worked my way through about thirty. It was interesting but only one reference that might be related to our Strong of Heart. How was your day?"

I gave her the rundown on what happened at the monastery.

She said, "All the problems we are having in Spain are because of the sexual abuse scandal. It seems a stretch to me."

I agreed. I asked her if she would give me half of the remaining references we needed to check and I would start in on them after my 8:30AM meeting with Major Campbell. We decided to call it a day and went to the dining hall for a drink and dinner.

I was up at the airfield at 8:15AM. Major Campbell wanted me to check the equipment that was being sent to Arequipa to make sure they had everything that was needed.

I was waiting for the plane to arrive when Mitch walked into the hangar.

She said, "Professor, are you here to see if I was going to show up?"

Mitch had dyed her hair jet-black. No more rainbow of colors. It was slicked back and straight. She had removed the jewelry from her body piercings. Her fingernails that were usually painted black, blood red, or bright green had a clear or light pearl polish on them. She wore a white button-down long-sleeved shirt, blue jeans, and tennis sneakers. Her only jewelry was very ornate silver cross about four inches long that was hanging around her neck on a chain.

I said, "I'm checking on the equipment. I don't want to send you to work without the proper tools."

She saw me looking at the cross. She held it out towards me and said, "It was my great-grandmother's. I use it to ward off vampires and zombies."

I said, "I didn't see any vampires or zombies at the monastery but it is a good idea to be prepared."

"That's me, Professor, just like a Boy Scout, always prepared."

She had a medium-size duffel bag with what looked like a straw yoga mat tied to it. I said, "Do you have all your gear?"

She said, "I packed light, I didn't figure I need to make a fashion statement at the monastery."

Sadako arrived just as the plane was landing. It was the Britten-Norman Defender. That seemed to be the workhorse plane between the Lima facility and the ranch.

Dona and Peter Frank got off the plane. An assistant started unloading equipment. We all said hello and I went on board to check the equipment. It was all there. Mitch and Sadako got on the plane and it taxied away. The whole process took only 10 minutes.

Dona Frank said to me, "Sadako and Mitch are going to be working in the Monastery of Saint Catherine in Arequipa and living in the cloisters. That should be an interesting experience for them."

I said, "We could use another woman. Do you want to go?"

She knew I was joking and I went on, "I hope it is only for a week or two. I am not sure it is necessary but both Laura and the Abbess seemed to think it would help. Plus Sadako and Mitch volunteered. I told them they didn't have to go." I went on to briefly explain the situation.

Major Campbell came over and discussed the day's drone test flights with the Franks. When he finished I walked back with him towards his office.

I said, "How are Ned and Fred doing?"

He replied, "I could use Fred for another week if you don't need him. I know you are short-handed now with Mitch and Sadako at the monastery. Did you give Mitch a dress code? That's a new look."

"Major, I know better than to give any woman a dress code. I didn't say anything to her. Would you? How is the investigation going?"

"It's proceeding. I'm sure Walter will brief you at the appropriate time. I understand the test of Elizabeth's software system went well. Walter is quite impressed with her work."

"She is quite a remarkable young lady. But we don't seem to have any shortage of those around here. It makes it a fun place to work."

The Major said, "Most of the time it is, Rob."

I thought he must have been dealing with some unpleasant aspects of his investigation. He had a drone test to set up for the Franks so I said goodbye and headed to my office.

Abbey and I worked the next two days to get through the rest of the 200 references to the revolt of the Wak'as and the Taki Unquy religious movement. We decided not to run searches on the small quantity of new digital documents we were getting from the monastery each day and focus on the finishing the review of what we had. We worked into the evening on Thursday but had the work complete for the Friday meeting.

Friday at 9:59AM I walked to the whiteboard and wrote:

THE REJECT TEAM: PROJECT "THE INCA'S DEATH CAVE." WEEK 5 DAY 5

It was a small group with Mitch and Sadako at the monastery and Fred and Ned working for Major Campbell.

Elizabeth reported that she had spent the time working on refining her software system. The Lima computer group that Walter had analyzing her test run requested she go to Lima to meet with them. She said she planned to go Tuesday and stay two or three days if she wasn't needed here.

Mike and Harrison had plotted the locations of the references we had given them. They had lots of specific questions mostly for Abbey. It seemed they regarded her as the most expert on the topic. That was probably true and it didn't make me jealous, it made me proud.

We decided that the three of them would plot all the valid references we had found on our master map and try running Mitch's probability software on it. They quickly agreed that they wanted to work the weekend so it was ready for our meeting Monday with Walter.

I thought again this is a great group. I don't have to give them deadlines. I just need to tell them to take some time off when they have been working too hard. It makes me feel like a great manager. I was very interested to see what they came up with. I asked them to give me what they had plotted on the master map so far. I wanted to review it over the weekend.

Back in my office I read a long email from Laura O'Hara. She told me that Mitch and Sadako were working out well. The group decided to work seven days a week while in the cloisters. Cardinal Eduardo Poggi's representative was due in early next week and Laura wanted to get as much done as she could before he arrived. She didn't think he would sway the Abbess, but she didn't know what kind of pressure the Cardinal's representative could bring to bear.

I sent Major Campbell an email asking if Fred and Ned could attend the Monday meeting with Walter. I wanted them to stay connected to the team and know what progress was being made. I also invited Major Campbell.

I spent the rest of the weekend rereading the references we thought had some bearing on our work. I also studied what Mike and Harrison had plotted on the master map.

Chapter 34

Monday morning Walter was going to meet me in my office in the research facility at 9:30. My instructions from the Abbess were to deliver her letter directly into Mr. Falone's hands. I was also wanted to explain about Cardinal Poggi's representative's upcoming visit.

He walked into my office precisely at 9:30 and said, "Good morning, Rob, I'm looking forward to meeting with your team."

I said, "Our team, Walter, is the best bunch of rejects I've ever worked with."

A slight frown crossed his face. Then he smiled, sat down, and said, "Tell me about your trip to the monastery."

I went over my discussion with the Abbess. Then I handed him the letter.

I said, "She insisted I personally place it in your hand. I was quite impressed with her."

Walter took the envelope. He turned it over in his hands and examined the wax seal. Then he reached across my desk and took the letter opener that was sitting there.

He looked up at me and said, "Let's see what the Abbess has to say."

I was quiet while Walter read the letter. He read the four pages quickly and then went back and reread several sections. Then he was thoughtful sitting and looking at nothing for a moment.

He said, "It seems the Abbess wants me to help her reshape the world."

I said nothing. Then he went on, "I believe I would like to meet the Abbess. Please see if Laura can arrange a meeting. I can go anytime tomorrow."

I said, "I'll send Laura a text now and then we can go meet with our team."

Walter went ahead to visit with the team. When I finished the text I went in and made my ritual start to our meeting. I wrote:

THE REJECT TEAM: PROJECT "THE INCA'S DEATH CAVE." WEEK 6 DAY 1

Elizabeth started with a short report on the minor modifications she was making to her software system. Walter was the only one who seemed to really understand what she was saying. He asked several detailed questions that it seemed Elizabeth had no trouble answering.

Next I said, "Ned and Fred, what have you been up to?"

Ned spoke up. "We have been helping Major Campbell fight crime." He didn't say any more and I took the hint.

I went to Abbey. "Please tell Walter about what we found in our review of the items identified by Elizabeth's search run."

Abbey ran through the number of references in each of our four search categories. Then she talked about the relevant ones identified by reading each reference. Next she explained each one that could be associated with a geographic location that was plotted on our master map.

Then Mike and Harrison went to the master map. They had it projected on the whiteboard. First they put up the entire permit area. Next they overlaid the areas eliminated as not likely to have any caves or caverns.

Harrison explained that they didn't add his weather data because it didn't give any additional information and tended to make the map more confusing. Then they put up a probability grid for how likely there were to be caves and caverns of each of the three sizes they established. The drone had given them magnetometer readings for most of the grid.

It was interesting but I had no idea how accurate it was. It also still left many hundreds of square miles of area. Next they plotted the points for each of our valid references. The references for our four different searches were in a different color. It was a bit confusing but there were a total of 23 points plotted on the map.

This was the first time I'd seen all the references, that we felt were relevant, plotted on the map. My first thought was this is like sightings of Bigfoot. They are all over the place. As I kept studying the map I saw references started in the Ancash and Huanuco regions at the south end of our permit area. They were scattered north and east on the east side of the regions of La Libertad and Cajamarca and on the west side of the regions of San Martín and Amazonas. We hadn't looked for references south of our permit area. I was beginning to wonder if that was a mistake.

Mike explained that they tried to run Mitch's probability software but the results didn't seem to mean much so they didn't present the results. They would wait for Mitch to return to help with that.

I kept staring at the map. Walter asked Mike about the probability function he used to map the likelihood of caves and caverns being of each of the three size ranges they had established. I was only half listening. Mike explained what he had done and where he felt the weaknesses were in his assumption.

I guess I must have totally tuned out because Abbey poked me. I looked over.

Walter said to me, "I was asking you, Rob, what your thoughts are on what we have so far?"

I had a whole jumble of thoughts. I said, "The first thing is that we now have independent collaboration that Friar Ortiz was a captive of our True of Heart group. Before all we had was Friar Murúa's account in the *Historia*. Second we have enough sightings of the True of Heart group to feel comfortable they existed and moved north as a group. I would like the team to see if we can establish a time line for the sightings. Were the southern sightings before the more northern sightings? We may find references to crop harvests, tax collection, festivals, the weather, etc., that might help us develop a time line. Finally I'm puzzled that only Friar Murúa uses the name Minchancaman as the leader of the group. We do have several references that suggest the group's primary god was the moon god but no other reference uses the name Minchancaman.

"I have a couple of other ideas but before I comment on them I'd like to study what we have a little more."

Abbey said, "Good job, Prof. I thought you had fallen asleep with your eyes open."

"I was thinking, Abbey. Didn't you see the smoke coming out of my ears?"

Walter said, "The team has made excellent progress. I'm excited to see what you discover next."

Abbey said, "Mr. Falone, would it be possible to have Dr. Frank and her husband give us a presentation on their work? When we get to the point of investigating specific sites on the ground the tools they have developed could be very helpful."

Walter said, "That is an excellent idea. Please invite them for next Monday. I'd like to attend."

Abbey said, "I'll arrange it for Monday morning."

Elizabeth said, "Mr. Falone, may I ask how the investigation into who sabotaged our test run is going?"

"Elizabeth, first I must apologize to you and our whole team for this. It is deeply disturbing to me that something like this would happen within our company. Second we are not going to jump to any conclusions on who did this or why until we have all the facts. Once all the facts are in I can assure you the appropriate action will be taken. Also I know this must feel like an attack on you personally. However I take it as a personal attack on me, and the values of our entire company. Again, I'm sorry this happened."

Elizabeth said, "Thank you, Mr. Falone. Thank you for caring about us."

She was holding back tears. I saw she was thanking Walter not just for this, but also for saving her job, the jobs of her teammates, and giving them this opportunity. It was also clear Walter was very mad. He held it well but you could see it.

Walter thanked them again. He said to me, "Walk with me a minute, I'd like to speak with you."

As I walked out with Walter I heard Ned say to Elizabeth, "Don't worry, Elizabeth, we'll get the fuckers."

Walter asked me as soon as I heard about the meeting with the Abbess to let him know. I took out my phone, which I had silenced, and read the text.

I said, "Laura says the Abbess will meet with you anytime tomorrow at your convenience."

"Rob, please see if Major Campbell can fly me to Arequipa tomorrow leaving at 7:00AM. Tell him I would like him to accompany me to the meeting with the Abbess. Then let Mrs. O'Hara know we should arrive at the monastery at about 10:00AM. I would also like to briefly meet with

Mrs. O'Hara and her team after my meeting with the Abbess. I haven't met her yet and I'd like to see Mitch and Sadako as well."

He said thank you and told me he was pleased with the team's work. After sending a detailed text to Major Campbell, I went back to the work-room. Ned and Fred were gone. Elizabeth was asking Abbey if she needed her help before she left for Lima. Mike and Harrison were waiting for Abbey.

When Elizabeth was done I said, "Abbey, let's talk with Mike and Harrison about trying to figure out how to establish a time line for the sightings."

We spent some time going over ways we might establish the relative time of each sighting. It didn't take long to give them all my suggestions. They would come up with ways I hadn't thought of. We all knew this was not going to be very precise but it could help.

I asked Mike to load the map on my laptop and I headed to my office. After a few minutes I decided I needed a walk. I went back to the guest-house and dumped my briefcase and laptop. I wandered up the trails to the north. After about an hour of walking, an idea in the back of my mind came into focus. I headed back to the guesthouse.

When Abbey came in after 4:00 I had maps and notes spread all over the large dining table.

She said, "Oh boy, another brainstorm. Let me wash up, open a bottle of wine and you can tell me about it."

I grabbed a beer and when she came back I said, "Let's not go all the way to a brainstorm. Maybe it is an idea or new lead. Two things came to-gether. First there is only one reference to Minchancaman as the leader of our True of Heart group. It was only in Friar Murúa's *Historia*. Why don't other references refer to the leader, who is well known and revered at least by his followers, by that name? The name Minchancaman was well known as the last great leader of the Chimor people. It would be known to people in the region of the Chimor Empire.

"The second is, if we look at all the references we have screened and plotted on the map, while they seem a bit scattered all over, there is a greater concentration of references in the areas that are now the eastern La Libertad region and the western half of the regions of San Martín and Amazonas. This is east of the old Chimor Empire and falls in the area of the Chachapoyas people. These people were also known the Warriors of the Clouds. The Incas conquered their civilization shortly before the arrival of the Spanish in Peru. When the Spanish arrived in Peru in the sixteenth century, the Chachapoyas were one of the many nations ruled by the Inca Empire. The incorporation of the Chachapoyas into the Inca Empire was not easy, because of their constant resistance to the Inca troops.

"So Abbey, I'm starting to think that our band of the True of Heart may not be made up of people from the former Chimor Empire but from the Chachapoya Empire. Perhaps Friar Ortiz didn't give Friar Murúa the name Minchancaman and just said something like, 'He took the name of their last great leader.' Friar Murúa assumes he is talking about the Chimor and uses the name Minchancaman in his *Historia*. The *Historia* was written at some point after the two friars met. It could have been a few years later.

"If we look again at our map and the work that Mike did with caves and caverns, we see the area of the Chachapoya Empire has lots of areas along the eastern side of the Andes that are suited to caves and caverns. Now this is also true with the western side of the Andes that falls within the old Chimor Empire.

"Then I started thinking about all the reading I've done over the last month when I was trying to look busy when you and the rest of the team were hard at work."

Abbey smiled, poured herself more wine but didn't say anything.

I continued, "I don't remember a single reference to cave burials in Chimor culture. However, there were two funeral patterns typical in the Chachapoyas culture and both involved caves. One used sarcophagi placed vertically and located in caves that were at the highest point of precipices. The other type were groups of mausoleums constructed like tiny houses located in caves worked into cliffs. The burial sites at Revash and Laguna de los Condores or Lake of the Condors are among the many sites of these two types.

"I read someone has estimated that only 5% of sites of the Chachapoyas have been excavated. So what do we know about the Chachapoyas? The Chachapoyas culture is believed to have developed around 750 to 800AD. The Inca ruler Tupac Inca Yupanqui conquered them in about 1475AD.

After the defeat of the Chachapoyas smaller rebellions continued for many years. Using ethnic dispersion, the Inca attempted to quell these rebellions by forcing large numbers of Chachapoya people to resettle in remote locations of the empire.

"Everything we know comes from Spanish chroniclers or the archaeological records. There is little firsthand knowledge of the Chachapoyas. Writings by chroniclers of the time were based on fragmentary secondhand accounts. Chroniclers such as El Inca Garcilaso de la Vega and Pedro Cieza de León wrote about the Chachapoya Empire. Cieza de León noted that, after their annexation to the Inca Empire, they adopted customs imposed by the Cusco-based Inca. Much about the Chachapoyas Empire prior to the Inca conquest was undoubtedly lost.

"The Chachapoyas' territory encompassed the triangular region formed by the confluence of the rivers Marañón and Utcubamba in the area of Bagua up to the basin of the Abiseo River, where the ruins of Pajatén are located. The center of the Chachapoyas' culture was the basin of the Utcubamba River. Because of the great size of the Marañón River, and the surrounding mountainous terrain, the region was relatively isolated from the coast and other areas of Peru.

"If we can establish with some degree of confidence that our True of Heart group is primarily made up of Chachapoya people we will be able to cut our search area to less than a third of what we currently have. Now here is what I want you to do."

Abbey said, "How did I know your bright idea was going to end up with more work for me?"

"I wouldn't want you to run out of work. Idle hands do the devil's work. Now here is a list of the chroniclers I believe have written about the Chachapoyas. I'm sure you will find more. I've also made a list of Chachapoya location names, gods, and a few other key words I could find. I would like you to take all the references we found from our mega search and run searches screening for the key Chachapoya terms. You should also focus in detail on the works of the chroniclers I've listed. By then I'm sure you will have figured out a much better way to do what needs to be done. So then do it your way and come back and tell me what you found. Now that's pretty simple and straightforward, isn't it?"

"Would you like me to start before dinner or is tomorrow soon enough?"

"Start whenever you want."

"Prof, you know this is actually quite interesting and quite good."

"Thank you, Abbey."

Chapter 35

The next Monday was the presentation by Dona and Peter Frank.

I started the meeting by writing:

THE REJECT TEAM: PROJECT "THE INCA'S DEATH CAVE." WEEK 7 DAY 1

Dona Frank gave most of the presentation. What the Franks were primarily working on was large area aerial survey techniques with unmanned vehicles. This would allow the company to cost effectively survey huge areas of land. What they were focused on currently was miniaturizing the existing type of sensing equipment to meet the weight and power limitations of the drones.

Once again it was clear that the combination of the company's huge database and advanced search technology gave the company a big advantage in analyzing data once it was collected.

It was interesting but it didn't really apply to what we were doing. If we ever reduced our search area enough we would need subsurface information at depth and in detail.

Everybody asked questions and seemed to enjoy the discussion.

As the questions wound down Abbey said, "What we need is the Goodyear blimp with powerful magnetometer and ground-penetrating radar units that can be lowered to just about the surface. It will give us much greater detail than we are getting from the magnetometer up in the drone and ground-penetrating radar doesn't really work unless it is in contact with the ground."

Walter got it first, next Dr. Frank and finally it sunk in with me. That was exactly what we needed.

Abbey went on, "It has to be cheaper to get a blimp than one of those fancy drones. They can fly low and slow. They can stay airborne far longer than any drone or helicopter. There must be a lot of those Skyship 500s or 600s around; you see them on TV all the time. Magnetometers are not that heavy. For power just fit the Skyship's two Porsche 930 turbocharged engines with generators. The service ceiling could be an issue but I'm sure Major Campbell's people can come up with some custom modification to handle that."

Walter said, "Dr. Frank, would you meet with Major Campbell and give me a preliminary feasibility study on that by Friday. Abbey, I like the way you think. But once again my schedule is overbooked and I need to leave. This has been a very interesting morning. Thank you, everyone."

Walter left and I thanked the Franks.

Dona Frank said, "I guess I better go find the Major and get to work. Peter, you may get a new toy to play with."

Peter Frank said, "I love new toys."

I said to Abbey, "Have you ever even seen a blimp?"

"On TV, Prof. Only on TV."

The next few weeks fell into a routine. We kept adding the new documents we received to our database. We ran more and more related search terms. We found more evidence that the group of the True of Heart did exist and seemed to be moving north.

I received an email from Laura at the monastery saying Cardinal Poggi's representative had come and gone. The Abbess told him she was reviewing all documents before they left and he didn't have to worry that any would embarrass the Church. Once he realized that the only documents being digitized were from 500 years ago and covered a period of less than 100 years, he seemed convinced. Plus he didn't really want a fight with the Abbess, who it turned out enjoys an excellent reputation in the Church hierarchy.

Laura said she was sending Mitch and Sadako back. They both had done an excellent job and fit into life in the cloisters smoothly. Her team would go back to their normal work schedule. She also said she had found a fourth person to continue work this fall. It was all in all a good report.

Major Campbell was able to fill me in on his meeting with Walter and the Abbess. It seemed the Abbess wanted to be provided with transportation so she could visit the Abbesses of the other South American monasteries and convents. She hoped to enlist their help with her plan to put the Church's sexual abuse and cover-up scandals behind it. Depending on her reception in South America she planned to go to North America, Africa, Asia, and finally to Europe.

Walter had agreed to provide a jet, pilots, and a security detail. I made the mistake of saying to Major Campbell, "The Abbess needs rent-a-cops?"

The Major replied, "Let me assure you, Professor, my security people are not rent-a-cops. I doubt the Abbess is in real danger from factions of the Church that disagree with her. However, they will have a rude awakening if they think she will be an easy target."

I knew over the course of its history the Church had experienced every kind of intrigue known to man. But I hoped the Abbess wasn't in any danger.

Major Campbell still said nothing about his investigation. He also asked to keep Fred working with him. That was fine since I didn't have much for Fred to do.

Elizabeth was spending two or three days a week in Lima working with that computer group on her software system. Now that everyone knew it worked and understood how powerful it was, they wanted to refine it and make it more user friendly. She was available to help Abbey when she needed help. Abbey had mostly figured out how to do the search runs we needed.

Towards the end of August, as I walked down the hall to my office, I heard singing. Well, I guess it was supposed to be singing. The voices were Ned's and Fred's and the song was from *The Wizard of Oz*. They sang, "Ding-Dong! The witch is dead. The wicked old witch is dead. She's gone where the goblins go ho-ho-ho the wicked witch is dead."

As I walked to the workroom they kept singing those lines over and over again. It was probably all they could remember. I walked to the door and looked in. Fred and Ned were swinging each other around in a jig-like dance step, singing the lines over and over and laughing the whole time.

They saw me and said, "Professor, the wicked witch is dead." Then kept dancing around.

Mitch said, "Professor, they are right, the witch is dead. Walter shit canned Dr. Stone this morning. It turns out she was behind the sabotage of Elizabeth's work. She went all the way around the bend. I could have told you she was a nut job time bomb. Some kind of paranoid breakdown."

Elizabeth said, "Officially she resigned for medical reasons and is voluntarily entering a clinic to receive treatment."

Ned said, "She is doing that in a deal so Walter doesn't press charges. I'd rather see the bitch in the slammer."

To try to change the tone a bit I said, "How many others were implicated?"

Ned said, "Three. Two were fired and the third is still with the company. Dr. Stone coerced him into being part of the sabotage and he came forward to confess the whole thing. So Walter went easy on him. I know him he isn't a bad guy really."

Well, after the way these folks had been treated by Dr. Stone I guess they had a right to celebrate. She must have become unbalanced. I don't see how someone in her position would do this otherwise. I was just glad to see the whole matter resolved and behind us.

It was the buzz around all the company for a few days and then we settled back into our routine. A few weeks later Walter wanted an update. He had missed our meetings for several weeks.

I started the meeting in my usual way. I went to the whiteboard and wrote:

THE REJECT TEAM: PROJECT "THE INCA'S DEATH CAVE." WEEK 10 DAY 1

The main focus of this meeting was on our master map.

Abbey started by explaining that as we received new documents, they would be run using the previous search terms. New references were checked. If they seemed valid and we had a location they were plotted on the master map. Additional search terms were developed based on what we found from the previous searches and the process continued.

Mitch would then do a computer probability run on the referenced locations. I still didn't really understand how this worked. The algorithm she developed took as inputs all sorts of factors the team developed and came up with an overall likelihood of it being useful. I just decided to look at the areas that her software said had the highest probability first and work my way down the list.

The pattern that was developing was that the True of Heart group was mostly made up of Chachapoya people. They were headed north to their traditional homeland that encompassed the triangular region formed by the confluence of the rivers Marañón and Utcubamba. We had references in this area. We knew that the Chachapoyas buried their dead in caves and the geography of the area was full of caves.

Given that we started with about half of Peru as our search area this was progress. The trouble was I wasn't sure where to go from here. We were receiving a trickle of new documents each week but so far not much new was being added. The new search terms Abbey was developing were farther and farther away from terms that were likely to help.

Walter seemed pleased with our progress. He commented on how much we had accomplished in just 10 weeks. I had to agree when you looked at it that way we were making a good start.

The meeting ended and we planned to spend the week doing about what we had been doing the last few weeks, the grunt work of a major research effort.

It is funny, when a breakthrough comes it is often from the most unlikely spot. I was in my office one afternoon when Ned came in. I said, "Hi, Ned. Have a seat and tell me about your day."

Ned sat and said, "Well, you know part of my job with Major Campbell is to monitor what goes on in Peru. Since we are focusing on the section of the Amazonas Region where the Chachapoyas Empire was I decided to give that area a little special attention.

"Last week park rangers at the Cordillera de Colán National Sanctuary found a 20-foot hole in the ground that wasn't there when they last patrolled the area. It appears that the top section on an underground cavern caved in. They didn't want to get too close to the edge in case more of the roof caved in. So they threw a few rocks in to see if they could tell how deep it was. They heard the rocks splash. Next they threw in a long rope they had with some kind of grappling hook on it. Guess what they came up with."

"Ralph Hardy's nucleon energy belt."

"No, a skull and this freaked them out. It turned out to be an old skull and around Peru they find old bones all the time so they decided it wasn't a crime scene and it must be some kind of burial site."

I was excited. "When did this happen and what are they doing now?"

"Professor, I knew this was a big deal so the Major and I discussed it. He called the Antiquities Department at the Ministry of the Interior and explained that this was covered by Mr. Falone's permit. They were very happy to help so they called the park and talked to the rangers who agreed to secure the area until we arrived. The park authorities seemed very happy that it was someone else's job to deal with it."

"Ned, you know all this because you listened to all their conversations?"

"It is part of my job, Professor. Plus I like to know what is going on."

Major Campbell walked in and said, "Interesting news and a good piece of work by Ned. I suggest we take a team up to investigate. I have several highly trained divers on my staff. Give me tomorrow to organize everything and we can leave at first light the day after tomorrow. Pack your stuff for a few days to stay out in the field."

I said, "I'll be ready and I want to bring Abbey."

The Major said, "By all means, we all know she is the real brains of our Cornell duo."

They left and I looked up the Cordillera de Colán National Sanctuary. The sanctuary is 247 square miles located in both the Bagua and Utcubamba provinces of the Amazonas Region. Over 150 species of animals are found there.

I found Mike, told him what we found, and asked him to put together as much information as he could on the topography, geology, and especially the subsurface hydrogeology of the park. "I need it by tomorrow afternoon. Sooner if you can. Get the others to help you," I told him. I gave him the coordinates of the park 5.35 degrees south by 78.14 degrees west. "Ned may be able to tell you where in the park the cavern is at least in general terms," I added.

Next I told Abbey and said we were leaving at first light the day after tomorrow.

She said, "Prof, it might be nothing but a few old bones. Don't get all excited until we know more."

She was right I was excited, and hopeful. I said, "It will be great to see the park. I understand it is beautiful. Plus I need to get out of here for a few days. I'm sick of reading references that mostly don't mean anything and staring at our master map. But you are correct, it may have nothing to do with our project."

Chapter
36

Abbey and I were up at the airfield before dawn. We each had a duffle bag and a small backpack. Major Campbell sent the divers and support crew north by truck yesterday with all their gear. They would meet us at the small airfield in the city of Bagua Grande.

We put our bags in the Cessna Skymaster. I told Abbey to take the co-pilot's seat for a better view. I had the pleasure of my full-day flying tour with the Major several weeks ago. I wanted Abbey to have a chance to enjoy the view. It was about 370 miles to Bagua Grande. We should arrive about 8:30AM.

Major Campbell flew straight to Bagua Grande. There was no detour to try to see the site from the air. At this point we didn't know exactly where it was. Bagua Grande's urban area is located on a hillside by the river Utcubamba at an elevation just over 1,400 feet. The population is about 47,000. We planned to stay in Bagua Grande because it was less than an hour's drive to the sanctuary.

Major Campbell landed and taxied over to the tie-down area. Three vehicles were waiting for us. It looked like the Major had planned for bad roads. For all I knew there might not be roads. There were two off-road Range Rover Defenders. They had big knobby tires and the mufflers that went up above the cab for crossing streams. The truck looked like a military style truck with two back axles and two tires on each side of each back axle. Like the one they called the "deuce and a half" in World War II movies. It had a crane-type boom fitted to the bed of the truck. All three vehicles had winches on both the front and back bumpers. If we couldn't get there in these then I guessed we walked.

David Fine from the ranch's security team seemed to be in charge. There were four others: two divers and two support people.

David said, "Good morning. I hope you had a smooth flight. I reserved rooms for all of us but I thought we could go straight out to the sanctuary and meet with the officials. It's about an hour drive."

We put our bags in the back of one of the Range Rovers and got in. David drove the three of us; two others went in the truck and the other two in the other Range Rover. The road was OK for about 20 miles and then became a rutted dirt road. The Major had picked the right vehicles.

This part of Amazonas Region consists of areas covered by rainforests and mountain ranges. It extends up to the north to the border of Ecuador. The Utcubamba River originates in the highlands of the central mountain range. It flows north before joining the Marañón River. This semitropical valley of the river was the heartland of the Chachapoyas culture. Important factors to its geography are the big valleys and plains that connect with the routes to the Pacific coast. It was beautiful country.

We arrived at the ranger station for the sanctuary and parked outside of the main building. Major Campbell and I went in and the rest of the group got out to stretch their legs. The Captain of the ranger station greeted us. He seemed happy to turn this site over to us under the authority of the Department of Antiquities. His primary job was to keep poachers and illegal loggers out of the sanctuary.

The Captain showed us on a wall map of the park where the cave-in was. It looked like it was only 30 or 40 yards off a dirt jeep track. That is why the rangers spotted it so quickly. He assigned a man to show us the way and gave us passes for each of the vehicles.

The ranger led the way in his jeep. We drove for another 45 minutes but only at about 15 mph. When he stopped the spot was clearly visible from the dirt road. It was a 25-yard circle of no vegetation. Once we got out we could see the hole.

The first thing the Major did was used his sat-phone to determine the exact coordinates of the site. Next one of his men started unpacking the Scout, that small vertical takeoff and landing quadcopter I had played with at the airfield. The plan was to film the cave-in and the area around it first.

Then I would walk the perimeter with a USRadar 100 series ground-penetrating radar unit. It is small, light, and offers the greatest realistic penetration that GPR can provide. It is used for locating targets up to 100-feet deep. We wanted to try to determine the depth of the ground around the hole. No one wanted to fall in if another thin piece of the cavern's roof caved in.

The Major flew his little quadcopter around the perimeter of the site. Then he flew it back and forth across the site. He hovered it above the center of the cave-in filming but didn't attempt to go in the hole.

I dragged the GPR unit around the perimeter of the site. It had two wheels and I was able to bump it along the rough path the rangers made when they walked around the site. I figured if the ground held when they walked around it should hold me.

Abbey took pictures from a variety of angles. We then decided to go to our hotel and analyze the data and develop a plan for tomorrow's work.

Back in Bagua Grande David Fine had booked rooms at a local inn. It was a large Spanish style house with a shaded courtyard. The owner gave us the first-floor library to use as a workroom. We took our bags to our rooms while the owner's wife prepared us lunch.

After lunch we set up in the library. Abbey started analyzing data from the ground-penetrating radar. Major Campbell and I watched the video on his laptop. The divers and their two support men were out on the truck unpacking and assembling the equipment.

Abbey overlaid the GPR data on to a photo taken by the quadcopter about 200 feet above the site. The cave-in hole was in the center and the photo went to about 200 feet from the edges of the hole in all directions.

What it looked like was the cavern ran east to west. The GPR showed that the wall on the north and south sides fell off sharply. That meant that just a few yards back of the hole to the north or south we would be on solid rock.

Since I had gone in a circle around the hole we didn't have any data on the size of the cavern in the east-west direction. I would go both east and west with the GPR unit tomorrow.

Major Campbell started talking with two of his men about setting up the truck on the south side of the hole. I reviewed the geological and hydrogeological information Mike had put together in more detail now that I had the specific location of the site. Abbey studied the video the Major and I had already watched.

I said to Abbey, "If I remember correctly what the Major told me about the Scout, it has a range of almost two miles if you maintain line of sight. We should ask him to film as large an area around the site as he can tomorrow. It would be a lot easier than trying to walk it."

Abbey said, "We just need to get the operator up high enough to maintain line of sight for a reasonable distance."

That evening everyone went to a local restaurant for dinner. We planned to make it an early evening. We would leave early in the morning because it would take over an hour and a half to get all the way to the site. I asked about using the quadcopter to video the area around the sight.

David Fine, who it seemed liked any chance he could get to play with it, said, "Great idea and the line of sight issue you mentioned shouldn't be a problem. We have a man-basket for the boom arm on the truck. I'll just get in that and they can raise me up to its full extent. From there I can fly the quadcopter in circles of increasing size around the site videoing the terrain. We can do that first. Also we have arranged for the big Heron drone to do a test run tomorrow over the site. It will give Dr. Frank a real company project to run her tests on. How does that sound?"

I said, "That sounds great."

Abbey asked, "I saw quite a bit of farmland as we came in. What do they farm here?"

The Major answered, "The agricultural production is mostly rice, corn, and coffee. The rice is said to be of especially of high quality. The industry of the area is largely related to supporting agriculture. There is also coca. Everywhere in South America where the climate is right for it they grow coca. There is just too much money in it for poor people to resist."

We had an enjoyable dinner discussing a variety of topics and then called it a night.

OpenROV (Note 4)

Chapter
37

We left the inn shortly after 7:00AM. They made us breakfast and packed box lunches so we could spend the entire day working at the site.

Once we arrived the Major and David walked the ground looking for a good spot to position the truck on the south side of the cave-in. They wanted to be close enough so the boom arm reached well out over the hole.

When they found the spot they cut back some of the brush and slowly backed the truck into position. I hadn't noticed them before but the truck had jack-down legs on each side to stabilize it, like you see on utility trucks in the States.

The Major came over and stood next to me, watching his men position the truck.

I said, "After the filming with the quadcopter what is next?"

He said, "I have another great piece of equipment to show you."

We walked to the back of one of the Rovers. The Major pulled out a suitcase, opened it, and said, "It is a remotely operated underwater vehicle, commonly called a ROV. Usually these things cost between $10,000 and several million dollars. This one is called OpenROV. An open source group developed it and you can buy it in a kit form for $850.

"OpenROV is a remotely operated mini-submarine that weighs about 5.5 pounds and is about 7 inches by 8 inches by 12 inches, and it is powered by eight C-size batteries. Its components are all common materials. The OpenROV is controlled from a laptop computer connected to the submarine with a cable. It is equipped with on-board LED lights and a video camera. We have about 325 feet of cable so it should be plenty to give us a good look around. If it looks safe we will send the divers in.

"Here's the interesting part, the project was started in a garage in Cupertino by a few guys who wanted to explore the deep water of a cave in northern California that legend had it contained stolen gold. According to legend, renegade Native Americans stole over 100 pounds of gold nuggets from miners in the 1800s. While being chased the Indians dumped the gold in the deep water of the Hall City cave. They were soon caught and hanged so they never went back for the gold.

"Of course they never found any gold but they invented this great inexpensive ROV that has all sorts of uses."

The Major did like his toys. But it made sense. It was a cheap and easy way to check out the cave to make sure it was safe for divers.

David was done videoing the area with the quadcopter. They lowered the boom and removed the man-basket. In its place they fixed a pulley system to the end of the boom. Major Campbell brought over the OpenROV unit. They hooked the mini submarine to the pulley and positioned the boom arm over the cave-in hole. One of the support team had the control computer. He sat on the back of the truck and had headphones on. He was apparently going to record what he was doing as the sub videoed.

He began, "I'm lowering the OpenROV into the cavern. With 28 feet of cable out I've made contact with the water. That puts the water surface at about 20 feet below ground level. I'm lowering to a depth of three feet below the surface. The light and video are on. The visibility is good and the water seems basically clear. There is a current running in a west to east direction."

First he went down in place. He reported on the visibility and current at intervals of 10 feet. He found the bottom about 40 feet below the surface of the water. Then he came to the surface and went north until he found the wall of the cavern. He again went down in intervals of 10 feet. At each depth he estimated the distance to the north wall. He repeated the process with the south wall.

When he started west he had to power against the current. On the surface he found the wall about 60 feet from his starting point. At a depth of 10 feet the west wall was 130 feet from the starting point. At 20 feet deep he couldn't find the west wall. It appeared to be an underground river that was flowing from the west into the cavern.

Finally he repeated the procedure to the east. At the water surface it was only 40 feet to the east wall. This wall actually sloped back into the cavern slightly and was just 25 feet from the starting point at the bottom. This is where the bones were piled up. He videoed up and down along the bones and then brought the OpenROV back up and out.

We were all eager to watch the video. My desire was to skip right to the sections showing the bones. But I knew we needed to watch the whole video. The cavern ran west to east. It seemed to vary from 30 to almost a hundred feet wide in the north-south direction. It was over 300 feet from the east wall to the west. We didn't know how much farther it went because that was as much cable as the OpenROV had.

This was all consistent with the geography and hydro geography I had been studying. We were on the east slope of the Andes. Everything flowed generally west to east and ended up eventually in the Amazon River flowing to the Atlantic Ocean.

When we got to the part of the video showing the bones I was surprised. There were lots of bones. A great big pile and it was hard to tell how deep the pile was but there were bones on top of bones. To me they all looked like human bones. There were at least a lot of human bones. We wouldn't know if there were also animal as well until we did a detailed examination.

I said as the video ended, "There has to be the bones of hundreds of people in that pile. The only way I see for the bones to get there is that the current carried them from someplace upstream. But the water must be getting out somehow."

The operator of the OpenROV said, "The wall on the east end is made up of boulders. It is like a big sieve. The water flows through and the bones get trapped. I could feel the current still at the face of the east wall."

I said to Major Campbell, "Is it safe enough for the divers to go in?"

He said, "I think so," then looked to his divers for confirmation and they agreed.

I said, "I'd like to run the magnetometer to the west to see what we can learn about where the tunnel goes. It looks very overgrown. I'm not sure if we will get accurate readings."

Abbey said, "Let's walk up that way and see what is there. Then maybe we can decide how best to proceed."

Major Campbell told his team to set up for the dive. The divers would wear helmets fitted with video cameras. They would also do voice recordings of what they saw as they went along. For the first dive they wouldn't touch or disturb anything.

Major Campbell said, "Let's take a walk."

He led the way. It wasn't that hard to walk but wheeling the magnetometer would have been difficult. We headed west up the slope generally along the line we thought the cavern ran. We had walked about half a mile over lightly wooded terrain when we came to a clearing. We were about 20 yards into the clearing when I heard automatic gunfire. Major Campbell slammed backwards into me and we both went down. I saw stars and I might have blacked out for a few seconds. Our legs were tangled and covered in blood. I wasn't sure if Major Campbell, I, or both of us were hit. I didn't feel any pain.

I heard a tap-tap sound. I looked up Abbey was flat on the ground in a military firing position. She had Major Campbell's Sig-Sauer pistol in her hand. One of three men running at us with automatic rifles went down. She moved the pistol slightly. Tap-tap the second gunman went down and the third dove for the ground. Abbey fired a shot in his direction. She then aimed the pistol to the far side of the clearing. I realized we were being shot at from the cover of the trees on that side of the clearing. She was slowly firing one shot at a time. I realized she was trying to keep them pinned in the woods.

Major Campbell shook my shoulder and said, "Give these to Abbey."

He handed me two ammunition clips for his pistol. I took them and squirmed my way towards Abbey.

I said, "I have two clips for the pistol."

Without looking my way she said, "Put them six inches to the right of my right arm."

I moved a little farther forward and set the clips down. She fired three rapid shots and the slide on the Sig-Sauer stayed open. In one swift motion she ejected the empty clip, reached across with her left hand, grabbed a fresh clip, and rammed it into the butt of the gun.

The third gunman in the clearing jumped up and started towards us. Abbey chambered a round and tap-tap. The third gunman went down. She again aimed at the far side of the clearing.

I crawled back to the Major. He was trying to get a small medical kit from his backpack. I took it and opened it.

He said, "You're hit."

I looked down and saw my left leg was bleeding. I still felt no pain.

He went on, "Put that field dressing on your leg and tape it in place."

I said, "You're in worse shape, let me help you first."

"No, you will be no good to me if you pass out. Do what I tell you, Rob."

I taped the field dressing on my leg and thought it is like what they say on the airlines. In an emergency put your oxygen mask on first and then help the others. I took out two more bandages and put one on each side of the Major's leg. Next I wound a rolled bandage around his leg and taped it all in place. Abbey was still firing one shot at a time and they were still firing back from the other side of the clearing. I wasn't sure if she was still on her second clip or the last one.

I said to the Major, "Any more ammo?"

He said, "No. I wasn't planning on a war."

From behind us I heard shooting and shouting. It was David Fine and one of the support techs. They each had an automatic rifle. I realized they were trying to make it sound like the cavalry had arrived. The tech took up a firing position next to Abbey. David took up a position on the other side of the Major.

He said, "Once the divers are out of the cavern the other three will be here. I called and there is a drug interdiction SWAT team flying in and a medevac helicopter following it. I also have the Heron drone arriving any second."

I said, "Tell me that drone is like the Predator drone and has Hellfire missiles on it."

David said, "It has no weapons but your CIA has put the fear of drones in all terrorists. I'm hoping the bad guys think it's a Predator."

As he spoke the drone flew low over the clearing and began circling the far side of the clearing. At this point the other three joined us and took up firing position. The combined fire and the drone seemed to be more than the bad guys could take. Their firing died down. Then I hear the distant sound of a helicopter. That must have done it. No more firing from the far side.

David said, "The drone has the bad guys moving away from us to the north. None seem to still be on the other side of the clearing."

One of the techs had medic training and starting tending to our legs.

Major Campbell said to David, "Go photograph the three dead guys and take a hat and put it in your pack before the chopper gets here."

One of the techs said, "Major, I'm patched though to the chopper on my phone."

He handed the phone to Major Campbell. The Major said, "Major Ian Campbell, Royal Air Force retired with Falone Advanced Technologies. I'm security director. Over."

"US DEA officer Manuel Garcia on loan to the Peruvian National Police drug enforcement unit. What is the situation?"

The Major said, "Our drone has about a dozen bad guys heading north from our position. There are three bad guys down here. We have two wounded. The clearing should be safe to land. We are at the southwest side of the clearing."

The helicopter circled in and touched down. Three men jumped out, the chopper lifted off and headed north. The two National policemen scanned the clearing and then went to the three dead bodies. The DEA agent came over to us.

He said, "Looks like a war here. How badly are you two hurt? They radioed us you were working on an archaeological site."

The Major said, "We were working on the site until they started shooting at us. Both Professor Johnson and I have leg wounds. I don't think we have any broken bones."

The DEA agent said, "It looks like you ran into one of the drug cartel's enforcement gangs. They send them over from their base in Ecuador to keep the coca farmers in line. The farmers don't usually shoot back. It must have been as much of a surprise to them as it was to you."

I didn't take much comfort in that and now my leg was starting to hurt. Abbey sat next to me, quiet, with her hand on my shoulder. We didn't say anything.

The tech medic said to the Major, "Lay back, sir. You need to have your head down."

The Major looked like he was going to say something but he smiled and put his head on the backpack the medic was using as a pillow. The Major looked as white as a ghost. He must have lost a lot of blood.

I heard the sound of another helicopter. It was the medevac chopper. One of the National policemen was talking to them on his radio. It landed in the clearing.

Then things seemed to happen in a blur. The Major and I were put on stretchers and loaded on the helicopter. Abbey was to come with us. One of the techs would drive with David and meet us at the hospital in Bagua Grande. En route David would phone in a report to the company. The other three would pack up our equipment and head back to Bagua Grande.

Both of us were on morphine drips now. Abbey had her hand on my shoulder. It was too noisy to talk in the helicopter. I saw the Major close his eyes and then I must have fallen asleep.

Chapter 38

At the hospital I received 19 stitches. My wound was relatively minor. A bullet grazed my leg causing a cut on the outside of my left leg below the hip. They gave me some pain pills and a cane. They told me to stay off it and have a doctor check it in a few days.

Abbey stayed with me. She was quiet. We didn't talk about what happened, we just focused on the process of getting treatment. David came in the room and said he had arranged for my discharge.

I said, "How is Major Campbell?"

He said, "He is sore but he should be fine. Here are some new clothes. Put them on and we can go see Major Campbell. Do you need help?"

I did need a little help with my pants. Then they put me in a wheelchair and David pushed me to Major Campbell's room. Major Campbell was propped up in bed. I was surprised to see Walter Falone sitting in the chair next to his bed. I wasn't sure how he got there so quickly. Then I realized I didn't even know what time it was. David had my watch and other belongings in a bag. Walter had one of Major Campbell's security men with him.

I said, "Ian, you look a lot better than the last time I saw you. How are you feeling?"

"I'm not feeling much, Rob, they seem to have me pretty drugged up. They tell me I have quite a hole in my leg."

I shook hands with Walter. He asked about me.

I said, "Just a cut on my leg. They put in a few stitches and I'll be fine in a week or so." I could tell we were trying to make light of the situation.

I guess we didn't want to think about what a close call it was.

The Major said, "Abbey, I know you told me you are from Plattsburgh, but where did you learn to shoot like that? Most of my SAS soldiers couldn't handle themselves that well."

Abbey said, "My grandfather was a Marine. He taught me stuff when I was a little girl. I never shot anyone before." Tears started streaming down her cheeks.

Walter put his hand on her shoulder and said, "You saved Rob, Ian, and yourself from certain death. I know it is hard but those were bad people and they might have killed all seven of you. Your grandfather must be quite a man."

"Yes, Mr. Falone, he is. He enlisted as a wild teenager and retired 40 years later as a Master Gunnery Sergeant. That's what my Grandmother told me. She said he had two wives, her and the Marine Corps." Then she was quiet but no longer crying.

Major Campbell said, "I'd like to meet him and thank him for saving my life. I don't think I even thanked you. As Walter said you probably saved seven lives today."

David Fine came back in the room. He said, "Looks like we have issues. I just finished talking with DEA Agent Garcia. The three bad guys were part of Gilberto José Rodríguez's drug cartel in Ecuador. The Rodríguez cartel works as an affiliate of the Colombian Norte del Valle Cartel, or North Valley Cartel. As Agent Garcia explained it, the Colombian North Valley Cartel is the big dog and they sort of franchise out territories to minor cartels that control certain areas and feed product to the Colombians. It turns out one of the dead men is Mr. Rodríguez's son, another is his nephew, and the third is a low level sicario or hit man. Garcia feels Mr. Rodríguez will be coming after us. Not only was family killed but even more important, he can't look weak to either his people or the Colombians. There is always someone looking to take his place."

Major Campbell said, "It will take them a little time to figure out what happened and who we are. But we should get to the ranch as soon as we can. It would be best if we drove back tonight. It would also be smart to let as few people as possible know where we are and where we are going."

David said, "I'll go arrange for an ambulance to take the Major. Our man with medic training can ride with him. I'll leave two men with the truck and the equipment. They can pack up and drive back tomorrow. We'll take the two Rovers. That leaves the two planes."

Walter said, "Both the people with me are pilots. They can each fly a plane back in the morning."

The Major said, "Walter, I'd like two men in each Rover and one man in the ambulance with me. Let's have one pilot go back with us and only leave one man with the truck. Tomorrow morning the other pilot can fly to the ranch and pick up another pilot and a second driver for the truck."

Walter agreed. Abbey looked worried and it seemed to me the Major expected trouble.

There was a commotion in the hall and a captain of the National Police came in with his chest puffed out and an air of self-importance. His demeanor quickly changed when he saw Walter. I thought we might have been in for a different kind of interview if Walter wasn't here. The captain's goal now seemed to make sure any report Walter gave to his superiors was positive.

The police captain said, "It is very nice to see you, Mr. Falone. I'm very sorry to hear about this unfortunate incident with the Ecuadorian drug gang. I came personally to check on your people and offer my assistance."

Walter said, "We greatly appreciate that, Captain. Were your men able to catch the rest of the gang?"

"No, Mr. Falone. They scattered and went to ground. They blend in well and know which farmers will hide them. We will keep looking of course."

Walter said, "If it is alright with you, my men will give the police a full report tomorrow and be available for interviews at that point. It has been a hard day for these people and I would like to focus on their medical needs now."

"That will be fine, Mr. Falone."

Walter said, "Mr. Fine here will contact you no later than noon tomorrow."

David said he would and took the captain's card. The captain left. I thought that was strange. I looked at the Major.

He said, "It is a fifty-fifty chance the Captain is in the pay of the cartel. It would be best to be back at the ranch and handle things from there."

I said, "Even the National Police?"

The Major said, "A few years ago Vladimiro Montesinos, the long-standing head of Peru's intelligence service under President Alberto Fujimori, was secretly videoed. The videos showed him bribing an elected congressman to leave the opposition and join the Fujimorist side of Congress. The ensuing scandal caused Montesinos to flee the country and hastened the resignation of Fujimori. Subsequent investigations revealed Montesinos was involved in drug trafficking, graft, embezzlement, and gun running. It was reported that the Colombian drug cartel paid him $50,000 for each planeload of coca he let them fly out of Peru. So it is best not to fully trust anyone other than our people."

He went on, "Walter, about that report to the police. Perhaps I should be the one who shot the people. It was my pistol. I'm head of security and ex-military. It would make sense. We are all targets but no need to make Abbey a bigger target."

I said, "Wouldn't the one that got away know Abbey was shooting at them?"

"Maybe, Professor, but they were on the other side of the clearing. Lots of shooting and they may not want to admit a young woman held all of them off. The cartel will bribe someone to get a copy of the report. It will at least make it a little more confusing for them."

Walter said, "I agree. I don't want this harder for Abbey and Rob than it is already."

Major Campbell said to David, "Once you have things here arranged, call the ranch and put them on alert. Then call our Lima office and have them send at least four more men tonight. Have the two drone pilots who are not at the ranch come up tonight or tomorrow. Then tell them we will need at least a dozen more men with a full complement of skills. We are going to need shooters so bring them in from all over South America if we need to. Try not to leave any one place with no security people."

David said, "What types of equipment?"

"Well, what we used to call Defensive Pack 332 would be good."

This was SAS army speak.

David said, "I can get most of it but I don't think we have man portable antitank or antiaircraft missiles."

The Major said, "I don't see them using tanks. Antiaircraft might be nice, but I don't think they will use a helicopter. It is too easy to track."

This sounded like the Major expected them to send an army.

I said, "Would it be better for Abbey and I to go back to Ithaca?"

The Major said, "There is no way to protect you there. A university campus is about the most open place there is. The Rodríguez cartel would just hire gang members in the US to kill you."

Walter said, "This should be a temporary situation. We need to have them capture or kill Rodríguez. As long as he is in power he will believe he has to come for us. We will work with the Peruvians, the Ecuadorians, and the US State Department to get everyone going after him."

I said, "How long will that take?"

Walter didn't look hopeful and said, "It could take a while."

I said, "Maybe we could pay the Colombians to whack Rodríguez."

Everyone just looked at me. I said, "Or maybe I've seen too many movies." I tried to smile.

Walter said, "Give me the information from Agent Garcia's card. I'm going to call the embassy and talk to the Ambassador in the morning. I want him to arrange for Agent Garcia and whoever else he needs to come to the ranch and give us a full briefing on this cartel. I want to know what we are dealing with here. I also want the Ambassador to start the ball rolling. I don't want my people under threat any longer than they must be."

David gave Walter the card and went to organize our vehicles. They brought in a stretcher and the doctor advised us against taking the Major out of the hospital for a few days. Walter said he had arranged to have a doctor and two nurses at the ranch for the next few weeks. The doctor would be there when we arrived and look after both of us.

Abbey looked a little better. But I was worried about her. Shooting three people had to affect a young woman. I had to remember she didn't turn 23 for another five days.

She looked at me, smiled, and said, "What do you think of Texas now, Prof?"

We left the hospital. The ambulance was parked between the two Range Rovers. We put the major in the ambulance. Abbey and I got in the back of one Range Rover and Walter got in the back of the other. David and one of the security men rode with Walter in the lead Rover. The other two security men were in our Rover with us and we drove behind the ambulance. A member of the National Security Police spoke into his cell phone as we drove out.

Chapter 39

We arrived at the ranch late at night without any problems. The gate was manned and I assumed security was tightened all around the ranch.

Despite the late arrival I was up early Thursday morning. I was glad to see Abbey heading out for a run when I started making coffee. I couldn't swim until after the stitches were out.

I said, "I'll make you breakfast when you get back."

"Great, Prof. I'm starving. How is your leg?"

"It's stiff and a little sore. The pills work well but I can sure tell when it's time for the next dose."

When I went out by the pool to drink my coffee, I heard the plane coming in from Bagua Grande. After a bit I went to the common kitchen to make breakfast. As always the kitchen was well stocked. I decided on tomato and cheese omelets with toast from the great homemade bread and fresh fruit. That was about as fancy as my cooking gets.

Abbey ate everything. I realized we hadn't eaten much yesterday. The day was a blur.

Abbey said, "What happens now?"

I said, "After breakfast we go talk to the Major and then we figure out how to proceed. I really want to find out about all those bones in the cavern."

"I agree, Prof. This trouble with the drug gang can't stop our project. We have all worked too hard. We can be careful and keep working."

I sent a text to Major Campbell to see how he was and if we could meet with him. He texted right back and said to come over to the security office when we were done with breakfast.

We walked into the security office area. It was a busy place. There were several people I hadn't seen before installing additional monitors on the wall. It appeared they were adding a lot more security cameras.

I knocked on the open door to the Major's office. He was in there with David Fine. He was in a wheelchair with his wounded leg up on a leg rest attached to the wheelchair.

I said, "How are you doing?"

He said, "It hurts no matter what I do so I decided it's better to be working than just sitting around. How are you two?"

Abbey said she was fine. I told him I thought I could beat him in squash today if he wanted to play.

Then I said, "What happens now? We want to keep working the site. When the truck gets back we will review all the videos and talk to the divers."

He said, "We will have a better idea in a day or two. For now do all your work on the ranch. We will decide who goes back to the site in a day or two. My thinking now is to send a totally new crew and let that be widely known. There should be no reason for the Rodríguez cartel to bother them. For now go through everything we videoed and gathered from the site. Then develop a plan of what you want done next. At this point assume you two will be directing the work from here. How does that sound?"

It sounded like a plan to keep us busy and out of the Major's hair for a while. I said, "That sounds fine to us. When do we get an update on the situation?"

He said, "Walter wants to meet with me this afternoon. I suspect he is working the phones now, calling the Ambassador, the State Department, Peruvian and Ecuadorian officials, and others. He will not let this stand. He wants it resolved. I have a lot to do. How about join me for dinner about 7:00 tonight and I fill you in?"

We agreed and headed to our workroom. On our way out of the security office one of the men said, "We put a copy of the videos from yesterday in your office. The pilot dropped it off this morning when he landed to pick up our other folks that will be getting the other plane and the truck."

I thanked him. We grabbed the package off my desk and headed to the workroom. It had a memory stick in it.

As soon as we arrived the team started assembling in the room. I sat. My leg was sore from the walk. Elizabeth gave Abbey a hug. Everyone sort of hung back not knowing what to say. It appeared they all heard the story of what happened yesterday.

Abbey finally said, "Hey, we're OK. Let's get some work done."

Mitch said to Abbey, "You rock, girl." Then she said to me, "Give me that stick. Let's see what this boneyard looks like."

The technician who stayed with the truck put the videos on the stick in the order we took them, starting with our first day's quadcopter flight. Then it had our magnetometer readings overlaying the still photo of the site. Next was the second day's quadcopter flight around the site.

Abbey and I hadn't seen this yet. It gave us a feel for the terrain around the site out to about 300 yards in each direction. The OpenROV video was next. We had seen it on site right after it was videoed but now I was more attentive to the details. The cavern was long and thin with the underground river running west to east. The east wall was made up of large boulders. This formed the sieve that trapped the bones and let the water keep running through.

Again I was struck by how many bones there were. From what you could see this had to be the bones from hundreds of bodies. We couldn't tell how deep the pile was. Next came the divers' video. Not much help there. They just got into the cavern when the shooting started and they had to be extracted.

I said, "I would like to outline how to proceed with our investigation of the cavern and then I'd like your help refining the outline and developing the plan. First I would like a couple of you to research what type of remotely operated underwater vehicle we need to go upstream in the cavern. The little OpenROV only went a couple hundred feet up. We need something much more sophisticated. I'm sure if we specify what we need, they can find it in Houston.

"Next we need a plan for examining and sampling the bone pile with the least possible disturbance to it. Then it would be nice to have a detailed aerial mapping of the area around the site, especially upstream to the west. We have video from the quadcopter but I would like a scale map with coordinates and elevations. Finally a more detailed understanding of the hydrogeology of the area around the site would be helpful. What else?"

Mitch said, "We could look into burial practices past and present in that area. There are pockets of local customs that can be quite different from the general practices."

I said, "Great idea. Other thoughts?"

Elizabeth said, "I assume this means you feel strongly enough about this site to suspend work looking for additional sites."

I said, "Yes, I want to focus on this site now. But not because of how strong the evidence is for this site. It is more that everything else we have is so weak. Please decide who will do what. Let's skip our Friday meeting tomorrow and meet on Monday. Unfortunately with the security situation up in the air we will all be staying at the ranch for a few days."

I went back to my office. I knew this group would cover in detail everything I outlined without any more direction from me. Again I thought it was remarkable how well this group worked together. They seemed like very different types of people, at least on the surface. One of Walter Falone's gifts was picking good people. Well, he wasn't perfect, he did make Dr. Stone Chief Technology Officer.

There was an email from Major Campbell saying Agent Garcia and others would be arriving early Friday afternoon to give us a briefing on what they knew about the Rodríguez cartel. Mr. Falone would like Abbey and me to attend the meeting. It was scheduled for 1:30PM in the security office conference room. He cancelled our dinner for tonight and said we could cover everything tomorrow after the meeting with Agent Garcia.

After working a while I went back to the guesthouse. My leg was sore. Major Campbell's leg must be killing him. When I took enough pain pills to make it better I was sleepy. So I spent the rest of the day resting and reading. It was what the doctor said to do.

In the middle of the afternoon the doctor Walter brought to the ranch came over to the guesthouse with one of the nurses to check on me. They changed the bandage and cleaned around the stitches. The doctor said the wound looked good but to stay off my leg as much as I could.

I said, "How is Major Campbell doing?"

He said, "Frankly he's doing too much. He won't stay in bed so I set up a wheelchair for him. I had to redress his wound twice today. He is a very strong man but he lost a large chunk of flesh on his leg. It will take quite a while to heal and I don't want it to become infected. Since he won't stay in bed, I will have to keep following him around cleaning and redressing the leg. He seems better at giving orders than taking them."

I thanked the two of them for their help. They said they would be back in the morning to check on me again.

Abbey came back about 6:00PM. She said, "How is the leg?"

I said, "It is sore but the doctor was here and he said it's doing well. He told me to stay off it as much as I could for a few days. Once the stitches come out I can start swimming again. Major Campbell cancelled our diner tonight and that is fine by me. How did the afternoon's work go?"

"Everybody is taking a part and diving in. We should have a plan together by Monday. Since Major Campbell cancelled I think I'll go have dinner with some of the team. Do you want to join us?"

"No, I'll just have them send something in and go to bed early."

Chapter
40

In the morning I decided to work from the guesthouse. Midmorning one of the ranch workers drove over in a golf cart. He set the charger up and plugged it in next to the guesthouse. He said I should use it as long as I needed it.

I was pleased. I was starting to go a little stir crazy and walking hurt. As soon as he left I got in the cart and went for a drive. The first thing I noticed was a crew putting up more security cameras. I drove to the airfield. It was busy and the Britten-Norman Defender had just landed. Six men got off and started unloading crates of equipment. All the men looked very fit. These were more of Major Campbell's security force arriving.

I drove my golf cart into the hangar. Peter Frank was working on the big Heron drone. I pulled the golf cart over and said, "Hello."

Peter said, "We should have your detailed mapping done this afternoon as long as we don't have bad weather."

I said, "That is fast. I only suggested it yesterday."

"Ned heard about it from Fred last night. He told the Major this morning and the Major said get it done ASAP. Once the mapping is done I'm going to change out the equipment in the drone and install defensive surveillance equipment. Major Campbell plans to use the drone to provide 24-hour-a-day surveillance of the ranch."

"How is he going to do that with one drone?"

"The Heron has a flight endurance of 52 hours. When we land it to refuel and service it we will launch one or more of the ScanEagle drones.

They can't do everything the Heron can but they will give us basic coverage when the Heron is down."

We visited some more and then I left him to his work. I drove around the ranch for about 20 minutes more. Everywhere I drove there were signs of increased security. When I got back to the guesthouse the doctor was waiting for me. He changed my bandages and told me to have a nice day.

At 1:00PM Abbey came to get me. I showed her my new wheels and we drove over to the security office for our meeting. There were two black Chevy Suburbans parked there. We went in. Agent Garcia was there with two people who were with the State Department. Major Campbell was there in his wheelchair. He looked better today. He was less pale looking than yesterday. He introduced us to the men from the State Department.

Walter came in. David Fine came in behind him and closed the door. We sat around the conference table.

Walter said, "I appreciate you gentlemen coming today. As I explained to the Ambassador, I am very concerned about the safety of my employees. We need to understand as best we can the situation we are facing. Then I need to know what is being done. Perhaps you can start by telling us what you know about this drug cartel."

Agent Garcia said, "I guess I know the most about this cartel. The men were part of Gilberto José Rodríguez's drug cartel in Ecuador. It was a group who was sent over to oversee the collection and transport of coca from the Peruvian farmers back to Ecuador. Their job is also to intimidate the farmers so they stay in line. It appears there were about a dozen of them. The group was led by Rodríguez's nephew who was 31 and one of Rodríguez's closest lieutenants. His 24-year-old son was also killed. The third man appears to be a low-level member."

He looked at Abbey but said to the Major, "That was nice shooting, Major. Two shots in each bad guy, both center chest just like they teach at the academy." It was his way of saying he understood the reason we put that in the police report and DEA would support the decision.

"Rodríguez was born in Ecuador. He moved to Colombia and began working for the cartels as a young man. The Northern Valley Cartel rose to prominence after the Cali Cartel and the Medellín Cartel fragmented. It was led by two brothers, Luis Enrique Calle Serna and Javier Antonio

Calle Serna. Their alias was Los Comba. The brothers were captured and delivered to us in 2012. Óscar Varela García alias Capachivo seems to now be in control of the cartel. He is a 54-year-old and known to be utterly ruthless. By the way he is no relation of mine.

"Rodríguez was sent back to Ecuador and set up to organize the peasant farmers producing coca paste in Peru and Ecuador. He was then to arrange for it to be smuggled to Colombia where the coca paste would be processed into cocaine. We are unsure of his current standing with the Colombian cartel. However we believe that he will feel obligated to avenge the death of his son and nephew. We have already received indications that he is trying to find out who was behind the killings. It shouldn't be long before his people bribe the right person and know who you are."

Walter said, "That is very interesting and in general what we thought. Now what is being done about it?"

One of the State Department officials said, "The Ambassador asked me to outline what we are doing and plan to do. First we have contacted the Peruvian and Ecuadorian governments at a high level and asked for a detailed plan of how they will step up their efforts to deal with this cartel. We have requested that the FBI put Rodríguez on their Most Wanted list and put a multimillion-dollar reward out for his capture. The Ambassador has requested that the DEA send additional agents to work with Peruvian and Ecuadorian law enforcement. Our people have put out the word that the people are United States citizens and if something happens to them the US government will respond."

I thought great, another "red line." I'm sure the drug cartels are shaking with fear.

He went on, "Finally we recommend the seven people involved in this leave the country."

Walter and Major Campbell asked several questions. Some were answered and some were not. I was having trouble deciding if we were getting real action or just lip service. The meeting ended. Walter thanked them for their help and they left.

I said, "Did we get a snow job or are they really turning up the heat and pulling out all the stops?"

Major Campbell looked at Walter. Walter nodded for him to go ahead.

He said. "I think they are making the requests they say they are making. The question is are they putting any weight behind them? It is easy for the Ambassador to call his counterparts in the two governments and ask them to do something about this drug cartel. It is much harder for him to put any teeth in the request. Especially since the US has been trying to stamp out the drug cartels for decades. We will see what the FBI and DEA do. As for the statement 'the US government will respond,' I'm afraid it is like the boy who cried wolf. Your government has ignored too many of its 'red lines' for that to mean much especially to the drug cartels."

Walter said, "I believe that is a fair assessment of the situation. As for leaving the country I believe we can protect you here far better than back at Cornell. Major Campbell is planning to stay so we will increase security to the same level whether you stay or not. In fairness to our team I believe we should ask the other members if they would like to leave. I have jobs for them in Houston and Sudbury if they don't want to stay. Professor, I would like you and Major Campbell to explain the situation to them and let them know it is completely up to them."

"Abbey, it is your birthday on Monday. I would like you and Professor Johnson to join me for dinner at 7:00PM if you would."

Abbey said, "Yes, of course. It's funny, I forgot all about it being my birthday. That would be very nice. Thank you."

He said to me, "I would like to attend your Monday meeting if you think it would be productive."

I said, "We should have a detailed plan of investigation for the cavern and its contents to present. I believe you will find it interesting. Also we will need some special equipment and I have no idea what it will cost. I'd like your approval before we proceed."

He said, "Great. I'll be there Monday. Now if you will excuse us I have things to go over with the Major and Mr. Fine."

I asked Major Campbell to come down to my office when he was done so we could talk to the team. Then we left.

Major Campbell arrived at my office about an hour later. Abbey let the team know there would be a meeting to discuss the situation with Major Campbell and me as soon as Major Campbell was free. They were all in the workroom when we came in.

I said, "First I want to make it perfectly clear that Mr. Falone said any decision you make is fine with him. He has interesting jobs for you in both Houston and Sudbury. I also feel that it is 100% up to you and I will support any decision you make. Now Major Campbell will outline what we know about the situation and what is being done."

The Major got most of the way through telling them what we had just heard when Mitch cut him off and said, "There is no F'ing way I'm being run off this project and the ranch by a bunch of scum ball drug traffickers. Besides I spent weeks in the monastery. I figure God owes me."

Fred and Ned both shouted out, "Right on, we are staying too."

Elizabeth said, "You should listen to what Major Campbell has to say. He wasn't finished."

Mitch said, "So you are ratting out?"

Elizabeth shouted back, "I'm not leaving! But it's rude to cut off Major Campbell when he is explaining something important."

Mitch shot back, "I'm just saving him time. He has other important things to do. By the way, Major, how is your leg doing?"

"It hurts, Mitch. But thank you for asking."

I said, "OK, I don't want an answer from anyone now. I don't want an answer until Sunday. Does anyone have a question for Major Campbell?"

Ned said, "Where is the hat?"

At first Major Campbell looked like he was going to get mad, then he smiled and said, "It is back with its owner."

I said, "OK, I'll bite. What hat?"

The Major said, "Remember back in the clearing when I had David photograph the dead men? I asked him to grab one of their hats and put it in his pack. I was thinking of the trick Ned here pulled on the people in Houston. I asked him to make up a memory stick. They took it back with them when the pilot picked up our other two people Thursday morning. I had them put the memory stick in the headband and drop it in the clearing. The police had already removed the bodies. I'm assuming Rodríguez will send people to look around the site and find it. We know they will be coming to find out what happened."

I said, "Even if they find the hat there is no guarantee they will plug the memory stick into their computer or that it will be a computer that belongs to someone high up in the organization."

The Major said, "I think because Rodríguez's son and nephew were killed his men will take it right back to the boss. With any luck the hat belonged to his son or nephew."

I said, "I can see why they would be curious but won't they be suspicious as well?"

Ned said, "Not when they see it. I loaded it with first-class porn. Just what you would expect to find in the hat of a hot-headed young man. If they do open it, we will not only be able to listen to what is being said but we can also read all their email. However I suspect they are careful about emails and the web given what the NSA can do."

I said, "I have found you never know what ends up helping so the more info the better.

"Any more questions? On Sunday please see me individually and let me know what you would like to do. Alright I managed to not interfere with happy hour."

Major Campbell and I left. He was wheeling his wheelchair and I was using my cane.

I said, "You could have Peter Frank put a motor on that."

"Rob, it is the only exercise I get. Let's get a drink. I know we shouldn't drink while taking pain pills, but let's have one beer and then I'm going to bed early. It will be a busy weekend."

We had a beer and a light dinner. I was in bed and asleep before 8:00.

Saturday I took a drive around the ranch in the golf cart. I found I enjoyed riding out in the fresh air. I had been feeling cooped up because I couldn't walk far on my leg. As I drove I saw signs of increased security. No chain-link fences. It was electronic surveillance mostly. The drone was high enough overhead that you didn't hear it. I noticed that there were several new rooftop guard stations. They weren't manned but they were prepared. There were new people I hadn't seen before. Everything was orderly and calm. People were going about their business.

On Sunday I went to my office so the team members could let me know what they wanted to do. Elizabeth came first. She said she would stay and continue to refine her program whenever she wasn't needed for something else. Sadako said she wanted to stay but would like to work with Dr. Frank as much as I could spare her. She felt she wasn't learning anything more from the study of the quipu. Dr. Dona, as she called her, told her she would like her help if that would be OK with me. I told her to plan to work with Dr. Frank full time and I would let her know when I needed her help.

Harrison said he was happy to stay but there didn't seem to be much need for a meteorologist. If a job were available in Houston or Sudbury where he could use his training he would prefer that, if I didn't mind. I told him I would check and have personnel get in touch with him. He could decide once he knew what was available.

Mike and Fred said they wanted to stay. Mitch and Ned never came to see me. I guess they figured they had clearly given me their answer the other day.

Bradford Wheler

Chapter
41

Monday morning at 9:59AM I hobbled into the workroom and wrote on the whiteboard:

THE REJECT TEAM: PROJECT "THE INCA'S DEATH CAVE." WEEK 14 DAY 1

Walter was already there visiting with the team members.

I said, "OK, let's see what we have for a plan of investigation for our cavern."

Fred said, "I'll start. Thanks to Ned telling the Major about the aerial mapping we wanted done, it is almost done. Peter Frank installed the camera equipment Friday and they ran the drone flight Saturday. The images are being processed in Houston and in a day or two we should have an extremely high-resolution, scale mapping of the entire area. When we get it I'll start looking for the hole where they dumped in the bones."

Next Mike gave his report. "The OpenROV was only able to go a couple of hundred feet upstream in the cavern. I'm assuming we don't want to send divers up the cavern until we know more about what is up there. That means we have to use a remotely operated vehicle with a longer cable or an autonomous underwater vehicle.

"I started by looking at ROVs with a longer cable that are commercially available. There is a company in Pottstown PA, VideoRay, that is the world's largest producer of underwater ROVs and the global leader in MicroROV technology. They have manufactured more than 2,500 VideoRay

ROVs. So we should be able to rent one. Their longest standard cable is 1,000 feet. But we may be able to add cable and increase that distance. Even with the standard cable we can go almost 800 more feet upstream than we did with the OpenROV.

"Another alternative would be the autonomous underwater vehicle. These are more expensive and usually used in open water. They are pre-programed with a route and turned loose. I'm not sure how we would pro-gram it for unknown twists and turns the cavern might make. If we go with an AUV perhaps Elizabeth can help me with a decision-making program to handle whatever the AUV encounters.

"My third idea is to see if we can modify the controls of the OpenROV to be able to be operated by divers under water. They could the send the OpenROV ahead of them, as they go up the cavern, checking to make sure it is safe."

Walter said, "It is easy to rent a VideoRay ROV in Houston. It could be here in a few days. Ask Major Campbell to arrange it. I also like the idea of modifying the controls on the OpenROV to be operated by a diver. See if Peter Frank can do that. He is a genius when it comes to customizing equipment. Let's hold off on the AUV for now."

Abbey went next. "The first thing we have to do is to complete the div-ers' survey and videoing of the cavern. We need a topographical survey and a site plan showing the location of bones and other items of interest. In this case the simplest way is for the divers to carry out the three-dimensional survey using depth gauges and tape measures. We should also do an envi-ronmental assessment of sites to determine the water chemistry, dynamic properties, and the natural organisms present.

"Once that is done we need bone samples from various locations in the pile. We will make a 3D map of where the samples should be taken. There will need to be a variety of different bones sampled in each location. Skulls will be the most useful. Teeth can tell you a lot about the age, diet, and health of the individual before death. In addition to the physical exam-ination of the bone we will do mass spectrometry and DNA analysis. I will provide the protocols for each work item.

"Based on what we find we will decide how to proceed. If Professor Johnson and I won't be at the site we should have a trained underwater field archaeologist as part of the dive team."

I said, "Mitch, you're on."

She said, "I plan to research the area to see if there is any history of water hole burials in the region. Local customs vary greatly and perhaps we will find something of interest. I will let you know. End of my report."

Walter said, "Excellent, please proceed as quickly as you can. Major Campbell can arrange for the divers. They should be able to start the videoing and the surveying of the cavern before the equipment to explore upstream arrives. Professor Johnson, what are your thoughts?"

I said, "I agree that the team has done a great job. I'm anxious to see what the next round of research in the cavern produces. In studying the video we have had several thoughts. First, as we have said, there are a lot of human bones. Second, from what I can see there are no jewelry or clothing fragments visible. Most burial sites we see in Peru the dead are buried with adornments of some sort. I will be interested to see what the environmental conditions are in the cavern water. It is hard to tell from the video but I believe you can see marine life. It looks like some type of small crustaceans, perhaps krill or shrimp. Both are found in the water of many underground caves and caverns.

"I'm starting with the assumption that bodies were put into this underground river somewhere upstream. They were carried down here and decomposed where we see the pile of bones. If bones had been introduced upstream I don't believe the current would have carried them all to one place. Since we see no hair or flesh I assume the bones have been there a while. Carbon dating will tell us that. Finally, if I can't be at the site when the work is being done, I would like to have a real-time audio and video link to help oversee the work."

Walter said, "Interesting, Professor. I'm also most interested in what we will discover in the next few weeks. Thank you again for all your hard work. I look forward to our next meeting."

Walter left and we spent the next hour deciding who would do what. I was hopeful that Major Campbell could schedule the divers later this week. I decided to drive the golf cart up to the airfield to talk to Peter Frank.

I found him at the workbench in the hangar. He told me he would have no trouble rigging the controls of the OpenROV in a Plexiglas box that the divers can operate underwater. It could be ready in a few days. I decided to tell Major Campbell to hold off on renting and flying in a VideoRay ROV from Houston.

After that I decided to go to the guesthouse and get off my leg for a while before we joined Walter for Abbey's birthday dinner. It was nice of him to invite us. At ten of seven we drove the golf cart over to the main ranch house. Mrs. Lopez opened the door and wished Abbey a happy birthday. Once again I thought she is just turning 23. We followed Mrs. Lopez to a double door. She opened it.

"SURPRISE! HAPPY BIRTHDAY!!"

I stood there with my mouth open. There were at least two dozen people in the room. It seemed to be everyone we had worked with at Falone Advanced Technologies.

Then Abbey cried out, "Mom, Dad!" She ran over to them and was trying to hug them both at the same time. Both mother and daughter were talking at once. Finally she stepped back and said, "Wow. Thank you, everyone. I guess you can tell I was surprised."

She looked over towards a table where Major Campbell had pulled up his wheelchair.

She rushed over. "Grandpa, Grandpa, you came too." More hugs and tears.

I said hello to Abbey's parents and then went over to the side of the room where Walter was standing.

I said, "Walter, this is very special and extremely thoughtful of you."

He smiled but said nothing. I greeted various people and then made my way over to the table where Abbey's grandfather and Major Campbell were sitting. I'd only met her grandfather once at Abbey's undergraduate graduation.

I sat with them. My leg was sore. I said, "Nice to see you again, Mr. Summers. Well, you were successful in surprising us."

He said, "Major Campbell was giving me a detailed account of your encounter with the drug gang. I suggest we not go into details of the event with Abbey's mother. She worries enough as it is."

Major Campbell said, "Abbey told us you were a gunnery sergeant in the USMC but I had SAS men who couldn't have handled that situation half as well as she did. She saved our lives and perhaps the lives of the other four on our team."

He said, "Well, as Professor Johnson can tell you, Abbey is quite an exceptional young woman. When I retired from the Marines my wife and I decided to move to Plattsburgh to be near our son, daughter-in-law, and Abbey. We looked forward to retirement together. Unfortunately my wife contracted cancer. She was dead in less than two years. Abbey's parents both worked so Abbey would stay with us after school. Abbey was wonderful with my wife. When she arrived my wife would just brighten up no matter how much pain she was in. Abbey would read to her and tell her about her day at school. Abbey was only about nine but she could read any adult book. As a matter of fact I can't remember a time when Abbey couldn't read. I think she could read before she could walk.

"When my wife passed it was my job to watch Abbey. I taught her to play chess. But in about two months she could beat me in 10 minutes. She was so quick at learning everything. So I started teaching her the only thing I really knew well, how to be a Marine. A big part of my career was in training. For a number of years I helped train the Corps' elite Force Recon units. The ones the media like to call 'the tip of the spear.' In all my years training I had few if any who learned as fast as Abbey.

"In the winter we would go to the shop of a friend of mine who is a gunsmith. Abbey would help us repair all sorts of small arms. We took apart every gun in his shop, then cleaned and reassembled it. Abbey could take apart and reassemble almost any gun blindfolded. We shot at the range together. She couldn't seem to learn enough. By the time she was 15 and able to be on her own after school, I think she knew more about being a Marine than I did. I was still down the street to drive places or help with anything she needed. But by then she had other interests and activities. She graduated at 16 and went off to Cornell. Those years with Abbey were the best transition I could have had after losing my wife."

I thought, I knew her grandfather was a Marine but I didn't know any of this.

Major Campbell extended his hand and said, "Gunny Sergeant Summers, I believe I also have you to thank for saving my life."

The two of them started talking about the places they had both served.

I got up to go visit with others. I wanted to talk to Dona Frank about her work with Sadako.

I said, "Good evening, Dona. This was quite a surprise. It seems everyone we know is here. I understand you have work for Sadako?"

She said, "I'd love to have her working with me if you can spare her. She seems very interested in what I'm doing and it should help advance her career."

"Yes, she can work with you as much as you want. I believe she has found out all we are going find in the quipus. She could write an interesting paper about her work if she wants to."

"I believe she might at some point. Now I believe a change of work might be the best thing for her."

"It may be more homesickness than anything else. I'm sure we could arrange for her to go home for a vacation for a while."

"I don't think she would go right now. It would seem as if she was running away. These people are too important to her. Let me work with her. In a few weeks when things settle down maybe I'll suggest she take a week or two vacation."

"Dona, when I signed up it seemed like the whole year was going to be a vacation."

"What does it seem like now, Rob?"

I thought and then smiled. "Now it seems like an adventure."

Walter gave a short welcoming speech. He thanked everyone for all the hard work and then dinner was served. It was a sit down dinner for twenty-two. There was a big cake with 23 candles. Everyone sang happy birthday. All in all it was a successful surprise birthday party.

Abbey's parents were staying in the third apartment in our guesthouse. Her grandfather was in the fourth apartment. They were going to stay two more days before going home. On short notice it was hard for them to take too much time off work. It was just as well because Major Campbell didn't want Abbey taking her parents sightseeing around Peru right now. We were more or less confined to the ranch.

In the morning I had a quick cup of coffee with Abbey and her family and then I went to the dining hall for breakfast. I wanted them to have as much time together as they could. I saw Major Campbell and asked him to arrange a tour of the National Park next door.

I said, "If we don't set up something I'm afraid they will wander off on their own."

He said he understood and would take care of it. I wanted them safe without it seeming like armed guards were following them. He also told me that we could send the dive team up to Bagua Grande on Thursday and they should be able to go back in the cavern on Friday.

It was a workday for the rest of us so I went to my office. Abbey came by with her parents and grandfather midmorning to show them what she was doing. I told them Major Campbell was setting up a tour of the National Park next door and to check with him about the time. I started writing the site investigation protocols for the divers so Abbey could spend the next two days with her parents.

Ned walked into my office, plopped in a chair and said, "Eyes and ears."

I said, "Ned, that was just what I was thinking. Tell me about it."

"Professor, I understand you want to have real-time, two-way audio and video with the divers when they are in the cavern."

"Actually only the audio needs to be two-way. I don't care if they can see me. However we need to be able to talk back and forth. I also want to see and communicate with them when they are on site but out of the water."

"I got it. What I plan to do is set up a station at the airfield. That is where we have all the satellite links for the drones. It will almost be like the drone pilot's station, multiple screens with video feeds. A helmet camera on each diver and two cameras mounted on site with 360-degree swivel, tilt, and zoom. It will have two operator chairs. You don't want to stand all day while you watch them. Not with that bum leg. How does that sound, Professor?"

"Like the captain's chair on the Starship Enterprise?"

"No. But it will be very cool. Trust me."

"Ned, any action on your spyware they left in the bad guy's hat?"

"Nothing yet, it is still early. I'm hoping whomever they sent to look around will take it back to the boss. Then we might get something useful."

"Have you heard any other info about our cartel friends?"

"Professor, I guess you are cleared for all this. I mean, since you are one of the people who they want to kill. We hear that there are people out there asking questions about who we are, what happened, and so on. By now we figure they know who we are and whom we work for. We made no secret about what we were doing. Lots of people in Bagua Grande saw the team. The sanctuary rangers all knew what was going on. It should be easy for them to find out we are at the ranch."

I said, "So do you think they will come for us?"

Ned said, "Major Campbell thinks they will and sooner rather than later. The faster Rodríguez acts the stronger he looks. The Major has some big-time shooter coming in this week. We'll be ready when they come."

Ned seemed a little too enthusiastic about this. I hoped he understood it wasn't a video game. "Any other interesting news?"

"Well, Professor, it looks like those bodyguards with the Abbess had to actually do some stuff."

That surprised me. "Is she alright?"

"Yes, she is fine. It seems Cardinal Eduardo Poggi's representative, the one who came to Peru, showed up at her hotel in Paris. He had three very fit young monks with him. They were surprised to be let into the Abbess's suite by two armed female attendants and quickly joined by the two pilots who are former Royal Air Force. They asked to speak to the Abbess alone. The Abbess refused. I guess they made some kind of veiled threat. Going forward they are not going to disclose where the Abbess is staying. Also she is due to come back to Peru soon.

"Professor, do you think these bones are the death cave?"

"Ned, I'm not sure. But whatever it is, it is interesting. It is different than any burial sites I've seen or read about."

"Maybe it is a grave from a mass murder during one of the military uprisings."

I thought of that but I didn't want to say so out loud. No one from the government seemed interested. I said, "I don't think so. Keep me posted if something new comes up."

I spent the rest of Tuesday and early Wednesday writing the protocols for the divers to use on the survey of the cavern. I also wrote protocols for the sampling of the bones, water, and sediment on the cavern floor.

I had arranged to meet the divers up at the airfield after lunch. There were two divers and two support people who met with me. David Fine made the introductions and then went back to his office. The four were new faces to me. The other divers and support men had be sent back to the States. The word would be put out in Bagua Grande that these were totally different people and that all the people involved had been sent out of the country.

The divers were both former military. One was a marine biologist and the other had extensive diving experience for the oil industry. They quickly understood what needed to be done. I was relieved to see how much experience they had. These two would be easy to work with even from a distance.

Once I finished they went back to packing up their gear. It looked like they were taking the same truck and two Range Rovers. I wondered how many people Major Campbell was sending with the dive team.

Next I found Peter Frank. He was busy working at the workbench. He had the OpenROV on the bench and had a different set of controls than we used at the cavern. He was fitting them into a Plexiglas box.

He said, "Give me about an hour and then we can go have some fun. We will test this in the guesthouse swimming pool."

I said, "I'll go see what Ned has put together for the audio and video link to the site. Come get me when you are ready."

Ned and two technicians were working away on the control system. They had taken over the office next to the drone operator's station. The wall had a bracket arrangement from floor to ceiling. There were four large flat-screen TVs attached to it. There was a table with two comfortable-looking chairs in front of the screens. In front of each chair was a keyboard. Between the two keyboards were two joysticks.

Ned said, "Sit down, Professor, I'll give you a demonstration."

I sat in one chair and he sat in the other. He went on, "The top two screens are the video feeds to the divers' helmets. We tested those earlier and the divers packed their stuff up to go in the morning. So we can't see those. The helmet cameras record everything the divers see. You will see it in real time only when the divers are attached to their tethers. They will be on during the cavern survey, mapping, and sampling. If they go upstream they will not be tethered but be recording. You can watch that portion when it is uploaded to us when the divers come out of the cavern.

"The bottom two screens are the cameras on site. I have them mounted on the truck now. Look. You can see them loading the truck and Rovers. Now use the joystick to pan and tilt. The toggle on the top zooms in and out. Give it a try.

"On your computer screen you can control the audio feeds. See the three buttons on the computer screen? One for each of the divers and there is one microphone with the support techs. You can listen to all three at once or just one or two audio feeds. You will have headphones so you can talk to all three or just one or two. All the video and audio will be recorded. Not the Starship Enterprise, but cool."

I said, "Very cool, Ned. Nice job." It was still amazing to me how quickly things got done here compared to the snail's pace at the University.

While I waited the Britten-Norman Defender landed. Eight very fit men got out and started unloading gear. They had ex-military written all over them. David Fine was talking to them as they unloaded the plane.

Ned said to me, "The shooters. These boys are the real deal. The Major checked each one of them out personally. There are four Brits, two Israeli, and two US. All former special forces of some kind."

Again I thought Ned was a little too enthusiastic about us being attacked by a drug gang. I was happy Major Campbell was taking the threat seriously but I didn't really know how scared I should be.

I said, "I'm surprised Walter didn't get the Peruvian National Police to give us protection."

Ned said, "Mr. Falone and the Major don't trust them not to be in the pay of the cartel. But Mr. Falone has arranged for a Peruvian Navy commando team to be stationed at the National Park next door. Their home base is all the way south on the border with Chile. It is unlikely the Colombian or Ecuadorian cartels have gotten to them. Professor, if they come we will be ready and we will spot them coming."

I had no doubt that Major Campbell knew his business. I decided to see how Peter Frank was doing with the control box for the OpenROV.

As I walked over to Peter's work area, he said, "All set, let's go test it out."

He had the OpenROV all packed in its case. We climbed in the golf cart and drove off to the guesthouse. Peter went in the pool house and came out in a swimsuit. He had a mask and snorkel. I sat in a chair while he unpacked the OpenROV and climbed into the pool with it. He seemed to be having a fun time floating face down with the control box under the water and the ROV running around the pool.

After about 15 minutes he came over and set the control box on the side of the pool near my chair. He said, "It works great. Do you want to try it?"

"I would love to but I can't go in the pool until the stitches in my leg come out, doctor's orders. But it looks like fun."

He said, "I need to adjust the ballast a little. I want it to have neutral buoyancy. Then I'll show the divers and then they can pack it up. Will you give me a ride back?"

"Sure. I wonder if they will let me keep the golf cart when my leg is better."

That evening our team was to have dinner at the dining hall with Abbey and her family. They came back from their tour of the park shortly before the dinner hour. They wanted to pack and clean up before dinner so I headed over to the dining hall.

At 6:30 the bar was busier than I had seen it. There were a dozen or so men and about half that number of women I hadn't seen before. Peter and Dona Frank waved me over to their table.

I said, "Good evening. It's a busy place here now." I sat and signaled the waitress for a beer.

Dona said, "I know, lots of security people from all parts of the company."

I said, "Are they all company employees?"

Peter said, "The ones that came in on the plane today, they're from a private security firm. I heard two of them served with Major Campbell in the SAS. They all have a Special Forces look about them. Major Campbell must be expecting trouble. We have all four drone pilots at the ranch full time and a drone in the air 24 hours a day."

I said, "What type of equipment is in the drone?"

Dona answered, "Both the Heron and ScanEagle drones have infrared and video cameras. The equipment is very good. No one will walk in on us without us spotting them coming."

Our team started arriving. I excused myself from the Franks and went over to join them. It was also Harrison's last night with us. He was going back to Houston to start work at a new job with the company. Everyone seemed happy and relaxed. All the additional security people didn't seem to bother them.

Abbey and her parents arrived. Mrs. Summers seemed a little sad but was trying not to show it. Everyone was milling around and talking. I sat because my leg was getting sore again. Abbey's grandfather came over and sat next to me.

He said, "These kids are a lot like Abbey."

I said, "It is an amazing group and a pleasure to work with them."

He said, "I'm looking forward to getting to know them better." He saw the look on my face and went on. "No one told you? Major Campbell hired me. He gave me a fancy title. 'Director of Security Training.' Pretty fancy sounding. He wants me to make sure all his people have a refresher in counterinsurgency. He said a lot of them have been mostly flying a desk for the last few years. He doesn't want them rusty. I'm looking forward to it. I've been sitting on my butt too much up north. Plus I'll be able to spend time with Abbey and your team."

"Great. I'm very pleased you are staying. It will be good for Abbey and I'll enjoy having you here. I won't be the old man in the group anymore."

He smiled and I went on. "Those boys that flew in on the plane today don't look like desk jockeys to me."

He said, "No, I reviewed their résumés. They're tough enough. One is a Marine. I haven't met him yet. Frankly I hope we don't need them. But the Major tells me the cartels here are really bad and wouldn't think anything of killing a dozen innocent people to get to the ones they want. Plus they have a lot of cash to spread around."

Abbey came over, put her arm around her grandfather and said, "Did he tell you he is staying? I'm so happy and Mom will sleep better at home knowing you are here with me."

In that moment, she again seemed the little girl who knew she would always be safe in her grandfather's arms. Having her family here helped her get over the shooting.

I smiled and said, "Yes, he was just telling me and I'm very pleased too. The dive team leaves tomorrow morning to drive up to Bagua Grande. They will head to the site first thing Friday. I went over our command station with

Ned. You should have him show it to you. I'm planning to cancel our Friday meeting. We should be up at the airfield by 9:00AM Friday. Let me get you two a drink."

The group enjoyed the dinner. I left early with Abbey and her family. They were leaving early and my leg hurt.

Chapter
42

Friday, Abbey and I were up at the airfield before 9:00AM. They had cleared out an area behind the main hangar and up into the hill beyond for Sergeant Summers' training ground. I drove over for a look. The Sergeant was directing about six of the ranch hands in building an obstacle course. There was a shooting range and other things I wasn't quite sure what they were. He had on fatigues and army boots. His sleeves were rolled up, hard at work, and he looked happy. I waved and went back to the hangar.

Abbey and Ned were in the two control seats with headsets on. Abbey was testing the site camera. I could see the site as she moved the camera around. It was mounted on the front of the truck on a pole. There was a clear view of the hole into the cavern. The divers were putting on their gear. Abbey was speaking to one of the techs. Ned hit a button on his computer and their conversation came out of the speakers on the desk.

One diver turned on his helmet camera. The flat-screen for that feed showed the site spinning back and forth as he lifted the helmet and put it on.

Both divers were ready to go. The first diver sat in a sling attached to the boom crane on the truck. The operator moved him over the hole in the top of the cavern and lowered him to three feet above the water. The diver jumped off into the water. The operator repeated the procedure with the second diver.

Ned gave me the second control seat. I let Abbey instruct the divers. They started the mapping on the west end and then they would work east towards the bone pile. Everything was being recorded so they didn't have to write anything down underwater. It was a methodical process but it seemed to move along smoothly. After a little while I took off the headset and left the room.

Ned's workspace consisted of a desk with folding tables on each side. It was covered with computers and electronic equipment.

I pulled up a folding chair. "Any new news from the spy department, Ned?"

He said, "Lots of stuff all the time. Let see. It doesn't look like the Ecuadorian police are going to do much about the Rodríguez cartel. They are saying yes, yes to our State Department but there is no sign of any action, at least not yet. My guess is that Rodríguez has paid them off. The Peruvian National Police have stepped up patrols along the border. So it looks like they are at least trying."

"What about your spyware stick?"

"Nothing yet, Professor. But I'm still hopeful. I know what else is new. The Abbess and three other Abbesses have a private audience with the Pope. Mr. Falone is lending her the Gulfstream G4. One Abbess is from Brazil, one from Africa, and the third is from Spain. I've been thinking about how I could bug the Abbess so we could listen to that meeting. How cool would that be? But I'm pretty sure the Major wouldn't go for that idea."

"Ned, you are probably right about the Major not liking that idea." I wondered what else Ned has bugged around here.

I decided it was time to give Abbey a break. I sat with her until I knew exactly how far along they were with the mapping. Then I told her to take a break. It would take all of today to map and take soil and water samples. The water wasn't deep so the divers could work for fairly long periods of time between breaks. They had the routine down and didn't need much help from me.

During the day various team members showed up to watch. Mike and Fred were ready to take the measurements from the audio recording and start plotting the map of the cavern. I transferred what we had done so far to Mike's laptop.

Abbey took over the control station again. I walked out back of the hangar to the new training area. Major Campbell was in his wheelchair at the edge talking to Abbey's grandfather. I hoped I was that fit at his age.

I hobbled over and said, "You put this training area together fast."

Abbey's grandfather said, "It is just the basic but it will do for getting the folks back in shape. Do you want to train with us, Professor?"

I leaned on my cane and said, "No, but thank you for thinking of me." I noticed the eight men that came in the other day that were from the private security company. "Are they going to train with you?"

He said, "No, they will train on their own but use the range and training area. They have their own routine. I'll work with the company employees. They seem to like the idea but I haven't started working them yet."

I pointed to the private security men and said, "They seem a long way from the targets."

The Major said, "Bad guys will want to be a lot farther from them than that if the rest of those guys are as good as my SAS men. It will be interesting to watch. They will start by adjusting their scopes after putting the rifles back together."

I said, "So Rodríguez will be coming for us."

"He won't come personally, but I'm willing to bet we will have trouble before too long. He must know who we are and that we are here on the ranch by now. My men will be prepared and everyone else should continue with their work. I know Walter is trying to turn up the pressure on the various agencies to go after Rodríguez."

They had work to do so I went back to the hangar office to work with Abbey.

I said, "How is it going?"

Abbey said, "The divers are taking a break. We should be able to finish the mapping of the cavern and the taking of environmental samples today. Tomorrow we will survey the bone pile and gather samples. We should complete that in one day. After that we start exploring upstream."

I said, "I'll see if Major Campbell is willing to have a plane fly up and get the samples Sunday morning. If so they can fly them to Lima for shipment to Houston. We may be able to have the basic water and soil tests done in Lima. Make sure there is a detailed video of each bone, especially the skulls. I would like to examine the actual bones but I don't want to slow down the process of getting the testing done in Houston."

Since the divers were on break I started to rotate the truck-mounted camera around the site. I saw that there were four security men with the two divers and two techs. There was also a jeep with two armed park rangers. No one wanted more trouble. I didn't think the drug gang had any interest in our work. If we hadn't walked right into them we probably wouldn't even have known they were there. That would have made life simpler.

The rest of the day went smoothly.

Saturday morning we were back at the control station in the hangar office area. First the divers mapped the bone pile. Then they began bagging bones from the locations Abbey had detailed. The first group of bones was from the top and the edges. Then they began to remove layers of bones to get samples at various depths within the pile. This had to be the bones of hundreds of people. It still looked like all the bones were human.

As they worked in the middle of the pile fairly deep down I saw something. I said to the first diver, "Stop, look towards your left hand. No, down more and a little left, it looks like a metal object."

He picked it up. It was a small gold-colored figure and a chain. He carefully bagged it. It was the first object we had seen among the bones. Again I was struck by that fact. I couldn't think of a single pre-Columbian burial site where there was no clothing, jewelry, and other items included with the bodies. I instructed the diver to mark that for delivery to the ranch.

By the end of the day the diver finished the first round of bone samples. Once these were analyzed we would determine what additional sampling should be done.

On Sunday one of the men took the samples to the airport and met the flight from the ranch. The others went directly to the site. The divers would start by mapping the first 200 feet upstream on the west end of the cavern. This was the part we had filmed with the OpenROV on our first trip to the cavern. Then they would send the OpenROV filming up another few hundred feet. If it was determined to be safe, the divers would map and sample that area. They would proceed in that way as long it was safe. It would be a slow process with the divers having to come out to decompress and get fresh dive tanks every hour or so. We had no idea how far the underwater river went upstream. But the bodies had to get in there somehow. The only logical place was upstream.

Shortly after noon the Cessna Skymaster landed. The bulk of the samples had been dropped off in Lima to be sent on to Houston. We decided to collect a few additional skulls and bones to examine at the ranch and we received the small gold-colored ornament. I left Abbey to work with the divers and I went out to the plane. The pilot handed me a clear plastic box. Two skulls, a few bones, and the ornament were in separate evidence bags.

First I took out the figure and looked at it through the clear evidence bag. The figure was fairly small, about two inches high, less than an inch wide and about one-quarter inch thick. It was a figure of the god Uku Pacha, which was the Inca god of the inner earth realm. It was made of gold.

That was interesting because in Inca religion the god Uku Pacha of the inner world was connected by caves and springs to the god Kay Pacha of the upper world that man occupied. What it meant I hadn't a clue, at least not yet.

I set that aside and took out an evidence bag with one of the skulls; it was intact. The second skull was smaller. Perhaps it was a woman's or child's skull. It was also basically intact. I looked at the bags with a few other bones. We would examine them in more detail at the research facility later. I put them all back in the plastic box. The really interesting information would come from the complete analysis done in Houston.

Monday I drove my golf cart up to the airfield at 8:00AM. Abbey was at the range working with her grandfather.

I drove over and said, "Good morning. What time did you two leave the guesthouse? I didn't hear you."

Abbey said, "Grandpa dragged me up here before 6:00. I told him I'd work with him if it didn't interfere with my other work. But I was hoping for a more civil hour of the day."

Sergeant Summers said, "I told Abbey if she was going to spend her career digging in the jungles of Third World countries she needed to know how to take care of herself. So in addition to her morning run I'm adding self-defense training and time on the gun range. Do you shoot, Professor? Maybe you should join us on the range."

I said, "No, I'm more likely to shoot myself or the good guys. I don't think it is a smart idea. I'll leave the protecting to the professionals. However, Abbey seems to be professional at just about everything she does."

"I'll get the divers started," I said to Abbey. "You finish up with your grandfather, get cleaned up and meet me at the workroom for our 10:00AM Monday meeting. The divers know what they are doing and they can keep working their way upstream. If they have questions we can answer them when we come back after the meeting."

As I drove around to the hangar entrance I saw her. Sergeant Summers had Abbey firing one of the rifles with a scope. They were way back from the targets.

At 9:59 I walked into the workroom and wrote on the whiteboard:

THE REJECT TEAM: PROJECT "THE INCA'S DEATH CAVE." WEEK 15 DAY 1

Our group was smaller now. Harrison was working at his new position with the company in Houston and Sadako was working with Dona Frank at the Lima facility. Ned was attending the meeting even though he was working almost full time for Major Campbell.

Everyone had apparently worked all weekend.

I showed everyone the gold figure and bones that were sent to the ranch. Then I asked Abbey to start.

She said, "The mapping of the cavern's central area is all done. Fred and Mike have a 3D computer map available. The water, soil, and bone samples have been shipped to Houston. We should start getting data back from them in a few days. When the data starts arriving we should know a lot more. The divers are working their way upstream now and I'll keep you posted."

Fred went next. "I've been using the high resolution map of the area and working westward trying to identify caves, sinkholes, rivers and streams that could be the location where the bodies were introduced to the cavern. My plan is to develop a description and GPS location for each item identified, then run it through Mitch's probability software to develop a priority listing. From there someone is going to have to hoof it in and look at the specific locations. I should be done this week developing the list and I'll need some help from Mitch running the software."

Mitch said, "I'd be happy to help with the software. It is easy to use once you get used to it."

I thought, easy for this group, and said, "Mitch, did you have any luck with local religious and burial practices?"

She said, "There are lots of interesting local practices. Many date back to pre-Columbian times. On the surface the Catholic Church is the main religion. But many indigenous people in this area mix their ancient religious practices in with Christian ones or simply practice both. Their traditional celebrations and their religious beliefs are mixed with fantastic apparitions and there is almost always a cave in them.

"Local shamans known as curanderos are very prevalent, well respected, and to some extent feared. Some curanderos make use of simple herbs, waters, and even mud to effect their cures. Others additionally employ Catholic elements, such as holy water and saints' pictures. They use a variety of magic wands. The curanderos' most important wand is the 'chonta defense.' If a curandero dies without disciples, the chonta is weighted with stones and is thrown to the bottom of a lake. Its power will reemerge when a new shaman takes office.

"However all the burial practices I could find use some kind of coffin. The Chachapoyas in pre-Inca times had elaborate burials as is seen in the Sarcophagi of Carajía. The Sarcophagi, or anthropomorphic coffins contained mummies that sat on an animal skins and were wrapped in mortuary cloths. Ceramics and diverse objects were accompanying the deceased as gifts. I found no evidence of water burials and no evidence of burials without adornments. I would like to visit several local curanderos to see if there is any verbal history or stories of this type of burial practice. Many things about these indigenous people are not recorded, let alone online. So we have caves but no nude dead bodies."

I said, "Well put, Mitch. Perhaps when Fred goes climbing into caves and holes you can go with him. Let's keep working the data we are getting from the divers. When we start receiving the test results from Houston maybe we will have some answers."

Abbey and I had lunch and went back up to the airfield. We checked in with the dive team. They had mapped their way up almost a thousand feet.

The lead tech said, "Professor, you better order us a couple of dive scooters. Swimming up against the current for that distance doesn't leave the divers much time to work. Talk to David Fine, he will know what we need. Hopefully they can rent them in Lima. If not we will have to have them flow in from Houston. Get a set of spare batteries for the units. That way we can always have a charged set."

I said, "Is it worth continuing today?"

"We will do one more dive and then call it a day. It would be good to get these guys out of the water for a bit. We will transmit everything to you and then work on our equipment and rest until the scooters arrive."

I found David and conveyed the message on what the divers needed. He said he could have the scooters on site in a day or two.

Chapter
43

Major Campbell was right, unfortunately. I was reading at about 7:00PM in the living room of the guesthouse. When Sergeant Summers came out of his apartment, I noticed he was wearing a sidearm.

He said, "It looks like we have company. Where is Abbey?"

I said, "She is over at the dining hall with some of the team having dinner."

He said, "That should be OK. If it is real trouble they will lock that down. Come on, Professor, let's go over to the security command center and find out what is going on."

I put my book down and followed the Sergeant. We took the tunnel to the research facility that housed the main security office. Major Campbell, David Fine, and a few others were watching an infrared camera feed on one of the flat-screens.

Sergeant Summers said, "Do we have company?"

From his wheelchair the Major pointed to the screen. You could see the hazy heat signature of men moving through the woods. Then he pointed to another screen. It had a map of the ranch and surrounding area. There was a dotted line moving forward towards the ranch buildings. At the starting point there were three small car icons. The circle at the front of the dotted line had an eight in it.

Major Campbell said, "The drone picked up the three jeeps parking a few dozen yards into the brush at the side of the road about 20 minutes ago. The men have been slowly working their way in towards the ranch. My guess is they plan to hold up at the edge of the clearing until sometime late tonight and then attack."

Sergeant Summers said, "We own the night."

I looked at him and he went on. "The Marines always want to fight the bad guys at night. We have better equipment and are far better trained in night actions than almost anybody. I assume the SAS is well trained for night engagements."

Looking at the screens he said, "They are just stumbling through the woods. There is no one on point and no recon. Do they know which building the people they want are in?"

Major Campbell said, "We are assuming they do. But we're not going to let them get that far. The Peruvian Navy Special Forces team will be moving in behind them. Look, you can see the heat signature of their vehicles at the edge of the screen."

I said, "Did the bad guys leave people to guard their jeeps?"

He said, "There are no heat signatures so I don't think so, unless the person has been in the vehicle the whole time and the engine heat is masking their body temperature. We will know that shortly. The jeeps are not running and the engines are cooling off. The Special Forces team will clear and secure the vehicles first in any event. Then they will move in behind the eight bad guys. Once we know exactly where on the edge of the clearing they stop, the Special Forces team will move in behind them on three sides. When they are in place then we will let all hell break loose. Searchlights, sirens, a large volley of flash bang grenades and sniper fire will go in their direction all at once. It should drive them back into the Peruvians. If the bad guys don't retreat into the Peruvian team they will attack them from three sides. In any case it shouldn't take long."

I could now see the Special Forces teams' vehicles arriving near where the jeeps were parked. Men fanned out and approached the jeeps from three sides. They moved in and nothing seemed to happen. So no one was left with the jeeps. It now looked like there were about two dozen men. It was eerie watching the shaky heat signature of the men. Three men stayed with the jeeps and the rest moved out following the path that the bad guys were taking.

The bad guys were near the edge of the clearing at the southwest side of the ranch. They were in a group together and were no longer moving.

Then the infrared camera showed a flare-up, then another.

I said, "What is that?"

Sergeant Summers said, "I can't believe it, those bozos are smoking."

Major Campbell said, "These drug gang enforcers mostly intimidate unarmed farmers. They probably have no idea we are watching. My guess is they plan to stay there until 2:00AM or 3:00AM when they figure they can walk in and shoot up the place."

I said, "Would shooting up the place and killing several people be enough for Rodríguez or does he have to specifically kill the three of us who were there?"

Major Campbell said, "That is a very good question. Perhaps if he shoots up the ranch and kills some people here it is enough to show he has gotten his revenge. That would explain the approach we are seeing. Send in his gunmen, shoot up the place, set some building on fire, and kill people who get in the way. It could be."

Major Campbell sent David Fine out to put everyone in place. David radioed he was all set. We waited another 20 minutes until the ready signal came in from the Special Forces. Then all hell broke loose.

A siren started blaring, searchlights came on and focused on the area where the bad guys were, explosions were going off by the hundreds it seemed. The drone had switched from infrared to regular video. On the screen I could see the searchlights criss-crossing the edge of the woods, tracer bullets were flying, and there was a steady stream of flash bang grenades flying into the target area.

I said, "Who is throwing all those grenades?"

Sergeant Summers said, "Not who but what. It looks to me like they are coming from an Mk 19 Grenade Launcher, also known as the Mark 19. It has been around since the Vietnam War. It can fire 40mm grenades at a top rate of 60 per minute. For night operation, an AN/TVS-5 night vision sight can be fitted. The US probably sold it to 20 different countries around the world."

Major Campbell said, "Not bad, Sergeant. It is the Israeli Maklar. It is the same launcher but manufactured in Israel under license from the US."

I saw a few shots coming back from the bad guys but not much.

Major Campbell said, "It looks like they are retreating. Stop the flash bangs and the tracer fire."

About two minutes later his radio buzzed. He listened and said, "They have them all. Three dead and five captured."

I said, "That was easy."

Sergeant Summers said, "Too easy. I don't like it. Not even druggies should be that dumb."

Just then we heard an explosion from the driveway. Someone put up cameras near the gatehouse. It was on fire. A truck had just crashed through the gate and following it were four jeeps with men shooting from the open back area. I could see at least one of our security men on the ground.

Major Campbell spoke into his radio. "All teams, building lockdown. Five vehicles and 20-plus bad guys just crashed the front gate. We have men down. Snipers to the ranch house roof, fire at will. All units west of the driveway assemble around the research facility, those on the east side converge on the ranch house."

Someone had opened a locked storage closet and was handing out automatic rifles. He handed me one. I shook my head and he said to take it.

I said, "We have my whole team in the dining hall."

Major Campbell said, "It should be locked down."

Sergeant Summers said, "We'll go. Come on, Professor." He was filling a knapsack with clips of ammunition and grenades.

Major Campbell said, "Take the tunnel and take a radio. Set it to channel 8. Go now."

Sergeant Summers put the radio in his pocket and a wireless earphone in his ear. I followed him at a jog, my bad leg hurting at each step. We went down the tunnel and then up the stairs to the dining hall. The door was locked.

Sergeant Summers pounded on it with the back of his rifle and said, "Sergeant Summers and Professor Johnson code 48 from Major Campbell."

Someone must have radioed ahead. The door opened instantly. There was only one security man there. He was holding an automatic rifle and the cook had his pistol. Everyone was seated at the back of the room.

The Sergeant said to the security guard, who was young and looked scared, "If they come, it will be through the ground level doors or the windows. Get everyone down in the back behind the bar. Take up a firing position to cover the two ground-level doors. Professor, give Abbey that rifle and take my pistol and spare clips. Where is there roof access?"

The cook showed him a ladder with a hatch to the roof in the kitchen. He said, "Let's go, Abbey. Hand me these when I get up top. Close and lock the hatch once we are up there."

I didn't like the idea of Abbey being in the middle of this firefight. But one look at the young security man and I knew Abbey was more qualified. I'd seen her in action in the jungle and she was with her grandfather.

I heard short controlled bursts of gunfire from the roof. They alternated first from the right side and then the left. No wild shooting, it seemed controlled and disciplined. I found out later it was also deadly accurate fire.

Then there were long bursts of return fire. Windows shattered at the front of the dining hall.

It seemed the shooting and explosions went on forever. But it was less than an hour and it was all over. The Sergeant and Abbey came down from the roof. They were sweaty and their clothes were dirty from lying on the roof.

Major Campbell radioed the Sergeant that it was safe to come out. Sergeant Summers unlocked the door. I gave him his pistol back and walked out the door. It was a scene from a war movie. Three of the five vehicles the bad guys came in were on fire. The windows in the buildings were shot out. The Peruvian Navy Special Forces team was loading bodies into body bags and then putting them in one of their trucks. Our wounded were being taken into our little makeshift clinic in the research facility.

I walked over there with Abbey and her grandfather. Both still held the rifles in a ready position as if more bad guys would pop up. I guess it is just standard procedure drilled into Marines by hours of training. We went into the security area.

Major Campbell was talking to the head of the Special Forces unit. Abbey's grandfather said, "If those Peruvians hadn't been here Rodríguez's attack might have been successful. Even though he probably didn't expect us to be this prepared. I don't know how big his organization is but he has to have lost 35 or so men."

As he spoke I saw more wounded men coming into the clinic. The doctor and nurse Walter brought to the ranch to look after Major Campbell's and my leg wounds were getting more than they bargained for. I could hear police sirens coming now.

Major Campbell wheeled his wheelchair by the Special Forces leader to go talk to the National Police who were just arriving. He said to Abbey and her grandfather as he passed by, "Nice shooting, you two. That one jeep got by all my men."

Sergeant Summers just nodded. Then he took Abbey's gun, went to the gun closet, took out a box and put it on the table. He started checking, cleaning, and oiling his rifle. Abbey went over, sat next to him, and began cleaning the other rifle. Not knowing what else to do I sat down with them and watched.

Abbey said, "The Marines have a saying 'take care of your equipment and your equipment will take care of you.' The Marines have a lot of good sayings."

Her grandfather patted her hand and smiled.

A minute later Mrs. Lopez, of all people, walked in. She had a double-barreled shotgun slung over her arm with the breach open. She walked over to Abbey who at this point had the rifle all apart and mostly cleaned.

Abbey said, "Sweet gun you have there."

Mrs. Lopez said, "If they got in the ranch house I wanted to be prepared. It belongs to Mr. Falone. I understand it is quite valuable."

I looked more closely. The wooden stock was beautiful. The metal was all engraved and inlaid with gold and silver.

I must have also looked confused. Abbey said to me, "It is a 12-gauge Purdey shotgun. Made by James Purdey & Sons Limited of London. It cost about as much as a Porsche. Mrs. Lopez, would you like me to clean it?"

Mrs. Lopez said, "I didn't fire it but it has been in the gun locker for a long time so I guess it can use a cleaning. Thank you, Abbey. Now I'm going to check on the wounded. Mr. Falone is waiting for my report. He arranged to be flown in as soon as he heard of the attack. He will be here by morning."

It was a beautiful gun and Abbey cleaned it with care. I decided I'd rather have a Porsche.

David Fine and one other man came in carrying several rifles. Sergeant Summers said, "Put then on the table. We will clean them. You have other duties to attend to. How bad were our losses?"

David said, "The two men at the gate were killed. They fired several RPGs at the gatehouse and then shot it up as the truck crashed through. Our men never even had a chance to clear their weapons. There are six wounded. Two looked serious and the others were mostly hit by flying chips from all the gunfire. The Peruvians had several wounded but no one killed. If you two hadn't been on the roof that jeep that got through would have doubled back behind us. No telling how many we would have lost then. Thanks, and thanks for cleaning the weapons."

The Sergeant said, "Keep bringing them. I doubt any of us can sleep so we might as well do something useful. The Professor wants to learn how to clean a gun."

I said, "I'm glad to help and I sure as hell can't sleep. Plus I'd like to see that Mark 19."

Various people kept bringing in company weapons. I noticed the men from the security company didn't. They would clean their own gear. Abbey disassembled the guns. Sergeant Summers and I cleaned the parts and Abbey put them back together.

Two men brought in the grenade launcher. It was a funny-looking thing. It was on a tripod and looked like a short, stubby machine gun with a shoe-box mounted under the barrel. The box was where the grenades were.

Sergeant Summers said, "The Mk 19 is a belt-fed, blowback-operated, fully automatic grenade launcher that is designed not to cook off. It fires 40mm grenades and can fire up to 60 rounds per minute. It operates on the blowback principle, which uses the chamber pressure from each fired round to load and re-cock the weapon. The Mk 19 can launch its grenade a maximum distance of over a mile and you need to launch them at least 100 yards to keep from blowing yourself up. We started using it in Vietnam and the Marines still use it."

I wasn't really sure what he was talking about and I said, "What is cooking off?"

He said, "Cooking off, or thermally induced firing is ammunition exploding prematurely due to heat in the weapon. Bad business."

I said, "Abbey, do you know how to take this thing apart?"

"Sure, Prof, I do it all the time."

"Good because with all the noise it made it must be ready for a bath.

I didn't think civilian companies were supposed to have things like this."

Abbey said, "I'm not sure they are but Walter and his company are very close to the Israelis. I think they will sell him just about anything as long as he doesn't take it into the US."

I looked at it again. It looked harmless enough just sitting there. Almost like a child's toy.

Major Campbell wheeled himself in. I said, "Are you OK, Major? How are your injured men?"

He said, "Fine, but tonight I could have used that motor you wanted me to install on this chair." He then became serious. "Two of our men are in serious condition. They are being sent by ambulance to the hospital in Lima with two others who are less seriously hurt. The final two have minor injuries and will be treated here. None of our civilian personnel were injured."

Sergeant Summers said, "They had pretty good intel on this place. But didn't seem to know the Navy Special Forces were here. My guess is someone sold you out."

The Major said, "It was most likely a contractor who worked here or a local policeman or inspector. I got word the Navy is sending in another full Special Forces team. Walter is bringing another dozen security men from the States on the plane with him and is contracting for more men from the private security firm."

"So the rent-a-cops held their ground?" Sergeant Summers asked.

The Major said, "They were better trained than many of my men. I reviewed each one's file before they were hired. Two of the six wounded are theirs. They did their job and then some. Many of my people are computer and information techs. Then there are the pilots, most have some basic military training but they're not shooters. We were lucky things held together until the Special Forces unit arrived. It is a good thing they were right at the edge of the clearing. A couple of them tied their prisoner to trees and left one guard. The rest came running as soon as I gave the lock down command. They took casualties and now they want Rodríguez. I hope that helps with the Peruvian police. They are taking the dead and wounded bad guys. Not many survived. They will be questioned and they will try to identify the dead ones."

Mrs. Lopez came in. She said, "I have them preparing pizza at the dining hall. Walter will be here in 45 minutes and wants to talk to everyone.

He said to tonight only do what must be done and make sure the bar is open and the drinks are free. I'll see you over there in a little while."

Major Campbell called David Fine and gave him instruction on posting guards. We cleaned and reassembled the weapons we had started. The rest we locked up to be cleaned tomorrow. My leg hurt and my pills were at the guesthouse so I went into the clinic down the hall. The doctor looked tired.

I said, "You look like you need a doctor."

He smiled and gave me the pills I requested. I said, "Is it OK to take these with beer?"

He smiled again and said, "Tonight it is doctor's orders to take them with beer." I think these were his first smiles in many hours.

I went back to the security room and then we headed to the dining hall.

People were arriving. They talked quietly in small groups. Some looked bewildered but mostly they just looked tired. My watch said 3:20AM. I had lost all track of time. My leg hurt but other than that I wasn't sure what I felt. Maybe I was just numb. My beer had no taste. I washed down the pills the doctor gave me.

Walter came with David Fine next to him. The dozen new security people he brought from Houston took over guard duty along with a few of the private security people. Against the doctor's wishes the two slightly wounded security employees were wheeled in. They insisted on being here when Walter arrived. I was struck again by how loyal these employees were to Walter. Showing up here from half the world away a few hours after the attack didn't hurt.

Walter went to the front of the room. You could have heard a pin drop. He said, "First let me say how sorry and disturbed I am by what happened here. My heart goes out for the two men and their families who were murdered tonight. The bodies will be flown home. Subject to the families' approval any employee who wants to attend the funerals will be flown to the funeral at the company's expense and on company time. I stopped at the hospital in Lima on my way. Our four injured there are now all in stable or better condition. They spoke to me of how well their fellow employees preformed and how brave you all were.

"Next, anyone who wants to be transferred to another place is welcome to do so. Your files will reflect the magnificent job you have done here. I am forever grateful for your service here."

"Twelve additional security personnel arrived with me tonight and more will be sent here. A second Peruvian Navy Special Forces team is in route now. The National Police will establish checkpoints on all the roads in. We will establish three rings of security. The outer one will be the National Police, the next will be the Navy Special Forces, and the inner one will be our security people.

"While flying here I spoke to our ambassadors in both Peru and Ecuador. They will meet with government officials of the two countries in the morning. I also spoke to the Peruvian Interior and Defense Ministers. They have promised to do everything possible to apprehend Rodríguez. I will be speaking with others tomorrow.

"We don't know what Rodríguez's reaction will be, whether he will redouble his efforts or if he has had enough. In any case the answer is to have him arrested and legally dealt with. I will stay focused on this until that happens.

"Tomorrow we will rebuild and move on with our work and our lives. We will not let drug gangs dictate to us. I will be here for several days. If any employees want to see me individually, Mrs. Lopez will arrange a time. Now I suggest you have a snack, a glass of wine, and then try to get some sleep. We will all have a busy day tomorrow.

"Thank you all again. I need to go thank the Peruvian Special Forces for their help tonight."

Everyone was quiet and thoughtful for a moment. Then the conversation began again, some left, others got food and a drink. I said to Abbey, "What do you think?"

She said, "Do you want the whole list? I think Walter genuinely cares about each employee. He controlled it but I think he is mad as hell about this and he is going to stay on it until they get Rodríguez. Also I think we should go to bed. We should start getting data from Houston on the bones tomorrow. I want to focus on that and forget tonight."

She turned to her grandfather and said, "No training for me tomorrow, and you can clean the rest of the guns. I have to get back to my real job. Now men, let's go before you have to carry me home."

Chapter
44

I slept until 10:00AM. When I came out to our common room Sergeant Summers was making breakfast. It smelled great. He looked younger, as if he had been energized by last night's events. I knew I looked like hell.

He said, "Pour yourself some coffee. I'll have eggs, sausage, and hash browns ready in a minute."

I said, "That sounds great. Is Abbey still asleep?"

"No, she left a little while ago. She wanted to check on the underwater scooters for the divers and talk to the team up at the site."

I said, "Did she seem OK? I worry about her, she is not a professional soldier, despite all the skills you taught her."

"I know and I'm worried also. She acted fine, her usual bouncy self, but we should keep an eye on her. I don't want her to be in situations where she needs to defend herself. But since I can't guarantee that, I want her to be able to take care of herself. I want her to continue to train while I'm here. Her career will take her to places with problems like this.

"It is strange, I prided myself on always being able to take care of my family. But when my wife got cancer I felt helpless. All I could really do was pray and be with her.

"Well, let's eat. Then I'll drive you around in your golf cart and we can see what a mess was made of this place last night. For Abbey probably the best thing is for her to get back to the work she loves."

After breakfast we took the golf cart. Sergeant Summers drove to the gatehouse area first. The gatehouse was burned out completely. Several rocket-propelled grenades had hit it. Just down the road we could see two army trucks blocking the driveway. There were members of the Special Forces team and two company security men by the trucks. Several of the Special Forces men had rocket tubes slung over their shoulders. I pointed to them.

The Sergeant said, "They are M72 light antitank weapons. The US started using them about 1960. It is a simple, one-shot, unguided antitank rocket. Point it and shoot it. It is good up to about 200 yards. It won't stop a main battle tank but it will blow a truck to pieces. If the bad guys try to ram through here again they will be in for a surprise. But I doubt they will try that again. If I was in their situation and wanted to kill you, Professor, I would use a sniper. One good man to slip into position somewhere with a good view and wait for his targets to walk by."

I said, "You should probably mention that to Major Campbell."

He said, "I bet the Major has already thought of that."

I said, "Well, it couldn't hurt to tell him, just in case."

We continued to drive around the ranch. They had towed away the five vehicles the bad guys used. It wasn't like the crime scene investigations you see on TV with the FBI going over everything with a fine-tooth comb. The Special Forces and National Police put the dead bodies in the back of a truck and collected the gang's weapons. Then they towed their vehicles away. Job done. They left the rest of the cleanup to us. There were broken windows and bullet marks on the ranch house, the research facility, and the dining hall.

I could see Sergeant Summers sizing up the entire area. It was as if he were planning for the next attack.

He said, "You and Abbey should use the tunnels whenever you can." Then he was quiet.

I said, "Do they make bulletproof golf carts?" He just looked at me. "Let's go up to the airfield. I want to check in with Abbey and the dive team."

He parked in the hangar, I went in the office, and he headed for the practice range. The screens for the cameras on the site were dark. No one was in that office. I went over to Ned's area. If possible he seemed to have even more electronic and computer stuff all around him.

I took a chair over, sat, and said. "How are you doing? How did you make out last night?"

"I'm OK, Professor. I watched the whole thing from the drone control room with the drone pilots. We locked the doors, a couple men stood guard, and the pilot kept relaying information to our men. Our people knew where the bad guys were all the time. That was how we were able to stop them without more of our men being hurt.

"Abbey was pretty cool on that roof with her grandfather picking off the bad guys. First they shot out the tires. Then they alternated shooting short bursts. First the Sergeant and then Abbey, no wild firing, all well aimed and controlled. Even the drone pilots were blown away by how cool and controlled they were. Just a couple of minutes and all five bad guys in the jeep were dead.

"Do you think Sergeant Summers would let me train with him? I'm not much for working out, but I'd like to be able to handle myself like Abbey. Oh, how is your leg by the way?"

I thought Ned was still treating this too much like one of his video games. Watching it from the control room TV screens it probably looked like a video game. I said, "Talk to Sergeant Summers, I bet he would love to have you running 10 miles and doing 1,000 push-ups per day. What have you heard from the Rodríguez gang?"

He said, "My bug is in. I'm not sure whose laptop it is in and the laptop is moving around a bit. I can only upload if they are online. The software will voice activate the microphone and record when people start talking. When they go online it will upload to me here. The only problem is if the laptop battery goes dead. I don't have much yet.

"What we are getting by monitoring radio transmissions and other stuff is that Rodríguez knows all the people he sent in were killed or captured. My count was 32 so it has to have hurt his organization. Thirty-two families mad at him that he has to now take care of. I think his problems just got worse."

I said, "Does that mean he gives up or does it mean he has to try harder so he doesn't look weak?"

Ned said, "I don't know. Also it seems the Ecuador police aren't doing much."

"Ned, Sergeant Summers said that if he were planning another attack he would send a sniper. The sniper could quietly sneak into a spot with a view of the ranch and wait for one of us to walk into his line of fire. What do you think of that?"

"Professor, come with me and I'll show you."

We went into the drone control room. The drone was flying a slow circle around the ranch, about 3,000 feet above ground.

Ned pointed to the screen with the monitor for the infrared camera. "Professor, this isn't just an infrared camera. It is extremely sensitive. It is set to pick up the body heat of animals as small as 40-50 pounds. The infrared feed goes to a software program as well as to the screen. The software is set to specifically identify human heat signatures. We have tested it and retested it. It works. Now the CIA may have a magic suit to avoid this level of infrared sensitivity but I don't think Rodríguez's gang does. If something seems like a person the software sets off an alarm. The pilots don't have to spot it on the screen."

I said, "You should show Sergeant Summers this. I think he would worry less if you did."

"Good idea, Professor. I'll go talk to him now. Then I can ask about some training. You were just joking about the running and push-ups, right?"

I went back into the hangar and got in the golf cart. Maybe I didn't need a bulletproof golf cart. I drove to the research facility and went to my office. Abbey was in her office working on her laptop.

I said, "What's up?"

She looked up and said, "The underwater scooters are arriving in Bagua Grande this afternoon. The divers will start exploring upstream again tomorrow. I'm starting to get some data on the samples from Houston. The water and soil samples look pretty much like what you would expect to find in a cavern around here. The bones are all human as we thought. They will send me the carbon dating and mass spectrometer as they do it. We sent them lots of bones. The forensic examination of the skulls and other bones will take a bit longer, the same for the DNA analysis. They are processing the bones in the order they were collected."

I said, "Good, maybe we will know more by later today. Did you recover from last night, you OK?"

"Sure, Prof. Work a full day, have some dinner, and then shoot some bad guys. It's just another day in a grad student's life. I don't know, sometimes I think I'm not normal."

I looked at her and said, "I've known a lot of students and grad students. You are off the charts in brains and talent. You are way better than normal when it comes to friendliness, kindness, and character. You are balanced and have a range of interests. We just happened to walk into a bad situation that day at the site. The training your grandfather gave you as a little girl saved our lives. You and your grandfather saved more lives last night. Those were bad people. I'm proud of what you did. I know I couldn't have. I also know it has to be stressful and confusing for you. That is another sign you are normal."

"Prof, it's more like I was a different person when the shooting started, I can't explain it, it was weird."

My phone buzzed as a text came in. It was from Major Campbell asking us to come to his office for a meeting with Walter. I texted back that we were on our way.

Abbey and I walked into Major Campbell's office. Walter stood and greeted us.

He said, "Please have a seat. I was just telling Major Campbell what I've been able to learn from the State Department and the Peruvian Interior Ministry. From what their sources can tell Rodríguez is feeling the heat after losing over 30 men. Some of his men feel he can no longer lead with so many families upset at him. He has asked the Colombian Northern Valley Cartel for men to help him control the situation. It isn't clear what they are willing to do. He also has gone to the South Pacific Cartel for more men. The South Pacific Cartel is a Mexican gang composed of the remnants of the Beltrán-Leyva Cartel. It is based in the Mexican state of Morelos. Although they call themselves a 'cartel,' the violent gang is known for having employed 12-year-old gunmen as executioners. They are very violent even by cartel standards. They will do just about anything if the money is right. It is unclear if Rodríguez will use these men to come after us or just to maintain his grip on power within his own cartel.

"Rodríguez has paid off all the right people in Ecuador. The police there are not likely to be of much help to us. I believe in Peru the situation is different. Enough high-level people are involved and enough important business people are concerned that the police and military will be serious about this. Plus Special Forces had people injured. They want to settle the score. But the Peruvians can't help inside Ecuador."

I said, "Sergeant Summers thinks their next logical move against us would be to send in one or two well-trained snipers. They would hold up somewhere in the jungle with a view of the ranch and wait for one of us to walk into their line of fire. Ned explained how good our drone sensors are, but what do you two think?"

Major Campbell said, "I agree that would be one logical move for them to make. I don't think they could get in undetected. Not at night. If they were smart they would come in during the hottest part of the day and then move under some type of ground cover to mask their body heat. It would cost Rodríguez some serious money to hire snipers with those skills but they are out there."

I said, "So do we use the tunnels to go everywhere?"

Walter said, "We may be able to find out if Rodríguez is trying to hire someone with those skills. I'll talk to the State Department. They can alert all their agencies that might hear of such activities. I wouldn't hide in the tunnels just yet. Our equipment is good."

Abbey said, "What about coming in during a really heavy rain and thunderstorm? Would that confuse the sensing equipment? Can the drone fly in a thunderstorm?"

Major Campbell said, "Yes, that would be another good time to sneak in. Stay in Lima until there is a storm forecast. Have someone drive you at the height of the storm, slow the car down, jump out, and have the car drive on. That might work well. If the storm is bad the drone would have to avoid it."

I said, "I was scared of lightning before I heard this."

Walter smiled and said, "How do you two feel about staying and continuing your work?"

Abbey said, "We are staying! They are not going to run us off this project, no way. Right, Prof?"

I said, "I couldn't have said it any better myself, Abbey. We'll stay."

Walter said, "Alright then I'd better get to work on this. As I know you are aware, I am more than a little upset by this."

Abbey said, "What about that Goodyear blimp for our investigation?"

Walter answered, "The experts tell me what you proposed is feasible. So OK, Abbey, I'll rent you one. Go work with the Franks on equipping it. It is the least I can do after all the lives you have saved here. I'll keep Major Campbell posted on any development I have. Good day."

When he left I said to Major Campbell, "How is your leg doing?"

"It hurts. How is your leg?"

I said, "It hurts less than it did, but I like the golf cart. If you don't need us for anything we'll get back to work."

"No, go ahead. However I think I'll send Abbey's grandfather out with a couple of my men to identify the best spots for snipers to set up. We can add wireless sensors in those areas and monitor them without having to use the drone."

We left and went to get some lunch.

Abbey said, "What do you think of us getting the Goodyear blimp?"

I said, "Actually I've been thinking about it since you brought the idea up. The magnetometer is no problem but ground-penetrating radar doesn't work very well unless it is in contact with the ground. Perhaps the Franks can rig up a super powerful one, but if not I have another plan. First map out the area we want readings on. Then identify the best spots for readings and clear out the vegetation in about a six-foot square. Fly over with the blimp, lower the GPR, take a reading, and move on to the next spot. Not as good as rolling continually on the ground. But since we are looking for caverns and caves not small objects it might work. Just interpolate between the points and go back for more readings in between if needed."

Abbey said, "I like it and since you are confined to the ranch you won't have to chop the vegetation."

I said, "I thought you would have learned by now that is what grad students are for, the grunt work professors don't like doing. Let's go back to our office. You contact the Franks. I want to study the mapping of the cavern to date. Maybe we will get some data from Houston."

The attack was Wednesday. Today was Thursday, I was losing track of my days. I spent some of my time that afternoon preparing for our Friday meeting. I made myself a sandwich at the guesthouse for dinner and went to bed early.

Friday at 9:59AM I hobbled into the workroom and wrote on the white-board:

THE REJECT TEAM: PROJECT "THE INCA'S DEATH CAVE." WEEK 15 DAY 5

I wanted to put our focus back on our work, not on the events of Wednesday night. So I said, "Fred, tell us what you and Mike have done."

Fred started. "I worked mainly on identifying possible entry points where bodies could be introduced into the cavern. Mike has been evaluating the cavern map and the underground geology upstream. I'll let him report on that. I defined a cone shaped area going upstream, widening my area as I went west away from the hole to the cavern. Then Mitch helped me with the running of her probability software. We now have a priority ordered list to investigate either on the ground or maybe with the ScanEagle. You will have to tell me how to proceed."

I said, "Great, I'd like to review the list with you and we'll figure out what to do next. Mike."

He said, "I've mapped all the information we have from the divers. It appears to be much as we thought. It is an underground river, similar to many that are found in this region. Much like surface rivers there are tributaries of various sizes flowing into it as you proceed upstream. So far we have found several small inflow points. I've marked them on the map. You could think of these as pipes connecting to the main tunnel that flows into our cavern. They vary in size from about four to 16 inches, but they aren't perfectly round. None seem large enough to be the entry point for a human body.

"Next I reviewed what was known of the subsurface geography and geology of this area. Unfortunately that was not much help, so I estimated and mapped what it might look like. At this point it is mostly guesswork. As we receive more information it will improve and become more useful. We are at the point that we need more data from the divers and to do field work up there."

I said, "Mitch, what do you have to add?"

She said, "Not much. We ran the probability software on Fred's list. The results look reasonable. Nothing that stands out as wacky. We won't really know how well it works until we field check the locations.

"On the local religious and burial practices that match what we have in the cavern, I still haven't found much. I contacted the Monastery of Saint Catherine in Arequipa. I remembered that one of the nuns I met was originally from this area. The Abbess has agreed to let the nun go with me to do my field investigation into the local religious and burial practices. This nun is not only a local with a large family, she speaks the local dialect as well as Spanish and English. The nun seems quite excited to help and can start any time we want."

I thought that Mitch must have made a good impression when she was at the Monastery. I also knew that Walter was helping the Abbess. I said, "Great, set it up and talk to Major Campbell about transportation, accommodations, and security. Elizabeth."

She said, "Walter has me working on a list of things to broaden the application of my software. He told me to stop and help you if you need my help."

I said, "We will speak up if we need help, Elizabeth. Abbey, you're next."

She began, "I spoke to the Franks about the magnetometer. They will fly in tomorrow with Sadako to work with me this weekend on it. I'm trying to find out when our Goodyear blimp will arrive."

The others hadn't heard about the blimp.

Fred said, "I wanted Snoopy One. That is so cool. I never thought Walter would spring for it. When can I have a ride? Ned, did you know about this and not tell me?"

Ned said, "I know everything."

Abbey went on, "In any event we should have the equipment ready when the blimp arrives. If you want a ride, Fred, you and Mike will have to help me develop the coordinates of where we want to take readings. I'm sure your list of potential entry points for the bodies will be helpful.

"I've started receiving data from Houston. As I told Prof the water and soil samples are pretty much what we expected. The bones are all human. The carbon dating for the first few dozen samples started to arrive. The bones get older the deeper in the pile the sample was taken from. Here is the really interesting thing. The newest bones seem to have been there about 40 years; the oldest to date are almost 200 years old. Those oldest samples are from less than halfway down the pile. If this trend holds there could be bones over 500 years old at the bottom of the pile."

Abbey hadn't told me this. Bodies being buried for a 500-year period, not the 500-year-old mass grave we thought we might find. I'd have to think about this and the bodies appeared to have stopped arriving about 40 years ago.

Abbey continued, "We will know a lot more when the rest of the data comes. That will include the DNA and mass spectrometry data as well as the rest of the carbon dating."

I said, "Are the same people doing all the testing? If so ask them to give priority to the carbon dating first. But obviously all the data at once is best if they can do that."

She said, "I'll check. But I know they don't work on the weekend like we do. I'll ask them to send whatever they have done at the end of today."

I said, "OK, folks I suggest we rest a bit over the weekend and only work as much as you feel like. It should be a busy week next week. I'll be in my office or at the airfield if anybody needs me."

I went back to my office and Abbey said she was going to spend the afternoon training with her grandfather. First I studied the carbon dating results. Abbey had plotted the bones' age on each sample site. The easiest thing to see was that the bones tended to get older the deeper in the pile you went. I guess that isn't surprising. Next I reviewed the water chemistry and the flow of water in the cavern. Finally I went through the list of possible entry points for the bones that Fred had compiled. I needed help.

I composed an email to a friend of mine who was a professor of hydraulics in the Civil Engineering school at Cornell. I attached the digital map of the cavern with all the flow and current readings the divers had taken. I included the video and the water and soil test results plus a few other things I thought might be helpful. I explained what we were doing and asked for his thoughts.

Next I sent an email to a biology professor friend. I sent all the data again but asked how long it would take for a body dumped into the underground river to decompose to just bones. I also requested that she include any other ideas she had about our bone pile.

It was after 4:00PM and the doctor wanted to see me. I went upstairs to his clinic. It was quiet and the doctor looked a lot better than last time I saw him. His natural friendly smile was back.

He greeted me and said, "Come, take off your pants and sit up on the examining table. Your wound is healing nicely. How does it feel?"

"It hurts a little less each day," I said.

"We can take the stitches out and you should be able to start swimming. I'd go easy on it for another week or two. No running or kick boxing."

I told him that wouldn't be a problem and thanked him for his help. He was headed back to Lima for a long weekend with his family. He earned his pay this last week.

I drove back to the guesthouse to take a swim. As I drove I couldn't help but look to see where a sniper might be. The other guesthouse on the far side of the pool was now full of the security people that flew in with Walter. That was fine by me. I liked the idea of them being close by.

I was paddling around in the pool when Sergeant Summers came out of the guesthouse in swim trunks and dove in the pool. He swam laps for 15 minutes and I continued to gently work out my leg.

He pulled himself out of the pool and said, "Professor, can I get you a beer? I'm going to grab one for myself."

"That would be great. I could use a beer about now." I got out and toweled off. It felt good to swim. As I toweled off I looked at the scar on my leg and thought I was lucky to be alive.

Sergeant Summers handed me a beer, we sat and I said, "Did you find all the sniper spots out there today?"

He said, "This company is pretty remarkable. Major Campbell sends me two men. One is a former Royal Marine recon expert and the other is a former SAS sniper. This is yesterday. He says identify all the feasible sniper locations. Put your list in priority order and get back to me by 16:00 local time in the hangar.

"Now these two men are good. In about three hours we have the list and we spend a little more time putting the list in priority order. At 4:00 we give it to the Major. He looks it over, asks a few question, and calls Ned in. He tells Ned to make a list of the monitoring equipment he needs to cover these sites and send it to Lima within the hour, tell them we need the equipment flown in here by noon tomorrow.

"Ned looks at the list, says 'cool' and walks away. The Major then says to us, Ned will call you when the equipment arrives. He will show you how to install it. I'd like it all in operation by tomorrow night. Then he goes back to working with the drone pilots.

"The equipment arrives at 11:45AM. It's state-of-the-art gear and this kid Ned knows his stuff. We had it installed just over an hour ago and Ned is testing it now. I tell you this company knows how to run a railroad."

I said, "It sure is a lot faster than the University bureaucracy I'm used to. So Abbey didn't work out with you this afternoon as she had planned?"

He said, "Not with me, but she was still training and working out with others on the range when I left the hangar. It looked like they were getting a good workout."

Just then Abbey arrived. She was dressed in blue jeans, a tee shirt, and hiking boots. She was sweaty but wearing a big smile. She said, "Hi. Let me take a shower and then how about a drink and dinner?"

I said, "Sure, I'll open some white wine and get your grandfather and me another beer. Join us when you don't stink."

She stuck her tongue out at me, then laughed and went in.

I said to her grandfather, "That seems like the Abbey we know and love."

He said, "I agree but it won't hurt to keep an eye on her. Being in two deadly firefights in just a couple of weeks is stressful to anyone."

Saturday morning after a swim and breakfast I went up to the hangar. The divers were going to work today and take Sunday off. The divers would video and record their progress mapping upstream. There would be no live feed because they were beyond the length of the tether. Abbey and I wouldn't be needed to help. Each time the divers surfaced then the crew would transmit their data back to us.

I found Abbey with Sadako and the Franks. Peter Frank was showing Abbey drawings. I said hello to everyone and looked over Abbey's shoulder at the drawing she was looking at. It was a frame that would fit under the gondola of the blimp. It had a magnetometer and a ground-penetrating radar unit on a winch system so it could be lowered to the ground to take a reading as the blimp hovered.

Peter said, "I've tried to design this to require the least modification to the airship. Since we are renting it and we need to return it in its original condition. I will install the controls for the magnetometer, GPR, and the winch in the gondola along with a propane generator to power them. Once the blimp arrives I'll figure out how to attach it. We will start working on the frame and winch system today. The rest of the equipment we need will be arriving this week. Dona found a new high-tech GPR unit that should work even if we don't have full contact with the ground."

It didn't look like they needed me here either so I drove back to my office. I wanted to see what else the Houston lab had sent.

I went through the carbon dating data of the bone samples sent to us at the end of the day. They had completed 14 more samples. The trend seemed to continue. The deeper in the pile the bone sample was taken the older it was. The oldest sample date now was over 200 years old.

Mitch walked into my office, plopped in to a chair. "Morning, Professor. Do you have a minute?"

"Mitch, for you always. Do you want to see something interesting?" I spun my laptop around so she could see the data on the oldest bone sample.

She said, "That is an old bone, 200 years old. Even your bones aren't that old. How deep in the pile was the sample taken?"

"Not even halfway to the bottom of the pile. What can I do for you, Mitch?"

She said, "I contacted the Monastery of Saint Catherine in Arequipa and the Abbess will be flying up with Sister Maria Monday. Walter invited her and she thought it would be a good idea to have Sister Maria come up with her so we could start our field research."

I started to ask but she cut me off and said, "Major Campbell has arranged for them to arrive Monday afternoon. Walter is hosting a dinner at 7:00PM. You and Abbey are invited.

"Tuesday Sister Maria and I will fly to Bagua Grande. I had to straighten out Major Campbell. He tried to book us in a hotel with a security detail. I told him we were staying with Sister Maria's family and the only thing we needed was a jeep. We agreed he could include a driver with the jeep."

She obviously had it all planned out. I think she was preparing for me to object. I said, "That sounds great. I may have some ideas for you to check out when you are there but I need to think about it some more."

She almost seemed disappointed with me completely agreeing with her. She got up and said, "I'll see you around, I got work to do."

I went back to looking at the bone data. But I was interested to see the Abbess again and I wondered if she would talk about her meeting with the Pope. I would track down Ned later and see what he knew.

Next to show up was Fred. He said, "Hi, can I tell you how I'd like to proceed and see what you think?"

His approach was a pleasant change from Mitch's. "Sure, Fred. Have a seat."

He started, "I'd like to get some more data from the divers as they move upstream before heading into the field. Now that they are using the scooters they can cover more ground. Given the security situation I'm not sure Major Campbell will let us take the ScanEagle and crew up to the site. Looking at the aerial-photo maps, it doesn't seem like an easy place to hike around. I'd like to eliminate as many places as possible before I try to hike in."

I said, "Talk to Major Campbell. Show him what you want to do. He may have some ideas or maybe the company has another drone they can send us."

We discussed his list of potential locations for a while longer and then he left. I understood why he wanted to wait for the divers to map farther upstream. The farther the divers went upstream without finding any point where a body could get into the underground river, the more places Fred could cross off his list. If he was lucky he might only have to check out a very few locations.

I decided to have lunch and then go see what the divers sent back from their morning's work. I went to the hangar office and watched some of the video from the divers. Then I sent the data from their morning work to Fred and Mike.

I walked over to Ned's workspace. It had still more equipment, now piled all over the floor.

I said, "Hi, Ned. Can you show me how your sniper detection system works?"

He said, "Sure, Professor. It is pretty simple. I can monitor it from my desk but it is easier to see it on the flat-screens in the drone control room. Since there is always a drone pilot on duty I set it up so they can monitor it from their station."

We went into the control room and said hello to the pilots. These were additional pilots in from Houston. They seemed young.

326

Ned picked up a remote and said. "We have infrared and audio sensors in 22 locations. I also had some cameras set up. I'm not sure they will be that effective but it is fun to see what is going on. The infrared and audio sensors have audible alarms. It also sets off my cell phone."

He clicked the remote and it showed the location of each sensor on a map of the area around the ranch. He said, "Look at that infrared sensor. See the low reading. A small animal is nearby. If the heat signature was higher it would set off the alarm."

He clicked the remote again and a video of the jungle appeared. He kept clicking and the screen went to another camera and then another. He said, "Well, you get the idea. Assuming we have the correct spots picked out we will know if anybody is there even without the drone. There is a thunderstorm predicted for tonight so maybe we will find out if they try to sneak in."

I thought that there goes tonight's sleep. We thanked the pilots and went back to Ned's area.

I said, "The Abbess is coming on Monday."

He said, "I know. Major Campbell is sending the Britten-Norman Defender to fly her in. She is bringing the nun Mitch is going with to hunt witch doctors."

I said, "Did you hear anything about her meeting with the Pope?"

"Just that she had it."

I was getting the feeling Ned was pretty good at keeping information to himself. He had been told by Major Campbell on instructions from Walter that I was to be kept informed. But he didn't tell me anything unless I asked for it specifically.

"What about your bug in Rodríguez's computer?"

"Not much yet. The men have started arriving from that Mexican cartel. I think there are more on the way, maybe two dozen in all. They don't seem to use that laptop that much. I'm a little disappointed."

I left Ned and went out into the hangar. The Franks and Sadako were working away on the equipment mountings for the blimp. I said, "Where is Abbey?"

Dona said, "We didn't really need her help so she went to the training range."

I went out back to the edge of the range. I saw Sergeant Summers there talking to David Fine. So I walked over. Abbey and about six others were running the obstacle course.

I said, "Ned showed me the sniper sensor system. It looks like it's working. Then he told me that there is a thunderstorm coming tonight. I hope he was making that part up."

The Sergeant said, "He is not a bad kid, really. He knows that tech stuff and Major Campbell trusts him. He asked me about training with us but didn't seem very interested in the conditioning part. I haven't told him yet but after I saw the great job he did with the sensors I guess I'll give him some pistol and rifle training. Maybe he will come to understand the need for being in shape as we work together."

I said, "I think he has spent too much time playing video games. Abbey seems to be getting serious about her conditioning. She was always a runner but that obstacle course looks like a real workout."

Sergeant Summers said, "There seems to be a little competition going on among the security folks about who is better at each routine. She seems to enjoy that and a little competition makes it more fun for everyone."

I looked at them out on the obstacle course and I was happy just to be swimming again. I drove back to my office, did some research, and then went back to guesthouse for another swim.

Sunday was a quiet day. We received a little more data from the divers late Saturday afternoon. I looked it over and forwarded it to Mike and Fred. Then I did a little more research but mostly I relaxed.

Chapter
45

Monday I swam and went to my office. At 9:59AM I walked into the work-room and wrote on the whiteboard:

THE REJECT TEAM: PROJECT "THE INCA'S DEATH CAVE." WEEK 16 DAY 1

Walter was attending the meeting. Sadako and Ned were also here. I saw Walter do a double take when he looked at Mitch. She had gone back to what I called her "convent look." The day before she had bleached blonde hair with bright green highlights. Today it was jet black and slicked back in the same style she wore when she went to the Monastery of Saint Catherine in Arequipa.

I said, "We don't have much new since our Friday meeting. But I'd like each of you to summarize what we have for Walter. We should receive a lot more data on the bone samples this week. That along with a full week of the divers mapping upstream should give us a much better picture of the site."

Each team member reported on his or her work. I asked Sadako to report on the equipment for the blimp. She said that they were waiting for some equipment that should be in this week and Major Campbell would try to get a firm date for the arrival of the blimp.

Walter asked Abbey a few questions and then said to me, "Professor, do you have any theories?"

I said, "I'm not sure I'm to the point of theory yet. But I have a couple of ideas.

"Un-contacted people, also referred to as isolated people or lost tribes, are communities who live in isolation. They have little or no significant contact with the larger civilized world. Few people have remained totally un-contacted by global civilization. But there are perhaps a hundred un-contacted communities located in densely forested areas in South America, New Guinea, and India. Peru has 15 confirmed un-contacted tribes. They can have as few as 50 people or as many as 400 in the tribe.

"Knowledge of the existence of these groups comes mostly from aerial footage or some infrequent encounters with neighboring tribes. Isolated tribes may lack immunity to many common diseases. Contact with outside groups often can kill a large percentage of their people.

"There are now five reserves in the Peruvian Amazon meant to protect the lands and rights of isolated peoples. It is not unreasonable to assume that 40 or more years ago there were more of these groups. We may have discovered the burial ground of an isolated tribe that was assimilated into the larger society about 40 years ago.

"Another idea, this was a religious group that may not have been isolated. It just continued to practice its ancient burial practices up until about 40 years ago.

"Mitch has agreed to research both these ideas when she travels to the area to research religious practices. Forty years ago is not so long ago. Some people in the area may remember something about the burial practice.

"Another interesting piece of information came from a hydraulics professor who is a friend of mine. I sent him all the data on the cavern and the measurement of the current that the divers took. He believes the flow rate of the underground river is currently too low to move bodies the distance we have currently mapped upstream. Since we haven't found it yet we know the entry point must be farther upstream. He suggests that in the past the flow rate or current speed must have been greater. He reviewed the video with a geology professor at Cornell. Based on the water wear of the cavern walls they both feel that the water level was lower and the current stronger in the past.

"I asked him what could cause this. He gave me several possibilities. There could be a partial cave in farther downstream or a change in water levels downstream. Both of these would cause a backing up of the water.

That would tend to slow the flow rate and raise the water level. There are any number of potential causes from earthquakes, to changing rainfall patterns, to mining activities, and so on.

"If the flow rate is no longer high enough for bodies to reach our pile and the burial custom continued beyond 40 years ago we should find more bones upstream. A biology professor friend tells me it could take up to several years to for a body to degrade to just bones. So we have lots of interesting possibilities. As Abbey said, once we get the rest of the data we will be able to answer some of the questions."

Walter said, "This is absolutely fascinating. The team is doing a wonderful job. I look forward to meeting with you all next Monday." Then he left.

That afternoon I went up to the airfield to check on the divers' progress and Abbey spent her time logging the new data from Houston.

At ten of seven that evening we walked over to the main ranch house to have dinner with Walter and the Abbess. I saw the Britten-Norman Defender land with the Abbess and Sister Maria at about 4:00PM. Mrs. Lopez was there to meet them and escort them to the ranch house.

There were eight for dinner. Walter had also invited. Mitch, the Franks, and Major Campbell. Major Campbell was on crutches. His leg was still bandaged.

When we all had drinks and were seated in the living room, Walter said to the Abbess, "To the extent appropriate, can you tell us about your travels and your meeting with the Pope? Were you able to persuade him?"

She said, "Again I would like to thank you for facilitating my travels. It would have been impossible without your generous help. I also want to say how sorry I am for the loss of life and injuries you suffered here. Drug gangs are a very big problem in my country. We suffer with this same problem in the south of Peru around our monastery. The Sisters of the Monastery of Saint Catherine in Arequipa have been praying for you.

"My trips were not meant to be secret or clandestine in any way. I visited major monasteries and convents on five continents. My goal was to gage the depth and breadth of support for needed changes to the Church. Once I had done this I requested a meeting with the Pope. His Holiness was kind enough to grant six Abbesses a private audience.

"We would not presume to persuade the Pope on anything. We were there to report to him on the level of support he had for changes we believed he wanted to make. As you perhaps know, women constitute the majority of members of the consecrated life within the Catholic Church. Once we clearly understood what the Pope hoped to accomplish, we explained the deep and wide support he had within the worldwide Church. Based on our extensive travel and discussions, we told His Holiness the changes he outlined had overwhelming support among lay and consecrated Catholic women around the world. We also expressed our opinion that a majority of lay and ordained men would also be supportive. We further expressed our opinion that the resistance to change at the Vatican did not reflect the opinion of Catholics worldwide.

"I believe we will be hearing major announcements from the Pope in the coming weeks. Now please tell, how is your work coming?"

I asked Mitch and Abbey to outline how we were conducting our research and what had been discovered to date.

They did an excellent job explaining in detail what we had found. I could see that the Franks and Major Campbell enjoyed it and learned a few things, even though they had been involved in much of what we did. Walter seemed pleased.

The dinner was understated but elegant. Walter said grace before dinner and at the end the Abbess gave a prayer. I found the evening a stimulating change from my routine. Even though I was excited about our work I was starting to feel cooped up on the ranch. The evening ended about ten and Abbey and I went back to the guesthouse. Tuesday would be a busy day and my leg hurt. I decided I didn't like being shot.

The next morning after a swim and breakfast I headed up to the airfield. It was a busy place. Abbey was out on the training range with her grandfather and several others. Both the Cessna Skymaster and Britten-Norman Defender were being pre-flighted by their pilots. Mitch was there with her duffel bag. The Abbess and Sister Maria were saying goodbye to Mrs. Lopez. I went over and wished them both well. I then asked Mitch to keep Abbey or me posted daily, and we would update her on the data that was coming in from Houston.

I went into the hangar. The Franks and Sadako were working on the

332

equipment for the blimp. I said good morning and headed for the office. Ned was behind his mountain of computer equipment doing something. The drone pilot was at his station. I sat at the deck with the link to the site and powered up the video and audio feeds. I said good morning to the techs. One jumped as my voice boomed out of the speakers mounted on the truck. I turned the volume down. I could see the divers putting on their gear. They gave me a quick update on the plan for the day and told me they would upload yesterday afternoon's data shortly. I said goodbye and powered off the links.

Major Campbell walked in on his crutches as I came out of the room with the link to the site. He said, "Good morning, Professor. That was an interesting dinner. I don't come in contact with too many Abbesses in my line of work."

I said, "A refreshing change. How is your leg doing? You seem to be getting around better."

"The doctor tells me it is doing fine. It hurts less and the hole is filling in. I've avoided getting any infections. The doctor said that is key to a rapid recovery. How is your leg?"

I started to answer when Ned yelled, "Holy shit. They're shooting at us." He ripped his headset off and ran to the room with the link to the site. I went after him and Major Campbell followed quickly on his crutches.

As Ned powered up the links I said, "What the hell is going on"?

Major Campbell in a calm voice said, "Report, Ned."

"Sir, there is a firefight at the site. It came over the park rangers' radio. I have a program running to alert me to distress calls over their communication radios. You know, with keywords like help, shooting, danger, and the usual stuff. Here comes the video and audio. I'll go real time with the rangers' communication radios."

There were no sounds of gunfire on the site audio feed. I couldn't see any of the techs on the video.

"This is Major Campbell, report in if you can hear me."

One of the techs said, "We're behind the truck. We have or had incoming fire. We are unhurt. The divers are in the cavern and out of communication range. The park rangers and National Police are returning fire. I have no more information at this point, Major."

I thought that is a pretty calm response for someone who is being shot at. But he was probably trained as a soldier. Most of Major Campbell's men were.

Major Campbell said, "When are the divers due to surface?"

"Not for another hour, sir."

The Major went on. "OK, stand by." He turned to Ned, "What are you hearing?"

Ned had headphones on and said, "It is a bit confusing but it seems four gunmen ran out of the jungle and started shooting. The police and/or park rangers returned fire. It sounds like they shot or scared off the shooters. They are calling for a medical team so someone is hurt."

Major Campbell began moving the control stick for the camera. As he focused it towards the road I could see the park rangers and police behind their jeeps with their guns pointed up the dirt road. There was no shooting. Two of the policemen moved forward. The Major zoomed in to the area they were slowly walking to. On the ground were three bodies. One was moving.

Major Campbell shouted into the microphone in Spanish, "Take him alive. We need to question him."

One of the policemen behind the jeeps repeated it as an order to his men.

Two more policemen went to help. While holding the one at gunpoint they checked the other two. Both seemed dead. They looked like boys. The third one was handcuffed and dragged back to the jeeps.

More park rangers arrived. Four of them went after the one gunman who had run away. There were broken windows and bullet holes in some of the jeeps but no one appeared to be wounded. They were bandaging the boy they had captured.

Major Campbell said to one of his men, "It seems the shooting is over. Go over and find out what is going on, from here the shooters look like young teenagers."

A jeep with medical signage on it pulled up and medics jumped out. A policeman waved them over to the boy. Major Campbell's man came into view and went over to the senior police officer.

Two rangers came out of the jungle with an automatic rifle.

After a few minutes we saw Major Campbell's man walk off to the side and take out his radio. "Major, can you hear me?"

"Yes, go ahead."

"Four gunmen came out of the jungle onto the road about 100 yards up. They began shooting wildly. The police and rangers returned fire and shot three of them. Two are dead, one wounded, and the fourth one ran off into the jungle. The rangers recovered his weapon and are still tracking him. The one they captured looks about 14. I don't think the others are much older. I'm not sure if he is able to answer questions at this point."

I said, "Not very professional. Not at all like last time. What do you make of it, Major?"

He said, "Even without questioning the one they captured I'm pretty sure I know what this is. I'd bet ten to one these are kids of some of the gang members that were killed during the ranch attack. They wanted to take some kind of personal revenge. Just dumb teenage boys. Tragic really. Ned, check to see what Rodríguez and his gang are up to. Excuse me for a few minutes. I need to report to Walter."

Major Campbell hobbled out to his office. A small crowd had gathered outside the control room. Major Campbell told Ned to fill them in on what happened then get to work on info about Rodríguez's gang.

Abbey, her grandfather, and others who had been training on the range joined the group. For as goofy as Ned could be, he also could be extremely precise and professional when he wanted to. He gave a clear report outlining what we knew and what we suspected. Then he went over to his pile of computer equipment and started working. He totally tuned out the people in the room around him.

I said to Sergeant Summers, "Do you agree with Major Campbell's theory? It was just dumb kids seeking revenge?"

He said, "It would fit the facts. Those kids couldn't shoot very well. They missed everyone and only managed to hit a couple of jeeps. But sometimes it is worse having irrational people after you."

That wasn't a very comforting thought.

Major Campbell came out of his office and said, "I'm going to pull our team off the site at least for today. They can stay in Bagua Grande until we decide how to proceed."

I said, "OK, we have plenty of other things to work on with the data coming in from Houston. If they take some time off it shouldn't hold anything up. Do you think Mitch and Sister Maria will be safe?"

He said, "I don't think they will even be connected with us. They should just stick to the story they are doing research on local religious practices."

I told him I was going back to my office. I hoped he was right about Mitch's safety. In my office, first I reviewed the latest data from the divers, and then sent it on to Mike and Fred.

I'd been working in my office for almost two hours when Abbey came in and sat in a chair.

She said, "Bingo, we finally have something useful from all those documents we have been searching. In the latest batch of documents from the Monastery of Saint Catherine in Arequipa there was a group of letters. One is from Friar Ortiz to his sister. In it he has almost a page on his time with the True of Heart or as I believe is more accurate the Strong of Heart. I cleaned up the English translation from the software program and emailed it to you. Let me know what you think."

I said, "Great. What have we gotten from Houston?"

"Prof, that is next on my list. I'll let you know later."

She got up and left. She was always in good shape but now with her new training routine she had a more muscular look. I should probably work out more.

I opened the attachment Abbey sent me and started to read. I heard a gentle knock on my doorframe. I looked up to see Walter, Major Campbell, and Ned. This probably wasn't good news.

I said, "Come in, gentlemen. Have a seat."

They sat and Walter nodded to Major Campbell.

He said, "Ned has been hard at work since you left the hangar. It doesn't appear the Rodríguez gang even knows about the attack today. So it is probably as I thought it was. What else Ned found out is that Rodríguez put out a contract on Abbey, you, and me to have us killed. He is paying $500,000 for killing me, and $250,000 each for Abbey and you. I guess he figures he has lost enough of his own men. For that amount of money a lot of people will be looking to kill us."

Walter said, "Professor, we will keep you safe until Rodríguez has been captured or killed."

I wasn't sure exactly what to think. I said, "Any progress on capturing Rodríguez?"

Walter continued, "Not the kind of progress I'm looking for. The Peruvians are seriously working on it but Rodríguez is in Ecuador. There is no love between the two countries. They have fought three wars. There was the so-called War of '41 in July 1941. Next the Paquisha War in 1981 and then the Cenepa War in 1995. There were also several minor border conflicts. Plus Rodríguez has paid off the right people in Ecuador. I'm working with the US State Department and I have some other ideas. Professor, we will get him. But for now I want you three to work from the ranch. I don't see any reason the divers can't go back to work. We will get increased police protection but I don't think we will see a repeat of that problem."

He turned to Ned and said, "Please see if you can find Elizabeth and see if she can join us."

When Ned left Walter said to me, "Would you like me to talk to Abbey about these developments?"

"No, Walter, I think it is better if I did that."

Elizabeth came in and greeted everyone in her cheery way.

Walter said, "As I've told you, I am extremely pleased with the work you have been doing. I believe I know the answers but before we proceed I need to ask you a couple of questions."

He had my attention. I wasn't sure where he was going.

He continued, "Am I correct in assuming that you developed your software program while you were in Peru and using our equipment in Peru?"

Elizabeth looked a little confused but said, "I developed it while I've been in Peru using equipment here. The only outside computers used were on the two test runs that included the servers in Houston and Sudbury."

"I don't mean to be mysterious but the software has potential defense and national security applications. Because it was developed outside the US we are not required to notify any agencies of the US government. I would like to work with the Israelis. Are you familiar with the Israeli defense forces' facial recognition software?"

She said, "I obviously haven't worked with it as it is all classified. However I've read about it. It is believed to be one of the most advanced systems in the world. It is known that their system combines several proven facial recognition methods. There is a great deal of disagreement over which methods have been combined.

"The list includes popular recognition algorithms such as the Hidden Markov model, the Principal Component Analysis using eigenfaces, the Linear Discriminant Analysis, the Elastic Bunch Graph matching using Fisherface algorithm, the Multilinear Subspace Learning using tensor representations, the neuronal motivated dynamic link matching, and possibly others. It is known to incorporate 3D recognition and skin texture analysis. The NSA probably has something just as good."

Much of what Elizabeth had just said was Greek to me.

Walter said, "Very good and yes the NSA probably has something like this but I don't think they would share it with us. Do you know what problem the Israelis have with their software?"

A word popped into my mind and I said, "Combinatorial explosion. And…"

Walter was looking at me. Everyone in the room was looking at me. He said, "Very good, Professor. You were going to add something?"

I said, "And that is just the type of problem the massive computing power of Elizabeth's software solves. So you are going to cut a deal with the Israelis, who you work closely with on many things. You will solve their combinatorial explosion problem, lease them Elizabeth's software for other national security purposes, and in return they will help us get rid of Rodríguez."

Walter hadn't expected me to connect so many dots. He said, "Professor, sometimes you amaze me."

I said, "Abbey keeps telling me one of your greatest gifts is picking good people."

He smiled and said, "The agreement will be a bit more complex than that but I believe you have clearly stated the key elements. I want everyone in this room to know this is top secret. All of you are deeply involved in this tragic situation that was not of our causing. I believe the Israelis have the skills to help us out of this mess without causing an international incident. There will be a great many commercial benefits to our company working with the Israelis on continued software development, and our lives will not go back to normal until Rodríguez is dealt with."

I said, "That works for me." Then I decided it was best for me to shut up for a while.

He continued, "There will be two teams arriving from Israel shortly. Elizabeth, you will be working with the two-person team on integration strategies for the two software systems. They will be staying in the fourth apartment in the guesthouse the Professor is using and work in the research facility. Major Campbell, you will be working with the second team. You will need to find accommodations for them in the second guesthouse and the security personnel bunkhouse. At this point you should be able to reduce the number of security people at the ranch. I doubt we will have another large-scale attack. They will work out of the airfield facility.

"Elizabeth, we are in the process of expanding the servers in Lima. There should be enough capacity for you to conduct your work without interfering with our other work at the Lima facility. If you need more capacity than that, you can arrange it with the manager of the Lima servers, please let me know.

"Major Campbell and I must leave now for a meeting in Lima. Again I'm sorry we are in this situation. We did not cause it but we must resolve it. Also thank you for all your hard work under these difficult circumstances."

They left and Elizabeth followed. Ned hung back. I said, "What else is going on?"

He said, "Well I would like to talk to you about something and I do have one interesting piece of breaking news. The Pope has asked to address the United Nations General Assembly. He also asked to have leaders from the world major religions attend."

I said, "Our Abbess seems to have motivated him. Can you record the speech? Now what can I do for you?"

"Professor, I'll record it for you, no sweat. I want to go to Cornell next fall and I want your help."

"I'm happy to help and I'm a firm believer in the value of a higher education. But you have a job that most graduates in your field would love to have and you have the respect and trust of all the people you work with."

"I know, Professor, but I promised my mother I would graduate from college. It would mean a lot to her. She never had the opportunity to go to college. My problem before was that if something bored me I wouldn't do it. Now I've learned that everything in life has boring parts. The best thing is to just do the boring stuff as fast as you can and then get back to the interesting things. I can do it now. So you will help me?"

"What about your job here?"

"Mr. Falone said he would give me a leave and pay my expenses if I returned to the company. That is what I want to do. I'm 25 now so I'm getting pretty old, I'd like to get this done."

"OK, but you shouldn't be in a regular undergrad program. That would be too boring and a waste of your time and talent. Make me a list of the credits you got before. Also list all the programming languages you know. You also know Spanish, put that and everything else you know on the list. Include as much as you can think of. Later you and I can pare it down. I'll talk to some folks at Cornell and we will see what we can figure out."

"So you think I can get in, Professor?"

"Ned, you will get in, we just need to make sure you have the right experience when you are there. Give me the list in a few days."

He left and I decided I had better find Abbey and tell her there is a price on her head. She was in the main workroom with her laptop.

Abbey said, "What the hell happened at the site? I heard there was shooting. I saw everyone in your office so I didn't want to interrupt. What is going on?"

I said, "Let's go in my office to talk." As we walk back to my office I told her what happened at the site. I then explained Major Campbell's theory on it being young sons of some of the gang members who were killed. I was trying to decide the best way to give her the rest of the news.

We sat and I said, "It looks like Rodríguez didn't even know about the kids' attack. But he is going after us in a different way now. He has put out a contract to kill us. He is paying $500,000 for killing Major Campbell, and $250,000 each for killing you and me." I stopped to see her reaction.

She just looked at me and then said, "What do you think of Texas now?"

I went on to tell her about what Walter was doing with the Israelis.

She said, "How soon?"

"I'm not sure but I think soon. The divers are going back in tomorrow. The blimp arrives within a week. Walter wants our lives to be back to normal. Tell me about the letter from Friar Ortiz to his sister."

Abbey said, "He talks about his trip north with the Strong of Heart. He used the term in the Quechua language. After reading this letter I more strongly believe 'Strong of Heart' is a better translation than True of Heart. He doesn't use the name Minchancaman. Friar Ortiz refers to their leader as Manqu Qhapaq. That means 'Founder Royal' in the Quechua language.

"The group appears to be made up primarily of people who originally came from the northern part of the Inca Empire. As they moved north anyone who was ill was left behind, and new healthy followers joined. I wasn't able to tell exactly how many were in the group from his letter. It seems it must be over a hundred. Those are the high points."

I said, "That is very interesting. However we may be looking at a totally different group of people in our cavern. The cavern bones are different than any other documented burial site in Peru. So we have something significant."

She said, "We are starting to get lots more data from Houston. I think I will just organize it as it comes in and not try to analyze it until we have most of the bone pile info. Now I think I'll go up to the range and practice shooting. It seems we may still need it."

I walked back to the guesthouse. I hoped Abbey was OK. It has been a rough few weeks since the first shooting. She could have been killed on two occasions and was forced to kill four or five men to save our lives. She seemed to be her upbeat self, other than doing a lot more training with her grandfather and the security people.

Wednesday morning I swam and was having coffee by the pool. Sergeant Summers came out and joined me.

"Good morning. How is the training going with Major Campbell's security people?"

He said, "They are almost all former military people. They are used to training and it just becomes part of their day. Most of them like the work on the rifle range and they don't bitch too much about the conditioning. Major Campbell told me about Rodríguez's hit contract."

I said, "How do you think Abbey is taking it? All of this seems like a lot for a young woman to handle in just a few weeks."

"Professor, I don't know. She seems fine but I sense a new hardness or edge to her. It could be the stress of our situation."

Just then Abbey came back from her morning run. She sat down and put her fanny pack on the table. It landed with a thud.

"Good morning, men." She looked energized after her run and sounded upbeat. "Prof, I'm planning to work on the bone data most of the day. Can you check on the divers at the site?"

I said, "That's what I'm planning to do this morning. I'll just get in your way if we both try to work on the data from Houston as it comes in."

Abbey said to her grandfather, "What time is your long-range target practice today? I'd like to join you if I can."

He said, "I can schedule it for 4:00PM so you can get a day's work done beforehand."

She got up, patted my shoulder, and kissed her grandfather's cheek. "I am going to shower and go to the research facility."

She grabbed her fanny pack and walked into the guesthouse. I said to her grandfather, "That pack seems a little heavy for a cell phone."

He said, "She has started carrying a mousegun."

I said, "A what?"

"A mousegun is the name given to a group of small revolvers, or semi-automatic handguns. They are intended for concealed carry self-defense. Abbey has the Beretta 3032 Tomcat. It is semiautomatic with a double action trigger and a magazine that holds seven .32 ACP bullets. It is quite effective at very close range but it's hard to hit anything more than a few dozen yards away."

"Does she need it?"

"She feels safer with it. Given everything that has happened I had Major Campbell get it for her. She is well trained in gun safety and use."

I thought he was right about that. I'd seen her in action. Her grandfather trained her and everyone here considered him a real expert. For me guns were something you saw on TV and in the movies. I'd be happier when this Rodríguez mess was over.

He went on, "Once this is over I hope she won't feel the need to be armed."

I said, "I know she is properly trained. I just worry about her. But I feel better with you here. I'm headed to the airfield. Do you want a ride in my golf cart?"

"No, Professor, I'll walk up later."

The divers continued to find small underground streams flowing in the underground river as they went upstream. But none were big enough to be the entry point for bodies. They were taking measurements every few yards for our detailed map of the cavern and river as they went along. It was slow going even with the scooters. I was tempted to tell them just go upstream until you find something interesting. However that went against all my training.

The number of police around the site had doubled. I didn't think there would be more trouble. The dive team didn't seem bothered by the shooting the other day. They went about their work professionally and they didn't need any more instruction from me. I forwarded all the new data to Mike and Fred.

I stopped by Ned's workspace and took a look at his list. I told him not to be so modest and add more to the list then bring it to me. I also told him to look through the Cornell website at the BS and MS programs in three departments in the Engineering College: Operations Research and Information Engineering, Computer Science, and System Engineering. We would meet in a day or two.

Ned told me some Israeli computer people would be flying in later today and the blimp would be here Friday. The blimp would be fun. Everyone would want to see it.

I cancelled our Friday team meeting and said we would meet on Monday. By then I hoped we would have more information. I decided the best thing I could do was stay out of people's way. I sent off some emails from my office and decided my leg was enough better that I should start working out in the fitness center.

On Friday the buzz was all about the blimp. It had been shipped deflated from the States to Lima by cargo jet and then refilled with helium. It left Lima airport first thing in the morning. Since it cruised at only about 40 mph it would take over four hours to get to the ranch. Once all the equipment was installed, the support team would go to the Bagua Grande airport and set up shop. Then the blimp would fly up to Bagua Grande.

The ground crew and their support vehicles arrived first. They could drive faster than the blimp could fly. Shortly after noon we got the word that the blimp was headed in. Abbey rode up to the airfield in the golf cart with me. She was wearing her fanny pack.

People were all around the hangar waiting for the blimp to come into sight. We heard it before we saw it. It was big. The Skyship 600 is 216 feet long and 72 feet tall. It can hold up to 12 people. It seemed to lumber through the sky, not at all like a plane. The ground crew was out on the runway to receive it.

As it touched down everyone started clapping. I thought I hope we find something with it because Walter has spent a whole pile of money on this toy. Major Campbell got off first. He looked like a kid on Christmas morning. Once it was secured the flight crew and support team went to meet with the Franks to discuss the installation of the equipment. Major Campbell was using only one crutch and getting around quite well.

I went to check on the dive team at the site. Things were going smoothly there and I transferred the latest data to Mike and Fred. Since Abbey and I were still restricted to the ranch, Ned was working with the Franks to set up an audio and video link to the blimp.

Saturday afternoon Abbey and I got a ride in the blimp when they were testing the equipment. We both wanted to be on the blimp when it was surveying west of the site. However Walter wouldn't hear of it and he was right. There was no real need for us to run that risk.

Sunday I spent a quiet day reviewing the data from Houston that Abbey had compiled.

SkyShip 600 blimp (Note 2)

Chapter
46

Monday I did my usual routine of a swim and going to my office. At 9:59AM I walked into the workroom and wrote on the whiteboard:

THE REJECT TEAM: PROJECT "THE INCA'S DEATH CAVE." WEEK 17 DAY 1

The group was small today. Elizabeth was working with the Israeli computer people, Ned and Sadako were working with the Franks on the final testing of the blimp equipment, and Mitch was still researching burial practices around the site. So it was just Walter, Abbey, Fred, Mike and me.

Mike started by displaying the 3D map of the underground river. It was quite detailed, which was the main reason the divers' progress was so slow. We still hadn't found any entry point large enough for human bodies.

Abbey went next. She said, "The bones at the bottom of the pile were carbon-dated to be from the 1500s. The newest was about 40 years old. The preliminary DNA indicated people native to northern Peru. Perhaps all these remains had a tribal relationship. Experts in the field will review the data and send us a detailed report. There were few signs of violent death as you see in battleground mass graves. The ages and sexes were varied.

"There is another interesting common factor among all the samples we took, they have low bone-mineral density, plus a high rate of osteomalacia. The leading cause of both these conditions is a deficiency in vitamin D. I've requested an experts' report on this as well."

She continued, "Mitch asked me to let you know that she is finding some interesting religious practices but nothing that fits our burial site yet."

I said, "The more we know the more it seems we have discovered something unique. We just have to figure out what it is. I'm hopeful between the divers and the blimp we can find out how the bodies got in the underground river. I still like my idea that we could be looking at an isolated tribe with a unique burial practice that became assimilated into the broader culture about 40 years ago."

Walter said, "However if your hydraulics professor friend is correct about the current being too slow now to carry bodies to the pile, we may find more bones upstream from a later date."

I said, "When Fred and Mike get caught up on the plotting of the underground river map, they will research what events occurred 40 years ago that could have caused the change in the river's rate of flow. Let's meet again next Monday. There is no point meeting before then."

Walter said, "It should be an exciting next few weeks. Thank you all for your continued hard work."

Walter was right but it turned out not to be the excitement we wanted.

After the meeting, Abbey and I decided to go back up to the airfield. The blimp was ready to go. It would leave first thing in the morning and travel over 200 miles up the coast road to the city of Trujillo. The support team would meet them there and spend the night. The next day they would go on to Bagua Grande and Thursday they could begin work. Everyone had high hopes for the blimp.

We checked on the dive team. Even with the scooter the work was slowing down. By the time they went against the current to the point they were to map, they had shorter and shorter time left to work before they had to head back for fresh tanks.

Major Campbell was ordering special air tanks that would attach to the scooters. The divers would use these tanks to travel up and back. The tanks on their back would be used when they were off the scooters taking measurements. But still it was only safe for the divers to be underwater for so many hours a day.

I went over to Ned and said, "How did the audio and video link to the blimp come out?"

He said, "It works great. Let me show you. I set it up in on the same control station as the site. You can do split screen if you want to watch both at the same time."

He powered it up. We could tilt, pan, and zoom the camera that was mounted on the bottom of the gondola. The audio feed was to the blimp's cabin. Both worked well.

I said. "It looks good. Do the readings from the magnetometer and ground-penetrating radar transmit in real time as well?"

Ned said, "Yes, I'll set up the monitors for those later today. Oh, here is the transcript and the English translation of the Pope's UN speech earlier today." He handed me a memory stick.

I said, "Thanks. I forgot all about it. How was it?"

He said, "World changing." And then he headed back to his pile of equipment and started working.

I wanted to talk to the Franks about details on the equipment sensitivity so I went back into the hangar where they set up shop. They were explaining it all to me when we heard a helicopter approaching. We walked to the hangar door. The helicopter landed and five men got off. Major Campbell met them, they got into two Range Rovers, and drove towards the ranch house.

I turned to Dona Frank and said, "Was that the Peruvian Minister of the Interior?"

She said, "I think so but I've only seen pictures of him. Looks like a high-level group. I wonder who the rest of them are."

I was wondering the same thing but I didn't say anything. As soon as I finished with my questions I knew whom I would see next. Once we were done I went back to Ned's workspace.

I said, "Who was that with the Minister of the Interior?"

He looked at me. I stared back at him. Finally he said, "OK, Walter said you were in the loop, but only on the QT. The other two Peruvians are the heads of DINOES or Special Operations and DINANDRO or Anti-Narcotics Unit of the National Police. The National Police report to the Minister of the Interior.

"The two Israelis are with Mossad. One is rumored to be the head of the Kidon. It is the elite group that undertakes overseas assassination operations.

Not much is known about this mysterious unit. The unit only recruits from former soldiers from the elite Israeli Defense Forces special forces unit. Wait until you see what arrives next."

"I guess Walter is tired of Rodríguez jerking him around."

Once again Ned seemed a little too excited about all this for my liking. I said, "Let me know when you want to go over your list for Cornell."

He said, "How about Saturday? The Major has me jumping right now."

I told him any time he was ready was fine with me. I checked the divers once more and then went back to my office to study the data Abbey had compiled. I gave up on that about 5:00PM and decided to go for a swim.

After my swim I got a beer and plugged in the memory stick Ned gave me. It had the Pope's speech video recorded on it and the words in English scrolling along the bottom. It was a 50-minute speech. I watched the whole thing and then clicked to the written transcript.

I really couldn't believe it. The Pope said that the entire Catholic Church would devote the rest of his papacy and he hoped beyond to the worldwide protection of children. The protection of children from the many evils they cannot protect themselves from. He included hunger, disease, child labor, child soldiers, child slavery, prostitution, genital mutilation, and sex abuse.

Then he said the Church would start this crusade by cleaning up its own child sex abuse crisis. "This is an abomination on our Church that I pray to God each day for forgiveness and the strength to properly overcome it."

I was stunned. In the video of his speech he was interrupted many times by the UN delegates standing and clapping. He briefly referred to the panel he had commissioned on the Church's sex abuse issue. Then he said the Church needed to go further. He was directing each diocese to convene a panel of inquiry. The panel was to be made up of laypeople and members of the consecrated life within the Catholic Church. However each panel must have at least half the members be women. No exceptions.

All documentation of abuse or the cover-up of abuse would be turned over to appropriate local authorities. The pope stated, "The only way for our Church to regain our moral standing was to put this scandal out in the open and behind us."

For priests who feel the temptation of this evil toward children, special monasteries would be set up where they could serve without the temptation of children being present. These monasteries would be set up worldwide. Brazil had already agreed that these monasteries would be welcome in their country. Priests living in these monasteries and obeying their rules would not be prosecuted and deported for past acts. It was hoped that other countries would follow.

The pope went on to invite all religions to join with the Catholic Church in this fight to protect children. He said he believed that governments and charities, led by the great religions of the world, would follow.

I was interested to read the way he addressed inequality. I knew he had spoken about this before. Rather than bash the rich or top 1% he acknowledged that many wealthy people are generous supporters of their religions and of charities. However he asked them to do more, to lead others, and use their God-given talents to further this great crusade.

At the end of the speech he received a standing ovation.

I turned on the TV and ran through several news channels. The commentaries were overwhelmingly positive. I believed our Abbess from the Monastery of Saint Catherine in Arequipa had given the Pope the additional support he needed to take this bold step. The devil is in the details but I was hopeful that much good would come from this.

Chapter 47

The blimp had already gone when I went up to the airfield. However two large tractor-trailer trucks and several other vehicles had arrived. I went into the hangar and in the back corner near the office area where men were installing equipment.

First I checked on the dive team and sent Mike and Fred the latest data. Next I powered up the camera on the blimp. The blimp was flying up Peru Highway 1. This road is the Peruvian portion of the Pan-American Highway. I panned the camera west and I could see the ocean and to the east were the foothills of the Andes.

I spoke into the microphone. "Anybody home?"

Peter Frank said, "Good morning, Professor. The view is beautiful up here."

I said, "I have the video camera on and it is quite a view. Is everything going smoothly?"

"Just fine. We will keep testing the equipment on the way, but it all seems to be working. I'll try transmitting the test data to you a little later."

"That sounds good, Peter. I'll let you get back to work." I powered off the audio and video feeds.

I went out to see Ned. "I was just playing with the video and audio feeds to the blimp. They seem to be working great. Is that the Israeli army we have setting up out in the hangar?"

Ned didn't answer me. I kept looking at him. Finally he said, "I know Walter told us to keep you in the loop. Officially these are all employees of

Elbit Systems Ltd. That is an Israeli defense electronics manufacturer and integrator. They also produce a line of drones. Elbit Systems and Falone Advanced Technologies are preforming joint testing of remote sensing equipment. The flight testing with the drones has been approved by both the Peruvian Ministries of Defense and Interior.

"What they will be assembling shortly in the hangar is a Hermes 450 drone designed for tactical long-endurance missions."

"Is it better that than our drone?"

"In many ways the Heron drone we have is much better. The Hermes only has 20 hours of flight endurance. But some of the Hermes 450 have been modified and equipped with two of the Israeli version of the Hellfire missile. So we use our Heron drone that has 52 hours of flight endurance to find Rodríguez and the Hermes 450 to blast him to hell. Pretty cool plan, Professor."

I thought there had to be a little more to it than that. I said, "Can your bug tell us where Rodríguez is?"

He said, "The bugged laptop belongs to one of Rodríguez's aides, I think. So Rodríguez may or may not be in that location. They are pretty careful about when they go online, so it is of limited help. My guess is the US State Department or DEA will give the Peruvian government info on where Rodríguez might be under some kind of inter-government sharing of information. Rodríguez operates in Peru so the information sharing is routine business. The Peruvians give it to us and we get our man. The US has no official role. That's the way I see it going down. Then you're no longer worth $250,000 dead, Professor, and we can get back to normal."

I thought of something else. "Doesn't our drone only have a range of about 200 miles even though it can stay up 52 hours? How is that going to work?"

Ned said. "That's why we have two tractor trailer trucks. We get the drones all ready, then remove the wings and load them on the trucks. They will go with the ground service crew to a Peruvian military base up close to the border with Ecuador. The pilot's station will be here. We hope to get the trucks on the road today. Like I said, pretty cool plan."

"Ned, let's hope we don't start another war between Peru and Ecuador."

He said, "The Peruvian Defense Minister doesn't seem to like Ecuador much."

"Do you listen in on everybody's conversation, Ned?"

"No, Professor, I don't have time for that. Major Campbell has me way too busy."

I just wanted my life back. I wanted to be up at the site working in the field not confined to the ranch. I went back out into the hangar. The Hermes 450 drone was already packed in the truck. The Heron drone was having its wings removed. I wondered what Walter had gotten for the Peruvians to get all this help. Probably some fancy Israeli military hardware. Maybe I'd go see if Fred had any new comics for me.

Instead I went to my office and started reviewing the data. I was curious about what might have caused the slower flow rate in the underground river. Mike had sent me a lot of info on earthquakes in Peru. So I started with that.

There's lots of earthquake activity in Peru. It seemed like three or four a decade. The Peruvian coast is located near the interface between the Nazca and South American tectonic plates. The South American Plate is moving over the Nazca Plate at a rate of 3.0 inches per year. This process has caused earthquakes, the rise of the Andes mountain range, the creation of the Peru-Chile Trench, and volcanoes in the Peruvian highlands.

Mike's list of earthquakes started in 1586 and went up to last year. There were over 40 earthquakes listed. For the quakes from 1619 on he included the magnitude, coordinates of the epicenter, area affected, and the number of fatalities caused by the earthquake. I looked in the period of 1960-70. Most of the earthquakes were either in southern Peru or near the coast on the other side of the Andes from our site. It was a totally different watershed. I found one earthquake in the Amazonas and San Martín regions but it was in May of 1990. I put everything I found into an email to my hydraulics professor friend. Maybe he could make sense of it.

Next I started reviewing the bone data in detail. My routine for the next few days was go to the airfield after my morning swim, check on the divers and the blimp, and then go back to my office to study the bone data.

Friday morning I was at the airfield. It had taken a couple of days to figure out how to get accurate readings from the blimp. They started over the areas of the cavern and underground river we had mapped. That way they could check the readings against our detailed map. Once they had the calibration and technique down, they were going back and forth about a half-mile on each side of the underground river working their way upstream to the west. They hadn't yet reached the point where the divers were currently mapping.

Our Heron drone had been flying into Ecuador for the last two days. The Hermes 450 drone was standing by at the northern military base ready to take off when needed. The Israelis with the control station here were a quiet group that kept to themselves.

Abbey, Ned, and two others were out on the firing range with Sergeant Summers. They were doing long-range target practice. There was the slow but steady sound of rifle fire. Major Campbell came out of his office.

I said, "I see Sergeant Summers relented and let Ned take target practice with the rest of the group."

He said, "I think Ned's calling is more as a cyber warrior. He was complaining about how much his shoulder hurt after target practice the other day. They are shooting the Remington model 700 that is the same gun as the US Marine M40 sniper rifle. It has a good kick to it."

I said, "I haven't heard Abbey complain about a sore shoulder."

He said, "No, she is a tough and determined young lady."

"You forgot smart, Major."

He laughed and said, "That is a given around this place. Let's go see how they are doing."

We walked out. The target was way off in the distance. I said, "How far does that rifle shoot? I can hardly make out the target."

Major Campbell said, "It has a maximum effective range of just over 800 yards. They are practicing with targets at 600 yards now."

Ned was rubbing his shoulder. Abbey was beginning to sight the rifle. Sergeant Summers had a telescope. He was acting as spotter and would report exactly where the target had been hit.

Then a shot rang out from our left and Major Campbell went down. I looked down at him. He was bleeding. He reached out his right arm and pulled my feet out from under me while shouting to get down. I fell in a pile next to him as a second shot rang out and hit the dirt near me.

Again it was all fast and slow at the same time. I wondered if this was always the way it was when someone was trying to kill you.

The two security men on the range drew their sidearms. One pushed Ned to the ground. Then both took up prone firing positions. Sergeant Summers scanned the tree line to our left. He said, "Abbey, your nine o'clock position, the second tree to the right." She looked and then swung the rifle over in that direction.

Another shot rang out from the trees. It hit me in the same leg. I screamed and grabbed my leg. A strange thought went through my head. Was it better to be shot twice in the same leg or once in each leg?

I heard Abbey say, "Target acquired, Grandpa."

The calm voice of her grandfather said, "Take the shot, Abbey."

The Remington 700 discharged and a body fell out besides the second tree.

Security men rushed out of the hangar. Sergeant Summers said in a loud but calm voice, "Major Campbell and the Professor are hit. One shooter is down. We don't know if there are more."

Two men rushed over to us with medical kits. Sergeant Summers studied the tree line and Abbey used the riflescope to study the tree line. Lying in the dirt I saw the Israelis all had guns and had taken up defensive positions around the hangar. They put a tourniquet and bandage on my leg. They gave me something and I fainted or passed out.

I woke up in the infirmary. Abbey and her grandfather were sitting next to my bed. I didn't feel any pain, just thirsty. I reach for the water on the bedside table. I took it, drank, and said, "How is Major Campbell?"

Abbey said, "He was taken by ambulance to the hospital in Lima. I haven't really heard about his condition."

Her grandfather said, "I'll get the doctor. He wanted to see you as soon as you woke up."

Abbey went on, "Major Campbell was shot in the chest or shoulder. I'm not sure but that was where they were putting bandages. How do you feel?"

"I don't hurt. But I'm probably drugged up. Thank you for saving my life again."

She sat quiet for a moment and then smiled. "I didn't figure just giving you an apple, like most teacher's pets do, would be enough."

I was glad to see she was trying to make light of the situation. The doctor came in.

He said, "You are a lucky guy, Professor."

Being shot twice in the last two months didn't seem that lucky to me.

He must have read the expression on my face. He said, "I mean your gunshot wound could have been much worst. No bones or arteries hit, even a few less stitches than the last time. Let me take your pulse and blood pressure, then check the stitches. I want you off it for a few days and then go easy until we take the stitches out. Same drill as last time."

I said. "Thank you, Doctor. I guess this isn't the peaceful retirement job you were planning on."

"No, but it is nice to know my skills are needed. However, it would be fine by me if I go back to treating sore throats and sniffles."

I asked, "How is Major Campbell?"

"He is listed in stable condition. He is a strong man, I believe he will recover. He was shot through the shoulder. X-rays were taken at the hospital so I really don't know the extent of the damage."

He left and I said to Sergeant Summers, "How did that guy get past all the sensors you and Ned put out?"

He said, "Two things. The gunmen picked a wide-open spot to shoot from. No trained sniper would have chosen that location. Second we didn't have the drone patrolling. We set the sensors to get what the drone might miss. This guy parked his motorcycle off the edge of the road and walked up one of the nature trails. The kind of money Rodríguez is offering will attract all sorts. He wasn't even a very good shot."

I thought good thing he wasn't. I was to spend the night here and go back to the guesthouse in the morning. So I told them I'd be fine and I shut my eyes again. Drugs are wonderful at times like this.

Later Ned told me Abbey's shot had gone through the center of the gunman's heart.

The next day they moved me over to the guesthouse. Much to my surprise I didn't feel that bad. I guess I was getting used to being shot. I was sitting by the pool with a book but I had trouble concentrating. Fred arrived with all 22 issues of *The Man from U.N.C.L.E.* comic books. They were more my speed today. We visited for a while, then I thanked him, and he left.

You learn something every day, Napoleon Solo, the lead character in *The Man from U.N.C.L.E.*, was created by Ian Fleming as a small-screen version of James Bond. Solo possesses a charm, sophistication, efficiency, and weakness for beautiful women comparable to Bond's. But Solo is considerably less intense and also less brutal than the English spy. I fell asleep in the lounge chair.

When I woke up Walter Falone was sitting in a chair next to me reading one of the comic books. From the way the two piles of comic books were arranged it looked like he had been there long enough to read six to eight books. I thought, there's one of the busiest men I know sitting quietly reading comics so he didn't wake me.

He said, "These are pretty good. I used to watch the TV show when I was a kid. How are you feeling?"

I said, "Surprisingly not too bad. How is Major Campbell doing?"

"He will make a full recovery. His collarbone was shattered but the doctors say they can fix it. It was his left shoulder and he is right-handed so he will have a little easier time during his recovery. Do you feel up to a ride in the golf cart to the airfield? With a little luck our Rodríguez problems will be over in about 20 minutes. You deserve to see this."

He brought the cart over and I got in. He drove slowly and carefully trying not to bounce me. He drove into the hangar and right up to the Israeli drone control station. Abbey and Sergeant Summers were there. The drone was in flight. I watch the screen from my seat in the cart.

The lead Israeli – none of them gave us names – said, "If our information is correct Rodríguez should get in the center Land Cruiser any time now. His bodyguards will be in the lead and following jeeps. We will wait until they are on the open road."

The picture reminded me of the footage you saw on TV during Desert Storm, but this was in color. It was surreal. Three men came out of the building with automatic rifles. They looked around and then more men came out.

The Israeli said, "That is Rodríguez in the blue shirt."

Someone opened the door for him and he got in the back of the middle car. No one spoke.

The drone was at 20,000 feet flying at 80 mph. The three vehicles were on an open stretch of road. One of the drone pilots said "target acquired," the senior Israeli just nodded, a few seconds later the Land Cruiser blew up. The pilot gave the thumbs-up sign and the senior Israeli said to bring her home.

I said, "Is that it? Are our problems over?"

Walter said, "It will take a few days for the word to get out that no one is going to be paid for killing you. Then it should be safe to get back to a more normal life."

The Israelis were already starting to pack up some of the equipment. As soon as the drone landed they would take apart the control station.

Abbey said, "Come on, Prof. I'll drive you back. You don't look so good."

I smiled and said, "It's time for another pill. Thank you to all of you. I doubt I'll ever see any of you again but I'll never forget you. Walter, I know you went to great lengths to make this happen, we appreciate it."

He said, "The world is a little better place now. But I have no illusions. Someone will replace Rodríguez in a few days. However that won't be our problem."

Abbey drove me back to the guesthouse and I hobbled on my crutches to the lounge chair. She handed me my pill and a glass of water.

She said, "More intellectual reading from Fred?"

I said, "How are you doing, Abbey? This can't be easy for you."

"Prof, I'm not sure but it must be better than being shot. Did you see Grandpa, both this time and last time? He never raised his voice or lost his cool."

I said, "Abbey, you didn't lose your cool either."

"I'm not sure I would have been so calm if he wasn't with me."

"You were the first time."

She smiled at me, sat in a chair next to me, and started to read one of the comic books. I closed my eyes and nodded off.

Chapter 48

Monday I hobbled up to the whiteboard on my crutches and wrote:

THE REJECT TEAM: PROJECT "THE INCA'S DEATH CAVE." WEEK 18 DAY 1

Sadako was in the blimp with the Franks, Elizabeth was working with the Israeli programmers, and Mitch was still interviewing witch doctors and medicine men. So the group was small.

Walter was there and I asked Abbey to start.

She said, "The rest of the bone sample data confirmed what we found in the sample data last week. We have the time period from about 1500 until about 40 years ago. The DNA data indicates pre-Columbian people native to this general region. The clan closeness of their DNA could be an isolated tribe as Prof has suggested. However it could just be a remote village. They tended to have most members loosely related. No sign of mixing with European DNA that could again be explained by it being a remote village. The members who did intermarry tended to move away. I still haven't found a good reason for the low bone-mineral density and high rate of osteomalacia. It is probably something to do with their diet. We have experts looking into that.

"Mitch has some interesting findings. There is a legend of people returning to the earth during the time of the great sickness. The stories vary depending on the source but there are common elements. These include references to caves, blaming the Inca for turning the gods against the people, and references to the moon god and earth god instead of the sun god. Some of the versions call the leader of the group Manqu Qhapaq or Founder Royal just as Friar Ortiz did in his letter to his sister. She still hasn't found anything that is related to the burial practice we have in our cavern. She said she will keep digging and doesn't seem very interested in coming back to the ranch any time soon."

I said, "She can keep researching. We have enough people to process the data here. Mike, fill us in on what you and Fred are doing."

Mike said, "We are continuing to map the underground river as the divers send us data. We may have the world's most-detailed 3D map of an underground river. The data from the blimp is just starting to come in. Dr. Frank seems quite good at interpreting it and she is helping us organize it. I gave you the info I compiled on earthquakes the other day. That is about it."

I said, "I went through the earthquakes and none seemed to fit our location or time line. I sent it all off to my hydraulics professor friend. He sent me a very short email back. It said 'look for dams.' So when you have time, check dams built in this watershed about 40 years ago. Walter, any questions?"

He said, "No questions really. It seems we are finding so many clues that it will have to come together soon. I'm very pleased with your progress. I would like Mitch to refine the probability software she developed. I've played with it and I believe with a few improvements it will have significant commercial value."

I said, "Do you want me to tell her to return to work on it now?"

"No, Professor, when she is done with her field research will be fine. Just explain to her my interest in it. Now I have other things to attend to."

I thought when Mitch finds out Walter's level of interest in her work she will hurry back. He sure has a way of motivating people. I again thought, Walter would end up making a nice profit from the spin-off software from our archaeological research.

I tried to follow the doctor's advice and stay off my leg. I worked mostly from the guesthouse. The blimp was having trouble getting good readings from the ground-penetrating radar. They had to clear out most of the vegetation to get a quality reading. So I asked them to do the magnetometer readings of the area first. We could then use the GPR only in the places of interest.

We got a report on the diet of the people we had bone samples on. I'm not quite sure how they determine the diet from just bones, teeth, and DNA. It concluded that these people eat a very high-protein diet of fish and meat. It reminded me of the diet of the Inuit Eskimos in the Arctic regions. I had read that studies showed that the Inuit's low-carbohydrate diet had no adverse effects on their health. Interesting but again I had no idea what it meant. I sent a text to Mitch to see if she could find anything about people who eat mostly fish and meat. Maybe it was due to some social or religious customs.

I also watched the news. It was fascinating to see how the Pope's speech and plans were being received. His approval rating was at an all-time high. This was for both Catholics and non-Catholics. The latest NBC News/Wall Street Journal Poll showed that the favorable rating of the Catholic Church was up over 10 points, again among both Catholics and non-Catholics who were polled. Attendance at all religious services seemed to be up. Many major religions had agreed to join the Pope's endeavor. It seemed everyone wanted to sign up to help. I thought here is a man brave enough to be honest and do what is right. I hoped he would set an example for all leaders.

The news from Ecuador was about a daring raid by the Ecuadorian Air Force's 22nd Combat Wing from Simón Bolívar Air Base. They successfully pursued and eliminated the notorious drug cartel leader Gilberto José Rodríguez. Acting on information provided by the Ecuadorian National Police's special drug unit, the 22nd Combat Wing used two Dhruv attack helicopters to eliminate Rodríguez and his key lieutenants with no casualties to military or civilian personal. A couple of generals, the head of the National Police, and several political figures went on TV to praise this great crime-fighting effort.

I thought they had spun that pretty well. No international incident. Ecuador received great PR and the Israelis quietly went home. A new drug lord would emerge soon. The crooked Ecuadorians would demand even more bribe money and say don't go on a shooting rampage in Peru. Rodríguez got what he deserved for shooting up a wealthy businessman's ranch. Everything would go back the way it was. Drugs would be produced, shipped, and sold. Politicians would be paid off. But at least Abbey and I would not be part of it.

The entire team at the site was taking the weekend off. The Franks were flown back to the ranch Friday night. Dona Frank wanted to review the magnetometer data with me. We would then decide how to proceed.

I drove over to the research facility in the golf cart Saturday morning. Abbey was already there and was setting up in the workroom. I hobbled in and sat down.

"Good morning, Abbey. What have we got?"

"Hi, Prof. How is the leg? I'm loading the magnetometer readings and video from the area Dona would like us to review with her. Then I'm taking the rest of the day off. Major Campbell has arranged for some special weapons training. We will be doing joint training with the Peruvian Navy Special Forces."

I said, "I didn't think Major Campbell was back yet. As for my leg I've decided I don't like getting shot."

She said, "It took you two times to figure that out, Prof? To answer your question, Major Campbell is arriving back from the hospital this morning."

Dona Frank walked in and seemed excited. After saying hello she said, "We have found something a little different and I want you two to give me your opinion on it."

She sat next to Abbey and began scrolling through the magnetometer data. "I'll start over our cavern. See the reading. I've edited the upstream readings to just give you the general idea without taking hours."

We followed the reading. They looked just like you would expect for the area we were working. It was all consistent with the published geographic and geological data we researched for the area.

She said, "Now look at this."

I looked and said, "Where were these readings taken?"

"About six miles west and south of the cavern."

I said, "It looks like another cavern. But larger than the one we are working."

She said, "Much larger."

Abbey said, "Like Howe Caverns?"

Dona didn't seem to know what Abbey was talking about. I said, "Howe Caverns is in Schoharie County, New York, a couple hours from Cornell. If I'm reading this correctly this is more like Mammoth Cave National Park."

Dona said, "No, nothing like that big, but quite large. We only have readings for about five miles. We don't know how much farther it goes yet. Now look at the video."

She ran a segment of video; it showed a ridge running up the mountainside.

She stopped the video and said, "There, see the long, dark area. It is a cave or at least an opening. I'll zoom in. It varies from one to almost three feet wide and looks about 20 feet long. If it connects to the cavern below it would be large enough to introduce a human body. We found a second smaller one farther along our route."

It was hard to tell. It could be just a few feet deep.

I said, "I don't see any path or trail up to it. But if it hasn't been used for 40 years it could be completely overgrown. I suggest you continue the magnetometer reading until you find the end of the cavern. But get someone on the ground to examine the cave. Lower a camera into it or something to see how deep it is. Once you have finished the magnetometer readings then select the spots to use the ground-penetrating radar to try to get more info on the cavern below.

"If you need a helicopter to get someone in there Major Campbell can arrange it. It looks like quite a hike and I didn't see trails close by."

Abbey said, "I'll go. I'm sick of being stuck on the ranch and Walter said we should be OK in a day or two to leave the ranch."

I was going to object but I would be going myself if it weren't for my leg. I said, "See if Major Campbell can arrange a helicopter to get you there and one or two people to go with you. Then go to the range and play with his new toy. I want to review all this again with Dona."

Abbey left and Dona Frank said, "Abbey looks like she has been taking her training seriously."

I said, "Yes, she was always in shape but now she is super fit. I hope everything that has happened in the last few months isn't too much for her. She has shot and killed at least six people and before this she never shot anything other than a target. I know she did it to save our lives but it still can affect you. She still carries that small gun in her fanny pack."

Dona said, "She is a strong, well-balanced young lady. I think she will be fine."

We reviewed the data again and decided on a plan for the rest of the magnetometer readings we wanted to take. When we were done I went back to the guesthouse, took a pain pill, put my leg up, and fell asleep.

I woke up about 2:00PM and decided to drive up to the airfield. I saw Major Campbell sitting in a golf cart at the edge of the range. I drove over and parked next to him.

"How is your shoulder doing, Major?"

"It hurts. How is your leg?"

"It hurts. What are they shooting? It looks like a cannon."

He said, "It is a Barrett M107 that is a .50 caliber, shoulder fired, semi-automatic, sniper rifle. It is considered an anti-material sniper rifle for taking out jeeps and trucks not just people."

I said, "A .50 caliber bullet like the machine gun bullets that are six inches long?"

"Well, Professor, they are actually 5.45 inches long. But it is the same one used in a .50 caliber machine gun."

"I'm surprised it doesn't knock the person over who is firing it."

"The rifle is said to have a manageable recoil for a weapon of its size because the barrel assembly is designed to absorb force, moving inward toward the receiver against large springs with every shot. Also the weapon's weight and large muzzle brake assist in recoil reduction. Now manageable is a relative term. Most people won't enjoy firing it. The target they are shooting at is almost a mile away."

I shook my head and said, "Did Abbey talk to you about getting into that area of the site?"

"She did and I agree a helicopter would be the best way. I'll arrange to have one stationed up at the airport in Bagua Grande. I have two of my men and Sergeant Summers going up with Abbey for the onsite work."

I said, "Isn't Sergeant Summers a little old to be jumping out of helicopters?"

"Do you want to tell him that, Professor?"

I looked at him out on the range firing the monster gun and said, "Good point. Plus he will keep an eye on Abbey and I'll feel better with him there. The divers are still over three miles downstream from where the blimp has identified the cavern. Do you think we should keep mapping our way upstream or wait and see what we find? I don't want to overwork your men."

He said, "Walter has put no restrictions on our budget. If he thought we were overspending, believe me he would let us know. If you have found something significant Walter will want the best possible documentation of it. My men are well paid, plus they enjoy their work and want Walter to be successful."

"OK, Major that sounds great. I'm going to the control room and see Ned." I drove to the hangar and Major Campbell drove out onto the firing range. I was sure he wouldn't be firing that gun with his shoulder. But I knew he wanted to see if he could outshoot Sergeant Summers. My money would have been on Grandpa Summers.

I hobbled into the office area, went over to Ned's area, and sat. "Ned, you're not out on the range firing that shoulder cannon?"

"Professor, that gun and military stuff is not all it is cracked up to be. It isn't cool like the video games. It hurts my ears even with those ear protectors on. Look at this bruise on my shoulder from firing the smaller sniper rifle. I'm not firing that other gun. Major Campbell says I'm a warrior of the future, a cyber warrior, and I should focus on that. I don't know why Abbey gets such a kick out of running that obstacle course and lifting weight and stuff. But she is scary good with those guns."

I thought it was a bit scary how good Abbey is and said, "Ned, I think Major Campbell is right. You should save the world by being a cyber warrior.

"I spoke to the Dean of the Engineering School and he is open to designing a directed studies program for you in computer science. You will get credit for some of the courses you have taken and can test out of others. If you go year-round you could get a BS and ME degree in about two and a half years. You can use the master courses to give you enough credits to meet the BS requirements. How does that sound?"

"Thank you, Professor, my mother will be very happy if I can do this."

I headed back to the guesthouse.

Sunday was pretty much a day of rest for everyone. I read the papers online. The polls showed the positive opinion ratings for what the Pope was doing were still going up as people saw there would be action and follow-through, not just words. Victims' rights groups were working in partnership with the Church now. In the US, participation in volunteer organizations was on the rise. In India there was a renewed effort and new laws to protect women. I must admit I was one who was coming to doubt that honest, selfless, moral leadership would accomplish much in this age. I'm happy to see I was wrong in this case. I still like to think our brave Abbess from the Monastery of Saint Catherine in Arequipa played a key role in making this happen.

Monday at 9:59AM I hobbled into the workroom and wrote on the whiteboard:

THE REJECT TEAM: PROJECT "THE INCA'S DEATH CAVE." WEEK 19 DAY 1

First thing Monday morning the Franks and Sadako flew back to the site. Walter was away, Elizabeth was working on her software, and Mitch was in the field.

I said, "I guess we can make this a short meeting." I then outlined what the magnetometer reading showed and our follow-up plan. The helicopter would arrive in Bagua Grande on Wednesday.

Everyone gave a short report. Fred and Mike plotted the divers' data as it came in and were getting bored. Ned had more time now that Major Campbell didn't need him full time on security. Mitch would be done in the field this week. The team was losing focus and I could feel the energy level dropping.

I realized we needed to get up to the site. My gut told me we were getting close. I just didn't know to what.

"OK, let's take this show on the road. Ned, start organizing the equipment for a mobile command center. We will either set up at the Bagua Grande airport or at the inn. Also arrange with Major Campbell for transportation and accommodations. I want the team moved on location in Bagua Grande this Wednesday. Mike and Fred, help Ned with whatever he needs. We are out of here Wednesday morning. Any questions?"

Abbey said, "Just one. Why?"

"Because we are about to rock the entire archaeological world with the biggest find of the century."

She said, "How many of those pills did you take this morning, Prof?"

The group needed to be reenergized and I felt this was the best way. If we came up empty, well, I'd worry about that later.

I said, "You can stay here and Mike can go do the ground survey if you like."

She smiled and said, "Fat chance!"

I adjourned the meeting and went to see the doctor to get my stitches taken out.

Chapter 49

Wednesday Abbey, Sergeant Summers, Fred, and I flew to Bagua Grande in the Britten-Norman Defender. Ned and Mike drove up with two security guards and two Land Rovers full of equipment. Major Campbell arranged for a hangar at the airport and the entire inn we had occupied before. Mitch was at the airport to meet us. The plane would fly Sister Maria back to the Monastery of Saint Catherine in Arequipa.

My leg was better and didn't hurt if I didn't do too much. My plan was to ride in the blimp and be driven to and from where I needed to be, at least for a while.

We spent the afternoon getting settled in and setting up our computers and other equipment. That night the inn had a big dinner for the whole team. There were two dozen of us including the blimp pilots and support team, the dive team, security people, and my group. This was a big payday for the innkeeper; he and his wife wanted to make sure we were well treated.

Everyone was in a festive mood. Now that no one was trying to kill us, we were away from the ranch, and seeming to make progress, people were upbeat.

Thursday morning the dive team went to the site and the rest of us went to the airport. It was busy. Abbey and her group loaded up the helicopter. The Franks, Sadako, and I went to the blimp. Mitch, Fred, and Ned would keep setting up in our makeshift office in the hangar.

Riding in the blimp wasn't at all like riding in a small plane. It went only 30-40 mph. It was like gliding through the air. We were only about halfway to the survey area when we saw the helicopter heading back to the airport after dropping Abbey and the team off. We could radio them but they had work to do. We waved as we flew over Abbey and her team.

Since the blimp team returned on Monday they had taken magnetometer readings back and forth moving up the line of the cavern another eight miles. From what I could tell the main cavern ran to the west and south for at least 13 miles. There were several smaller caverns that seemed to run off to the sides.

Dona and I discussed the readings. I said, "How far do you think it goes?"

She said, "It's not the size of Mammoth Cave National Park. That has over 400 miles of caverns. But it could be two or three times larger than what we have surveyed so far."

I was tempted to say, just fly up the centerline until we know how big it is, but that wasn't the proper way to do it. We would continue taking readings back and forth a half mile on each side of the cavern centerline. This was done at 100-yard intervals. So by the time we turned around it took over an hour to survey a mile up the centerline. We worked almost five hours, covering just over four miles, and then headed back to the airport.

Abbey and her team were already at the airport. Once the blimp was moored I went into hangar to see what they had found.

Abbey seemed excited and said, "We might have something. The large opening goes a long ways down and I believe it connects to the cavern. But it doesn't go straight down. It goes at an angle so I will have to modify the camera system. I think I'll need some help from Peter Frank.

"It took a while to get brush cleared away and secure ropes so we could look over the edge. If you don't need him I'd like to have Peter help me rig up a camera system that we can slide down the cave tomorrow. My other team members can clear the brush around the second cave."

I said, "All the equipment on the blimp seems to be working so we don't need Peter tomorrow. I'd talk to him now in case he needs to get parts sent in."

Sergeant Summers said, "I think I'll let the three young guys chop brush tomorrow and I'll relax here."

I said, "Would you like to go in the blimp with us?"

"No thanks. I'm a Marine grunt. I only go up in the air when I absolutely have to. I'll just hang here tomorrow if you don't mind, Professor."

I didn't blame him for not wanting to spend the day cutting brush on a mountainside. But I suspected what he really wanted to do was keep an eye on Abbey. We all hoped the threat to our lives was over, however we really didn't know.

Ned, Fred, and, Mitch had all our equipment set up. Fred was talking to the divers.

I said, "We have room for one of you on the blimp tomorrow if you want to go."

Fred said, "I'm going to the dive site to help out. You two fight over it."

Mitch said, "Ladies first. I'll go. Thank you very much, Ned."

Ned didn't bother arguing with her. I said, "Tomorrow, Ned, could you review the video we shot today and see if you can find more caves?"

"No problem, Professor. I like to do meaningful work," Ned said.

Mitch made an obscene gesture towards Ned and walked away.

Ned smiled and said, "Not very ladylike."

Friday was much the same as the day before. The divers left from the inn, the helicopter took Mike and the two security men to the second cave, and we lumbered off in the blimp.

Saturday we weren't going to work the site. People would be analyzing data or maintaining equipment. I wanted to review the magnetometer data in more detail. Most of us headed to the hangar at the airfield.

I saw Peter Frank working on the on the blimp equipment. I said, "I thought you and Abbey would be building something to customize the camera so we can get it down into the cave."

He said, "We thought about it but when we did a little research we found iRobot Corp. made just what we need. It is the company that makes the little round robot vacuum cleaner called Roomba. They make ones that clean your pool and mow your lawn. Well, they also make a little robot called FirstLook. It has visible and thermal cameras and infrared sensors to gather and transmit images of buildings, caves, or other locations. It only weighs five pounds and runs on small tank tracks. So rather than spend a lot of time making something that might not work we just ordered one. They already shipped it from Houston to Lima and we should have it in a few days."

I told him that sounded good to me and went to a table where I could study the magnetometer data. We had readings for over 20 miles and we still hadn't found the end. I started at the northeast end and slowly worked my way through the data. After three hours and four cups of coffee I decided to take a break.

I had worked with a lot of magnetometer data over the years. There were some small things in the data that didn't look right. Without mentioning anything specific I asked Dona and Abbey to review the first five miles of data.

My leg was still sore so I slowly walked around. Ned came up and told me Walter Falone would be landing in a few minutes for a short visit.

When the plane landed and taxied over I was there to meet it. I said, "Walter, what a pleasant surprise."

He said, "I can't let you have all the fun."

We walked around and Walter greeted everyone. He had a way of asking questions and then listening intently to the answers. People were always glad to see him. I brought him up to date on what we had found.

When we got to the table where Abbey and Dona were reviewing the magnetometer data, I said, "Walter, you have spent your entire career looking at this type of data. Tell me what you think."

He sat down and started reviewing the data. He spent about a half an hour slowly going through the data. No one spoke. He seemed totally focused.

He looked up. I said, "What do you think?"

He said, "It looks like mining activity has gone on in there. There is definitely some measure of alteration of the natural shapes. Look at the reading here. That is too uniform of a rectangular shape to be by nature. This reading indicates something like a straight wall. I only looked at the first few miles but there are several data points that tell me some kind of mining or other human alteration has occurred."

I said, "I couldn't put my finger on it but I knew it was off. There are those types of readings in place over the five miles I've reviewed in detail. Well, once again it seems to me that we have found something significant, we just don't have a clue what it is."

Walter said, "We don't have a clue yet."

The four of us discussed where would be the best spots to try to get ground-penetrating radar readings. Abbey filled him in on the first of the two caves that could connect to the cavern. Everyone agreed that we should continue with the magnetometer readings until we found the southwest end of the cavern and then use the ground-penetrating radar.

Next Walter spent time with Mitch discussing the additions and modifications he would like to see in her probability software. After that he worked his way around for a short visit with everyone. Then he got back on the plane and left.

After he left Abbey came up to me and said, "If there was mining or some other human activity down there, there must be a way to get in. Ned, where is that videotape from the blimp? Let's get to work."

I went back to reviewing the magnetometer readings. At 6:00PM I said to Abbey and Ned, "Let's lock this place up. You two can continue to review the video at the inn if you want."

Abbey said, "Ned, just leave it. We will come back in the morning and start then. It is Saturday night, let's get a drink."

The rest of the team had no problem with that idea.

However, back at the inn it was hardly a wild night. The buzz was all about Walter's observation that mining activity appeared to have taken place in the cavern. Speculation ranged from a lost gold mine worth billions to cavemen tens of thousands of years ago. We had cocktails, a wonderful dinner, and by 10:00PM pretty much everyone had gone to bed.

I didn't get up Sunday until well after 8:00AM. I had a leisurely breakfast and coffee in the courtyard. Mitch came in from somewhere and sat down.

"What's up, Mitch?" She was still sporting her conservative look.

"Prof, I learned a lot about all sorts of local religious and cultural practices. But I'm not sure it was much help."

I said, "It is like a jigsaw puzzle. You discover pieces here and there, and try to fit them together. You found several things that indicate our Strong of Heart existed. Or at least the legend of them existed."

"What do I do with the rest of it?"

"Write it up in a paper and publish it. It could be very helpful to future scholars."

"If you don't need me, I think I'll go back to the ranch and work on my software program. I'm going to need help from Elizabeth."

"That is fine. Walter seemed very interested in your software. Your work and Elizabeth's will probably pay for all of us, and more. But you should document your fieldwork even if you don't get around to publishing it for a while so you won't forget anything. I think Walter would encourage you to publish it."

"If you need me I'll come back." She got up and left.

I had more coffee and decided I was procrastinating. There was a lot more magnetometer data to review, so I got a ride to the airfield.

Abbey and Ned were working away viewing the video. I walked over.

Abbey said, "We have six more possible caves into the cavern. But with all the vegetation it is hard to tell. We need to hike it or something."

I said, "That would be a nice hike. We are up to 20 miles of cavern length. Then check each side out to half a mile. The hundred yards spacing we used in the blimp is too large for a visual inspection on foot, so say 20-yard intervals. That would be over a hundred miles of cutting your way through the jungle."

Abbey said, "I can do the math, Prof. What would you suggest?"

I said, "Well, since I'm not really fond of hacking my way through jungles, I would say, identify all the spots on the video that look promising. Then take the helicopter and go video those areas you identified in more detail from various angles. Also video anything else that looks promising."

Ned was looking at the helicopter. He said, "I could rig a camera on each side. Abbey and I could each operate one. I've never really done it but I don't think I'd like cutting my way through the jungle."

I said, "Until the FirstLook robot camera gets here it is probably our best option."

Abbey said, "I'm going to see if Mitch can run her probability software on this video. Maybe it will help us.

I said, "Great idea. Mitch is going back to the ranch soon so you should talk to her right away."

Abbey called Mitch and Ned went to find Peter Frank to help him mount cameras.

I went to the table and spent the rest of the day studying the magnetometer data.

Monday we held our weekly meeting in the hangar at 8:00AM.

There was no whiteboard so I wrote on a paper flip chart:

THE REJECT TEAM: PROJECT "THE INCA'S DEATH CAVE." WEEK 20 DAY 1

We quickly reviewed what we had found and what each team would do for the next few days. There were a few questions and by 8:40AM everybody headed to their task.

I found I enjoyed riding in the blimp. It peacefully lumbered through the sky. We were fortunate that the weather cooperated with us. There were no storms or high winds.

On Tuesday morning we found the end of the cavern. It was about 26 miles long. That is big but no kind of a record. Mammoth Cave is over 400 miles in length. There are at least half a dozen caverns over 150 miles long in North America. The deepest known cave is Voronya Cave in the country of Georgia. It is 7,208 feet deep.

We kept going to the southwest for the rest of the day taking magnetometer readings but we had found the end of the cavern.

Ned and Abbey spent the two days videoing from the helicopter. They would drop Mike and the two security men off to clear brush at the locations we were going to use the ground-penetrating radar and then go video. I was surprised Mike didn't seem to mind doing this work. He looked happy and fit. Wednesday they would spend the day viewing the blimp video we took Monday and Tuesday, plus studying the video from the helicopter. Mike and his team kept cutting the brush.

Peter Frank removed the magnetometer from the blimp. He then installed the ground-penetrating radar and the winch power plate that could be lowered to the ground. It worked well parked at the airport.

The next day we started taking GPR readings. Most of the first day was spent trying to figure out how to get accurate readings. The blimp didn't stay perfectly still. We needed someone on the ground to hold the plate in position, while we played out enough cable to compensate for the blimp's movement. The helicopter would land two people on the cleared spot and they would guide the plate in place, then we would take a reading and move to the next spot. By Friday evening we only had about a dozen valid readings. However the readings confirmed that there were rock structures that were manmade.

The FirstLook robot camera arrived on Friday. Peter Frank figured out how to operate it. We decided to try it in the first cave and see whether it connected to the cavern.

The helicopter took Abbey, Mike, two security men, and me to the cave opening. It was at the top of a ridge. Fortunately both the security men were experienced mountain climbers. Also Abbey enjoyed rock climbing and was super fit. I, on the other hand, was still recovering from the gunshot wounds. But I wanted to be there and I would leave the gymnastics to others.

The cave opening ran across the top of the ridge and was about 20 feet long. It varied in width from about one to three feet. The FirstLook robot camera was 10 inches long, nine inches wide, and four inches tall. There were four cameras on the robot. It was remotely controlled but we tied a heavy fishing line to it that we could spool out as it went. We didn't want to lose the thing on the first day.

The cave went in a few feet and then straight down about eight feet. From there it looked like it sloped to the north.

Abbey had a climbing harness on and a helmet with a light and camera attached. She went in a few feet and lowered the FirstLook to the sloped area. Mike handed her the controls. The cameras transmitted to the control unit and to a laptop we had. The laptop recorded everything as well as Abbey's helmet camera.

The cameras were on and Abbey slowly started the robot down the slope of the cave. It widened out as it went. About 25 feet down the slope it drove into a seven-inch crack. It was nose down in the crack. She tried backing it up and then pulling on the line tied to it. But it was stuck.

Abbey said, "I can see it. I'll crawl down and get it. Give me some slack on the rope to my harness."

Mike and the security guard played out the rope as Abbey inched forward. I crawled a few feet into the cave so I could see Abbey. I wasn't sure this was a good idea.

She went carefully forward on her stomach. When she was about 10 feet away she tried pulling the line again, with no success. She went closer until she could get one hand on it, but the FirstLook's tank style tracks had wedged it firmly into the crack. She got a little closer and tried with two hands. But she couldn't get any leverage and the FirstLook remained stuck. Next she turned over and slid so she was sitting with one leg on each side of it. She put both hands on it and pulled straight out. The FirstLook unit popped right out.

Next we heard a loud crack and a 10-foot square of the ledge with Abbey on it broke away and fell into the darkness below. I screamed, "Abbey!" As if that would do any good.

As I backed out of the cave Mike said, "We've got you. Abbey, can you hear me?"

Abbey, as cool as a cucumber, said, "I'm just hanging out, boys. Nothing to get excited about."

I said, "We'll pull you up."

"Sit tight, Prof. When I'm ready I'll climb up. Since I'm here I might as well look around."

I tried to relax and tell myself she was in the safety harness. They had tied her rope off to a series of pitons that they had previously pounded into the rocks.

Next she said, "Mike, I have the FirstLook in my hand. I want you to slowly play out more line to me and I'm going to lower it down and see what we have here."

She held the FirstLook so she was looking into one of the cameras and said, "See, Prof, I'm fine. Don't have a cow."

She put the unit under her arm and began looking around. The light on her helmet interfered with the helmet camera so it was hard to see much. She appeared to be looking straight down.

Then she said, "Holy shit! Holy shit!"

I said, "What? Are you all right?"

"Prof, there is a whole city down here. A whole underground city and lots of bones!"

EPILOGUE

Well, it was the find of the century and we did rock the entire archaeological world. It wasn't really a city, it was more a large underground village. Abbey and I had a lifetime's worth of research work here.

There will be a National Geographic TV special on our find next year. Abbey and I hope to publish the first volume of our book series in about 18 months.

Walter made a sizeable donation to Cornell to fund the research and insisted that Abbey and I be in charge of it. The University was only too happy to oblige. Cornell was getting wonderful worldwide press from the find.

I received a generous offer from the Harvard Dean to take over as head of their Archaeology Department. This was the same guy who wouldn't even acknowledge my presence at conferences in the past. I politely told him he could put his offer where the sun didn't shine. However, it did enhance my bargaining position with Cornell.

Abbey's thesis committee was falling all over each other to help her finish her PhD as soon as possible. Everyone wanted her as a faculty member at Cornell and the sooner the better.

Ned was at Cornell getting his combined BS and ME from the Engineering College. Elizabeth had been promoted to Chief Technology Officer at Falone Advanced Technologies. Mitch was admitted to Princeton to get a doctorate in religious history. Our other team members had their pick of jobs within Walter's company. Sadako said to me that her parents told her she brought great honor to her family. Sergeant Summers decided to stay on with the security team at Falone Advanced Technologies. He would work on training and develop a rapid response team for the company.

The Pope had appointed our Abbess of the Monastery of Saint Catherine in Arequipa to head up his program for the protection of children for all of Central and South America. I thought he should make her a saint.

We had thousands of documents that we had digitized from the period put online for scholars all around the world to study.

Carbon dating showed that humans up to 10,000 years ago used parts of the cavern. Prior to their conquest by the Inca, the Chachapoyas used the cavern for religious ceremonies for their royalty. Its location was a closely guarded secret known only to the royal family and high priests.

Manqu Qhapaq, or roughly translated "Founder Royal," must have been legitimate Chachapoyas royalty who had the secret of the caverns location passed down to him. He led his band of the Strong of Heart north to the cavern to escape the disease and slavery brought by the Spanish. The group of about 400 went in through the secret entrance and then sealed it behind them.

There have been many examples of small communities living in isolation for hundreds of years but no others have been found that existed underground. It was a fascinating system and in many respects it resembled the Inuit Eskimos of the Arctic.

The Inuit survived on fish, seal, whales, caribou, and birds. The diet of the community in the cavern was mainly fish and peccary, or New World pigs. It is a pig native to Central and South America. They grow to between 45 and 90 pounds. The Strong of Heart evidently brought in a herd of these pigs.

The fish were a species of catfish, or Astroblepus rosei that are commonly found in caves in Peru. The Strong of Heart created stone walled ponds and farm raised the fish. They also created ponds to raise other fresh water troglobites. These included crustaceans such as shrimp and crayfish and cave salamanders. The catfish fed on the shrimp, crayfish, and salamanders. The pigs ate the scraps from the catfish plus shrimp, crayfish, and salamanders. The people ate all of them.

The pig's skin was made into hides. The teeth and bones were used for tools and implements. There were designated places for cooking. The fuel was primarily fish oil and pig fat.

There were several caves that connected to the cavern roof similar to the one Abbey fell in. They let in some sunlight. Small garden plots were set up to grow plants adapted to low light. But plants appear to have made a limited portion of their diet. Polished copper plates were set up to direct the sunlight to other parts of the cavern. However it was dim to dark everywhere.

There was no evidence of mining for metal work. All the metal items must have been brought in when they arrived. There is extensive stone carving and stone building. Pig and fish bones were also carved, often with beautiful designs. Most of the tools were stone or bone.

Our theory on the burial practice is that the deceased was stripped of clothing and jewelry. Then they were anointed with fish oil and placed in the underground river at the downstream end of the cavern. The deceased's belongings were given to their family. The in-ground burial or cremation of bodies would be unworkable in the cavern. This method was both sanitary and efficient.

It appears one wall contains a carved history of the life in the cavern. We hope to be able to decipher it. Life went on in this underground village for 400 years. Fred discovered the cause of the village's sudden demise. Starting in the early 1960s a series of hydroelectric dams were built on the rivers in the region. When the new dams were filled the water level rose rapidly in the cavern. This destroyed the delicate balance that the Strong of Heart had survived on for all those years. All the bones in this cavern dated from about 40 years ago. Once again we see that when civilization crosses paths with isolated people, the isolated people suffer greatly.

We have years of work to discover the archaeological, anthropological, and historic treasures this cavern contains. I wanted to name it Faloneville, but Walter vetoed that idea. So for now our cavern has no official name.

NOTES

Note 1. The photos on pages 6, 32, 52, 93, 94, 135, & 163 are in the public domain.

Note 2. These photos are being used under the Creative Commons License. Individual photo credits are listed below. They may be reused under the terms on the Creative Commons License.

Photo on page 32
Description: A set of pre-Hispanic Sican culture (9th-11th century) beaker figure gold cups found in Lambayeque, Peru. From the Metropolitan Museum of New York.
Date: 30 December 2005
Source: http://www.flickr.com/photos/rosemania/86743151/in/set-7205759 4048518296/
Author: Rosemania

Photo on page 45
Description: Florentine Codex Smallpox
Date: 23 January 2009
Source: Own work
Author: Jaonitveros

Photo on page 45
Description: Mummies and archaeological rest in cemetery of Chauchilla, 30 km away from Nazca, southern Peru
Date: 2 May 2006
Source: Own work
Author: Colegota

Photo on page 45
Description: An Inca quipu, from the Larco Museum in Lima
Date: 29 October 2007
Source: enWiki, hochgeladen von User Lyndsaruell
Author: Claus Ableiter nur hochgeladen aus enWiki

Photo on page 94
Description: British Army's 651 Sqdn. landing at RAF Waddington
Date: 22 March 2010
Source: Flickr: ZH002 Britten-Norman Defender AL.2 British Army's 651 Sqdn. landing at RAF Waddington
Author: Jerry Gunner

Photo on page 106
Description: Political map of Peru
Date: 21 July 2009
Source: Peru_-_(Template).svg
Author: Peru_-_(Template).svg: Huhsunqu derivative work: Huhsunqu (talk)

Photo on page 114
Description: Cessna O-2 Skymaster
Date: 29 September 2007
Source: Own work
Author: Kogo

Photo on page 135
Description: The complete Scout system including the touch screen interface, carry case and vehicle
Date:
Source: Available online on the Aeryon Labs website
Author: Aeryon Labs Inc.

Photo on page 150
Description: Bridge in use during the rainy season
Date: 24 June 2008 (first version); 24 August 2005 (last version)
Source: Transferred from en.wikipedia; transferred to Commons by User:-Jalo using Commons Helper
Author: Photo courtesy of Rutahsa Adventures - uploaded with permission by User:Leonard G. at en.wikipedia

Photo on page 151
Description: Inca road system
Date: 13 April 2008
Source: Made from the images in the book *The Inka Road System* by John Hyslop
Author: Manco Capac

Photo on page 345
Description: Blank Skyship 600 at Floyd Bennett Field in Brooklyn, New York
Date: September 2007
Source: Airship Management Services
Author: Company Employee

Note 3. The photo on page 223 was purchased from Dreamtime.com.

Note 4. The photo on page 252 is credited to OpenROV.

About the Author

BRADFORD G. WHELER is the former CEO, President and Co-owner of Allan Electric Company. He sold Allan Electric to a New York Stock Exchange listed company. After staying on as President during the transition, Brad retired.

Brad's lifelong love of history, art, books, and the inherent humor in man's nature led to the founding of BookCollaborative.com and the publishing of *Inca's Death Cave* as well as *GOLF SAYINGS: wit & wisdom of a good walk spoiled*, *CAT SAYINGS: wit & wisdom from the whiskered ones*, *HORSE SAYINGS: wit & wisdom straight from the horse's mouth*, *DOG SAYINGS: wit & wisdom from man's best friend*, and *SNAPPY SAYINGS: wit & wisdom from the world's greatest minds*.

His community involvements include being a Trustee of Community General Hospital in Hamilton, NY, and chairing their Finance Committee. He is the former Chairman of the Board of Trustees of Cazenovia College, and former Chairman and member of the Board of Directors and Alumni Association and President of the Sigma Phi Society at Cornell University in Ithaca, NY. He is also a former member of the Board of Directors of the Greater Cazenovia Area Chamber of Commerce and several other boards.

Brad played polo on the Cornell University men's polo team for four years and was a member of the Cazenovia Polo Club. In 2012 he was inducted into the Manlius Pebble Hill Athletic Hall of Fame.

He holds a BS and ME in Civil and Environmental Engineering from Cornell University in Ithaca, NY as well as an MBA degree from Fordham University in New York, NY.

Brad, his wife, Julie, and their golden retriever Quincy live in Cazenovia, NY and Fort Pierce, FL.

Acknowledgments

A few clarifications first, this book is a work of fiction. However the regions, cities, archaeological sites, rivers, and national parks of Peru are all real. Walter Falone's ranches and the death cave are not. The major historical figures and their works are real. Characters such as Friar Ortiz, Sister Ortiz, and the True of Heart are all fictional.

To the extent of my ability I have tried to accurately describe the pre-Columbian cultures of Peru. The same is true with the technology. Most of what I describe exists in some form today. The super-computing program developed by Elizabeth Walters was made up. But who knows, the NSA may have this type of software? Any errors are completely my fault.

First and foremost I would like to thank the readers of this book. Thank you for giving it a chance. I hope you enjoyed it. If you did a review on Amazon.com would be helpful to other potential readers and I would appreciate it.

I would like to thank the following individuals for their direct help with this book.

My wife, Julie, not only encouraged me to write the book, she did the first proofread of the book when it needed a lot of work.

Marcia Abramson for her professional proofreading and editing.

Lorie DeWorken at Mind*the*Margins for her wonderful book design work and producing the e-book files. She was also great about answering many questions I had about publishing e-books.

My website consultant Brian Hoke of Bentley Hoke Consulting who continually helps with all things web related.

Finally I'd like to thank all those book consultants and experts who help authors and small publishers survive in today's rapidly changing media world.

Buy These Books at a discount on www.BookCollaborative.com

They are also available on Amazon.com and Barnes&Noble.com. You can order them at any bookstore in the US, UK, and Canada for delivery within a few days.

GOLF SAYINGS
wit & wisdom of a good walk spoiled

Five 5 Star reviews

Lots and lots of wisdom on these pages and a lot of chuckles

By D. Blankenship, Amazon top 50 and Hall of Fame reviewer.

I have quite a few books whose subject matter deals exclusively with "golf sayings." I have been collecting these books since I first started playing some 55 odd years ago. Of all the wonderful reading I have on my shelf; all the wisdom, humor and frustration documented in their pages concerning what is probably the greatest game every invented, this little work is most certainly in the exclusive top five I own.

CAT SAYINGS
wit & wisdom from the whiskered ones

Thirteen 5 Star and three 4 Star reviews

Feline Art and Words: For cat lovers and those who attempt to understand them

By Grady Harp, Amazon top 50 and Hall of Fame Reviewer

Brad G. Wheler has curated an art and words spectrum devoted to Cats (note the capital C and you'll get the gist of this book!). There is about as much variety of artwork reproduced on every page of this enormously entertaining book as is mirrored in the variety of excerpts of words from the ancients to the moderns. Wheler wisely keeps the reader's interest by dividing his book into chapters: Cats Rule, Wild Cats, Kittens, Humor, Of Cats and Dogs, The Cat Personality, Death of a Friend, Love Of, Cats Vs. People - each topic is generously illustrated with art and comments pertinent to each subsection.

HORSE SAYINGS
wit & wisdom straight from the
horse's mouth

Nine 5 Star and two 4 Star reviews

Horse Enthusiasts Rejoice!

By Dr. Joseph S. Maresca, Amazon top 1000 and Hall of Fame reviewer

Horse Sayings; Wit and Wisdom Straight from the Horse's Mouth by Bradford G. Wheler depicts the horse in all of its glory together with the continued human interest in the equine. The presentation has pearls of wisdom from horse humor, competition, ancient wisdom, training and many other aspects of horses unbeknownst to the public generally but well known to horse enthusiasts. There are illustrations by 61 artists from 11 countries.

DOG SAYINGS
wit & wisdom from man's best friend

Three 5 Star reviews

A Choice Read, Solidly Recommended

By Midwest Book Review

The simple mutts can be far wiser than they let on. *Dog Sayings; Wit & Wisdom from Man's Best Friend* looks at a collection of humor and knowledge as well as plenty of art focusing on man's constant canine companion. For centuries, there has been much said about the relationship of man and dog, and much inspiration has been drawn from them. Presented in full color throughout, *Dog Sayings* is a choice read, solidly recommended.

SNAPPY SAYINGS
wit & wisdom from
the world's greatest minds

Four 5 Star reviews

A Top Pick for Anyone Looking for
a Solid Collection of Humor

By Midwest Book Review

The best wit and wisdom comes from the best minds.
Snappy Sayings is a compilation of quips from countless
brilliant minds throughout history, from hundreds of years ago to the modern
day. Divided into the many aspects of human nature and the unique quips delivered from these individuals, *Snappy Sayings* is a collection that will lead to hours
of entertainment. *Snappy Sayings* is a top pick for anyone looking for a solid collection of humor.

EIGHTEEN 6/10/71

The Poetry Of John G. Hunter III

is a collection of poems written by John G. Hunter III
and given to Bradford G. Wheler for his eighteenth birthday on June 10th 1971. Each poem is accompanied by a
color photograph. The layout and design was done by the
renowned Italian book designer Adira Cucicov. Wheler
has said many times, "I'm sure I received many fine gifts
on my 18th birthday but this is the only one I remember
and still treasure."

www.ingramcontent.com/pod-product-compliance
Lightning Source LLC
Chambersburg PA
CBHW080859020726

47502CB00008B/2279